"*A*re you always this trusting?"

She fell back a step. "If you mean to be wicked, I shall run away. But actually"—she inspected his face carefully—"I'm not afraid of you." She smiled triumphantly. "You don't desire me, and I can tell."

His tool had recovered from the icy loch and was making its interest known—because she was wrong, wrong, wrong. "I've never forced myself on a woman," he said with disgust. "I was talking about the way you showed up here with not more than a few scraps of flimsy stuff covering your bosom."

This time she laughed, a beautiful sound. "That's funny . . . I can't tell you why, but it is."

"It's the truth," he said flatly. "You're an idiot to stand near a naked man while wearing that gown."

"You're not—"

He saw the exact moment that she remembered he was wearing nothing under his kilt.

"All right," she conceded. "I'll take your advice the next time I encounter a naked man in a stream." Her lips tilted up into a smile.

Caelan had the mad thought that kissing her lips would be a good idea, so he turned on his heel and started walking down the path. He'd been so tempted that he almost reached out for her, pulling her against his chest and then settling into a deep kiss, a searching one that would have her trembling against him.

Bloody hell.

She was *married*.

Also by Eloisa James

ELOISA JAMES

HARDLY A GENTLEMAN

An Accidental Brides Novel

AVON

An Imprint of HarperCollinsPublishers

HARDLY A GENTLEMAN. Copyright © 2025 by Eloisa James, Inc. All rights reserved. Printed in the United States of America. No part of this book may be used or reproduced in any manner whatsoever without written permission except in the case of brief quotations embodied in critical articles and reviews. For information, address HarperCollins Publishers, 195 Broadway, New York, NY 10007.

First Avon Books mass market printing: April 2025

Print Edition ISBN: 978-0-06-334746-5
Digital Edition ISBN: 978-0-06-334744-1

Cover design by Amy Halperin
Cover art by Alan Ayers
Cover images © Depositphotos

Avon, Avon & logo, and Avon Books & logo are registered trademarks of HarperCollins Publishers in the United States of America and other countries.

HarperCollins is a registered trademark of HarperCollins Publishers in the United States of America and other countries.

FIRST EDITION

25 26 27 28 29 BVGM 10 9 8 7 6 5 4 3 2 1

*This book is dedicated to all the friends and readers
who applauded my idea of a naked laird
fly-fishing in the stream . . . with a special shout-out to those
who shared inspiring photos*

ACKNOWLEDGMENTS

My books are like small children; they take a whole village to get them to a literate state. I want to offer my deep gratitude to my editor, Tessa Woodward, and my agent, Kim Witherspoon, as well as to my personal team: Leslie Ferdinand, Sharlene Martin Moore, Isabelle Guergolett, and Braden Mayer. My husband and daughter, Anna, debated many a plot point with me, and I'm fervently grateful to them. I consider myself tremendously lucky to be assisted by the PR firm Kaye Publicity and the website developers Wax Creative. In addition, people in many departments of HarperCollins, from Art to Marketing to PR, have done a wonderful job of getting this book into readers' hands: my heartfelt thanks go to each of you.

Hardly
a
Gentleman

CHAPTER 1

April 10, 1803
Scotland

Caelan Eneas MacCrae, Laird of CaerLaven, was up to his thighs in freezing water, his bollocks flinching with every splash.

Spring was finally fighting off winter: the heather was turning purple, and he had a hatful of wild garlic sprouts waiting for the two trout he'd already caught.

Aware of a dim feeling—icy bawbag or no—that life didn't get much better, he flipped his long rod forward and let the silk spin out, his fly splashing down with a sound better than bagpipes or trumpets.

His sister's voice interrupted the delicate process of snapping his rod just enough to set his fly bobbing. "You'll catch your death, standing in that loch like a naked gowk."

Caelan bit back a curse, turning his head to find Fiona on the bank in a muddy dress, hair blown out around her face like red clover. She must have walked across the two fields separating his estate from that of his brother-in-law, Rory McIntyre.

"Turn around if you dinnae want to see me in the altogether," he said by way of greeting, beginning to reel in his line. Fiona wouldn't pay him a visit unless she wanted something, and she wouldn't leave until they'd argued it out. He was stubborn, but his sister was twice as obstinate.

She threw a dramatic hand over her eyes. "What would Mother say?"

Mother would have ranted. The poor woman had waged a relentless, failing campaign to civilize her family.

"She'd be calling on the world, the flesh, and the devil," Fiona said, answering herself. "All of them in one package, when the laird himself is naked in the out-of-doors, teasing local lasses with his muscled thighs and burly chest, with nary a fig leaf covering the family jewels."

"There's naught but my crofters between here and the village," Caelan said, tossing his rod onto the bank. "They have more to do than gawp at me."

"My better half wants one of those newfangled twirly things," Fiona said, pointing to Caelan's reel. "I suppose I might get him one for his birthday, except I wouldn't want the maids admiring Rory's naked arse in a stream."

"As I said, there's no one to see. I have only Mrs. Baldy, and she—"

"I regret to tell you that I had a dispute with that woman over rotten mutton, and she's left in a huff."

"Bloody hell." He plucked his kilt from a bush, buckled it on, and turned to pull his creel out of the stream. "She's the first housekeeper who stayed more than a few weeks."

"I threw the mutton over the wall," Fiona said, "thereby saving you from a nasty death by dysentery. According to her, she's been feeding you porridge—"

"Nothing wrong with that."

"Porridge, cabbage soup, pigs' thinkers—which she clarified as brains—and mutton stew."

"Sounds right," Caelan said, going down on his haunches next to the flat boulder he used for cleaning fish. "I cook trout myself, and otherwise I don't care much what I eat."

A fact his sister knew perfectly well.

"How's the Bean?"

"You have to stop calling him that. *Alfie* is seven years old and tall for his age." Fiona squatted down beside him, pulling a knife from her skirts and slicing open a trout while he started on the other.

"And?"

"He's a pain in the arse," she said darkly.

"He seemed fine at the kirk last Sunday."

"He's obsessed by his pet chicken, Wilhelmina. He says that he can tell from her expression that laying an egg is hideously painful, 'like passing a shite the size of a boulder.'"

Caelan's bellow of laughter echoed over the water.

"Aye, you can guffaw," Fiona said. "You don't have a son who refuses to eat chickens *or* eggs."

"What kind of chicken is Wilhelmina?" Caelan asked, still grinning.

"A silkie, so called: a chicken with a mop of white feathers on top of its head. A grifter at the market rooked Alfie into believing she is half rabbit, half chicken."

Caelan groaned. "That's so wrong."

"Rory offered to turn her into rabbit-chicken stew, which resulted in tears and screaming accusations of cruelty, capped by Alfie being sent to bed with bread and milk for supper."

"Happened to you many a time without stunting your growth."

"And to you," his sister retorted. "I do understand the appeal of the carnivorous wilderness, Caelan. *But*—and I mean this—would it emasculate you to live in a sanitary dwelling? With a pantry that had more than a few withered carrots and some fly-blown mutton?"

"There's a partridge hanging off a hook in the courtyard," Caelan objected. "And these fine trout. What more do I need?" He meant that sincerely. The castle was merely a place to live and food just something to eat.

"A housekeeper, a cook, two housemaids, and a scullery maid," his sister said, flipping gills into the heather.

He hated fuss and noise, which servants brought along with them. "Mrs. Baldy was no bother. She made a cup of tea when I shouted for one and didn't mind serving me outside."

"Aye, but she's gone, remember?"

"I'll have to hire another housekeeper," Caelan said, resigned. "And a maid or two."

"You'll have to start wearing a shirt. Decent women aren't used to seeing brawny chests. A pair of smalls under your kilt, as well."

"I don't see any reason to stain a shirt with fish guts if I can avoid it."

Fiona sighed. "You can't live like this."

"All signs are that I can."

"The castle is filthy."

"That's an exaggeration," he said, wondering if it was. He didn't tend to notice dirt.

"Your study is littered with books, fifteen dirty teacups, piles of horsehair, and drifts of foolscap around your desk. I assume from the horsehair that you're still writing a guide to fly-fishing?"

"That, and a book about Scottish whisky."

"I dinnae know how you survive without an estate manager. Father was besieged by crofters on open days."

Their father had refused to make repairs of any kind and had spent open days brawling with his tenants. Caelan considered himself lucky to have escaped his father's red hair and temper, along with his tightfistedness. The former laird would have exploded with rage if he knew about the money his heir had sunk into improvements.

The upshot was that CaerLaven crofters could support themselves and their children, not merely by farming but also by brewing small batch whisky. "I don't find the crofters unreasonable."

Fiona tossed two fillets into the creel, rinsed her hands in the stream, and carefully wiped her knife on the moss.

"Lunch?" Caelan suggested.

"I'd be taking my life in my hands eating anything from that kitchen."

"I do my cooking on the courtyard hearth. Look, I found wild garlic."

"All right," Fiona said, shaking out the skirts of her riding habit. "I can't believe you're using that fireplace. I remember Mother refusing to allow the cook to go near it on the grounds that we were no longer living in the dark ages."

"It works," Caelan said, leaving it at that. "Why are you paying me a visit, Fiona? The Bean's not the first nor the last laddie to be obsessed by shite."

"I mean to talk to you seriously about your future," his sister declared.

"Ah, bloody hell," he muttered, picking up the creel and his rod. Sure enough, she lectured him about the benefits of marriage all the way back to the castle, not even stopping when they got home.

"There's a good example of what I mean," she

said, pointing at some large stones lying under the south tower.

Castle CaerLaven was one of the smallest castles in the country, but it was one of the oldest as well. To Caelan's mind, it had everything a castle should have: two towers linked by a stone rectangle set at right angles, and an interior courtyard with room to house fifty crofters if the MacCraes were ever besieged.

Which they never were, being as his ancestors had been quick with a claymore and more than capable of fending off aggressive clans and stray Englishmen who thought to steal CaerLaven land.

"What do the rocks have to do with this wife you're proposing?"

"CaerLaven is going to rack and ruin," Fiona declared, crossing her arms over her chest. "You're letting our ancient holding decay inside and out."

"I am not," he said, stung. "Those stones were left over from repairing the battlements in the north tower, and they'll be used for the south in the summer. I've had the stonework repointed and most of the beams replaced. Remember how the nursery ceiling was always sifting wood rot?"

"The nursery won't be the same without that frightful creaking during windstorms," Fiona said nostalgically. "I always pretended that I was sailing the seven seas, not realizing I was in mortal danger."

"Mortal danger is an exaggeration. Magnus got up in both towers and tapped the beams. The termites haven't weakened the structure."

Fiona rolled her eyes; their mother's injunctions against graceless gestures never caught on with her. "The castle is decaying inside, if not outside.

There's a foul, boggin smell in the kitchen. I swear our chicken coop is in better shape."

"You already made your point about a house-keeper."

"Yes, but a wife *keeps* a housekeeper. You rattle around like a pea in a pod, not even noticing your surroundings. I worry for your sanity."

Caelan pushed open the front door, refusing to dignify that foolishness with an answer. Fretting over nonsense like a smell in the kitchen was a waste of time.

"*And* your body as well," his sister continued, walking into the castle before him. "Eating little more than porridge and pigs' thinkers. Did'ya never wonder what happened to the rest of the pig—which you undoubtedly paid for?"

He frowned.

"Mrs. Baldy was selling some lovely bacon out the back door, I've no doubt," Fiona declared. "I know you hate fussing, but bow to the inevitable, Caelan: I've decided you need a wife. What kind of lass would you consider? I'm not talking about the women down at the tavern."

"I will not marry again," he said, as firmly as possible.

Fiona turned and put a hand on his cheek. "Caelan, dearest. I ken you fear losing another wife, but that's no reason not to live."

Fire burned under the surface of his skin because he hated it when people talked about Isla.

His sister rattled on. "Don't I know how much you loved Isla? But it's going on two years. You're twenty-seven next month, and the time has come to move on."

Jesus. She had no intention of giving up.

"You need an heir," she announced, "and for that you need a wife."

She was like a damned dog with a bone. Aggravation curled in Caelan's gut as he lit a fire in the old stone hearth and threw the trout on the rack. "I have an heir. The Bean."

"Alfie is Rory's heir, not yours. Remember how he got that name? The Bean was born far too early, and it's been seven years since he was conceived. I'm thinking the chance of me producing a spare for you is slim."

"I don't give a damn about having my own heir. Our lands adjoin, which would make Alfie the only laird in these parts to brew two different whiskies."

"Sometimes I see that square chin of yours, and I feel as if Father has risen from the grave. You got the best of him otherwise," Fiona said. "You got his jawline, thick hair, and those gray-blue eyes."

Thankfully, the trout were cooked to crispy perfection. He dropped them onto a bed of wild garlic. Mrs. Baldy had left a stack of tin plates and some forks on the hearth.

They ate outside at a stone table that had reportedly been used by their ancestors to gut their enemies. More prosaically, in the last two years, he'd got in the habit of eating there unless it was raining or snowing.

"I've no plans to marry again," he stated.

"You have to—"

"I do *not* have to do anything I damn well don't want to do. And I don't want another woman. *Ever.*" Fiona looked so shaken that Caelan tried to lighten the mood. "No lady knows how to clean a fish the way you do."

Fiona wrinkled her nose. "Me? I never would

have caught a man if Rory hadn't been right next door, bent on seducing me in the barn."

"I don't need to know that!"

Fiona laughed with the confidence of a woman whose husband had fallen in love with her at the age of fourteen. "My point is that I'm rawboned and better suited to being a lumberjack than dancing a quadrille."

"What's a quadrille?"

"A new dance that's all the rage in Edinburgh. Thank God the Bean isn't a girl. I despair to think what a mess I'd make rearing up a young lady." She put down her fork, her eyes softening. "I know how you're feeling, Caelan. You may never fall in love again, not after Isla. She was lovely as a rose in June. The world knows you were desperately in love with her, but it's been two years."

He took a bite of trout. "Aye."

His sister's smile wobbled. "I'll never forget when the two of you left the kirk together. The sun came out from behind a cloud, and apple blossoms blew across the churchyard as if the world itself was celebrating how lovely the two of you were together."

He stood up, picking up his plate and Fiona's.

"I can't help worrying about you," she burst out. "Living alone, turning into a curmudgeonly widower with no one to share your kitchen or your bed."

Caelan turned around and scowled. "I'm happy as I am, Fiona. Leave it be."

CHAPTER 2

*W*hen the Honorable Miss Clara Vetry's fourth Season came to an abrupt and ignominious end at a garden party thrown by the Countess of Jersey, everyone in the beau monde agreed that she had no one to blame but herself.

She could have headed off disgrace in any number of ways—by jumping into the Thames, for example, or by throwing herself over a hedge into a neighboring garden. By dropping into a dead faint . . . or even dying on the spot.

But assaulting a future king?

Not recommended.

"Leave the room the moment Prince George enters," her mother, Lady Vetry, had ordered at the beginning of the Season. "His attentions are *disastrous*."

Clara was already in the habit of running from His Majesty; ever since she caught the Prince of Wales's eye at her debut ball, the man never stopped hunting her. Every Season he'd grown bolder in his pursuit, more avid in his attentions, wetting his fat little lips in a manner that he apparently considered provocative. One of the lowest points of the previous Season had occurred at Carlton House, when His Majesty drew her aside to admire a Roman vase featuring men with extremely large (and erect) private parts.

She was cautiously dancing a quadrille while trying not to topple off the raised dance floor onto the grass when a butler emerged from the house.

"*Attend!* His Royal Highness, Prince George

Augustus Frederick of Wales," the butler bawled. He cleared his throat. "Accompanied by Caroline, Princess of Wales."

Excited chatter replaced the music, but Clara didn't care why Her Majesty was accompanying her estranged husband to an event hosted by his mistress, Lady Jersey.

Her heart plummeted, and panic fluttered in her stomach as she and the other guests stepped down from the wooden dance floor. No sanctuary could be seen, since the garden was enclosed by tall flowering hedges running down to the Thames. And her mother, Lady Vetry, had retreated indoors to chat with other chaperones.

Horrifyingly, His Majesty caught sight of her and began waving, his red face and unsteady gait suggesting he was already drunk. When His Majesty was sober, he gawked at Clara's bosom and paid her lavish compliments, but when he was drunk, he was insufferable.

Arguably, at this point Clara should have turned about, run to the bottom of the garden, and thrown herself into the Thames. Instead she froze like a fictional heroine encountering a ghoul.

Lady Jersey hastened toward His Majesty, arms outstretched, uttering little squeals of joy, but the prince tottered down the short flight of steps from the terrace, walking straight past his mistress as if he didn't see her. All the guests sank into bows and curtsies as His Majesty skirted the dance floor, ignoring them and beaming at Clara.

Despair gripped her, and *bollocks, bollocks, bollocks!* went through her mind—that being the rudest word that she knew.

"Miss Cherry Vetry!" His Majesty boomed, as

he bowed with a wobbly flourish. "My favorite cherub."

A compliment that was only marginally better than his usual assertion that if she were an actress, he would have bought her a circlet of diamonds by now. Along with her virtue, presumably.

"Where have you been hiding? I find you more ravishing than ever." Prince George's eyes fastened on her cleavage. "I approve of this gown." His voice fell to a throaty whisper. "I would venture to say that I am enthralled by its . . . elegance."

Elegance? He was enthralled by her scanty French bodice.

"Miss *Clara* Vetry, Your Highness," she murmured, dropping into a curtsy that unfortunately lured him to step closer and gawp at breasts no cherub possessed.

"I know, but you remind me of cherry brandy," His Majesty replied, slurring. "It's m'favorite."

She could have guessed, since the odor was not merely floating from his breath but emanating from his entire body.

"Don't say another Season began and"—he cast a furtive glance at his wife—"you are still unmarried? The men of this country are fools. A Frenchman would have jumped to it, though of course most of the good ones were beheaded a decade ago."

Clara had paled from anxiety, but now she felt herself turning a sweaty puce.

"Who wouldn't want to marry you? You've the figure of a pocket Venus. A most delightful arse." He hiccupped. "If you were an actress—or at the least, married—I'd buy you a house."

Despair pooled in her gut like acid. There went her fourth Season the way of her first three. A man would have to be daft to court a woman so obviously heralded as a prince's next mistress.

Clara cleared her throat. "Your Majesty, please—"

He bent close to her ear and whispered, "You need a moment in the limelight, since you're having trouble popping off the market. My good deed for the day."

"Please *don't*," Clara gasped.

To her utter horror, he snatched her hand and stepped up to the dance floor, dragging her with him.

"Silence!" he bellowed. "I've a mind to entertain."

A Mozart sonata halted mid-note as the musicians put down their instruments. Out of the corner of her eye, Clara saw Princess Caroline coming down the steps from the terrace. Her heart pounded in her throat, and blood rushed to her head so quickly that she felt dizzy. "I—I—"

"I give you . . . a ballad!" Without further introduction, Prince George opened his mouth and sang, "'Cherry ripe, cherry ripe.'"

Clara flinched, thinking that he couldn't possibly be referring to her breasts? Or worse, her *nipples*?

He sucked in a breath and continued with surprising tunefulness, "'Cherry ripe! Ripe I cry. Full and fair ones, come and buy.'"

In case anyone was confused by the implication of "full and fair ones," he waved his free hand in the general area of Clara's bosom. Guests, musicians, and waiters turned speculative eyes to her cleavage. The princess, who was herself quite buxom, squinted before her brows drew together into a scowl.

Clara was seized by panic. Sweat broke out all over her body, including on her upper lip, where everyone would see it. She stared at the prince, unable to believe that this was truly happening. He had put her up for sale.

Not that she hadn't been already up for sale—no young lady could fool herself about the nature of the marriage market. But he was auctioning her off like a suspect heifer at a county fair.

She looked around at the circle of avid faces reflecting amusement, shock, and, in some of the debutantes' faces, gratitude that they weren't her. Nor would they ever be in her position. Most of them would be scooped up in months.

Her heart plummeted to her feet as shame tightened her throat. She tried to pull away, which merely led to her hand being crushed by the prince's grip.

"'Cherry ripe, cherry ripe!'" His Majesty caroled and then paused, seemingly forgetting the rest of the ballad.

When Clara dared raise her eyes, she was met by Princess Caroline's furious gaze.

She found herself in the grip of an overwhelming wish to never see any of these people again, which led to the realization that she didn't give a damn if the prince toppled over. She pulled back again, with all her strength. Prince George kept his balance—and her hand.

"We should have a sing-along," he bawled. "Because . . . Because . . ." Along with the words, he had apparently forgotten the reason he began singing. "Ah, I remember! None of you bachelors have looked closely at Cherry."

Bollocks didn't cover this humiliation. She didn't deserve it, not after years of mortification at the hands of this man. Tears stung her eyes as fury replaced shame.

"'Ripe I cry,'" he sang.

"Darling, why don't you let Miss Vetry go?" Lady Jersey stepped up to the dance floor in a flutter of skirts and tapped Prince George's fat chin with a finger. "The lady appears distressed."

"She's distressed because no one will marry her!" The prince's voice carried easily through the entire garden, alerting the few guests who weren't already spellbound. "From the moment I first saw Cherry— was it six or seven years ago?—I realized that I would have happily taken her to the altar myself."

"Four," Clara gasped, as despair swept over her, adding in a whisper, "Only four."

"Only thing stopping me was that wretched Marriage Act."

"Schlampe!" Her Majesty spat, turning away.

Clara had no idea what the word meant . . . but she could guess.

Lady Jersey's eyes narrowed, and she stepped down from the dance floor. "I have arranged a special entertainment in honor of Their Majesties' presence at my garden party," she announced.

"Come on, all of you," the prince said, ignoring his mistress. "Sing with me or go hang!" He started over. "'Cherry ripe, cherry ripe. Ripe I cry, Full and fair ones, come and buy!'" Thankfully, no one joined in.

Clara felt as if she were outside her body, watching a garish prince auction off a girl who wasn't *enough* to attract a spouse. Not slender enough, charming enough, nor rich enough to be a wife.

Merely buxom enough to be a mistress.

She began struggling for breath, which unfortunately made her bosom swell and the prince's eyes bulge.

"Loose the doves at once!" Lady Jersey shouted. On the terrace, the butler whisked the cover off a large cage and opened a door, releasing thirty or forty white doves. Diverted, the guests applauded as birds circled the garden like a whirl of snow-flakes.

Until a goshawk shot down from the cover of clouds, and the terrified birds scattered. One swooped over Clara's head, and disgustingly warm white slime splatted on her breasts and slid down her cleavage.

"Bloody hell!" Prince George squealed, drop-ping her hand and pulling out a handkerchief. He slapped his hand to her chest, pushing the fabric straight down inside her gathered bodice.

The sound of rending fabric followed . . . and warm fingers curled around her breast. A dark sound of greedy lust, like the snort of a hog, wheezed from his mouth.

Instinctively, Clara jerked away and swung her reticule, hitting the prince as hard as she could, straight in his gut. "Unhand me!"

He fell back a step, taking most of her bodice with him.

Freed of fabric, her breasts jiggled like jellies on a platter. Clara drew the ragged scraps of her bodice together with trembling fingers, but the surviving cloth didn't even cover her nipples.

Not a single guest stirred to help her. She might have been a butterfly, pinned under glass to be sold at auction. They all stood there staring, their eyes gleaming like brass buttons. Unfeeling, metallic buttons.

Then the silence broke on a raucous laugh; Princess Caroline had finally found something she approved.

Clara pressed her reticule to her chest, but since the small bag was shaped like a mouse's face, it covered only one nipple. From the corner of her eye, she saw her mother come running from the house into the garden.

"That wasn't very nice," Prince George said petulantly, dropping his stained handkerchief and the tattered remnants of her gown to the dance floor.

Lady Vetry arrived, gasping for air, wrenched off her gauzy wrap, and whipped it at Clara's head. "My daughter is sorry," she managed.

As Clara took in a sobbing breath, an instinctive response came unbidden to her lips.

"She don't look it," the prince retorted. "You said 'bollocks,'" he told Clara. "Heard it with my own eyes. No, *ears*. I am shocked to think that a young lady knows the meaning of the word, let alone to hear it from her lips."

He scowled in a disgusting show of hypocritical displeasure, given that he had used that word when pointing out said appendages on the Roman vase.

Before she could defend herself, he added, "You struck me with that rodent." He pointed. "You poked me in the belly with wire whiskers. A lady carrying a rodent! What will we see next in polite society? Gingham aprons worn by duchesses?"

As one, each guest turned to their neighbor and agreed that whiskered reticules would never be in fashion.

Clara's mother mouthed a sharp command.

Clara's wobbling knees dipped so low that she

almost sank to the wooden floor as she forced herself to murmur, "I apologize, Your Majesty."

He turned, nose in the air. "Brandy," he ordered as Lady Jersey caught his arm and bore him away.

"You've done it now!" Clara's mother hissed, grabbing her arm.

Indeed.

CHAPTER 3

"There's a dog in the kitchen!" Fiona squealed, as if their father's dogs hadn't followed him everywhere, including the privy.

"That's Ivy. I shut her in because I don't want her puppies born in the stables. There are too many rats out there."

"I wouldn't be surprised if there were rats in this very room," Fiona said darkly, walking over to the hearth where Ivy was lying on an old blanket. "She's an odd animal. Thin as a starved weasel, except around the belly, of course. What is she?"

"A snap-dog bred for rag-racing. The men were done with her, since bitches never race as well after giving birth. They were about to drown her when I happened by."

Fiona crouched down and scratched Ivy's head. "It's a sweet dog you are, aren't you? No good for anything but chasing rags, and what's the point of that?"

Ivy nudged her hand. "You are a beauty, a weasel-like beauty," Fiona crooned, stroking her sleek neck. "At the very least, Caelan, you could put Ivy in a box. Don't you remember when one of Father's dogs ran around the Great Hall with puppies dropping out along the way?"

"Mother was wildly offended," Caelan said, grinning. Their mother had been strident at best, and though she was regularly aggrieved by the state of the world—and her marriage—she never gave up her attempts to civilize the household. She would have been appalled by the state of the castle these days.

"Don't you dare give the Bean a useless puppy," Fiona tossed over her shoulder.

"I thought he was Alfie now."

Fiona straightened up. "I actually feel sorry for Ivy, giving birth in this pigsty."

Caelan looked around, and while he didn't *think* there were any rats, he took her point. His late wife had fussed until he'd put in a Rumford stove, but it showed little sign of use. Shortly after she'd been hired, Mrs. Baldy had informed him that she held with the old ways, by which she meant an open fireplace.

"Caelan!" his sister said sharply. "Do you see that pile of cabbage leaves in the corner? Not the one where Mrs. Baldy piled spare pans—because supposedly it was too much trouble to hang them back up."

He walked over and kicked the large drift of withered leaves; an indignant squeak suggested he was disturbing a mouse. "I take your point," he conceded.

"You need a housekeeper. One who will stay in place."

"As I told you, I hire them, but since Isla died, they never stay. Not until Mrs. Baldy."

"That's because they fall in love with you and wither from lack of attention."

"Nonsense," Caelan said.

"Remember Mrs. Garnet last fall?"

He shrugged.

"She made up the name. She was one of the unmarried Mclean daughters, and she thought you'd see her flitting around with an apron and feather duster and fall in love with her delectable domesticity. When you paid her no attention, she had a breakdown and had to be sent to the Lowlands for a rest cure."

"She wasn't here more than a month or two!"

"She was too young to understand that you were still grieving Isla and had no interest in another woman. Here's my point, Caelan: you can get anything in London. If we think creatively, we could even order a wife."

"Absolutely not."

"Think of getting a wife as a . . . transaction. We all know there isn't another Isla out there. I could order you a perfectly sound wife from London, perhaps even one with a dowry. Who wouldn't want to marry a fairly young, healthy laird? I hear they sell ladies there, two for a pound."

"God, no."

"All right, then, a housekeeper."

"Why from London? Why not hire one here?"

"Because no decent Scotswoman will remain in this castle," Fiona cried, obviously exasperated. "That dog will be giving birth in the kitchen, won't she, right there on the blanket? Any minute, from the looks of her."

"Aye."

"I need say no more."

"Why would an Englishwoman stay longer than a Scotswoman? I haven't met many, but my impression is that they are easily horrified."

"An English housekeeper who agrees to come all the way to Scotland is *desperate*. Fleeing an abusive husband, maybe. From what I hear, Englishmen are quick with their fists. What's more, she'll stay in place because she won't have a way to get back home. It wouldn't be like the Mclean girl, who ran straight back to her mum."

Caelan scowled. "I don't want anyone trapped here."

"I have a confession," Fiona said, grinning like a loon. "I posted the advertisement a few months ago, and I hired the best of the lot. The woman may be on her way to Scotland already and should arrive by the end of the month. But don't worry: she won't be able to say that she wasn't warned. I described your situation in bald terms."

Caelan clenched his teeth. He loved his sister. He just couldn't remember why, since she was an interfering busybody.

"I also ordered you a bathtub from Glasgow," Fiona added.

"Why? I bathe in the loch."

"Because you need a housekeeper and a bathtub before a woman would consider marrying you."

Caelan dropped the dirty plates on the counter, leaned back against the sink, and folded his arms over his chest. "Your expression belongs to our father. No mistaking it."

Fiona ignored the insult. "The privy off your bedchamber is big enough for a plumbed bath."

"Plumbed bath? Where would the water come from?"

"Rory mounted a tank on our roof that collects rainwater. It sits atop a stove and heated water flows down to my bath when I turn a spigot."

"Men are hauling wood up to the attic for your bath?"

"Coal," Fiona retorted. "The stove is a good, solid one, and a kettleful of coal keeps it warm for hours. Used water goes straight down to the moat through the sewer channel—and that helps clear the pit. It's a brilliant design."

"Who's hauling all that coal?"

"Our footmen!" Fiona cried. "You *are* living in the dark ages, Caelan. Mother had three footmen, don't you remember? Isla had four."

Four footmen? Hell, no. He picked up the dirty plates rather than answer. Mrs. Baldy had apparently been soaking dishes in a pail, so he stuck them in with the others.

"That water is as black as the Earl of Hell's waistcoat," Fiona said, promptly pulling them back out and setting them in a tub in the stone sink. "Get me a pail of clean water. I should order you a sink as well. This one must date to the birthday of Bonnie Prince Charles."

Caelan shrugged, pumped some water, and brought it over, filling the tub.

"I'm getting you a bath and a housekeeper because someday you'll see a lady coming toward you with dainty feet, shining eyes, golden hair, and a sweet expression—a cherub! You'll fall in love and ask her to marry you on the spot," his sister said, grinning because she knew it would snow in hell before that happened.

"I've no interest in angels."

"I know your heart aches," his sister said, bumping his shoulder with hers. "But it will get better, Caelan."

He didn't bother answering, just nudged her to the side and began washing the plates, adding those from the dirty pail as well. If Mrs. Baldy was gone, Fiona was right. He did need help.

Behind them, Ivy yelped. When Caelan turned

his head, the dog was standing up and looking at him in confusion.

"Oh, bloody hell," Fiona muttered. "The puppies are coming."

"Go fetch the Bean. He'll enjoy it as much as we did, and it'll teach him that not everything is born from an egg."

"I will not!"

"He'd love a puppy," Caelan remarked, putting the last plate to the side.

"I already put up with that chicken roosting in his bedchamber at night. I'm not adding a dog to the mix."

"Chickenshit in your son's bedchamber," Caelan said musingly. "What would Mother think? Pot . . . meet kettle."

CHAPTER 4

"Shredding one's reputation along with one's gown might be spurred by failure to find a spouse," Lady Vetry snarled the moment they sat down in their carriage. She fixed Clara with an eagle's eye. *"But only in pursuit of a husband!"*

Clara didn't bother to reply. She was huddled opposite her mother, trying not to think about the fact that she could still feel the imprint of Prince George's fingers.

"If you must expose your bosom," the lady ranted, "why before a married prince? Why not a mere duke? Or even a rich grocer? If you'd lured an *unmarried* man into fondling you in public, you'd be betrothed this moment!"

"That's not fair," Clara protested, praying that the carriage would miraculously circumvent streets clogged with traffic and arrive at their house in the next minute or so. "His Majesty ripped my bodice while groping my breast. I had nothing to do with it."

"Your response was impetuous and thoughtless, as always!" her mother retorted, her voice rising. "How many times have I begged you to think before you act? Remember that wretched dog, the one you found in a drain, who gave fleas to the boot boy and the cook?"

"Patsy," Clara said. "That wasn't the same."

She didn't know why she bothered defending herself, since her mother had never hidden her exasperation with the fact that Clara was ungainly, impulsive, and deficient in most ladylike arts. Lady

Vetry couldn't reconcile herself to her only daughter's inadequacies, since she prided herself on her beauty and grace.

"You've been on the market for years!" her mother cried now. "It's a national disgrace, given the size of your dowry. That absurd reticule made things worse." She pointed to Clara's latest creation, as if the bag was responsible for its inability to cover a pair of large breasts.

Clara swallowed hard. She adored the reticules she painstakingly shaped into charming animal faces with wire whiskers, but obviously she wouldn't be able to carry her favorite mouse ever again.

"Your figure is acceptable, you don't squint, and you have that bosom, so that's not the problem. The truth is that beauty is only skin-deep."

"No one ever fell in love with an attractive pair of kidneys," Clara retorted, trying not to sound too resentful. When her mother was in a temper, she brooked no disagreement.

"Kidneys?" Her mother narrowed her eyes. "Precisely what I mean! You can't stop yourself from saying peculiar things. It's unfortunate that Prince George became so obsessed, but that's not the reason why you're unmarried."

Clara made a tactical decision not to comment, because to her mind, he *was* the reason she was unmarried. Without his attentions, someone would have come up to scratch, if only to get hold of her dowry.

Market rules dictated that a gentleman without money was in need of a wife.

"The truth of the matter is that you're an *eccentric*. I can't imagine why." Her mother was as outraged as the prince had been when Clara's reticule bounced off his round stomach. "I myself am perfectly normal. My mother had a haughty temper, but she never had a fanciful thought in her life! Your father, God rest his soul, was remarkable only for his luxurious sideburns. He read the Bible, and that rarely."

"Are you criticizing my reticules or my reading habits?" Clara inquired.

"Both, but particularly the reticules!" her mother replied, her voice rising again. "They're an oddity, don't you understand? One day you're carrying a rat, the next a rabbit. No one wants to end up with an eccentric in the family, let alone a woman who reads all the time. A woman like *that*."

"Like what?" Clara managed, feeling as if she were choking.

"Like Lady Berne, who dyed the feathers of the estate pigeons bright pink. Or that man who invited his giraffe to tea."

Clara ran her fingers under her eyes.

"Are you sniveling?" her mother demanded.

"Yes," Clara said baldly. "You compared me to a pigeon-tinting spinster. I'm sorry that I wasn't able to bring any of my suitors up to scratch, but I don't think it was the fault of my reticules." Her breath caught on a sob. "Are we stopping for traffic *again*? I have to wash. My breasts are covered with excrement."

"I blame the fashion for teaching young girls to read. Hermione Willis bored me silly, raving about a peanut plant she's growing in the drawing room."

"She plans to cultivate peanuts and feed the poor," Clara said dispiritedly.

"I suppose her charitable zeal is attractive, but she's ignoring English rain," her mother scoffed.

"Not only are peanuts disgustingly greasy, but they won't grow here."

Since all Clara cared to do was lie on a couch and read about ghost-ridden castles, it was no wonder gentlemen flocked around Hermione.

"Whereas you've got yourself a reputation for frivolity and oddness," Lady Vetry continued. "Young men are cowards, you know. They don't want to be laughed at."

Clara felt another stab of humiliation. "A man would be mocked for courting me?"

"Put all that's *you* together with Prince George's attentions . . . Yes. Although it's irrelevant now. That's all over." Her voice trembled with emotion as she patted her chest, for all the world like Sarah Siddons playing Cleopatra stinging herself to death with an asp. "I must face my own failure. At the advanced age of twenty-five, my daughter will never marry into the best circles. I shall make immediate arrangements to sign over your dowry."

"I needn't go back?" Clara asked, her voice cracking from pure relief.

"You foolish chit, you *can't* go back," her mother snapped. "The prince is furious; Lady Jersey is outraged. It might have blown over if you hadn't struck him, but *you struck the future King of England*."

"That future king tried to auction me off, then pawed me after a bird excreted on my breast," Clara said. Still feeling as if she couldn't breathe, she sat bolt upright on the opposite seat from her mother, her hands shakily straightening the whiskers of her mouse reticule.

"His Majesty assisted you out of pure benevolence," her mother said. "You should have taken it as an honor and kissed his hand. Look." She withdrew a stained handkerchief from her reticule. "I saved this for you, a memento of the time when a future king came to your aid."

Clara snatched the handkerchief, wrenched down the carriage window, and threw it out.

Lady Vetry cried out as if she'd been poked by a wire whisker. "Valenciennes lace, embroidered with the royal crown! Yet another example of your foolish impulsivity. You could have shown that to your children one day!" Her brow crumpled into a scowl. "Yet I ask myself: What children? Who will carry on our august line? *Who will marry my daughter?*"

Clara had asked herself a version of that question a thousand times since she debuted and had yet to find an answer.

"I can console myself with the thought that I have done everything in my power to find you a spouse," her mother proclaimed, her voice throbbing. Now she was Lady Macbeth before the queen lost her mind and started washing her hands. "I ordered you an entirely new wardrobe every Season. A month ago I paid a fortune for your new maid, Hortense."

Clara felt somewhat cheered by the idea of saying farewell to her maid, who brought with her a reputation for buffing pebbles into pearls. She was nice enough, but she had a fake French accent and a conviction that low bodices were vital for catching a spouse.

"She forced me to *prepay* for the entire Season, arguing that you might elope," her mother grouched. "Elope! That was never in the cards, and the woman still has five months left on her contract."

"Hortense would have been a far better prospect on the marriage market than I."

"The best maids are like that," her mother said airily. "Perfect manners, perfect waistlines, all the rest of it. In Hortense's case, she actually has the bloodline, albeit tarnished by scandal and Gallic associations. At any rate, she can chaperone you, since I can't leave London."

"I'm leaving London?"

"Of course. As a pillar of society, I shall remain for the Season to mend the family reputation as best I can."

Clara glanced down and discovered that she'd wrenched out one of the mouse's whiskers.

"You can use your dowry to buy a spouse next year, if you wish. All the second and third sons already had a look at you, so it'll have to be someone disgraced. A gambler or a drunk. Depending on the man you acquire, I'll publicly acknowledge the connection—or not." Lady Vetry's lip curled.

Clara had been cursed with an infinite wish to please her mother—together with a complete inability to do it. She tried not to dwell on it, but in truth, her heart had been stamped on so many times that it was as cracked as her dreams of romance.

"What would you think of an actor?" For the last few years, she had nurtured a hopeless infatuation with a spectacularly good-looking actor named Mylchreest.

Her mother jerked in her seat. "Absolutely not! I've noticed you attending the same play over and over in order to watch that man perform, Clara. Whomever you . . . *acquire* must have a decent heritage. We cannot allow you to pollute a noble lineage that dates back to King Henry VII with the blood of a hempen homespun from Wales."

Clara had once investigated her mother's fondest claim about their ancestry and discovered that it didn't hold water. Her supposedly noble blood traced back to a wealthy merchant who bought the title of baronet from King James for £1,095. Being a shrewd man, he had kept the receipt but scrawled an insult in the margin. Apparently he felt he'd overpaid, since he labeled the king a pilfering swindler.

She hadn't had any real hope when it came to Mylchreest: he was so handsome that if she ever had the opportunity to speak to him, she would be dazzled into silence. Or blurt out an offer that included the precise amount of money he would receive in return for wedding her. That would be even more embarrassing than being openly marketed for her breasts.

"I could travel to Bath," she said. Bath was crammed with lending libraries and bookstores.

"You must be joking! I heard last night that Prince George has bought more land around the Royal Pavilion. Apparently he means to plant an onion garden." Lady Vetry shuddered. "As if he didn't already reek of the vegetable."

Onions would be a relief. Clara doubted she'd ever be able to stomach the sickly sweet smell of cherry brandy.

"If you were seen in Bath, everyone would assume that you had succumbed to his advances. Polite society needs time to forget this regrettable incident." Lady Vetry scowled. "It would be best if you married before the next Season begins and attend at most one or two balls next year, in company with your husband. Someone ferocious."

Disgraced and ferocious. Marvelous. "Why?"

"Your bridegroom must be good with a rapier. A few duels and everyone will forget about *you* attacking the prince. Instead, they'll be worrying about *him* attacking any man who insults you, including the Prince of Wales, should His Majesty's inadvisable infatuation continue. Though you might have nipped that in the bud today," she added on a slightly more positive note.

Why would a peppery man be more interested in her than all the soft-spoken men who regularly forgot her name? Clara turned her head and stared out the window, letting tears roll silently down her cheeks. Long experience told her that her mother responded with irritation to obvious signs of distress.

She didn't want a bad-tempered husband, a man as available for sale as she was. In fact, she didn't want to marry at all, nor did she ever want to attend a society event again. But what could she do instead? She wasn't good at anything other than making reticules.

Back when she and her best friend Torie had first debuted, she hadn't cared much about being labeled silly and frivolous, since Torie—who couldn't read—was tarred with the same brush. But now Torie was a viscountess, and her husband had proudly informed everyone in polite society that she was a brilliant painter. The king himself owned one of Torie's paintings of rabbits.

Clara didn't have a secret talent that would make a husband proud. All she was good at was reading, and even then she only liked to read frivolous novels, not the enlightening, somber ones. Novels in which a heroine was kidnapped from her convent, fled across France wearing boy's clothing, and somehow found her way to a duke with flashing eyes who took her in his arms and—

"Wait!" her mother said suddenly. "I have an idea."

Clara wiped her face and managed a shaky smile. "Yes?"

"Scotland," Lady Vetry said triumphantly. "Most of them loathe British royalty. They'll probably throw you a parade because you rebuked a corpulent, lascivious royal!"

"So you *do* understand why I struck him!" Clara cried, heartened by this show of loyalty.

"Absolutely not," her mother retorted. "It showed a sad lack of forethought and poor etiquette. It was practically . . . *republican*." Her face lit up. "America! Those rebels will love the fact you attacked the future king."

"No," Clara protested. "Lord Durden told me that Boston has more kangaroos than books."

Her mother scoffed. "What does that fool know? He's never been farther than Brighton. He certainly hasn't crossed the sea. What's more, I've never heard of kangaroos, and you know I regularly correspond with a childhood friend living there."

"Kangaroos are like giant rabbits with whiskers," Clara explained.

"I don't want to hear about whiskers ever again," her mother said flatly. "There are no reticules in your future." She glowered at Clara. "No reticules *and* no novels."

It didn't seem to have occurred to Lady Vetry that if Clara married someone on the other side of the ocean, she might never see her daughter again. Clara was fairly certain that her mother would consider that a benefit.

At the beginning of every Season, even knowing

that she had only a slim chance, Clara had always prayed that a man at the rank of viscount or above would fall desperately in love with her. Anyone at a higher rank than her mother, because the only thing that quelled Lady Vetry's critical comments was blood bluer than her own.

In more imaginative moments, Clara envisioned her husband reprimanding her mother for unkindnesses. "I fell in love with my wife at first sight," the viscount would snarl. "I would have married her were she selling flowers at the opera!"

A viscount had fallen in love with her dearest friend . . . and like all the other available bachelors, he had never taken a second glance at Clara.

"I prefer Scotland," she stated, taking a deep breath. She refused to imagine a life without novels. She had subscriptions with every press, and they could post new books to Edinburgh, but it would take months for packages to reach Boston.

"I suppose that's far enough, if you prefer it. We'll have to dispatch you tomorrow, before gossip filters up the country, though as I say, Scotsmen might embrace the story." Her mother leaned forward and caught Clara's eye. "You'll take *any* gentleman. Cast your net wide."

"I'm not sure what you mean by that." She yanked another whisker from her reticule.

"No man should be rejected on the basis of his age," Lady Vetry said, settling back in her seat. "Or his figure, schooling, accent, or estate. A vagabond will do, as long as his bloodline is respectable."

Clara bit her lip. "Where will I stay in Scotland? How am I to meet these aged vagabonds?"

"Don't be sarcastic," Lady Vetry snapped. "It's a

most unattractive trait in a lady. Do you remember your old nanny, Mrs. Wisk?"

"She used to read to me."

Her mother winced. "That started you down the path to eccentricity. At any rate, Mrs. Wisk is a Scotswoman. When it was time for you to have a governess, your sainted father sent her to Scotland to be a companion to one of his relatives, Lady Esther Ferguson, who had been recently widowed. I suppose she's your great-aunt . . . or perhaps great-great-aunt?"

"Have you ever met her?"

"Certainly not. I have never seen reason to venture farther than Britain's exquisite countryside. Your former nanny will be happy to see you, though now I think on it, I believe Mrs. Wisk has gone blind."

"Oh, dear," Clara said. "She loved reading."

"If worse comes to worst, I suppose you can read to her," Lady Vetry said with a sigh. "I have come to terms with your indolence, Clara, but you must think of your future. Mrs. Wisk won't last forever, and then what will you do? You have to marry."

Was she supposed to welcome the prospect of marrying a vagabond with a temper?

"There might be a fuss when you first arrive," her mother remarked. "It will quickly pass."

Clara shuddered at the idea of showing up unannounced. "How will I explain why I'm visiting? What if Lady Esther thinks I'm an impostor?"

Her mother scoffed. "You will have my letter, be dressed in an exquisite gown, and be accompanied by a French maid. You don't suppose that Hortense would allow anyone to offer disrespect, do you? She'll brazen it out, and you follow her lead."

Lady Vetry sighed. "Were Hortense my daughter, this would all be playing out *very* differently."

Clara burst into sobs.

"Now don't you wish that you still had His Majesty's handkerchief?" her mother demanded.

CHAPTER 5

April 11, 1803

𝒜 few hours after Lady Vetry and Clara arrived home, Hortense walked into the drawing room wearing an enchanting walking gown that might have graced a duchess.

A moment later, she had shed her dignity along with her French accent. Clara sighed. She tried to let her mother's criticisms roll off her back, but Hortense's temper flared every time Lady Vetry criticized her.

"I cannot produce miracles! Your daughter is not slender enough for current fashion, charming enough to draw suitors, nor articulate enough to intimidate them," she said with stinging clarity. "She can't even watercolor!" She turned to Clara and said, "Forgive me for my bluntness. You do make those ravishing little reticules, but gentlemen have no taste."

"Don't mention those whiskered eccentricities," Lady Vetry ordered, without disputing Hortense's assessment. "You put my daughter in a corset that hoisted her bosom to her chin!"

"If you want to sell an apple, you polish it," the maid snapped back. "But if I understand you, Miss Vetry slapped the heir to the throne. If you'd warned me of her reckless disposition, I'd have never taken the position!"

"Warned *you*? I consider you to be responsible for the scandal," Lady Vetry retorted. "*You* dressed Clara in a gown that made the prince mistake her for a strumpet. Not only that, but apparently the Princess of Wales called my daughter—who traces her ancestry to King Henry VII—a trollop, albeit in that confounded language of hers."

Hortense's lip curled. "No one could have foreseen this debacle. Tomorrow's gossip columns will speak of nothing else."

"You won't be here to read them," Lady Vetry said triumphantly. "The two of you are off to Scotland first thing in the morning. I've sent the butler to hire a post chaise that will take you from the Parrot and Pickle straight to the Great North Road. You'll live with our dear relative Lady Esther Ferguson through the summer at the least. As a titled lady, she is at the pinnacle of Scottish society . . . such as it is."

Hortense recoiled. "You are sending us in a public vehicle? I have *never* been asked to travel in such a ramshackle fashion!"

"It's not the public stagecoach," Lady Vetry retorted. "I have only one carriage, which I shall require here. Of course my daughter—and her maid—will travel in comfort. I shall dispatch linens and silverware with you."

"If you think—"

Clara sat to the side of the room, trying to ignore the escalating battle, wondering if she should retreat upstairs and take another bath. She'd had one as soon as they entered the house, but she could still feel the impression of Prince George's fingers—and the slimy warmth of bird excrement.

"I paid you a great sum of money on the premise that you would find a husband for my daughter," her mother hissed.

"No one could have anticipated this development."

"That's not what you said when you demanded hundreds of pounds paid in advance!" Lady Vetry snapped. "Tomorrow morning you will accompany my daughter to Scotland *and* act as her chaperone. Clara must be adequately turned out to catch a suitor's eye, but not so much as to attract lascivious attention."

"She slapped the future king, and no matter whether His Highness deserved it, which he surely did," Hortense said, with a surprising flash of sympathy, "now your daughter is"—snapping her fingers—"how do you say? Anathema!"

Her French accent had abruptly returned.

"Not in Scotland!" Lady Vetry said in triumph. "Highlanders are patriotic. Find her one of those. Find her a lard."

A moment of puzzled silence followed.

"Not 'lard'—*laird*," Clara exclaimed. "Highland chieftains are lairds."

"The word is 'lard,'" her mother said coldly.

"A man named Walter Scott wrote a long poem, 'Glenfinlas,' about a *laird*, Lord Roland, who was torn to bits."

Her mother frowned. "Was it historical? I don't think the Scots are at war."

Clara shook her head. "'Twas done by a fiend, who sailed away on the midnight wind."

"Utter rubbish!" Lady Vetry said. "I blame myself for the warping of your imagination. I should never have allowed you to move on from *The Book of Common Prayer*. Even the Bible contains overly stimulating material for an innocent mind."

"Miss Vetry's unmarried state cannot be blamed on a penchant for reading about dismembered bodies," Hortense pronounced, rising to her feet. "I shall do my best in Scotland, Lady Vetry. I think it only fair to warn you that I have grave reservations about my ability to succeed."

"Noted," Clara's mother said sourly.

"If we are to leave tomorrow morning, I must begin to pack. Especially since we are traveling so haphazardly."

"You'll not include a single whiskered reticule in my daughter's trunk," Lady Vetry ordered. "Throw them all out. If one is seen in public, it will stir up the scandal all over again."

A few minutes later, Clara sank into a chair in her bedchamber. She still felt shaky and had decided that she definitely wanted another bath. She opened *Lady Maclairn, the Victim of Villainy*, but the heroine was endlessly "giving herself up to tears," and because Clara wouldn't have minded doing the same, she put it to the side.

Ten minutes later, Hortense swept in with Betsy, one of the upstairs chambermaids, followed by a footman carrying a double-layer trunk with a curved top banded with etched brass.

"Wrap Miss Vetry's clothing in cotton, but the evening gowns in silk," Hortense instructed Betsy. "Daily garments, underclothing, necessities, and so on at the bottom. The removable shelf at the top should contain only evening gowns so they aren't crushed. I shall be in my chambers."

"'Chambers'?" Clara repeated after the door closed.

"Miss Hortense uses the room next to hers as a dressing room," Betsy explained. "Did you know that she was about to be presented to the King of France when he had his head chopped off? Her aunt was poor Queen Marie Antoinette's lady-in-waiting."

Right. Hortense would have been around ten years old during the Terror.

"I need a trunk for my books."

The maid's hands twisted together. "She said no books."

"Oh, for God's sake," Clara cried, exasperated. "*I* am your mistress, not Hortense."

"I didn't mean her," Betsy said. "It's Lady Vetry, miss. She said no books and no reticules."

Bollocks.

"I shall pack them myself while you fetch more hot water from the kitchen."

Betsy gaped. "Another bath?"

"With my apologies to the footman for asking him to drag pails up the stairs again. Since I'll pack my books, you can answer with complete honesty that you had nothing to do with it."

After Betsy left, Clara put a layer of favorite novels on the bottom of the trunk, followed by eight reticules, nicely padded with white cotton and held in place by another layer of books that she could not leave behind. The rest would have to be sent to her later.

Then she sank into the bathtub while Betsy packed the rest of the trunk.

"These evening gowns won't fit," the maid exclaimed, dismayed. She was holding a stack of three dresses, carefully wrapped in silk.

"Put them on a chair to the side," Clara suggested. "They could be accidentally left behind."

"That would be worth my position," Betsy gasped. "I'll take them upstairs to Hortense. She has two trunks, and she can fit them in somewhere."

"*Two* trunks?"

"That's why Lady Vetry allowed her to use an

extra room as a dressing chamber. You can't see the floor for her belongings."

When Betsy returned, Clara reluctantly climbed out of the bath and began drying her hair before the fire. She was lucky that her hair could be coaxed into fashionable ringlets—and unlucky because its yellow color had lent itself to Prince George's obsession with cupids.

The following morning, she once again found it hard to climb out of her bath. She was still plagued by the visceral memory of the prince's grasp—and no matter how much she washed and perfumed her breasts, she kept catching a whiff of cherry brandy.

When she was finally dressed for travel, and Betsy was packing her brush and other accessories into small cotton bags that fit neatly into the corners of the trunk, her mother appeared in the doorway.

Clara turned about and curtsied. "Good morning, Mother. We're finished."

"*We*?" Lady Vetry repeated magisterially. "Where is Hortense? Why is my daughter engaged in menial labor?"

Hortense strolled in the room and dropped a shallow curtsy. "Good morning, Lady Vetry."

"I have money to give you," Lady Vetry said to Clara. "Hand me your reticule."

"You demanded that they all be thrown out."

"You had *only* animal reticules?" her mother cried. "I suppose you may use this." She handed over a velvet bag edged with pearls. "These sovereigns should keep you for six months, but you may contact our man of business in the Inns of Court if you need more. I have written to instruct him that your dowry *and* choice of husband are now in your hands."

Her wrinkled nose made it clear that she was washing her hands of the situation—along with her unsuccessful daughter.

"Thank you," Clara said quietly, slipping the sack into her left pocket. When one's own mother couldn't muster up affection, hadn't it been rank stupidity to dream of a love match? She had hoped to meet a man as wonderful as the heroes in her favorite novels. She'd also hoped for a castle, so maybe she should give up men and focus on that. Reportedly Scotland had as many castles as daisies in a ditch.

"Here's another bag with farthings, ha'pennies, shillings, and a few florins that you can use for tipping the coachman," Lady Vetry instructed. "Your coachman is not our employee, so don't forget to give him a shilling every morning. You'll spend at least ten days on the road, and he must ensure that the innkeeper gives you an excellent room."

Clara nodded, pushing the second bag into the same pocket, leaving a visible lump against her thigh.

"Put my letter into your other pocket," her mother said.

"Thank you," Clara murmured, taking it.

"Finally, I shall give you a miniature of me made by that fellow Joshua Reynolds. I've decided to commission a more flattering one by James Northcote."

Lady Vetry handed the oval frame studded with pearls to Betsy, who promptly began rolling it in layers of cotton. "I would hope that my image will remind you of the precepts I have tried to instill in you. Why aren't you wearing the red mantle with the squirrel trim?"

Clara had chosen a rather shabby cloak that had

the advantage of covering every inch of her body, including her neck.

"Due to the quality of vehicle we're traveling in," Hortense cut in, "I thought it best if we dress in colors that disguise dust."

Lady Vetry narrowed her eyes, but the maid gave her an innocent look. Clara felt a wash of gratitude; Hortense might shout regrettable things when she was in a fury, but she always apologized and tried to shield Clara from her mother's displeasure.

Once in the carriage taking them to the Parrot & Pickle, Hortense removed a small mirror from her reticule—green silk with a fringed ruffle—and powdered her nose. "Who is Lady Esther Ferguson? Is she in fashion?"

"I have no idea," Clara said dispiritedly. "I've never met her. She's a distant relative who married a Scotsman. My former nanny serves as her companion."

"Have you seen your nanny in recent years?"

"Mrs. Wisk is blind, so she doesn't travel to London, and of course we don't correspond. Actually, I didn't even know where she was until my mother informed me yesterday."

"This sounds rather awkward. Don't you know anything about your relative?"

Clara shook her head.

"Your mother is remarkably callous," Hortense said abruptly. "You should not have raised your hand against a man of royal blood, but everyone acknowledges that Prinny is a bully and a cad."

Prinny?

"We will have a king who barely has the wherewithal to keep his numerous mistresses happy—given the time he spends in brothels—let alone to rule the kingdom," Hortense added.

Clara couldn't argue with that assessment of Prince George. She nodded and stared out the window as the carriage trundled through the streets to the Parrot & Pickle. She couldn't stop thinking about the disgusting moment when his hand closed around her breast, his fingers digging into her flesh, his breath quickening with excitement.

"Whatever you're thinking about, *stop*," Hortense ordered. "You're crumpling your mother's letter. Why haven't you put it in your pocket as she instructed?"

"I am carrying my favorite novel, *Love in Excess*," Clara said, deciding that if Hortense tried to enforce her mother's ban on novels, she would stop the carriage and put her out.

But Hortense plucked the letter from Clara's hand and began to flatten the sheet against the seat.

The only thing Clara wanted to do was enter the inn and wash her breast until she erased the feeling of a royal hand clawing at her. When the door opened, she hurtled out of the coach.

"Please find the post chaise that Mother rented and arrange for transfer of our trunks," she told Hortense, walking away before the maid could respond.

The hostelry was four stories high, each level faced with a railing. The courtyard was crowded with postboys in green uniforms and grooms in livery standing beside fine carriages. When she burst through the door, a kindly housemaid eyed her shabby cloak and refused the ha'penny she offered, giving her a pitcher of warm water and ushering her into a bedchamber.

Clara undid the ribbon gathering the bodice of her traveling gown and began washing her breast again. It didn't help. *It didn't help.* Her mind kept rocketing between sensations of disgusting slime and clutching fingers.

She was still washing when the innkeeper called that her carriage was waiting. Clara wrenched up her bodice, tied the ribbon, and wrapped the cloak tightly around herself.

The Parrot & Pickle was a large staging inn with carriages trundling in and out of several huge gates every five minutes or so. Clara hadn't noticed the cacophony of activity when she dashed from the carriage, but now the sound of coachmen bawling, whips cracking, and horses neighing buffeted her ears. She hadn't the faintest idea how to find the stagecoach her mother hired until she finally asked an ostler, who said that long-haul carriages bound for Scotland could be found next to the gate closest to the North Road.

"You the housekeeper bound for a Scottish castle?" a coachman shouted, waving at her as she picked her way across the courtyard, her thin soles slipping on the cobblestones. "You're a day late!"

Clara blinked. *A castle?* As in the novel that she adored, *The Castle of Otranto*? Or even better, *The Castles of Athlin and Dunbayne*?

"Miss Vetry!" She turned at the sound of her name and found Hortense standing beside a different carriage. One of her trunks was strapped on top, and a large coachman was overseeing two groaning grooms as they hoisted the second in the air.

Clara had always wanted to live in a castle—and now one was being offered to her. Her heart began pounding. Adventure beckoned, *if* she was brave enough. She waved at Hortense before she turned her back and walked over to the castle-bound coachman.

The man was rougher than the driver her mother had hired; he was wearing a thick woolen coat buckled around his waist rather than a crimson cloak with three capes, and he was chewing on an unlit cigar. The hair on his upper lip stuck out to the sides, curling up in a style she'd never seen before.

"You the housekeeper?" he demanded without a trace of civility. "You was supposed to be here yesterday. I was thinkin' you'd scarpered and weren't coming at all!"

Her breath started coming quickly; agreeing with him would be the bravest thing she'd ever done—and that included slapping the prince. "I won't get into a coach with just anyone," she declared. "Who are you waiting for, and what is your destination?"

He rolled his eyes. "How many housekeepers are headed for the Highlands, then?"

She only barely suppressed a gasp. The Highlands! A castle was one thing . . . but a castle in the *Highlands*? She mustered up a cool look. "I might be the only such housekeeper, but I'd still like to know your destination and the name of the woman you're waiting for."

He took out a piece of paper and squinted at it. "Mrs. Potts, bound for Castle CaerLaven. That you?"

Clara's heart was beating in her throat. Who could say no to *Castle CaerLaven*? What a darling name. Her mother's voice echoed in her head,

declaring that this would be the most impulsive
and stupid decision of her life, surpassing her so-
called assault on Prince George.

"Yes," she croaked. And then, when he scowled,
she raised her chin and said, "I am Mrs. Potts."

"Where are your things, then?"

She nodded at her trunk, on the ground beside
Hortense.

He grunted, took his unlit cigar from his mouth
and stuck it in his pocket before striding over to the
other coach.

Clara ran after him.

"That man is touching your belongings!" Hortense
cried. "Here, you—"

Clara caught her arm. "I'm going with him."

The maid's mouth fell open. "What did you say?"

"He's fetching a housekeeper to a castle in the
Highlands."

"What are you talking about?"

"I can't visit an ancient aunt who's never met me
in my life," Clara said. "I can't . . . I can't do it any
longer, Hortense. I don't want to marry a drunken
Scottish vagabond. In fact, I don't want to get married at all."

"I don't blame you, but what has that got to do
with anything?"

"I've never been good enough for Lady Vetry.
Never, Hortense, and I never will be."

"Your mother is a—"

"I have to *escape*. If I take this position as a
housekeeper—"

"You can't be a housekeeper!" Hortense cried,
interrupting in turn. "*I* couldn't be a housekeeper.
You'll be fired within the week. If you don't mind
my saying so, I consider you intensely unpractical,

which is *not* a desirable attribute for that particular position."

"That's all right," Clara said, giving her a giddy smile. "I don't mind. I have my dowry. I can live in Scotland quite happily. My mother told me to buy a husband, but I don't want one. I think I'll buy a small castle instead and fill it with books."

Hortense gaped at her.

"*Please* don't tell my mother where I've gone. *Please*." She swallowed, her throat suddenly tight. "Lady Vetry would vastly prefer not to think about me. I've always been a disappointment. I want to stop trying to make her happy, and the best way to do that is to live in another country."

"You shouldn't have to *try*!" Hortense cried without a trace of a French accent, her voice as aristocratically English as cut glass. "I truly can't bear your mother."

"Thank you," Clara said with a wobbly smile. "She prepaid you through the summer, right? So please, could you simply do something out of society's view for a few months? That way she'll assume we're together."

"Nonsense. I shall come with you. A *housekeeper*?"

"Only until I am fired," Clara told her. "I'd rather go alone, Hortense."

Her maid's brows drew together. "You won't be safe. This is a very reckless decision, and I can't allow—"

"You have no choice," Clara said, breaking in. "I've spent my life doing everything Lady Vetry ordered me to, and I am *done*, Hortense. I am certain that I can keep myself safe—safer than I was in a garden party, in company with a good many noblemen who didn't lift a hand to help after I was accosted."

"I'm very sorry that happened to you," Hortense said. "Miss Vetry, you have no idea how to be a servant."

"You'd better call me Clara, don't you think? We shall both be living belowstairs, after all. When you're not pretending to be French, you sound as much a lady as I do."

Hortense winced.

"You are a lady who learned to be a servant, and so shall I."

"But traveling alone? Your mother would . . . No, I can't say that she would worry about you."

Hortense had a remarkable ability to voice unpleasant truths.

"She'd worry about damage to the family name," Clara said. For that reason, Lady Vetry would have hysterics at the idea of her daughter accepting a post as a housekeeper. "Running away is better for my mother and for me."

"But you have no idea how vulnerable young women can be belowstairs."

"Did anything unpleasant happen to you at our house?"

Hortense blinked. *"Me?* No one would dare."

"I'll imitate you, then," Clara said.

"You *did* slap the future king," Hortense remarked with a reluctant smile. "I'm not sure even I would go that far."

"His Majesty isn't the first man to be poked by the whiskers on my reticules," Clara admitted. "If I hadn't been raised to revere royalty, Prince George would have felt the sting of those wires years ago."

"I did notice the reticules are no longer in your bedchamber. I suppose they are in your trunk?"

"My mother has washed her hands of me, and I

have taken the opportunity to wash my hands of her commands," Clara said, the truth becoming clearer to her with every word. "I shall never return to English society. *Ever.*"

Hortense looked reluctantly admiring. "Be careful. Men can be vile. Maids and housekeepers are seen as fair game, and wire whiskers won't be effective in every situation."

"In the last years I learned a great deal about lustful men while trying to avoid His Majesty's advances."

"You'd better take this," Hortense said, twisting a ring off her finger and handing it to Clara.

It was a pretty gold ring, chased with ivy. "I couldn't take your ring."

"My mother would want you to have it," Hortense said, stepping back. "She loved adventure. The only way you'll escape being accosted is if men think you're married. And in any case, every housekeeper is supposedly married."

"The coachman did say that he was waiting for Mrs. Potts." Clara glanced down at the band. "I could buy a ring."

"This one will bring you good luck," Hortense said. "I'd rather you have it than me."

Clara slid it onto her ring finger, and it fit perfectly. "Thank you," she said. "I'm so grateful, Hortense, truly."

"Your mother paid me a great deal, more than the ring is worth. Wear it always, Clara. Without it, any man on the street might feel emboldened to drag you into an alley and kiss you, or worse. You don't know what life is like without a maid or a chaperone at your heels."

Clara nodded. "I promise I won't take it off." She

waved at the vehicle her mother had hired. "This carriage has to go somewhere outside London, or Lady Vetry will discover the truth. Perhaps you might visit your family, if they live in the country?"

Something flickered in Hortense's eyes. "I could do that."

"Do you have enough money?" Clara began to drag out one of the velvet bags.

Hortense caught her wrist. "I'm fine. As you said, your mother prepaid me. Despite my better judgment, I think you're doing the right thing. I can imagine you in a castle full of books. Perhaps you'll meet a man like Valancourt."

Clara grinned at her. "I didn't know you read novels! I adore *The Mysteries of Udolpho*."

"I like Valancourt, but Emily? All her 'timid sweetness' made me sick to my stomach."

The coachman bound for Castle CaerLaven had finished strapping her trunk atop his coach and had started bellowing.

"Time to go," Clara said. She hesitated and then leaned in to drop a kiss on Hortense's cheek. "I wish I'd known you were a reader. Thank you for your help this Season. It wasn't your fault that I was such a dismal failure." Without waiting for a reply, she dashed over to the other coach.

"Get in," the coachman said, pulling open the door. "I hope to God you used the necessity, because we won't be stopping except to change horses until nightfall."

Nightfall?

"I need a mounting block," Clara pointed out.

"Poppycock!" He turned to a postillion lounging at one of his horse's heads. "Fred, jump up, blast you. We're off immediately."

Clara narrowed her eyes at him in a reasonable simulation of her mother. "I'll beg you to be more civil, sir."

Without a second's hesitation, the man grabbed her around the waist and tossed her into the coach, slamming the door behind her. Clara only escaped smashing into a closed wicker basket by throwing herself onto one of the leather seats. The carriage jolted into motion.

They were off.

To Scotland!

CHAPTER 6

*C*aelan strolled down the aisle of St. Andrew's Kirk in Lavenween, feeling profoundly grateful that the service was over. The Bean—*Alfie*—ran down the aisle ahead of him; by the time Caelan made it out the door, the boy was veering around the right of the building into the weedy little cemetery, shouting for his chicken.

Apparently guests were not allowed to cluck during a memorial service.

His brother-in-law, Rory, came up beside him and said, "Gloomy affair, death services," adding hastily, "I don't mean to diminish your grief, but I expect you'd rather remember Isla in your own way."

Caelan didn't answer Rory, just glanced at him. They'd known each other since they were boys, skipping school together to explore the dense woods that spanned their adjoining lands. Rory couldn't possibly think that Caelan was on the verge of tears.

His brother-in-law cleared his throat. "It's been two years, of course."

"How's your whisky coming along?" Caelan had persuaded his brother-in-law that the liquor would someday be one of Scotland's main exports.

"The home farm's stinking with fermented barley and burning peat. The men think you're daft, aging whisky in casks used for sweet wine."

"It's cheaper than buying new ones," Caelan said. Even more importantly, his first brew had racked up a bidding frenzy among London merchants because traces of Madeira wine lent it a smoky sweetness.

Ahead of them, one of Isla's friends, Lady Bufford, sauntered over to her carriage, her aging husband at her side. In the shadowed chapel behind them, Fiona was comforting Mrs. Gillan, the minister hovering nearby. Poor Mrs. Gillan seemed as inconsolable after two years as she'd been after one. Her husband had thought that another memorial service for her daughter might put her grief to rest, but Caelan hadn't held out much hope.

Caelan started down the steps, Rory following.

They could hear Alfie's voice off in the cemetery, rising with anxiety. "Wilhelmina, where are you, girl? Come out of there!"

"Fiona had to tell Alfie that the good Lord Himself doesn't allow chickens in church," Rory remarked. "He was inclined to argue when she attributed the rule to a mere bishop. We'd better go see if we can find the bird. He'll be in floods of tears if she escapes."

"I can't stop thinking of him as the Bean."

"Fiona thinks being called by a grown-up name might make him less emotional." Rory glanced sideways at Caelan. "I don't recall the two of us weeping daily, do you?"

Caelan couldn't remember ever crying. It wasn't in him—luckily, because his father would have belted him for being girlish. The former laird had stern ideas about what made a man. "Isla always said that I was rubbish at expressing myself. Alfie will do better."

"Let's hope his future wife has already started embroidering handkerchiefs for her trousseau," Rory said morosely.

The cemetery's wrought-iron gate was hanging askew. Upkeep for the Lavenween kirk and its cemetery fell to the MacCrae family, but if a task would cost more than a ha'penny, the former laird had refused to pay it as a matter of principle.

Rory strode into the cemetery, while Caelan swung the gate to and fro, determining that the hinge needed replacing. In the graveyard, Alfie was on his hands and knees, imploring his chicken to emerge from a thicket of lilac bushes.

A snowy-white bird with a startling crown of feathers peered out from the brush and clucked with a rebellious air.

"Wilhelmina!" Alfie cried, opening the cloth bag he was holding invitingly. "Here you are, old girl. Let's go home." Unsurprisingly, the chicken responded by rocketing from the thicket, clucking at the top of her lungs. "Get her!" Alfie screamed. "She might fly!"

Rory went left and Caelan ran to the right—as did the chicken, since she was shrewdly making a beeline for the broken gate. As she neared it, Wilhelmina thrust her head forward and spread her wings.

"Catch her, Uncle Caelan!" Alfie shrieked.

The hell if he'd be responsible for more tears today.

Caelan dodged a tombstone and lunged forward, managing to catch the bird before she launched into the air—but he tripped. Since the bloody chicken would be a pancake if he landed on it, he thrust out his arms.

He hit the ground with a thump that rattled his teeth and punched every bit of air from his lungs, but somehow he managed to keep hold of the bird.

Rory was laughing like a loon as he took the

struggling chicken. "We're lucky that earthquake didn't knock over every tombstone left standing."

Caelan shook his head, trying to catch his breath.

"Oh, my sweet lord Jesus!" he heard from the gate. "He's collapsed on her grave! He's lying there, a broken man!"

"Caelan, that's Isla's plot." All humor had disappeared from Rory's voice.

He hadn't fallen into weeds; he was face down in a bed of bluebells, his dead wife's favorite flower.

Crap.

The story would be all over the village tomorrow; hell, it would probably be talked about in Inverness. The Laird of CaerLaven had thrown himself on his wife's grave to mark her death anniversary.

He pushed himself to his knees, but his mother-in-law hurtled across the yard faster than a speeding chicken, casting herself in a puddle of black cloth by Caelan's side and winding her arms around his neck. "Your heart is broken! You're a broken man. We are all *broken*."

Keeping one arm around his neck, she put her other hand flat on the purple blossoms. "Isla, my dearest Isla, know that while you sit on the side of Jesus, we haven't forgotten you for a moment. Your husband will never recover from your loss. *We* will never recover. *Never, ever, ever!*"

Rory gently kicked him in the leg, muttering, "Get up, man."

Caelan slipped an arm around his mother-in-law's waist and hauled her to her feet.

"That's enough, Mary," Mr. Gillan said to his wife. "Let the poor man go."

"We had twenty-three years of perfect and unalloyed happiness with our beloved Isla," she wailed, hiccupping as she took the handkerchief her husband gave her.

"Many can't say as much." With an apologetic grimace, Mr. Gillan took his wife back from Caelan.

Alfie popped up at their side, Wilhelmina safely tucked into the cloth bag he wore by a strap over his shoulder. The chicken seemed resigned to having been caught and was glancing about with curiosity.

His nephew's forehead puckered. "Are you very sad?"

"He's heartbroken," Mrs. Gillan said. "Broken."

"Are you *serious*?" Alfie asked her, his head swiveling between her and Caelan.

Caelan could have answered that. His mother-in-law was serious about the statement—and about sharing it. Sometimes it felt as if the whole of the Highlands had been informed of his broken heart.

Fiona strolled up and said, "We all miss Isla, but it's time that Caelan thinks about marrying again. I've been talking to him about taking a wife."

Mrs. Gillan sucked in a breath. "No!"

"You know how fond I was of Isla, but the bald truth is that CaerLaven needs an heir. We all know that."

At that, the poor woman started sobbing so hard that she choked, and finally the minister and her husband drew her back to the kirk.

Once his mother-in-law was out of earshot, Caelan asked, "Did you have to?"

"Yes," Fiona said. "I don't want my favorite brother in the grave with his dead wife. I wouldn't want it for Rory, either, if I slipped off this mortal coil."

"I'm your *only* brother," Caelan pointed out.

"I'd have to grieve my first wife for at least a decade," Rory said, his eyes dancing. "I'll never find another with such a blunt way with the truth."

Fiona smiled up at him; he bent his head to kiss her. Caelan turned away. Most of the gravestones were old and mossy, and many had tumbled over, their inscriptions covered by ivy.

Not Isla's, of course. Reportedly poor Mrs. Gillan sat by her daughter's tombstone every day of the year. A weed wouldn't dare sprout there.

A small hand crept into his and clung tightly. "I'm sorry you're broken," his nephew said earnestly. "I can lend you Wilhelmina, if you'd like, as long as you give her back before bedtime. Stroking her topknot always makes me feel better."

Wilhelmina cocked her head and gave Caelan a look that promised a bloody hand if he ever touched her again.

"Are you certain she enjoys being in that bag? Most chickens are fond of their coop."

"She doesn't live in a coop," Alfie said airily. "She's lucky that I bought her at market and made her my friend. I keep her with me all the time. If I put her in the coop, she might get made into stew. Also, the other chickens might peck her, since she's rabbity." He fluffed Wilhelmina's topknot, which did have a vague resemblance to a rabbit's tail.

Caelan nodded. "I understand your reasoning."

"I would be *broken* if she died," Alfie said.

"I hope not," Caelan said. Behind his nephew, his sister was rolling her eyes.

Thanks to Fiona sharing her marital ambitions with Mrs. Gillan, he was dead certain that the morrow would bring his former mother-in-law to his doorstep with tears and recriminations.

"You know, I have some puppies that are too

young to leave their mother, but old enough to play with," he said, coming damn close to smirking at his sister. "Why don't you come visit tomorrow?"

Fiona's eyes narrowed. "Traitor," she hissed under her breath.

"I'm not sure that Wilhelmina likes dogs," Alfie said. "I'm pretty sure she doesn't."

"We can leave her at home," Rory said. He held out his hand. "Come along, Alfie. Time for Sunday dinner."

Alfie hung back. "I'm sorry about your broken heart. I really am." His eyes glistened with tears. "I wish that hadn't happened to you—losing the person you love, I mean."

Caelan smiled at him and then ruffled his hair. "You make up for it, because you're the best nephew any man could be lucky enough to have, Alfie. Let's get Wilhelmina home and give her some grain."

"I'm eating at the big table with you, and we're having jam roly-poly," Alfie said, cheering up instantly. "Mama says that you're starving to death, and that any day you'll die of disserary." He hesitated. "*Dysentery*. We need to fatten you up."

His sister reached out and pinched Caelan's waist. "You're wasting away," she told him, dancing back before he could swat her.

As Caelan strolled after his family, he decided that he would like to have a kindly, intelligent son or daughter like Alfie.

And he *definitely* would like to stop being viewed as a tragic Romeo.

He narrowed his eyes, thinking it over. Who cared if his wife couldn't clean a fish? He needed a mature and measured woman, as buttoned-up as

Lady Bufford. He refused to be seen as Romeo ever again.

Or was it Hamlet who jumped into his beloved's grave?

Irrelevant. He wasn't a man to leap after a woman, dead or alive.

CHAPTER 7

The carriage was of a good size, but its leather was cracked, and an odor of beer and pickled herring hung in the air. The glass windows had rolled leather shades rather than the silk curtains of Lady Vetry's traveling coach.

Clara climbed up to stand on the seat, steadying herself as it rocked out of the gate. Then she banged on the trapdoor in the ceiling. It shoved open.

"Is the castle near Glasgow?"

She heard the coachman snort even over the noise of a London street. "The castle's in the *Highlands*. Past Inverness."

Inverness? She'd never heard of it. "We're stopping for luncheon!" she shouted.

"No, we ain't! You have a basket there with meat pies and other vittles."

"I'll buy your meal."

The trap slammed shut, but Clara had the impression that she'd won that round. She pushed the trap open once again. "What's your name?"

"Cobbledick."

Cobbledick? This time she closed the trap rather than snicker while he might hear her. The coach sped up; presumably they'd turned into St. John Street, which turned into the North Road leading to Scotland.

Clara sat down before she fell over, suddenly realizing that her mother's letter had been left behind with Hortense. She didn't even have her great-aunt's address.

If her employers in the castle fired her, she wouldn't have anywhere to go.

She was alone.

After a pulse of fear, she took a deep breath. It was *fine*—and anyway, she might have found herself on her own whether she went to her great-aunt's or not. Lady Vetry didn't seem to have considered that an estranged, aged great-aunt may well be dead.

It was Clara's very first adventure, and she refused to return home. She was lucky enough to have the dowry her father left her, and she simply had to keep reassuring herself that she could use her money to buy a castle. A very small castle.

To have an adventure, one had to risk everything. That was true in every novel she'd read, including the ones featuring evil fiends and malicious fairies.

With that thought, she slipped off her boots, took out her book, and wadded up her cloak to serve as a pillow.

Melliora, the heroine of *Love in Excess; or, the Fatal Inquiry*, went through far worse travails than traveling to Scotland on her own. The poor woman suffered through endless adventures, as when an evil rival invaded her bedroom and seduced her true love, Count D'Elmont—who thought he was bedding Melliora, of course.

Clara opened to the first page with a satisfied sigh. Was there anything better than reading a beloved novel for the eighth time? Or perhaps it was the fifteenth. Who cared how many times she had read it?

As the coach rumbled on, she munched happily on apples she found in the basket, forcing herself to concentrate by reading aloud every time Prince George and his grasping fingers came to mind.

Around noon, the carriage turned into a courtyard. Clara had no idea where they were—and she didn't care, either. When the coachman opened the door, she handed him a farthing, which was surely more than his daily wage.

"Mr. Cobbledick, I'll thank you to request a private room where I can relax for an hour or two, along with a warm meal for the two of us."

He blinked, and she thought he was about to refuse. But then his fingers closed around the farthing, and he stamped away, returning a few minutes later to toss the mounting block at her feet.

Clara took his hand and stepped down. She refused to be so chicken-hearted as to fear adventure when it presented itself. All the same, if there was one thing she'd learned from Melliora's many calamities—for example, when she was kidnapped from the convent where she'd taken refuge—it was that every heroine needed a protector.

Novelists introduced tall men with flashing, dark eyes, but one had to take what one could get, and all she had was an irascible coachman with an unusual mustache.

"You will join me for luncheon," she informed Mr. Cobbledick.

He scowled but followed her into a private parlor lit with a good fire. Clara took off her cloak, washed her hands at the basin, and sat down before the table. "I've never been anywhere without a maid in attendance."

The coachman's frown deepened.

"My maid didn't care to travel in a hired coach," she said. "So I'm relying on you, Mr. Cobbledick, to keep me safe."

"I've never heard of a housekeeper with a personal maid. It sounds as if you're a proper lady," he said, standing uneasily in the middle of the room.

"I am," Clara said. "Or rather, I was. Now I'm a housekeeper."

"I would never have laid hands on you."

"It's fine that you tossed me into the carriage," Clara reassured him. "Adventures always begin in a most astonishing way."

He was twirling one side of his mustache, perhaps in a sign of nerves. "I can't eat with the likes of you."

"Yes, you can," she said, smiling at the innkeeper's wife, who appeared with a heavy tray.

"Now you're out of that cloak, I do see that you're no servant." His eyes skated away from her bosom, even though her traveling dress was quite modest. Finally he agreed to sit down, but stayed on the far side of the room.

"I'm sorry that I delayed your departure."

"I had to sleep on the box," the coachman said, jerking his head toward his carriage in the courtyard. "To make sure that me equipage wasn't stolen. Several of us Scotsmen go back and forth to London, but none of us like to stay in the city. Terrible reek of coal smoke. I can't abide it."

"Do you have a wife and children?" Clara asked as she took a hearty serving of stew, a small meat pie, a chicken leg, and some boiled spinach. "Come and get a plate of food. I can't eat all this by myself."

"Aye, I do." He came forward with as much enthusiasm as a man threatened with being hung, drawn, and quartered.

It took a good half hour, but she discovered that Mr. Cobbledick was a widower who'd had two wives and been graced with two girls, the youngest of whom was Clara's age and had taken her first position as an upstairs maid in Inverness.

He spent his time going back and forth to London and had been irritable when she arrived because "Mrs. Potts" was supposed to join him the day before.

"It took me longer to prepare for the journey than I thought," Clara said, crossing her fingers under the table.

"What of your husband? What'd he think of your moving to the Highlands?" Mr. Cobbledick clearly smelled a rat.

Clara's shudder came from the heart. "I had to flee, Mr. Cobbledick. That's the truth of it. I couldn't be treated like that any longer." She put her fork down, feeling suddenly sick.

"Ach, I've heard that about English men," the coachman said with a ferocious scowl. "You'll be safe in the Highlands, lassie. A true Scotsman would never raise his hand to a woman."

Clara managed a shaky smile. "I've heard that your Highlands are filled with fairies who'll lure a person under a mound, and they find on return that the world's aged a century or two."

"Pshaw!" he snorted. "You sound like me grandmother. I've lived in the Highlands all me life, and I ain't met a single fairy, giant, nor a demon, either. Those are tales spun by those who fell asleep at their post, I'd say. Had to explain themselves, so they talk of fairies and the like."

"You must be tired after such an uncomfortable night," Clara said sympathetically. "Do you want to take a nap before we leave? When we travel to Bath, our coachman always has a nap around midday. I know it's not easy sitting on the box, with the dust kicking up in one's face from all the traffic."

Unfortunately, Mr. Cobbledick pounced on that. "You had a carriage. And now you're to be a housekeeper?"

"It was my mother's."

That didn't make things better, and finally the truth tumbled out.

"You're fleeing the future king of England?" Mr. Cobbledick's eyes were wide. "I wouldn't put it past an Englishman, but I would have thought better of them that wear ermine, if you see what I mean."

"It's more that I'm fleeing the scandal. No gentleman would want to marry me now, and my mother washed her hands of me."

He started ferociously twirling his mustache. "I've never thought much of the English," he said gruffly.

"It's not her fault," Clara said. "I have been a terrible disappointment."

Mr. Cobbledick shook his head. "My sainted wife—"

"Which one?"

"Both of 'em. I am lucky that they were wonderful mothers. Be that as it may, now you're trying to be a housekeeper?"

"I like to sew, and I was taught how to run a household."

"Knowing the work and doing the work are two different things," he objected.

"Actually, I did learn how to do a few things. I know how to make potted mackerel," Clara countered. "Also orange fritters and Spanish onions. I know what a banister brush is and how to revive a carpet with oxgall. I can use a pudding boiler, darn a sheet, and keep a linen press. I've seen a wringing machine. How hard can it be to turn the crank?"

"*Hard*," Mr. Cobbledick said. "Mighty hard. Why did these people hire an Englishwoman from London rather than a good Scotswoman?"

Clara shrugged. "Perhaps the mistress of the castle is English and married a Scotsman. Now she's widowed and lonely for someone from her homeland. I can read to her."

"You have too much imagination for your own good," the coachman muttered.

"Have you tried this excellent ale? It's one of the best I've had," Clara said.

In truth, it was the *only* ale she'd had, since people didn't offer young ladies the beverage, but she definitely liked it.

After two tankards, Mr. Cobbledick cheered up, and they came to an agreement.

He would keep her safe and stop the coach two or three times each day, including once for luncheon and a nap. Every night he would find her a safe room at a decent inn, order a hot bath, and assign Fred, the postillion, to sleep outside her door.

"You and I will get along together very well," Clara said, smiling at him.

His mouth twitched into something like a smile, which felt like a triumph.

CHAPTER 8

April 12, 1803

Caelan was working his way through a snarl of estate accounts when he heard a carriage scrape over the gravel drive. Fiona would never come over this early, which suggested that Mrs. Gillan hadn't slept all night.

He stood up and stretched with a groan. He'd been working for hours, and his desk was as cluttered as it had been when the sun rose.

Thankfully, when he walked outside, his mother-in-law wasn't sobbing; once she launched into a fit of tears, she didn't find her way out of it for an hour or more. Instead, she stood on the far side of the moat, staring down at the flowers. "Isla's flowers are doing well," she said by way of greeting.

He walked across the moat and bowed. "Good morning, Mrs. Gillan. Would you care to enter the castle and have a cup of tea?"

She shook her head so violently that the black veil she'd thrown back from her bonnet trembled. "The place where my dear Isla died? No. Besides . . . it's known to all that you're having trouble keeping staff. If you had a housekeeper, I'd be glad to give you a scullery maid. I could spare my housekeeper's daughter, but with you a single man and she a maiden, I couldn't do it in good conscience."

Was his *own mother-in-law* implying that he might take advantage of the lass?

She caught something in his face, because she started clucking like Wilhelmina and talking about the scullery maid's reputation. When he didn't respond, she took a fresh breath and said, "I've no wish for tea. I'll remain here, next to the exquisite blooms my beloved daughter planted. Isla had such an eye for beauty."

Caelan nodded.

"I thought about the service and our conversation all the night through, laird. Your sister is right. You must have an heir." Her reddened eyes flicked to the boulders lying by the south tower. "Your grief mustn't result in Isla's beloved home falling to ruin."

He cleared his throat. "Well—"

"As I said, the state of your castle is gossiped of all the way to Edinburgh. My cracked heart and my sensibilities cannot stand in your way. A man needs a helpmeet, as the Good Book says."

Caelan frowned. "I doubt—"

"I have a request." She put a hand on his arm. Mrs. Gillan had lost so much weight since her daughter died that her fingers curled around his forearm like little claws. "You and I both know that you will never recover from Isla's loss. Yet as my husband reminded me last night, a laird has a responsibility to his land."

Caelan held his tongue. He'd have done damn near anything to shake his reputation as the grieving widower. Getting remarried was sounding better every minute.

"Just don't take up with a local woman!" Mrs. Gillan burst out. "I couldn't bear that, I really couldn't. To see another Highlander usurp my Isla's place, living in her castle, with the man she loved so much. She told me when she was eight years old that she meant to marry you, remember? And then she did."

Her voice cracked, but she managed not to break down.

"She was so proud when you singled her out from all the lasses. 'Twould break her heart to see you pair yourself with the likes of Helen Inglis or Rebecca Frasier. They were always jealous of her beauty, you know."

Since he'd never met a woman living nearby whom he'd care to marry, the promise was easily made.

"Nor one of those women who come to the kirk of a Sunday!" Mrs. Gillan added.

At that, Caelan frowned. He wasn't what one might call a religiously observant man, but his mother would turn in her grave if he didn't make his way to the top pew and sit opposite old Lord Bufford, an English lord tolerated for his long roots in this area.

Mrs. Gillan caught his expression. "I'm not saying you should become a godless fiend," she gasped. "There's Isla waiting for you on the side of Jesus. It's just that those women throng the kirk every Sunday hoping that you'll notice them, coming from three hours away, as far as Inverness—"

"You must be jesting," he muttered.

Her hand fell away, and a smile wreathed her face. "You haven't even noticed those bold wenches, have you?"

Bloody hell. "I have not."

"No more than you entertained that hussy from the Mclean family who had the effrontery to pretend to be married so she could become your housekeeper!" Mrs. Gillan bared her teeth at that memory. "I had words with her mother, I promise you that!"

He cleared his throat. "I haven't met anyone in the locality whom I'd wish to marry, Mrs. Gillan."

"You will *never* feel the urge to welcome another woman to your home, laird."

Though he had entertained the same thought, the words struck a sour note.

"When a heart is truly broken, it never mends. The best you can hope for thereafter is a civilized arrangement. I have a suggestion that you might take amiss, but it's worth consideration." Her hand clamped on Caelan's arm once more. "I think you should get yourself a wife from England."

He blinked, stunned by the local shift from seeing England not as a powerful neighbor but as a hothouse of available spouses.

"You know how we all thought Lord Bufford had made a fool of himself when he took that young wife?" Mrs. Gillan asked.

"Aye."

"I've changed my mind. A Scotswoman would have felt threatened by three previous wives, but the new Lady Bufford is cold as ice. She's a good wife to Bufford, partly because she doesn't care about those who came before."

Caelan tried to pick his words carefully. "His lordship is elderly but seems fit enough."

"I didn't mean you should wait for Lady Bufford to be widowed! Lord knows, Bufford might live to be one hundred. You need an heir, and there's no bairn in that house. Mayhap she's not fruitful."

According to Isla, Lady Bufford had eschewed the marital bed, which explained her lack of children.

"My point is that an Englishwoman won't care whether you love her, the way that the young

Mclean did. Scotswomen are passionate, and your second wife might wither on discovering that your heart is in the grave with Isla."

Caelan cleared his throat again. "My sister also suggested an English bride." Fiona had been jesting. Perhaps.

"There, I knew that Lady McIntyre couldn't be as cruel as she seemed when she blurted out your need for a wife," Mrs. Gillan exclaimed. "Not the lady whom Isla counted as a dear friend and sister."

Caelan was at a loss for words.

"We could ask Lady Bufford," Mrs. Gillan mused. "Unfortunately, someone told me her only sister is a viscountess."

"Right."

"There, that's settled," Mrs. Gillan said.

"It is?"

"You'll marry an Englishwoman with a stony heart, and the fact that yours is broken won't bother her. Anyone can tell that Lady Bufford doesn't give a fig about being the fourth of her husband's wives. She's not the love of his life, but that's irrelevant to her."

"Indeed?" Caelan asked.

"If there's one thing that you and I understand, it's that deep love—the kind that Romeo and Juliet, and you and Isla, experienced—comes only once in a lifetime, and most people don't experience it at all."

"Hmmm."

"As I said to my husband in the middle of the night, thinking on that image of you stretched over my darling's grave, we must be grateful to the Almighty that you didn't take your own life from the agony of your grief. You showed courage and restraint, knowing you'll suffer your entire life."

"I don't think I'm the type who would ever take my life," Caelan said, startled.

"Of course you wouldn't, because that would threaten your afterlife with dear Isla! I shall speak to Lady Bufford about her acquaintances," Mrs. Gillan said with sudden energy.

Apparently his former mother-in-law meant to personally shove him down the aisle to wed a stonyhearted woman with an English accent.

"You'll have to go back to wearing breeches," Mrs. Gillan added. "No Englishwoman will appreciate a kilt, any more than Isla did. It isn't clothing fit for a lord."

Caelan almost made the point that a laird is not the same as a lord but thought better of it. Isla had adored being addressed as Lady MacCrae. She had wanted him in breeches and a cravat, mincing around his holdings in polished shoes.

They had been furthest apart in those moments, since he was a man who cared nothing for appearances, and his wife emulated Marie Antoinette. To put it another way, he preferred reality but Isla, fantasy.

He stood watching as Mrs. Gillan's carriage rocked its way toward the pass leading to Lavenween, wondering why two women were searching out a wife for him, although he'd clearly informed both that he didn't want to marry again.

It was perplexing. His crofters tended to treat him with respect, and if he made his wishes clear, they took notice.

On the other hand, Mrs. Gillan seemed more cheerful than he'd seen her in two years. He turned away with a sigh. In addition to his estate responsibilities, he had to make it through the monthly accounts, meet a crofter with a leaky roof, drop in at the mill and find out why Ross the Younger hadn't paid the multure owed for grinding his corn. Then there was a parcel of bullocks due to be sold off, and that crofter had sent a message telling him to come take one animal in lieu of rent on his holding.

No time for fishing. No time to write, nor even to read a page or two of the new books delivered from Edinburgh.

Sitting down to the accounts, he caught sight of a scrap of paper he'd overlooked: he was due to sit in judgment over a small meadow claimed by two crofters, one as a matter of inheritance and the other through marriage.

That meant that both sides would show up at the castle, bellowing about dowries, jointures, and their respective fathers' attachments to that patch of land.

Bloody hell. He'd have to put off the bullocks.

He didn't have time to find a wife.

CHAPTER 9

April 14, 1803

Clara and Mr. Cobbledick were now friendly acquaintances, so that when a wheel spun off the coach within view of a pub, the coachman walked her into the yard and bullied everyone into entering the building so that she could sit at one of the outdoor tables without being gawked at.

The innkeeper's wife emerged with a glass of cool lemonade. "Would you like me to take your cloak, miss? I could beat off the dust, and sponge it down."

"That would be marvelous," Clara said gratefully. She'd had no trouble dressing herself since her traveling garments were designed for ease, but it had been demoralizing to watch her clothing and her boots, sewn from the softest pale yellow kid leather, turn brown with dirt. She stood up to pull off the cloak and handed it over. "Do you think you might wash some of my other garments as well?"

After the innkeeper's wife bustled over to the carriage and returned with an armful of dusty clothing, Clara opened up her book and plunged back into Melliora's adventures. Sometime later she took off her bonnet, because she liked to feel the sun on her face, and moreover, because she had decided that she didn't care about freckles.

Her mother cared about freckles. Adventurers like herself and Melliora didn't have time to worry about such trivialities.

A few hours later, she became gradually aware

of the conversation happening on the other side of a large window standing ajar at her right shoulder. Two men were talking about a woman, but not, thank goodness, in the disgusting manner that the prince used when muttering to his friends about her.

"If Venus had a figure, that'd be it," said one man, who sounded quite young.

"Course Venus has a figure. She's a goddess, ain't she?"

"Yeah, but does she have that . . . is she like *that*?"

"No one's like that, not normally," the other man said after a pause. "She might be one of the princesses, one of the king's girls. There's three or four of them."

"Look at her on top," the first man whispered, an ache in his voice that made Clara blink. "I know she's not for the likes of us, but I never seen a woman like that. You can tell she's sweet, and I bet she smells sweet too. I'd wager she bathes every week."

Clara couldn't help smiling. If anyone was sweet, it was that boy.

"Her hair is like a field of daisies with the sun shining on them."

Her eyes widened. He was talking about *her*. She was *stupefied*, like when Violetta—the other heroine in *Love in Excess*—disguised herself as a boy, Fidelio, and then revealed herself to her true love.

"You're right about that. She's *definitely* too good for the likes of you," the second man said, sounding amused.

"I cannae believe what I see," the longing boy continued. "She knows how to read, and she's more beautiful than I ever thought I'd see in my lifetime. If she was mine, I'd stand beside her all day long."

The yearning note in his voice was oddly healing. Clara glanced over her shoulder at the window, but leaded glass caught the sun and cast the indoors into shadow.

"Don't let her hear you!"

The boy sighed so deeply that she had to squeeze her lips together so as not to burst out laughing. Cobbledick waved at her from the gate, so she finished her lemonade and stood.

Before picking up her bonnet, Clara turned slightly so she was facing the window, raised her hands, and tousled her hair so that curls tumbled down her back. Then she said cheerfully, "Good day!" before whipping around, grabbing her bonnet, and heading off.

From inside the pub, she heard "Jesu alive, son, did you faint?" She arrived at the coachman's side giggling madly.

He smiled. "It's good to see you smiling."

"I'm a very sunny person." But then . . . she hadn't been, had she? Not lately. "Normally I'm sunny," she amended.

That evening she looked at herself in the glass after climbing out of her nightly bath. Prince George's attentions had made her loathe her breasts, but that was absurd. Her breasts were nicely shaped, and before George came along, she liked them.

She still had no wish for a husband, but there was something very heartening about realizing that the opinion of London society was not necessarily that of the world. Now that she was on an adventure, she was part of *that* world, not the London world.

When they reached Edinburgh a couple of days

later, Clara insisted on touring all the bookstores before they set off again. Back in the carriage, she happily sorted a tall stack of novels. She'd even found a new work by Walter Scott, *The Lay of the Last Minstrel*, that hadn't been published in England yet!

Thinking that perhaps the inhabitants of the castle liked books as much as she did, she had bought another copy of *The Castle of Otranto* as a welcome gift—and also to reread, since she had left hers at home.

Of course, CaerLaven Castle wouldn't be haunted the way Otranto was. She and Mr. Cobbledick had taken to eating their meals together, and when she shared a few details about that particular haunted manor, he rolled his eyes and snorted.

"Manuscript found in a Catholic household, you say? Dating back to the Crusades? Them's all madmen; I've heard it's eating moldy bread that drives them round the bend. I rarely go to the kirk meself."

"It was a literary ploy," Clara said, trying to explain that the novel was only disguised as a manuscript belonging to an ancient Catholic family. In reality, it had been written by the son of one of England's prime ministers.

"That don't make any sense," Mr. Cobbledick declared. "Either it is or it ain't. If there's ghosts running around, it's due to the Catholics for certain. They have all sorts of beliefs about devils and the like. Me mam told me that if I met a ghost, I should break a string of rosary beads at its feet. That's evidence right there."

When they reached Inverness, Mr. Cobbledick

took the opportunity to visit his youngest daughter while Clara browsed the city's only bookstore, emerging with the postillion carrying another stack of books.

"Elsbeth says the master of the house is making advances on her," Mr. Cobbledick told Clara that evening. They were only an hour or so away from CaerLaven land, but they had stopped at a large inn, as Clara wanted to bathe so that she might arrive the next morning properly attired for a castle.

"That's horrid," Clara said. "As I told you, my betters have done the same to me. You scarcely know what to do, because you can't kick a man who's more powerful than you, can you? I lost . . . well, I lost more than a possible spouse when I fought back. Elsbeth has to be careful."

"I don't know why he's after her. Elsbeth ain't like you. She's well enough, but not beautiful as you."

"You think I'm beautiful?"

Mr. Cobbledick snorted and said, "I thought that bookseller would follow you into my carriage like a duckling, he was that infatuated."

"Because I bought so many books."

"Nay, I heard him. He called you something. I didn't like the sound of it, but he didn't seem to be offering offense."

"Erato." Clara could feel herself turning pink. "The muse of lyric poetry, romantic poetry in particular."

"There you are," the coachman said. "Elsbeth ain't brave the way you are."

Brave and beautiful?

"I'm not very brave, actually," Clara confessed.

"When that future king pawed you, you didn't faint, did you?"

"I struck him," Clara acknowledged.

"Kept him off you, didn't it? Very brave. Men don't like to be struck, least of all kings."

"He wasn't pleased," Clara agreed. "I have an idea, Mr. Cobbledick. As you know, I left my maid, Hortense, back in London. Why don't you fetch Elsbeth tomorrow and bring her to me at the castle? She can be my maid!"

"I told you, housekeepers don't have maids of their own."

"I don't see how they can complain if I pay her wage myself. You'll take me to the castle early tomorrow morning, Mr. Cobbledick, and I'll explain that my maid will arrive soon. It's only three hours to Inverness. You can bring her back before nightfall."

The coachman couldn't get his head around the idea. "You'd be the only housekeeper in this country with a personal maid."

Clara tossed her head. "They'll take me as I am. They sent all the way to London for a housekeeper, which suggests they are desperate."

"Elsbeth don't know about curls and frills the way such a lass might do," Mr. Cobbledick objected, his eyes caught by Clara's hair. "From the sounds of it, she's up at dawn, hauling ash buckets and spending half the day in hiding so as to stay out of the way of that lascivious master of hers."

"We have to rescue her!" Clara declared.

"Elsbeth will be fine where she is," he said uneasily. "Perhaps she's exaggerating her master's interest. Why would he pay attention to a wee beastie like my daughter?"

Clara leaned over the table. "I don't suppose you've read *Pamela*?"

He shook his head. "I don't read. That is, I *can* read signs and the like, but I don't read as a matter of course."

"Poor Pamela is a fifteen-year-old maidservant who is assaulted by her employer. She ends up married to him—"

"Well, that ain't happening, since Elsbeth's master is married already."

"Even worse," Clara said. "The future king of England is married as well. More to the point, I've read the novel twice, and I still cannot reconcile myself to Pamela's marriage, being as her master assaulted her several times and kidnapped her as well."

Mr. Cobbledick frowned. "That don't sound like the kind of book that a young lady should be reading."

"It's considered an improving text," Clara told him. "The subtitle is *Virtue Rewarded*. Why, I expect that thinking about Pamela's plight as deeply as I had led to me striking the prince!"

"I would blame it on His Majesty's English blood," Mr. Cobbledick said heavily, "but Elsbeth's master is a Scotsman born and bred."

"Tomorrow morning you'll take me to the castle, then turn around directly, help Elsbeth pack her trunk, and bring her there as well."

"*Trunk?* She don't have a trunk. She's got a satchel, if that. She won't know how to be a maid to the likes of you."

"I'll teach her everything she needs to know. She has to keep my ringlets under control."

Mr. Cobbledick eyed her head and said nothing.

"I know," Clara said with a sigh. "My hair's twice the size it was in London, don't you think? I wash it every night with soap, but it's as if all this fresh air is making it puff up like a dandelion."

He cleared his throat. "I'm not sure that Elsbeth will know the solution."

"We can figure it out between us, Mr. Cobbledick. I need her help, I truly do. Most of my bonnets won't fit on my head any longer."

"I have to return to Glasgow directly," the coachman admitted, twirling one end of his mustache. "I'd rather do it without worrying about Elsbeth. I'm supposed to fetch a glass bathtub, if you can credit it, to this same castle."

"Bathing in glass sounds dangerous," Clara said dubiously.

"They're paying me double because it will take the whole of me carriage."

"If Elsbeth is anything like you, I will be happy to hire her," Clara said, beaming at him.

She smiled even more widely the next morning when they arrived at the castle bright and early. The castle was . . .

It was *everything*.

CHAPTER 10

April 19, 1803

*O*ne round turret stood to the right, with another shyly hiding behind. Bathed in morning sunlight, the stone had a lovely sheen that set off a moat planted with bluebells. Clara had never imagined anything as dazzling as a castle swimming in a pool of blue-and-purple blossoms.

Mr. Cobbledick moved to unstrap her trunk, but she caught his sleeve. "You have to leave it on your coach, because my maid would never travel in a separate carriage apart from my clothing."

"Why the dickens not?"

"Because she's in charge of my garments," Clara explained, turning back to the castle. "Isn't this gorgeous, Mr. Cobbledick? I've never seen such a romantic place in all my life."

"Romantic? I'd say deserted."

"No, not at all! See that magnificent arched doorway? It's ajar. People are already up and about. And all the rows of studs! Do you know why they're there?" She didn't wait for an answer, because while the coachman knew everything about horses and coaches, he didn't seem to have broadened his knowledge beyond that. "It's so that marauders can't chop into the door with their axes!"

Clara clasped her hands together, imagining hordes of warlike Highlanders, faces smeared in blue paint, wearing those funny plaid skirts while besieging the castle.

Mr. Cobbledick grunted and jerked his head at the postillion, who jumped back onto one of the lead horses.

"Go on," Clara told him. "You'll be in Inverness in three hours."

"Aye, but where are the footmen?" he said, scowling at the open door.

"If they don't have a housekeeper, the servants may be taking advantage," Clara said. Her mother was always complaining about that. "I'll get everything sorted out."

"I suppose you have it to rights," he said dubiously. "You'd better take this." He took out the picnic basket. Up in the Highlands, you couldn't count on an inn popping up every hour or so, offering a hot meal no matter the time of day.

"I'll take my books as well," Clara said. After all, what if the coach overturned? All the books she'd bought in Glasgow and Inverness would fly around the vehicle and get damaged.

Mr. Cobbledick piled all her new novels on a flat stone inside the gate. "They'll never believe you're a housekeeper, not when you've arrived with a load of books but nary a stitch of clothing."

"I'm an unusual housekeeper," Clara said. Then she added, "I'll try not to be fired before you return, but you might find me here waiting."

"I'll be back in seven hours, mind. If there's naught but cackling ghosts in residence, don't go inside." With a crack of laughter that would make a fiend proud, he climbed back onto the box.

Clara watched as the coach trundled out of sight before she turned back to the castle. Her cheeks hurt from smiling so widely.

The sunlight was warm, but she was reluctant to take off her elegant French pelisse before she met the inhabitants of the castle.

Housekeeper she might be, but she'd decided that—like Hortense—she needed to make an immediate impression and ensure everyone knew her rank. She had every intention of working hard, but she couldn't pretend to be someone other than who she was. She would do anything they asked of her, as long as she had breaks to read and have a cup of tea.

Before they set off that morning, she'd put on a white morning dress topped by her favorite pelisse, pale pink with lace trim and tulle at the neck. It had been designed to be worn alongside a lovely straw hat with silk scarves that tied under her chin. Unfortunately, her unruly hair made the hat sit so high on her head that it felt as if it might catch the wind and blow away, so she had left it in her trunk.

There wasn't a sound to be heard other than a couple of larks trying to outdo each other and from somewhere behind the castle, the rushing of a stream. No, that must be a *loch*!

"'Where wild Loch Katrine pours her tide, blue, dark, and deep, round many an isle,'" Clara whispered. "'Our fathers' towers o'erhang her side: the castle of the bold Glengyle!'" Walter Scott was a marvelous poet—but she pushed the thought away. It wasn't the right moment to be thinking about literature.

She had to find her employers.

Despite her bravado while speaking to Mr. Cobbledick, she felt a bit shy about introducing herself. Ladies were always introduced; they didn't do it themselves. To be totally honest, she was also slightly unnerved because Walter Scott's Castle Glengyle *and* Horace Walpole's Castle of Otranto housed shrieking ghosts—with "bursts of ghastly laughter," as Scott had put it. Yet surely no ghost would dare inhabit an adorable little castle encircled in flowers.

And this was an *adventure,* after all.

She walked over the narrow pathway that crossed the moat, admiring the flowers blooming on either side. What a marvelous idea to plant blue-and-purple blossoms to simulate water. Not that she knew much about gardening, but there seemed to be two types of bluebells intermixed. Her employers obviously appreciated beauty and elegance.

Squeezing sideways through the heavy door, she found herself in a vaulted corridor that butted into a spiral staircase at the far end, presumably leading up the foremost tower. Halfway down the corridor, an open archway to the left allowed a glimpse of a kitchen.

Clara reached the arch—and her mouth fell open.

It was filthy.

Not *at all* charming, flowery, or romantic.

She froze, reluctant to walk on grubby bricks in pink silk slippers. The fireplace was massive and clearly in use for cooking, although the spit and the huge iron pot were so blackened by burnt food that she couldn't imagine how to clean them.

A tall dresser to one side held stacks of plates that seemed to be the same thin, delicate kind that her mother preferred, with gilded rims. Even from here she could tell they were dusty, and the matching teapot had a broken spout. The sink was full of battered pewter plates, the kind that not even servants in her mother's home ate from. Pots and pans were piled on the floor in one corner of the room.

The tricks her mother's housekeeper had taught her so that she might instruct future housemaids—to press uncooked dough into nooks and crannies to remove dust, for example—felt thoroughly inadequate to address disorder of this scale.

Were there no servants at all?

The owners of the castle must be as poor as church mice. They should sell the enormous gold-plated soup tureen that sat on top of the cupboard, dulled by grime. Perhaps it belonged to an ancestor, and they couldn't bear to part with it.

Thank goodness she had her own money, because presumably they were offering poor Mrs. Potts a few ha'pennies a week. No wonder they had sent for a housekeeper from England! Anyone who lived close by would throw an apron at the laird's head and take herself home.

Turning around, she found that an arch opposite the kitchen opened onto a room that resembled a huge beer barrel. A long table ran down the middle; its legs had a delicate curve and might have been inlaid with veneer, but it was impossible to see through the thick dust. On one wall, a motheaten tapestry hung by a single nail.

Where were the maids? The footmen? Who could live like this?

A horrendous thought struck her.

Perhaps the mistress was bedridden and had no idea about the state of her castle. No one was ensuring that the servants did their tasks. Where was the cook, for example? The household ought to be awake and at work by now, preparing morning tea.

An even more terrible thought followed: perhaps the owner of the castle was *dead*.

Perhaps evil servants left the poor lady to starve. Her body lay upstairs in the dusty bed hangings, her face upturned to heaven, one skeletal hand outstretched toward the bedroom door.

Clara flew out of that castle as if she had wings on her feet. She ran far enough to be out of the castle's shadow, hand on her pounding heart. Surely that wasn't the case. Mr. Cobbledick was right: she had too much imagination.

Out here in the bright sunshine, her fear seemed rather foolish. All the same, after she calmed down, she decided that she wasn't going back inside until someone emerged or Mr. Cobbledick returned. Instead she began following the moat around the left side of the castle.

A rectangular part of the castle was set at an odd angle between the front and rear towers, presumably containing the grimy kitchen and perhaps a walled courtyard. It was thrilling to see narrow slits for arrows and battlements in the towers, alongside regular windows. She'd seen them on Windsor Castle, of course, but that was huge and royal.

This was far more . . . adorable.

Well, on the outside. Not inside.

Up the whole length of the tower were extra rooms, each with a window, sticking out over the moat and held up by buttresses. She was wondering what those rooms could be for when she realized that a stone shaft extended down to the moat and perhaps below into a pit—those were the privies, then.

As she padded around the curve of the rear tower, the sound of the loch grew louder, so she decided to search for its banks. Perhaps it was washing day, and the maids were scrubbing laundry in the water.

Finding her way was easy enough. A narrow footpath wound through a wood carpeted with moss and ferns under towering pine and hazel trees. The moss had crept across the path in places, as if hardly anyone walked on it. High over her head, trees bent to and fro in a breeze she couldn't feel, casting sunlit spangles over her arms and face.

The whole day felt magical, the best possible adventure she could have wished from the Highlands. The castle had been so very quiet, and this path was even more still. She found herself almost tiptoeing, her slippers making no sound.

If this was a fairy story, she would soon meet a prince. Or a stag that could talk. Perhaps a child who had lost a golden ball. Or the path would lead to a well, and in the well would be a frog—a frog *prince*—though she couldn't quite remember the end of that tale. It had been years since her nanny told her the story.

The path ended quite suddenly. She emerged through a leafy archway into bright sunshine as the sound of rushing water leapt to her ears.

And there . . .

Well, *there*.

He was not a frog.

He was standing in the midst of rushing water. Naked. Completely naked.

And he was so *large*, like a giant. A Scottish giant.

Clara clapped a hand over her mouth. She should have stopped, run away, respected his privacy.

Instead she stared.

The man had tousled chestnut hair that gleamed with deep red highlights. His eyebrows were thick and darker than his hair, and his face was stubbled in a way that suggested he had risen from bed without bothering to shave.

He was standing with his side to her, and what she could see of his face was spectacular, rough-cut and masculine, with a strong jaw. Her eyes drifted down to bulging shoulders that rippled as he flicked a fishing rod, then down the ridges and valleys of a strong back that tapered to lean hips. Below his waist, she could see taut buttocks and heavy legs set apart to fight the current.

Suddenly he caught a fish on the rod, and the muscles on his back and shoulders tightened as he backed up, pulling on the line. He muttered something that sounded like *bollocks*, then jerked the rod into the air. At the end of his line, a glistening fish threw drops of water into the sunshine, its scales shining like golden ingots.

"Oh, bravo!" Clara shouted, not thinking—until she heard herself, after which she wanted to die of shame. Before she could turn away, he pivoted to face her, water frothing around his thick thighs.

My goodness.

He was . . .

Both hands slapped over her eyes, but every detail of Prince George's Roman vase—that lascivious brute!—came clearly to mind.

Mylchreest was famous for walking across the London stage without a shirt. The Scotsman's shoulders and chest were twice the size of the actor's, and he was just as handsome. But the . . . *that* part of him?

She had suspected the Roman vase exaggerated a man's parts. This Scotsman was considerably less worrisome.

Less fearsome.

From the point of view of a virgin, anyway.

CHAPTER 11

Caelan was struck dumb. His sister loved a good jest, but this was taking it too far. How in the hell had Fiona managed to wrangle a lady into sticking a halo on her head and accosting him while fishing?

Presumably her prank was designed to shame him into wearing clothing in the loch.

He squinted. Not a halo, just a huge pile of hair backlit by sunshine.

Actually, she couldn't be a lady, since Fiona knew that he'd be naked. His sister would never play such a trick on a lady. What's more, he had the distinct impression that the woman was peeking at him between her fingers. She was no innocent.

Any moment now, Fiona would pop out from the bushes, chortling about having made her point. He'd give her the win this time: he'd probably start wearing a pair of smalls in the water once the English housekeeper showed up, which should be any day now.

"Who the bloody hell are you?" Caelan barked, tossing first the fish, then the rod to the shore. He stood with his hands on his hips and let her look her fill. For all she was pretending to be shy, she must be experienced, if not a strumpet altogether.

Her hair told him as much. She appeared to have risen from a man's bed, her hair tangled by his hands—

If the stream hadn't been fucking freezing, he'd have reacted to that thought. As it was, his cock didn't even twitch.

"Oh, for Christ's sake," he continued when she

didn't reply. "Cannae you put two words together? Where did my sister find you?"

"I can speak!" she exclaimed, hands still plastered to her face. "You heard me speak! I said bravo, because . . . because you caught a fish. Are you clothed yet?"

Her voice betrayed her: she was English *and* a lady—and apparently not peeking between her fingers. "Not quite." He splashed toward the shore. "Where's Fiona? She'll have to bring you back, because I've a long day ahead of me. Where are you from?"

"*Fiona?* I'm from London, but I'm—"

"Ach and begad, I told her no buying a wife from England!"

"That seems like a wise precept," she said from behind her hands. "There's a good deal too much buying and selling of spouses, in my opinion. Just out of curiosity, how much would such a wife cost?"

"Two ladies a pound, according to Fiona. All right, I have my kilt on."

Her hands dropped, revealing smoky green eyes the very color of the loch on a cloudy day. "That would be quite a bargain. Your sister is right about the market, but wrong about the price. I'm afraid that you wouldn't be able to afford a lady."

Jesus. She talked even faster than Fiona.

She perked up watching him buckle his kilt. "Your skirt is shorter than I've seen on the London stage," she observed. "No shirt?"

"No," he said curtly. "And it's not a skirt. It's a kilt."

"Do men not wear shirts in these parts? There's a London actor famous for taking off his shirt on stage. I don't think the audience has any idea that they could travel to Scotland and see such a sight in the wild."

Caelan couldn't think what to say about such a rubbish idea, but then, he'd never been one for the theater.

"Men seemed to be fully dressed on the streets of Edinburgh and Inverness," she said blithely. "I kept an eye out for kilts, as you call them, and didn't see even one. I suppose it's too much to hope that the long day ahead of you includes coloring your face with streaks of blue paint and storming the neighboring laird's castle?"

"That laird would be my brother-in-law," he said dryly. "My nephew would love it, but no, and those who fought in blue paint were an ancient people called Picts."

She wrinkled her nose. "How annoying. Last year's *Macbeth* at the Theatre Royal featured hordes of Scotsmen in kilts with blue face paint." She cleared her throat. "I watched the performance three times."

She had dimples. And a sweet little gap between her two front teeth. That smile was as lethal as any weapon.

"Do you suppose you could put on a shirt now?" Her eyes slid away from his chest. "I've discovered that it's one thing to see a man on a stage without a shirt, but like this, close, it's a bit . . . much."

"I don't have a shirt with me," he said, crossing his arms over his chest so at least she wasn't confronted by his nipples, but that led to her inspecting his forearms. He was getting an uneasy feeling about the English housekeeper, the one due to arrive any day. "So you've come up from London, but *not* because you answered an advertisement for a wife."

"You actually advertised for a wife? How brave."

He leaned down to grab his trout.

She was an odd little creature; as he watched, she plopped down on the boulder he used for gutting fish.

"No, I didn't. Do you mind stirring yourself so I can clean this fish? You're sitting on my butchery, to be blunt about it."

She jumped up, saw the blood that covered the rock, then squeaked like a mouse evicted from its home. The back of her pink coat had taken on some rusty stains. She took it off, regarding it with dismay before draping it on the same shrub where he'd laid his kilt.

Trying valiantly to ignore her low-cut gown, Caelan came down on his haunches and split open the fish.

She moved to another rock, dusting it off before she sat down. "I'm your new housekeeper."

Caelan swallowed a curse. *She* was a housekeeper? Only if he was a hairy cow, and he hadn't started mooing that he'd noticed. This is what came of the utter stupidity of hiring someone sight unseen from England, of all places. He should have advertised in Glasgow, if anywhere.

He glanced over to confirm his assessment. The woman had her elbows propped on her knees and her chin cupped in her hands. She was so delicious that it made him feel prickly and bad-tempered. What was she doing, wandering around on her own?

Another naked man might have posed a danger to her.

"You're no housekeeper," he said, stripping out fish innards and throwing them over his shoulder into the loch. Then he remembered the supposed

"Mrs. Garnet"—the Mclean girl who had hoped to marry him. "And if you're a lady thinking I'll fall for your charms once you're in an apron, I wouldn't choose you."

That came out a bit more vehemently than was entirely polite, but he'd meant it when he said he wanted a woman like his sister. He didn't fool himself that Fiona's freckled face and strong jaw were celebrated by anyone other than those who loved her. In short: he didn't want another beautiful woman. They were too much trouble.

Luckily, she just smiled. "Don't worry about that." She held up her left hand. "Even if you *were* a frog, I wouldn't kiss you."

"A frog?"

For the first time, he registered that she wore a wedding ring. No wonder she was unmoved by his nakedness. All the unmarried ladies he'd met would have fainted from shock; this woman trusted that her marriage lines would keep her safe.

They would, of course.

"I was remembering a fairy tale my nanny told me about a frog who had to be kissed in order to turn into a man."

He didn't know what to say to that nonsense.

"I am a housekeeper with no need for a husband," she added.

That was rot. Anyone could tell by looking at her that she wasn't a servant. She had to be in the gentry or even above. Her dress was so white that it resembled an eggshell. Her breasts were shining too, set off by ruffles.

Fancy didn't cover her appearance. Did she have any idea that propping her elbows on her knees made her breasts . . .

No, she did not. His holdings were the largest in these parts, which meant that unmarried women fluttered their eyelashes, cooed, and plumped up their assets when he walked down the street, even as far away as Inverness.

Whereas this particular woman was gazing at him as if he were a family member, a thought he found surprisingly unpleasant.

"You're not the kind of housekeeper I want."

Her face fell so abruptly that he felt a pang. Her lips moved, but surely she wasn't saying "bollocks." Not a proper lady like herself.

He'd been sent to university in Edinburgh, and wasted more than a few nights in ballrooms. Ladies acted as if a curse would tarnish their lips.

Then she brightened again. "I may not be the most experienced housekeeper in these parts, but frankly, I'm the only one you can afford."

"What do you mean by that?"

"You're poor, aren't you? You don't even own a shirt. I'm sorry about your lack of funds, but I suspect I am the only housekeeper who could afford to work for you. I entered the castle. I know how you are living. There isn't a servant in the place."

Mrs. Gillan was still holding out the promise of a scullery maid, but only after the new housekeeper was in place.

Caelan frowned at her. "But *are* you a housekeeper? I'd guess all you're good for is sitting on a cushion and sewing a fine seam."

She didn't seem to take that as an insult. "I'm rubbish at embroidery, but I can mend sheets. Do you *have* sheets?"

"Of course I have sheets!"

She regarded him skeptically. "It's a fair question, as it seems you don't have the money for clothing, if you'll forgive my bluntness. What is your name?"

"Caelan MacCrae, Laird of CaerLaven."

"So, Laird of CaerLaven, I know precisely why you advertised in London. Any Scottish housekeeper worth her salt would catch sight of that kitchen and walk out the door."

"My sister, Fiona, thought that a desperate woman might be interested enough to take the post," he admitted.

"The ethics of that idea are questionable," she said, narrowing her eyes at him. "You wanted to find a woman desperate enough to not only tackle that kitchen, but to work *for free*?"

He snorted. "Who said anything about free? I offered twice the going price. What's your name?"

"You don't know the name of the woman you hired?"

Fiona presumably knew, but she hadn't bothered to share it. And this woman was definitely planning to give him a fake name. She was desperate, all right. Her husband must be abusive. The thought made him want to kill the lout.

Not enough to travel to England, but almost.

He whacked off the fish's head. To her credit, she didn't show any signs of being squeamish, even when it flew past her cloud of hair. Isla had never liked to watch a fish being cleaned.

"Did you flee to Scotland because an Englishman wronged you?" He truly didn't like the idea that she was an abused wife.

She bit her lip and finally said, "That's none of your business."

"Then you did."

She was silent a moment and then said, "So to speak."

He let his knife thump down on the fish tail so firmly that she startled. "He should be shot."

Her eyes lit up.

"I'm not volunteering," he added.

"No, no! I was thinking of Walter Scott, the poet."

"Who?"

She straightened up. "One of Scott's heroes speaks in 'a voice of thunder that shook the—'" She frowned. "I haven't got the line exactly right."

"Bollocks."

"I *thought* you said 'bollocks' when you were fishing!"

He raised an eyebrow. "I thought the same of you, but then I remembered that proper ladies don't know the word."

"That's exactly what—" She broke off.

"So you don't want me to shoot him?" Caelan was rethinking his reluctance. He could go down to England, put a bullet through her beastly husband, and come back home directly.

"Shooting the man I've in mind would cause a great furor," she said, a smile playing around her lips.

He got up to dip the fillets in the loch, as much to stop himself from staring at her mouth as anything else. Then he started scraping off the scales.

"I suppose you can take the bloody job. After all, I paid for a housekeeper to come all the way to Scotland. What's your name?" He glanced at her again, because she was the sort of woman whom one wanted to look at.

"Clara."

She quickly shut her mouth before she added a last name. She didn't want the abuser to find out where she was. Or she didn't want Caelan to slap on blue paint, go down to London, and take him out.

She took a breath and said, "Clara Potts. Mrs. Potts."

Like hell she was Mrs. *Potts*. He had a bad feeling that she might have a title attached to her. Lord Such-and-Such would show up any moment and demand she return.

"You ran away from a man, the one who abused you," he said flatly.

"I'd say *accosted* is more accurate. But also because—well, just because. At any rate, why don't I take the position temporarily? I can help you sort the house and then leave. I'm happy to pay you back for my journey."

And . . . that wasn't happening.

It was too late.

"Where in Scotland do you think to live?" She'd be living in the Highlands, but he might as well hear her out.

"I plan to go around Scotland until I find a wonderful house that I will fill with books. Perhaps a little castle."

He had a castle. And books.

Caelan threw the fillets into his creel and stood. "Come on, then."

She stood. "Where are we going?"

"Back to my castle. Are you always this trusting?"

She fell back a step. "If you mean to be wicked, I shall run away. But actually"—she inspected his face carefully—"I'm not afraid of you. I know what lustful men look like. I can recognize the expression in their eyes. You don't have it." She smiled triumphantly. "You don't desire me, and I can tell."

His tool had recovered from the icy loch and was making its interest known—because she was wrong, wrong, wrong. "I've never forced myself on a woman," he said with disgust. "I was talking about the way you showed up here with not more than a few scraps of flimsy stuff covering your bosom."

This time she laughed, a beautiful sound. "That's funny . . . I can't tell you why, but it is."

"It's the truth," he said flatly. "You're an idiot to stand near a naked man while wearing that gown."

"You're not—"

He saw the exact moment that she remembered he was wearing nothing under his kilt.

"All right," she conceded. "I'll take your advice the next time I encounter a naked man in a stream." Her lips tilted up into a smile. "Not only is England short of such occasions, but I never had a conversation like this in London!"

Caelan had the mad thought that kissing her lips would be a good idea, so he turned on his heel and started walking down the path. He'd been so tempted that he almost reached out for her, pulling her against his chest and then settling into a deep kiss, a searching one that would have her trembling against him.

Bloody hell.

She was *married*.

The woman followed him down the path back to the castle like a lamb, because before God and man, "Clara Potts" was an innocent, for all she might be married. He could see it in her eyes—the same as he could see the pain there when he asked her if she'd been abused.

When they reached the kitchen, she stopped as if her feet were glued to the doorframe. "You can start your housekeeping by cleaning this room," he told her, waving at the sink full of dirty dishes.

She blinked at him. "You don't have any household staff?" She glanced around, one of her eyebrows arched. "Did the dust on that cupboard first land in the days of King Henry VIII?"

She was married. One didn't kiss a married woman because her tone made you want to laugh. Even if you hadn't laughed in . . . years.

He cleared his throat. "No, it didn't. My housekeeper, Mrs. Baldy, left over a week ago." Though she never bothered much about dust.

"I shall repay you for my journey immediately," Clara told him with what sounded like genuine regret. "I've had a marvelous adventure so far, and bought at least forty novels, and become friends with Mr. Cobbledick. And now I've met you, a proper laird." Her cheeks were turning pink; the wave of her hand must refer to his naked state in the loch.

Mr. Cobbledick?

"But I can't work miracles." She nodded at the floor. "I don't know what color this stone was back in the 1300s. I don't think it used to be black, and it's definitely not supposed to be mossy."

Caelan was rather surprised to see she was right about the moss. "Only where rain came in the window," he pointed out. "I could be more careful about closing it."

That explanation didn't seem to make a difference.

"I advertised and paid for your trip," he said before she could start arguing.

She bit her lip. "Your housekeeper didn't appear, which is why I got into the carriage."

Because she was running away.

"That's not fair. You owe me a housekeeper." The words came out fast, like the bullets he meant to aim at her husband. He'd never seen the point of a duel, but now he did.

"That wasn't my fault! Mr. Cobbledick had been waiting over twenty-four hours. The housekeeper you hired obviously thought better of the position. The poor man had to sleep in his carriage to make sure it wasn't stolen. And now he has to go all that way back to Glasgow for your bathtub. What on earth do you want a glass bathtub for?"

"Glass? Another mistake by my bloody sister. It's supposed to be ceramic, and now I'll be taking a bath in a transparent bucket."

She giggled—a pleasing sound, one had to admit.

"How old is this Cobbledick?" Caelan asked sharply.

"Too old to be traveling back and forth from London," she told him, eyes shining with earnestness. "His bones ache after hours on the box, and one night he almost fell off. Another day we had to stop twice so that he could lie in the fields until his back unknit. If you had more money and a carriage and some horses, you could hire him to work here in the castle."

He managed not to roll his eyes. "I might consider hiring Cobbledick after he fetches my bathtub . . . *if* you clean up the castle. You owe me a housekeeper, and I can't live like this any longer."

Never mind the fact he'd been living perfectly happily for a couple of years. He didn't even care if she was lying to him. He wanted her to stay.

She was stuck in the doorway, like a groundhog in a burrow with a hawk circling overhead, except she was eyeing the mossy floor. "Even if I tried to be your housekeeper, I couldn't do it forever. Nor could I do it alone. I would need housemaids. I can tell people what to do, but I don't know how to do it myself."

"I can get you a scullery maid tomorrow," he said, refusing to think about why he was being so stubborn, insisting a born-and-bred lady clean his kitchen. "So far maids have left because I don't have a housekeeper, but with you on the premises, they'll come."

"Will you be able to pay them?"

"Of course. I have plenty of money. And shirts," he added, goaded by her dubious look.

"You *choose* to live like this?" She glanced around again and took a cautious step forward. "Perhaps I could remain until Mr. Cobbledick returns with your bathtub. Just so you know, I can only cook fancy food, like orange fritters."

"No oranges in Scotland," Caelan said dryly.

"I was taught how to go over menus with a cook," she said, shrugging. "I can't wash clothing, either, because that's done by housemaids."

Caelan sighed. "I told you, I can pay others to do that labor. Mrs. Baldy preferred to work alone."

"Mrs. Baldy is your former housekeeper? That's another thing. I have to know what happened to her." Interest sparked in her eyes. "You didn't dismember Mrs. Baldy and cook her up in that black pot, did you?"

"No. Were you this fanciful as a child? First I was a frog in need of a kiss, and now I'm a murderer?"

"I didn't believe it, or I would have run away,"

she pointed out. She gave him a wry smile. "Normally I don't tell anyone what I'm imagining, and certainly not a man I scarcely know."

"Your husband?"

She blinked. "Ah, no."

Good.

"So why did Mrs. Baldy leave?" she asked.

"My sister fired her, thinking I'd get dysentery from some mutton she planned to serve for supper. I would have fetched her back, but the woman had been selling bacon out the back door."

Clara seemed to find that a reasonable response. "And the housekeeper before her?"

"She was a laird's daughter, hankering after me," he said, scowling at the thought.

"That won't be a problem for me!" she said, dimpling at him.

Right. Of course not.

"You can start by cleaning this room," he repeated. "Since you know how to clean, but you don't know how to cook, or sew, or wash linens."

"There is something very impolite about your tone," she observed. "I might as well say that I was taught to use skim milk to clean a stone floor, but I doubt you have any, nor do I think it strong enough to scour off moss. Do you have soap?"

"Of course." He walked over to the sink where he kept the cake that he'd been using to wash the dishes, but paused for a moment and stared out the window.

Why should he hire her? A lady could tell people what to do, but she didn't do anything herself. What was the point of having someone like that around?

Unless they were in one's bed.

He heard an indrawn breath and turned around.

"Puppies!" Clara was on her knees next to the box where Fiona had stowed Ivy and her puppies. As soon as they saw her, they started climbing over each other to get out, tumbling down to the hearth and scrambling up her legs.

"You're darlings, utterly adorable," she cooed.

"Am I to call you Clara? Because you're *not* Mrs. Potts. You need a better name than that."

"I could be Mrs. Athlin—or perhaps Mrs. Dunbayne." She certainly was an unusual woman; her eyes were shining with excitement. "Or I could dress as a boy!"

Despite his better impulses, his eyes fell to her bosom.

She scowled and tugged at her bodice. "You wouldn't believe how much trouble dressing in gowns has caused. I would do better in a shirt and breeches."

Her hair was billowing around her face and tumbling down her back like spun sugar. The lass had enough hair for three women. What's more, he'd seen her rear end. One glimpse of her in breeches, and the men in these parts would lose their collective minds.

She was delicate and luscious all at once. Curvy and strong, and yet fragile.

"No breeches," he declared. How could she have thought that anyone would believe she was married to a man called Potts? She was holding a puppy up to her face, the daft one whose eyes were two colors. She cuddled him against her chest and laughed down at the three puppies jumping at her knees to get some attention.

What creature wouldn't want to be nestled against that breast? One fat little pup managed to get his foot on the head of one of his siblings and then snagged his claws into the front of her gown.

Caelan heard a rip and turned away in time. Perhaps not quite in time.

"Oh, bollocks!" he heard quite clearly.

"I'll get your coat." He said it over his shoulder because he *was* a gentleman.

Almost a gentleman.

CHAPTER 12

Clara disentangled the puppy's claws from her ripped bodice, unsurprised to find that another of the gowns ordered by Hortense had ripped. She felt unsettled. The laird's voice had poured through her like rich, dark coffee. No, like sweet port wine.

"My breasts are too heavy for French gauze," she told her favorite puppy, the one with different colored eyes.

Behind her, the laird cleared his throat. "Here." She turned her head and found him staring at the hallway while holding out her pink pelisse. She felt a flash of embarrassment that he'd overheard her description of her breasts . . . but honestly, the evidence was overwhelming. He had described her gown as little more than tissue, and he had been right.

She scrambled to her feet, a puppy squeaking as he rolled off her knees onto the bricks, righted himself, and attacked one of her slippers.

"Are you clothed?" the laird asked a moment later, when she was wrestling her hair out from under her buttoned-up pelisse.

"Yes." She turned around, a little afraid that his eyes would show the nasty appreciation Prince George and his cronies always leveled at her bosom, but the laird was scowling. Definitely not appreciative. Thankfully—because *of course* she was glad!—he now wore a billowing shirt made of clean, if slightly grayish, linen.

Dingy shirt or no, he was blazingly handsome,

even more so than the actor Mylchreest. Oddly enough, she had started talking with Caelan Mac-Crae as easily as she might with her friend Torie, whereas if she ever met Mylchreest, she would have been silenced by shyness.

Likely it was because Caelan thought she was married. She didn't have to worry about him making improper advances.

She hesitated, but it had to be said. "I covered my eyes when I arrived at the loch, but I didn't do so immediately. I apologize."

"My sister would say that I deserved it, being out of doors without a fig leaf covering the important bits."

She laughed. She had been told that men loved to boast of their private parts, but he called them "bits." By rights she should be shocked to the bone by the conversation, but instead she found herself respecting his honesty as regarded his own measurements.

"My puppies led to the destruction of your fancy gown," he said. "Would you like to wait until tomorrow to begin housekeepering?"

"'Housekeepering'? Is that a word?"

He shrugged.

She looked around again. "I suppose I could help you, but only until Mr. Cobbledick returns with your bathtub. After that, I shall hire him for myself. He's bringing his daughter to act as my maid, and I'll need a carriage and a driver. It'll be the start of my own household."

"My housekeeper will have her own maid?"

"Strange, isn't it, since you haven't even one of your own? If Elsbeth is anything like her father, she'll lend me a hand. They should be back with my clothing in a few hours."

His jaw twitched. "You don't have any clothes? I mean, you can't change out of that ruined gown?"

"Not until Mr. Cobbledick returns. I'll keep my pelisse on." She turned around once again, examining the kitchen. "I have a basket of food. Would you like to have luncheon, perhaps outdoors?"

He sighed. "I've never contracted dysentery, no matter what my sister thinks. I usually eat in the courtyard. We could have the trout."

"I love picnics," Clara said. Something was living in that pile of withered cabbage. She could see leaves trembling out of the corner of her eye.

"I still don't know what to call you."

"What do you think of Mrs. Fialasco?"

"I don't like it."

"Then I'll remain Mrs. Potts."

"We're more informal in the Highlands than in British society."

His voice was so deep that it melted her bones, and she could scarcely follow his words. Or maybe it was because of his accent. Would living here give her a lovely burr like a Scotswoman? It seemed doubtful.

"I'll call you Clara," he announced.

Clara? Like a housemaid?

"Do I address you as Laird CaerLaven?"

He shook his head. "Caelan."

So he wasn't thinking of her as a housemaid. A friend?

His eyes sharpened. "Are you insulted if I call you by your given name? Does it make you uncomfortable?"

"No," Clara said instantly, though she wasn't certain why. It wasn't merely because she was wearing a wedding ring.

Maybe it was because he seemed aware of *her* as a person. Gentlemen usually kept their eyes fixed on her bosom or glanced past her to see if a prettier lady with a bigger dowry was waiting for their attention.

Whereas this laird—Caelan—was looking at her intently, as if he could see her inadequacies but also who she truly was.

"You must address me as Mrs. Potts after the scullery maid arrives," she told him. "As for the trout, going over menus is not the same as cooking. I wouldn't have any idea what to do with it other than pot it like a mackerel."

He seemed entirely unsurprised by this revelation.

"I do own a copy of *The Frugal Housewife*—which is a good thing, given your financial situation—but I left it behind with my other books."

He frowned at that. A bigger frown, she meant, because he was awfully prone to frowning.

"I'm not even certain I can make potted mackerel," Clara added in a rush. "I *watched* the cook make it, because my mother said . . . well . . . Never mind. I'm a fraud, and Mr. Cobbledick can leave me at the nearest village, and I'll be out of your way."

His eyes darkened. "Some things you said are true. You're married, and a man accosted you, presumably your husband. I would guess that you haven't been married long."

She should confess, obviously. But she was an unmarried lady, and he was an unmarried gentleman, and never the twain shall meet, at least when alone.

And she *didn't want to leave*.

It was an odd thought, because she rarely paid attention to her own desires, other than in a small way, such as desire for a new novel. Her wishes were subsumed under large categories that required someone else's approval. She wanted a gentleman of high rank to fall in love with her. She wanted Prince George to forget that she existed. She wanted her mother to be proud of her.

Staying in the castle as a housekeeper wouldn't be approved by anyone, particularly her mother.

"I ran away," she said, telling him the most important truth.

"Aye, I guessed as much." The laird folded his arms over his chest, and she couldn't help seeing how his forearms bulged. "I'll be going down to England to take care of that spouse of yours in time, but not yet."

Clara's eyes widened. "Ah—"

"Nothing to worry about now," he said, turning away. "I'm so hungry that I could eat a horse."

He moved back toward the dirty dishes, but she let out a little squeak. "Not those! I have dishes in my basket." The very idea of eating off those greasy plates was revolting.

Clara ran back out the front door and bent to pick up the basket, grimacing as her nipples brushed against the wool of her pelisse. She was tired of clothing that fell to pieces; the very idea of putting on another dress that covered her breasts with no more than a stretch of gathered gauze caught in her throat like a fish bone.

Once her trunk arrived, she would toss out her small French corsets and return to wearing stays over a sturdy chemise. Perhaps she would use her comfortable traveling gowns, designed to be worn without stays, allowing her to lie down on the seat of a carriage without shaping her breasts into twin mountains jutting into the air, or even worse, smashing them into her armpits so that she appeared more fashionably slim.

When she turned around, she discovered that the grimy building had morphed back into a fairy tale: charming, flowery, sweet, gleaming in a puddle of bluebells.

Caelan definitely qualified as the dark, brooding laird of a novel. He seemed sincere about slaying her abusive husband, so it was a good thing that she didn't have one.

Perhaps Melliora hadn't been as lucky as Clara had thought, since after all her adventures, she married a broody man who had chased several women. Caelan seemed more like the type who would fall in love once and stay in love for his whole life.

She slipped a new novel into the pocket of her pelisse and carried the basket into the kitchen. The laird was nowhere to be seen, but fresh air was blowing through an open door leading to a courtyard. Before she followed him outside, she knelt down again by the fireplace. A mama dog had appeared, and all the puppies were lined up next to her stomach, blissfully suckling.

Curious, she leaned over and poked the round, tight belly of a suckling puppy. When its mother raised her head, Clara withdrew her hand but hovered for a moment longer, watching the satisfied puppies fall asleep. Perhaps someday she could nurse her own children, even though ladies employed wet nurses.

The courtyard was generously sized, with an elderly crab apple tree covered in blossoms shading a slab of stone that had been fashioned into a table.

Caelan was crouched down, building a fire on a stone hearth.

The castle was so odd: horrible inside, but appearing charming out of doors. Yet when Clara approached the table, she saw brown stains on the granite, as if fiends had been sacrificing maidens on its surface. Which—obviously!—they had not. All the same, dried blood turned her stomach.

It was time to prove her worth as a housekeeper. She marched back into the kitchen, pumped a pail of water, staggered back, hoisted up the bucket, and threw it at the table.

The water slapped the stone and then plunged straight off, the wave striking Caelan's back. He flinched at the cold water and uttered a curse that Clara hadn't heard before.

Bugger.

It sounded like *bollocks*, but meaner.

"I'm sorry!" she called.

He didn't turn around, just added another log to the fire he had going. "Don't throw any more water at me."

His linen shirt clung to his back in an extremely attractive fashion. Clara forced herself to look away. "You oughtn't to curse so often . . . So what does that word mean?"

"Says the lady who knows 'bollocks'!"

"Is 'bugger' the same as 'bollocks'?"

"No! Don't repeat it." He stood up and turned.

Clara had never felt smaller than when this particular laird loomed over her. She was delicate in comparison. Or rather, she *felt* delicate, because of course she was herself: short and sturdy.

"We'll wait for the griddle to warm," Caelan said. "Then I'll throw on the trout."

"I think I have enough food in the basket. You could save the trout for your supper."

"*Our* supper," he corrected her. "I shall eat with my housekeeper, because it makes no sense to prepare a separate meal."

He liked to stand with his hands on his hips, and when she glanced away from his burly arms, she caught sight of his unclothed legs. She had noticed them in the stream, of course, but now? Framed by the fire crackling behind him? They resembled tree trunks.

Why were tree trunks attractive? Romantic heroes were never praised for that sort of thing. D'Elmont was praised for the "gaiety of his air." Caelan had no "gaiety" in his air. For one thing, he was glowering at her again.

"Sorry, what did you say?" she asked hastily.

"I said the trout will be *our* supper, because you can't cook," he said, exasperated.

"I suppose we could eat together until you hire a cook and a few maids," Clara said. "After that, I shall eat with the household staff until I depart."

"Why do you look as if you're about to burst out laughing?"

Normally she'd never tell anyone the truth, but normally no one asked her what she was thinking. "From the outside, this castle resembles one in a novel."

"So?"

"That would make you the hero."

He seemed appalled.

Clara couldn't help grinning. "One of my favorite heroes, D'Elmont, was celebrated for the 'unequaled charms of his conversation.'"

Caelan let out a crack of laughter. "I've heard about my deficits in that area from other women."

The sentence stung Clara's heart like a needle, but that was merely because she liked him. As a person. Not because she was jealous of those women.

He turned away and poked the fire, sending roaring sparks up the stone chimney and giving her another close look at the way his wet shirt outlined every muscle in his back. All right, she *was* jealous.

"Do you have another shirt you might wear, or was that your only one?" Clara asked, pulling herself together.

"Of course I have more shirts." When he was annoyed, his voice dropped to a deep rumble.

This was one of the moments she had prepared for, when she had to stand up for herself. "Luckily for your clothing, I was hired as a housekeeper, not a laundry maid. Who's been washing your clothes?"

"I drop them in the village," he said.

"The village laundress is not doing a very good job," Clara pointed out.

He glanced down at the dingy fabric and shrugged.

"Put on another shirt, if you please. One sees a hero's chest in a single act of a play, if then." She couldn't help smiling at his grimace. "If we drank hot chocolate every day, we wouldn't desire it as much, would we?"

Oops. That sentence rushed out of her mouth, and the sentiment was entirely inappropriate. Plus, she had the feeling that most women would be entirely happy to examine this laird's anatomy every single day. Many times a day.

"What's hot chocolate?"

Clara felt her eyes widen. "The best drink in the world. I'll ask Mr. Cobbledick to fetch some, and I can leave it with you as a farewell gift."

Caelan appeared about to say something, but instead he strode by her. "I'll put on another shirt."

"You might wash your hands too." And then, when he turned back: "Because you had them inside a fish."

"I rinsed my hands in the loch."

"That's not the same as *soap*." Her mouth fell open. "Don't tell me . . . you haven't a bathtub until Mr. Cobbledick returns. You just wade into the loch!"

He rolled his eyes. "Cleaner than washing with a pitcher of water."

"I take a *bath*. Every day. With *soap*."

"Not here, you don't."

Clara felt a wash of pure panic. She had been fighting back her memories of the prince's grope, but a daily bath was *key*. Every single day. Dots appeared in her vision, and she swayed, catching hold of the wet edge of the table.

She heard a curse, and then an arm wrapped around her waist. "Bloody hell, Clara. What's the matter?"

"Nothing," she gasped. Caelan had pulled her against his chest—and he smelled *so good*. Better than anyone she'd ever been close to. Like fresh air and fresh lake.

Like a man who was so clean he didn't need soap.

Apparently.

She leaned against him until her breath calmed. Then she moved away. "I'll happily eat with you, but I must leave later today." He was scowling at her yet again. "I know I owe you a housekeeper, but I cannot . . . You don't have a bath. Or soap. I can't."

His arm tightened for a moment, and then he said, "My wife used to—"

"You had a *wife*?"

CHAPTER 13

Clara's heart stuttered as the state of the kitchen jumped into her mind. "Your wife died." The house had fallen apart around Caelan, because he couldn't bear thinking about her. He couldn't live without her.

"She did." His voice was curt, but of course he wouldn't want to talk about his late wife to a stranger. No wonder his eyes were so dark and his face so grumpy; he was grief-stricken. Clara's heart skipped a beat at the thought.

"I'm so sorry for your loss. Was she lovely?" she asked impulsively.

His expression didn't change. "Very."

Of course she was. He was so handsome that he could have chosen any woman in the whole of Scotland. If he took off his shirt, he could choose from all London as well.

Why had she ever imagined that a man like him wouldn't have had a love story in his past, or present, for that matter?

"I will scrub the table while you are finding another shirt," Clara said, changing the subject. "Do you have a banister brush?"

"What's that?"

"A brush with stiff bristles. How about a mop-stick?"

After Caelan shrugged again and went back inside, Clara took a bottle of wine from the basket and unceremoniously yanked it open. She wouldn't have been able to do that two weeks ago, but Mr. Cobbledick had shown her how. Then she returned to the kitchen and looked around, holding a wineglass to her nose to smother the reek of decaying onions, stemming from a bunch that had first sprouted and then moldered.

The bread oven built into the fireplace was filled with kindling that had rotted to pieces. One corner held a broom with half its bristles and another, pots and pans. A third had that suspicious pile of leaves, and a fourth had a built-in pantry holding nothing but withered carrots.

The carrots were a metaphor for Caelan's sorrow. His suffering.

Clara couldn't help feeling as if her heart was breaking for him. How much must he have loved his wife? It truly was like a novel. After his lady died, the laird fired his servants and let the castle fall to ruin.

Actually, it was like that story about a princess who fell asleep for a hundred years. Rosebushes entwined and grew all around her castle, until a prince cut back the overgrowth and kissed the princess awake. Clara had always wondered why the hero started cutting through all those brambles, because in her experience, nothing stung as much as a rose's thorn. Evidently, the reward of a lovely princess was a compelling motivator.

She put a hand on her heart and took a deep breath—and instantly regretted it, given the stink coming from a disgusting bucket of dingy water with a fish tail floating on top.

Caelan could take that to the refuse heap himself, along with the onions.

Thankfully, the bowl of brown goop on the windowsill was recognizable as wood ash mixed with lye. She almost picked up the stiff brush next to it before noticing that something had nibbled the wooden handle.

Luckily her gloves were in the pocket of her pelisse, so she put them on before taking the brush and wood ash outside. She began scrubbing at one end of the wet table, precisely as housemaids scrubbed the floor. When she threw another pail of water, it rolled across the stone and sizzled into the fire since Caelan's body wasn't there to block the wave, but luckily the flame didn't go out.

By the end, she'd thrown three pails at the table, scrubbing between each one, until she felt satisfied that it was clean enough to lay down her checked cloth.

Arms aching, she hoisted the basket to the table and began taking out apples and pears, delicious gingerbread, meat pies decorated with flowers cut from golden dough, as well as clean plates and silverware. When Caelan still hadn't returned, she went back outside and cut some bluebells from the moat and put them in a glass on the table.

Feeling quite worn out by all this "housekeepering," she sat down and opened her new novel. A couple of chapters later, Clara was ravenous. A lady would never eat before her host arrived—but she wasn't a member of polite society any longer. Gentlemen didn't walk around naked, so Caelan didn't get that label either, title or no.

As far as she could tell, the laird wasn't even in the castle; the only sound she could hear was a bird determinedly chirping in the apple tree.

After reading another chapter, she picked up a meat pie and began eating it. An evil bailiff was threatening Felicity's virtue, and hopefully the handsome squire would soon come to her rescue.

Felicity was hankering after the squire, but why not push the bailiff into a stream herself? Or hit him with her reticule? Clara's stomach twisted at the memory. She could never kiss a frog, because it was probably as slimy as a seagull's . . . at which point she began rubbing her chest and made herself turn the page.

Felicity had tamed the squire's wild stallion and escaped the clutches of the bailiff when Caelan finally emerged from the castle wearing a shirt that was almost white.

"I'm sorry to say that I began eating without you," Clara said, putting down her book.

Caelan dropped a loaf of bread on the table. "I apologize for not returning immediately. I sent a groom to the village asking for a scullery maid and another to my sister asking to borrow her maids. While I was in the stables, a bullock was dropped off, and we had to find room for the beast."

"You have stables? Where? Why do you have no household staff, but you have grooms? Where did you get the bread?"

Caelan sat down opposite her and shrugged. "The stables are out of sight to the east. We used to house staff in the south tower, but after my father died, I built a new stable with living quarters. Bread and milk are delivered there daily. Is that meat pie for me?"

"I ate two," Clara said, feeling her cheeks glow with embarrassment. "But the basket was large, and there's still one left, along with a whole chicken, jam tarts, and those lovely pears, grown in a conservatory in Glasgow." She handed him a glass of wine.

"A feast," Caelan said. "Are those French sweets?"

She nodded. "They're marvelous! I was so happy to find the store in Glasgow that I bought almost everything they had."

"In my experience, ladies avoid candies, fearing for their waistlines."

Was he pointing out that she was plump? Humiliation washed over her. She'd eaten before him, scavenging the table, leaving him only one pie. She was—

"No." Caelan said it severely, his eyes holding hers. "That's not what I meant, and you know it."

Clara slowly, slowly let the breath out of her lungs. *Did* she know it? Neither of them was as refined as they ought to be. Proper gentlemen rubbed scented lotion into their hands and wore gloves to keep their hands white. When Caelan reached for a pear, she could see that his hands were brawny, veined, brown from the sun. Powerful, not gentlemanly.

"So, you did not choose to become a housekeeper due to a lack of funds."

She shook her head.

"You are not poor," Caelan clarified.

"No, I'm not. And you own two shirts, at least," Clara said brightly, warning herself yet again that ogling the master of the household was rude. As was brooding about the unfashionable yet surprisingly desirable qualities of large hands.

"I almost put on a cravat before I remembered that you are supposed to be my housekeeper," Caelan remarked. "By the way, I'm not poor, either."

"One doesn't wear a cravat to dine with a housekeeper," Clara agreed. She could feel the wine in her stomach like a dozy sweet glow.

He reached toward a jam tart—but froze. "You picked some flowers."

"Yes, from the beautiful ones growing in the moat," Clara said, wondering if Mr. Cobbledick would arrive soon.

Something about this day had begun to feel a little dangerous. Caelan's throat showed golden-brown from sun against his white shirt. Of course, now she thought of it, he had been a glowing color all over, due to running around naked.

His tumble of hair seemed thick and soft; she reached up to touch hers knowing that it looked awful, like cow parsley stuck on top of her head. More importantly, it was shameful to ogle a man, and yet she seemed unable to stop savoring the memory of his naked body.

Shameful.

Or did she mean *shameless*?

Covetous. Desirous. All those words that she had never considered relevant to herself, only to horrendous men like the prince. And yet here she was, thankful that her eyelashes were long enough that he couldn't see that she was watching him. It had been a mistake to drink wine; she felt flushed, and as if she might giggle for no reason.

She had to face facts. She'd desired Mylchreest. She hadn't wanted the actor's approval, but the man himself. So telling herself that all of her desires stemmed from other people's approval wasn't honest.

Now she desired the laird as well.

"Why did the flowers startle you?" Clara asked, scrambling to think of something to say.

"Isla, my wife, planted the moat."

The words had an instant sobering effect, sweeping away her irresponsible daydreams.

"We call these grannie's bonnets." He reached over and tapped a nodding head. "See the bonnet?"

"They smell like vanilla."

He sniffed. "To me, they smell like flowers."

Clara hesitated and then asked, "How long has it been since your wife passed away?"

"Two years."

Two years during which blue-and-purple brambles had grown around the castle and around his heart, obviously. How mortifying that she had been sitting opposite a grieving man, feeling base lust. "Were you married long?"

"Three years."

She cleared her throat, desperately trying to think of something to say. "Isla is a lovely name."

"Aye, it is."

Isla probably resembled a wild Scottish rose, willowy and graceful. Clara was grateful that a rasp of grief didn't underlie his words. This particular fairy tale was like one of the novels she loathed, the ones without happy endings.

"Had you known each other long?"

"She grew up in the village on the other side of the pass."

"Childhood sweethearts?" She was starting to feel a little nauseated. Surely it had been six or seven hours, and Mr. Cobbledick would arrive any moment.

"More or less. I was older than she."

"I wonder what time it is. I don't suppose you have a sundial, do you?" Not that she knew how to read one, but he obviously didn't own a pocket watch.

He glanced at the sky and said, "Round about twenty past five, I'd say."

"That's impressive."

"Worth a 'bravo'?"

"Mr. Cobbledick should be here any moment to fetch me," she said, looking away before she started blushing again.

Caelan picked up a piece of gingerbread. "He won't make it back tonight."

Clara froze. "What? Why not?"

"The storm."

The sky was a sunny blue.

"Not here. There." He nodded over her shoulder. When she turned, she saw that thunderclouds had piled up over the hills that lay between the castle and Inverness.

"See those blue streaks? That's rain." As if the skies were listening, a breeze sprang up, ruffling Isla's bluebells.

"Why can't Mr. Cobbledick fetch me in the rain?" Clara asked.

"Because of the craggy pass between here and the village, Lavenween. You didn't notice?"

"I was reading."

"You read straight through one of the most dangerous mountain passes in Scotland. The pass is surely closed, and your Mr. Cobbledick stuck in the village. You'll have to spend the night here."

"Oh." Her hand curled tightly around her glass. "I couldn't."

He spoke to her anxiety, not to her words. "Lucky you're married, because you'd be compromised otherwise."

She could wash with a pitcher of water the way she did in the Parrot & Pickle. She hardly ever thought about the prince's fingers. She wasn't prone to tears or attacks of sensibility, the way some heroines were.

She was *strong*. Resolute.

"Yes," she said hollowly.

"What's the matter?"

Clara felt herself turning pink at his expression, on the verge of blurting out the sad saga of Prince George. "Oddly, you don't feel like a stranger," she said instead.

"I feel as if I've known you for at least six months," Caelan said, nodding. That secret smile in his smoky eyes? It was devastating, because it looked as if he *liked* her.

"I am used to bathing nightly," she said, choosing her words carefully. "I'll be fine with a kettle of water." No, that wasn't good enough. "Though I'd prefer a pail."

"We can heat water in the large pot," he offered.

"That black pot?"

"The very one where I would have cooked up my last housekeeper, except that I'm not an ogre. Moreover, Mrs. Baldy was old and tough."

"Ogres don't *cook* their food," Clara said, startled into correction. "They snatch up humans and pick bones out of their teeth after the fact."

"I'm starting to feel some concern about your childhood," Caelan said, picking up a second piece of gingerbread.

Clara smiled at him. "Yours must have been remarkably deficient, since you don't know even the simplest of fairy tales. Do you recognize this? 'Fie, foh, and fum, I smell the blood of an Englishman!'"

"Is that an ogre speaking?"

"Of course. I couldn't bathe with water from that pot, and not because of its nefarious connotations," Clara said. "Because it's filthy."

"Unless you'd care to jump into the loch, that's all we've got. The tin bath rusted out, and I tossed it."

The loch? Naked, the way he had? Absolutely not. Not in a million years.

"You'll have to help me clean the pot," Clara announced, giving him a fierce look. "This castle is in a terrible state. Since you have no servants at the moment, you must clean it yourself, the way normal people do their houses."

He appeared truly surprised. "Men don't clean."

"Nonsense. If they live alone, they either clean or pay someone to do it for them. We're both here, aren't we? If no one is coming through that pass, we shall have to do what needs to be done. Where will I sleep?"

"The housekeeper used to sleep in the stables, but I can't put you out there with the grooms. I suppose you could sleep in the nursery. It might be dusty."

"We'll scrub the pot, heat water, then mop the nursery floor at the least." She jumped to her feet but froze. "Except . . . did your wife die in childbirth?"

The tragic novel was getting sadder every moment.

"She did not," Caelan replied. Before she could open her mouth, he added, "Isla died of a fever. There hasn't been a child in the nursery since my sister took a room of her own in the south tower. That said, I don't think I'll be much good at cleaning."

"I may not be either, but that doesn't mean I won't try."

She gave him a direct look until he grunted, which seemed to indicate acceptance.

"Are you still planning on leaving tomorrow?" he asked. "Your Mr. Cobbledick is supposed to turn around and fetch my bathtub. You'd be leaving me without a housekeeper *and* a bathtub if you take him away."

Clara felt a guilty pang. "How long will it take him to return with the bathtub?"

"Three days, perhaps four," Caelan said promptly. "He'll be here by Sunday. I could fetch a scullery maid first thing in the morning."

She stole a glance at Caelan under her lashes. Would it be wrong to ogle her employer? After all, she wouldn't want her employer to ogle her.

"Not for money," she stated.

He frowned.

"I'll help clean the castle, but not for money. I don't need it." She jumped up. "First we must rescue my books before they are rained on. I left two stacks on a rock before the castle."

Caelan picked up the last tart and followed her through the kitchen. "You don't have any clothing, but you have books?"

"I bought most of them on the journey from London. They wouldn't fit in my trunk, and they were covering the floor, which might have made Mr. Cobbledick's daughter uncomfortable," Clara explained.

She snatched up *Gulliver's Travels*. "In this book, a doctor discovers a race of giants. I found it quite inspiring—as far as seeking adventure, I mean."

"No giants in Scotland," he said.

"You have a way of laughing, even when you're not laughing. I might point out that you are practically a giant compared to me."

He laughed aloud at that.

"I suppose you think I'm outrageously fanciful," Clara said, resigned.

"Aren't you?"

"Yes," she said, sighing. "Life would be much easier if I thought only about my next cup of tea."

"But much more boring," Caelan pointed out.

His accent—brogue—sounded thicker, and Clara's breath hitched at his expression. The fact he was *interested* in her stories seemed to be an aphrodisiac; her primary response was a wish to lean toward him and wait to be kissed.

Which was absurd.

"Time to clean!" she said brightly.

He narrowed his eyes. He was obstinate, clearly. So was she.

CHAPTER 14

April 20, 1803

$\mathcal{J}$t was dark before Clara and Caelan finished washing dishes, making up the narrow bed meant for a nanny, and heating a pitcher of water. She was so exhausted that she washed without thinking twice about the prince, putting on one of Caelan's dingy-but-clean shirts and falling promptly into dreamless sleep.

She was awakened by a voice. "Mrs. Potts?"

"Who?" Clara asked, sitting up.

Sunlight was pouring into the room. The young woman standing at her bedside had a sharply pointed chin and a bright smile. "I'm Elsbeth, ma'am, Mr. Cobbledick's daughter."

"Good morning," Clara said groggily. "Thank you for agreeing to be my maid."

Elsbeth bobbed a curtsy. "I was grateful to escape that household." She grimaced. "I don't know what an upstairs maid does, my lady—I mean, Mrs. Potts."

"First of all, you must call me Clara. I'm not really Mrs. Potts."

"I know that, my lady." Elsbeth gave her a shy smile. "My father told me."

"Please don't tell anyone. The most important thing about a lady's personal maid is that she knows *everything*. All the secrets. And she never shares, not even with her father."

Elsbeth nodded earnestly.

Clara could feel her curls billowing around her head as she moved to the edge of the bed and swung her legs over the side. "I'm sure my hair is frightful."

"It's not like hair I've ever seen before," Elsbeth said carefully. "Have you tried braiding it at night?"

Clara felt a pang of embarrassment. "I don't know how. All the way from London, it's become worse and worse. My maid had a salve that she rubbed into it, but it must have been left behind."

"You're a proper lady, aren't you? Like in a play. My father said as much, but I couldn't see a lady taking up a position as a housekeeper." Elsbeth lowered her voice. "Let alone in *this* castle."

"It's more accurate to say that I was a lady, but now I'm an adventurer. And temporarily a housekeeper. What do you mean by *this* castle?"

"The state of it," Elsbeth said. "I'd heard tell. My father is downstairs talking to the laird. He scowled something fierce when he saw the kitchen, and I think he'd prefer to take us away, though the laird says you're staying until the bathtub is delivered."

"We washed the crockery last night, but—"

"*We?*"

"The laird helped."

Elsbeth's eyes were as big as sovereigns. "I've never heard of such a thing."

Clara shrugged. "He's hardly a gentleman. Why should I treat him as such? A gentleman would not live in a pigsty."

"I take it that shirt you're wearing is his," Elsbeth said, nodding. "It's dingy, and the cuffs are frayed. Fred brought up your trunk, by the way. It's on the landing."

"Let's pull it in. For today, I'll wear a traveling gown, and we can bind up my hair in a scarf, because I must tackle this pigsty. If you were a proper lady's maid, you would be very offended by this question, but seeing as you are not, do you know anything about cleaning?"

"I'm not offended! I like cleaning."

"Marvelous. Then we can do it together," Clara said, feeling rather faint at the idea of the work awaiting them downstairs. "The laird said that a scullery maid would join us."

"Cleaning is easy. Taming your hair, though?"

"You're eyeing me as if I have a live animal on my head."

Elsbeth giggled, not denying it.

They bound up her hair in a white lace fichu, winding and pinning until an unsteady mound balanced on top of Clara's head. "This way it won't collect dust," she said, wiggling it from side to side. "More to the point, I won't terrify the scullery maid."

"Do you want to carry a reticule?" Elsbeth asked, holding up a cat. "Are these the fashion in London?"

"No, I just enjoy making them."

The maid turned the small bag over in her hands. "It's adorable. You could sell these in Edinburgh."

"Housekeepers carry keys, not reticules," Clara announced. "As it is, I suspect that I don't resemble any housekeeper you've seen."

"No," Elsbeth agreed. "But then, you aren't a housekeeper."

"When your father returns, we shall leave and find a castle to buy."

Elsbeth's eyes widened. "A *castle*?"

"Growing up, I dreamed of living in a castle,"

Clara confessed. "They're few and far between in England, but we passed masses of them on the way here."

"Like a fairy tale," Elsbeth said, nodding.

"Hopefully without an ogre inside, but yes." Clara felt enormously relieved. Hortense's propensity to lose her temper and offer critical—if honest—comments had made Clara wary and even a little afraid of her own maid, but Elsbeth was obviously kind.

"I think we'll get along well," Clara said, and Elsbeth's grin was as large as her own.

Downstairs there was no sign of Caelan or Mr. Cobbledick.

"First we must have breakfast and tea," Clara said. Thankfully, the coals just needed a poke to bring the kettle back to a boil, and there was still food left in the basket. She and Elsbeth ate at the stone table.

"It's a shame to ruin those pretty gloves by cleaning," Elsbeth said as they rose from breakfast.

Clara looked down at her brown suede gloves with fringes. "Sacrifices must be made."

"You could simply wash your hands," Elsbeth said, a somewhat admonishing tone in her voice.

"That's true! I have to get used to not being a lady." Clara stripped off her gloves.

"You'll always be a lady. You can't escape it. We said that the laird isn't a gentleman, but that isn't true. Even in that terrible shirt, he still looks like a laird. There's something about him, and you too."

Caelan did have an intrinsic air of . . . of command. And decency. It didn't matter if his shirt was grimy and his castle nigh uninhabitable.

"Though the laird isn't like any gentleman I've seen," Elsbeth said, reversing herself.

"My father would have had a heart attack if he hadn't been served a proper breakfast with a butler and at least one footman in attendance," Clara agreed.

Elsbeth nodded. "The master I had in Edinburgh had a fry-up every morning." Her eyes darkened a little. "Along with too many mugs of beer. It pickled his brain. That's what the cook reckoned."

Just then, Caelan stuck his head out of the kitchen. Clara and Elsbeth both curtsied. "Good morning, laird," she said, smiling.

He froze for a moment, then strode over and grabbed a hunk of bread. "Morning."

Clara swatted his hip. "His lordship is supposed to eat in splendid solitude. We were planning to serve you a withered carrot in your study, since the dining room is uninhabitable."

Caelan showed no sign of being insulted by her impulsive gesture, since he rolled his eyes at her.

"Mr. Cobbledick is waiting to say goodbye to you, Elsbeth," he said. "You'll be boarding with the new scullery maid, as your father is worried about the proximity of stable lads."

Whereas Clara could sleep alone because she was married. Supposedly.

"I'll be in the study if you need me." Caelan grabbed another piece of bread and a chicken leg and walked back into the castle.

Mr. Cobbledick was waiting for them, leaning against the coach with his arms crossed over his chest, his mustache looking particularly fierce.

"I'll handle this," Elsbeth said. She marched right up to her father and said, "We're staying until you return with the bathtub, and that's that."

"I don't like it," he barked. "The place is filthy."

"We shall clean it," Clara told him. "We already cleaned some last night."

"Aye, the laird told me as much." He scowled at her. "Ladies don't clean."

"I do," Clara said stoutly.

"She can if she wants to," Elsbeth chimed in.

"Why aren't you wearing gloves?" he demanded.

"Because I can wash my hands afterwards. I don't have to have lily-white hands."

"I told her that," Elsbeth said with satisfaction.

"I don't hold with the idea of a lady working for a living. It's not right."

"He's not paying me," Clara said.

"Then why are you cleaning his castle?"

"Because he needs help. His wife died, and the brambles grew, and the castle fell to pieces, and he needs help."

Mr. Cobbledick groaned. "You've talked yourself into one of those novels you're always telling me about, haven't you?"

"Maybe," Clara said, giving him a big smile. "Keep your eye out for a castle that I could buy, won't you? I'd like one like this: not too big, and not too small."

He opened his mouth again, but Clara gave him a look. She'd made up her mind, and that was that. After the carriage rumbled out the gate, she led the way back into the kitchen.

"I suppose we should begin by taking stock of what needs to be done. The moss on the floor will have to be scraped off," Clara said, poking at it with the stick end of a broom.

"This pot seems clean," Elsbeth said, peering into the fireplace.

"I scrubbed that yesterday. Did you see that set of bell pulls by that wall?"

Three ragged rope ends emerged from holes drilled into the mortar. Tarnished brass plates beneath them read *Butler, Housekeeper, Kitchen*. Elsbeth darted out the door to take a look and reported, "They go into a lead pipe and then under the flagstones and probably ring in the other tower."

Clara tried pulling one, but neither of them heard a bell. "We'll ignore that tower for the moment," she decided. "I'll heat water."

"I'll sweep the floor." Elsbeth took the broom and headed for the pile of cabbage leaves.

Whereupon she met the rat who'd made it his home.

He was clearly terrified by having his leafy home swept away. He turned around, looking for an exit, his tail whipping after him, but Clara was standing between him and the door into the courtyard.

Elsbeth squealed, but Clara had more powerful lungs.

Upstairs in his study, Caelan leapt from his chair. Damn it, Clara's sodding husband must have made his appearance. He threw himself down the steps—

No man, noble, married, or otherwise.

The new maid was standing on a rickety chair, and Clara was waving a broom at the corner. "Caelan, what do we do about this animal?" she said, not turning around.

He walked over to take a look. The rat had pressed his plump body into the corner. If he had been human, he'd have had his eyes squeezed shut. Caelan put an arm around Clara's waist and placed her gently behind him.

"Don't kill him!" she cried.

Bloody hell.

Behind him, Mrs. Gillan walked into the kitchen, followed by a scullery maid who—as it turned out—had as fine a set of lungs as could be found anywhere in the Highlands.

Caelan caught the sluggish rat by the tail and carried it past the shrieking women to the front door, transporting it over the moat and then tossing it into the grass, where it scrambled away. He stopped to have a word with Mr. Gillan, who was leaning against his carriage, peacefully smoking a pipe.

"As you see, we had a rat."

"Aye, I thought it'd be something like that," his father-in-law said around his pipe. "Apologies if the missus fusses at you about marrying again. She was up half the night thinking about it. Finding you a spouse has given her a new lease on life."

Caelan nodded and raised the question of Young Ross's unpaid multure. As the head of the local burgh council, Mr. Gillan knew everything that happened in Lavenween.

"You might remember that his wife had a glad eye," Gillan said, knocking his pipe against a carriage wheel.

"Aye," Caelan agreed. Mrs. Ross had "tripped" and thrown herself into Caelan's arms a few months after Isla's death.

"Two weeks ago, she stole away with a traveling knife grinder. Young Ross has been spending all his time down at the pub. If his brother didn't go over and feed the animals, they would have starved in their pens."

A broken man, in other words.

Back in the castle, Caelan found the women had retreated from the kitchen to the courtyard. He stifled a grin on discovering his temporary housekeeper at the head of the stone table, pouring tea as elegantly as if she were in a duchess's parlor.

Mrs. Gillan announced, "We are discussing how to tackle the kitchen. Quite naturally, Mrs. Potts has no experience with a task of this magnitude." His mother-in-law's glare clearly blamed him for the sad state of Isla's castle, as she liked to call it.

He had a daft impulse to walk over and stand behind Clara, then put a hand on her shoulder until she smiled up at him, and he could be certain that Mrs. Gillan wasn't babbling about Isla.

Even more daft: he'd like to kiss her good morning. Instead he leaned against the wall and enjoyed looking at her, even with a tangle of lace covering her hair.

"Have you washed your hands after touching that rat?" Clara asked, narrowing her eyes at him. Kissing was obviously not foremost in her mind.

"I have."

"Market is held on Tuesday," Mrs. Gillan said, ignoring him. "You and Elsbeth will join me for coffee thereafter. You'll enjoy that. Bring your needlework."

"Me?" Clara asked. "With you, Mrs. Gillan?"

"All the village women come, and we do our mending. I'm afraid you'll find there's much to be mended in the castle."

"Excuse me, Mrs. Gillan. I want to show you something." Elsbeth jumped up and ran back into the castle, and Caelan heard her dashing up the steps.

"I shall return with two more maids to assist you in the Herculean task that awaits," Mrs. Gillan said. She turned to Caelan with a frown. "I too have been grieving, laird, but I did not neglect my household. I thought the rumors about the state of the castle had been exaggerated."

"Sadly, vermin can be found in every kitchen in London," Clara said.

Was she defending him?

"Nay, this castle is infamous," Mrs. Gillan retorted. "Didn't you wonder why you were hired from England? It's because the laird's own sister knew that no good Scotswoman would take on the task—not unless they were hoping to marry him." Her chin trembled. "Thank goodness my Isla can't see what's become of this place. She took such pride in her castle." She blotted a tear.

Caelan couldn't muster up a guilty expression, because he simply didn't feel the emotion.

Elsbeth ran back into the courtyard waving two small bags, the kind ladies carried to balls. "Look at these bonnie wee bags, Mrs. Gillan! Mrs. Potts made them with her own hands."

They were far better than the bejeweled French reticules that Isla had collected. Now he thought of it, those bags disappeared along with his wife's personal maid, who left the day after she died.

"Is that a *mouse*?" Mrs. Gillan asked, looking taken aback.

"Mayhap you can make a special rat for wearing around the castle," Caelan suggested.

Clara rolled her eyes at him.

"I wouldn't mind a cat," Mrs. Gillan said, turning it over. "I must be off home. Seeing Isla's castle in this state is breaking my heart." Her eyes welled up, and she took out a handkerchief.

Clara gently helped her to rise. "We'd be grateful if you could send maids to help, but you must stay home and put up your feet. Next time you see the castle, I promise that it will shine from the parapet to the kitchen. Does your housekeeper know how to make a posset of calf's-foot jelly? It would be very sustaining for you at this difficult time."

"I don't think she does," Mrs. Gillan replied. "I can see that you're used to the very best households, as you're wearing such beautiful lace on your head. I'm ashamed of Isla's home."

"It will be clean in no time," Clara said soothingly.

"Her linens were her pride and joy," she said, with a sob.

They walked past Caelan without a second glance, Clara's voice receding as they moved down the corridor and out the castle.

Now a good half of Scotland would think not only that he'd fallen on his wife's grave but also that he was so grief-stricken as to live in filth.

"Me and Maisie will be at it now, laird." Elsbeth stood up and curtsied, and then yanked the scullery maid to her feet. Clara's maid was clearly a force to be reckoned with, unsurprising after meeting her father. Cobbledick had demanded a tour of the staff's living quarters before he would consider parting from his daughter; thankfully the rat hadn't yet made its presence known.

Before he left, the coachman had served up a homily on the importance of a woman's virtue, by which Caelan understood that Cobbledick, like him, had concluded that "Mr. Potts" might be fictional.

Yet Caelan was keeping an open mind as regarded a forsaken nobleman. *Someone* had sent Clara fleeing to the Highlands.

That someone was going to pay for his crimes.

CHAPTER 15

*W*hen Clara returned to the castle after dispatching Caelan's mother-in-law to the village, she was in possession of several new facts, not a single one of which made her happy.

"The rot in the castle is the outer sign of the laird's grief," Mrs. Gillan had told her several times, catching her breath between sobs. "It's the wrapping around a broken heart."

The sturdy man whom Clara saw fishing in the stream hadn't seemed anguished, but what did she know? She was a fool who thought she saw a spark of desire in the eyes of a man who had married the most beautiful woman for a hundred miles.

"The laird married my daughter for love. She was no more than a village lass, without a dowry to speak of. But the laird—his lordship—scarcely danced with another. He described Isla as a willow bough in spring."

Eccentric Clara, with breasts and other curves, could never compare to that willowy beauty. Thankfully, Caelan had no idea she was attracted to him.

"Isla loved being called Lady MacCrae," her mother continued. "The title meant the world to her. I wouldn't be surprised if he started living like a peasant because of that, because his lady isn't with him any longer. You will clean her castle?"

She only left after Clara promised repeatedly that Isla's castle would be restored to its former glory.

But not before Mrs. Gillan told Clara that hardly

more than a week ago, Caelan had thrown himself down on the bluebells he'd planted on Isla's grave. It sounded like something that happened in a novel, a depressing one. It was hard to imagine the laird in such agony, but perhaps that was because she didn't like to think of Caelan in pain. He was already a friend, after all. No one wanted their friends to suffer.

When she walked back into the kitchen, Elsbeth and Maisie were on their hands and knees, scrubbing at the blackened stone around the fireplace. Clara stopped long enough to remind them to take a tea break after they finished that foul task before she climbed the tower steps. She needed to get a sense of the task ahead.

When she reached the top floor and opened the door, her mouth fell open. She had anticipated dust—but not grandeur. The floor was covered by a silk rug woven into a pattern of birds in flight. Given its tattered appearance, mice had been raising babies in luxurious nests.

To one side of the door, a gilded cabinet lacquered with fantastical beasts stretched all the way to the beams. Clara gently rubbed a griffin with a handkerchief, and its blue eyes promptly fell out. She guiltily pocketed them, hoping that she could glue them back in. The wood itself was pockmarked with holes, as if a flock of tiny woodpeckers regularly searched it for breakfast.

Apple-green curtains hung around the enormous bed, the damask dulled by grime, the sheets gray with dust. A draped dressing table was topped with a gold-trimmed looking glass, tarnished silver candlesticks, and a crystal bottle that must have held perfume. Clara couldn't help thinking of the tragic young queen Marie Antoinette taking a last spritz before being marched away to the tumbril.

But this tragedy was Isla's, not a French queen's.

Her throat tightened at the thought. The bed had no coverlet; Caelan hadn't been sleeping here. Likely he couldn't bear to be in the chamber he shared with his wife. She had a feeling that the door had closed behind Isla and never opened again. Wax had run down the candlesticks and puddled on the dressing table, and no one scraped it off.

She blinked away tears and had turned to go when a pair of malevolent yellow eyes caught hers. She shrieked before she could stop herself—and instantly heard Caelan pounding up the stairs.

"Clara?" His eyes were wild. "Is there another rat?"

"I'm sorry," she cried, hand on her thumping heart. "I caught sight of that bird, and I lost my composure."

He followed her gaze to the stuffed owl perched on a shelf over the door. It was falling apart, one wing hanging loose at its side.

"God, that's revolting," Caelan said. He reached up and grabbed it by one leg. A trail of feathers followed him as he walked to the window, unlatched it, and unceremoniously tossed the bird into the moat. "Queen Marie Antoinette reportedly had a stuffed crane, and Isla desperately wanted a bird. The owl was the best I could find."

"I apologize for being in your bedchamber," Clara said.

"You have every right to be here." His mouth crooked into a wry smile. "You're my housekeeper, remember?"

"Of course!" Clara said hastily. What did one say about such a bleak room? "Do you happen to know when the bed-curtains were last taken down and washed?"

"Never."

"Do you know what made these small holes?" She pointed to the dressing table.

He grimaced. "Worm rot. The piece will have to be burnt to stop the worms from spreading." He didn't seem distraught at the prospect as he peered closer at the wardrobe. "This one, too."

Clara cleared her throat. "Did you inherit the furniture from your parents?"

"No."

Isla must have chosen them. "The room needs a thorough cleaning." She walked over to the bed and wiggled one of the bedposts back and forth. "I want to be sensitive to your feelings, but I don't think this bed is sound."

"Sensitive to my what?" He glanced around. "Jesus, it looks like the chamber of a beheaded queen."

"I thought the same thing! There's a story—" Clara caught herself.

"Did a bed come alive and swallow Her Majesty?"

"Thankfully, no. A princess fell asleep for a hundred years. I would guess magic kept the termites and woodworms away."

"One would hope," he agreed. "Is she the one who fell asleep in a glass box?"

"Rather like your bathtub," Clara said, giving him a lopsided smile.

"Considering the dearth of magic in this castle, I should have climbed the steps to this room now and then." He gave one of the bedposts a gentle push. It groaned and leaned in, releasing a billow of dust from the brocade gathered above.

"Good thing you tied up your hair this morning,"

he said once they both stopped coughing. "You'd have never got it clean without plunging into the loch."

Clara patted her head, giving him a rueful smile. "Elsbeth and I compared it to a wild animal this morning."

"True, you could be hiding anything under that scarf," Caelan said, eyeing her.

"Household staff should be neat and clean at all times," she told him, a giggle escaping. "My mother would chide the housekeeper if even a strand of hair escaped a chambermaid's cap."

"In your case, a curl has fallen down your back and now it's as tarnished as the candlesticks." He turned her around and poked it back into the fichu. "I like your hair better when it's not all bound up."

"You do? Never mind!" she added quickly. "As I said, I don't know if the bed is safe. That bedpost seems rickety."

Caelan reached out and gave it a proper shove. Naturally it collapsed, dragging down another bedpost and ripping the bed canopy in half.

This time Clara retreated out the door to escape the cloud of dirt. "Did you have to?" she asked, shaking out her skirts.

He followed her out onto the landing. "Yes."

"Like the wardrobe, the bed will have to be replaced."

"Would you suggest that I get another one like it?"

"Well," Clara said awkwardly. "What if your next wife—if you take one—is not very tall? Personally, I'd have to climb that bed like the mast of a boat."

His mouth twitched. "Your husband would volunteer to be the mast."

Clara peered at him. "Was that an uncouth jest?"

"Yes," he admitted unrepentantly. "Perhaps you might clean my study instead? I never noticed the dust before this morning, but now I see the room differently."

She let out a crow of laughter. "Every lord should be forced to clean his own house at least once."

He snorted. "Could we say the same about ladies?"

"I saw people working, but I had no real idea how hard it was," she agreed. "I thought that pot last night would never come clean."

"After you, *Mrs. Potts*," he said with a sardonic wave of his hand.

Something in his gaze made Clara hurry down the circular stone steps, past the nursery where she had slept the night before. On the next level, Caelan reached over her shoulder to push open the door.

"Oh my goodness," Clara said faintly.

"I sleep in that bed." The laird nodded toward a narrow bed to one side. Taking her expression for horror, he added defensively, "I change the sheets weekly. They're stacked over there in the corner."

"Like the pans," Clara murmured, moving into the room.

"It's easier."

His life must be very easy, because everything was stacked on the floor: papers, sheets, a pile of quilts, shirts, breeches, mugs . . .

Books.

CHAPTER 16

Clara had only seen so many books in a library. Every wall was lined with rounded bookshelves crammed with books standing upright, with more laid horizontally on top. What might be a comfortable red velvet sofa was covered with stacks of papers held down by large leather-bound volumes.

"You ridiculed me for bringing books rather than clothes, but you're in the same situation!" She waved her hand. "Two shirts and . . . two hundred books?"

"A fair summary," Caelan said, putting his hands on his hips, which emphasized how large his shoulders were. He leaned back against the door.

Clara hastily turned away, because somehow her eyes went instinctively to his waist. "You must have laughed when I said I wanted a castle filled with books."

"Mine isn't filled yet. Isla felt books didn't belong in the drawing room, and they all ended up here."

"My mother would agree with your wife," Clara said awkwardly.

"The same mother who would berate a scullery maid for showing a lock of hair?"

"I only have the one." Clara sidled away, because something in his eyes suggested . . . No, she must be wrong. "Do you have any novels amongst all these volumes?"

"My mother did. They're over there." He nodded at a section on the other side of the room.

Flustered, Clara walked to the shelf and took down a battered copy of *The Castle of Otranto*. "She must have adored this one, as it's so well-read. Don't you love the scene where the helmet falls from the moon like a mountain of sable plumes?"

"How could a helmet fall from the moon?"

"You never read your mother's favorite novel? It's a most delightfully spooky story."

"I suppose there's a ghost?"

"*Two* ghosts, not to mention the helmet—which crushes the prince after it falls from the sky. Of course, everyone is terrified." She struck a pose. "'Are the devils themselves in league against me? Speak, infernal specter!'"

Caelan gave a crack of laughter. "Was that line addressed to the helmet?"

"Yes," Clara confirmed.

"Does the helmet reply? Because tumbling off the moon is one thing, but a talking helmet is even better. 'Fie, foh, and fum, I smell the blood of an Englishman—and now I shall swallow you with my rusty visor'!"

Clara couldn't help laughing. "Unfortunately, the helmet can only make a rustling sound with its plumes. Although there is a sighing portrait."

"My nephew, Alfie, has a chicken with a topknot of feathers. He already interprets her facial expressions for the rest of us, but if you read him this book, he might expand his interpretative abilities."

Clara paused. "Perhaps I could become a governess! I would enjoy teaching someone to read."

"No, because you want a castle of your own, filled with books and presumably children, who will constantly be on guard lest a suit of armor drop from the battlements. They'll think every glass bathtub should contain a sleeping princess and every loch a talking frog."

"I am coming to the conclusion that my being a housekeeper is not a natural fit," Clara acknowledged. She put *The Castle of Otranto* back on the shelf. "I brought a copy of this novel with me as a gift for my employers."

He looked dumbfounded. "Why?"

"I thought the owners of a castle ought to have a copy. The author, Horace Walpole, set it in Italy, but I heard he was thinking of the Scottish Highlands."

Caelan snorted. "You imagined that your new employers would enjoy reading about a sentient, homicidal suit of armor? You weren't even trying to disguise yourself as a housekeeper, were you?"

"Of course I was! The kind of housekeeper whom I'd like to hire. Whom I *will* hire," she added. He looked confused, so she said, "If people didn't have to work for so many hours, they'd take more pride in their work. If they had time to read, in other words. My mother barks at anyone she sees putting her feet up, from the housekeeper to the scullery maids."

"Literacy and laziness will be a requirement for employment in your household," Caelan interpreted. "Is this the novel where the hero is an excellent conversationalist?" He strolled over and leaned against the bookshelf next to her.

Clara's heart skipped a beat. The laird's shirt was dingy, and he wore no cravat and no coat. By all rights she ought to find him decidedly unattractive. "No, that's a different novel. The hero of this one has large black eyes, a smooth forehead, and 'manly curling locks like jet.'"

"'Manly curling locks like jet'?" He let out another crack of laughter. "You must be jesting."

"I am not!" Clara took the book from the shelf

again and began flipping through, but she was so flustered that she couldn't find the correct page.

"A smooth forehead?" Caelan pushed back the thick locks that covered his. "How am I doing? Any wrinkles? I'm coming up on twenty-seven."

Clara's fingers trembled to reach out and touch his face. He had a few wrinkles but would be just as handsome when his hair turned silver. His laughter gave her a disconcerting melting sensation. She clapped the book shut and jammed it into the shelf again. "We should continue our tour."

Below the study was a room as grand as Isla's bedchamber, hung with rotting tasseled silk drapes and crowded with equally unsuitable furniture, all of it pocked by woodworm. "My wife labeled this room the drawing room," Caelan said. "Before it was so grand, it was a sitting room."

"I see." Clara had a strong feeling that a family of mice—a village of them—had made their home in the drawing room. Whole generations had been raised in comfort. "I'm afraid this rug will be impossible to repair."

"It's dirty, I suppose." Caelan stared around, his entire body indicative of pure disinterest.

"Holes," Clara said, pointing to the largest.

He grunted.

"We could try washing it and arranging furniture so that the holes aren't as evident."

"No, throw it out." His voice was uncompromising. "The furniture too."

"That would be foolish," Clara said, schooling her voice to patience. "The rug must have cost the earth. I've never seen a *round* carpet, for goodness' sake."

"Ordered from Flanders." His jaw shut so tightly

that she was surprised he got the words out. Perhaps Isla's expensive tastes had bankrupted the estate?

"We could cut salvageable pieces into chair seats or ottomans and sell them," Clara said, inspired. "Or trade them for new sheets."

"I have money for sheets," he growled, kicking at the rug—which promptly ripped straight through a field of silken flowers. "The threads are rotten."

"The window leaks. Thank goodness books weren't kept in this room, or they'd have mildewed."

"I replaced the glass in the study last year." He grimaced. "I've been a fool, trying to pretend these rooms don't exist."

Clara's heart pinched, and she couldn't stop herself from reaching out to touch his arm. "Mrs. Gillan told me how much you and Isla loved each other."

"I don't want to talk about it." He looked down at her. "Let's talk about *your* marriage." His eyes didn't seem dark with pain, but obviously she was rubbish at interpreting men's expressions.

"Let's not," she said instantly. "We should eschew the whole subject of spouses."

"*Eschew?* What housekeeper uses that word?"

She was glad that his eyes had lightened. Clara poked him in the chest. "I'm only a housekeeper until Mr. Cobbledick returns with your bath. But before that happens, I've made a vow to Mrs. Gillan to leave Isla's castle shining."

"It's not Isla's castle, despite Mrs. Gillan referring to it as such." His jaw turned stony hard again.

"*Your* castle," she amended, wondering what the problem was. She was trying hard to think clearly.

Caelan was mourning his dead wife. *But Isla died two years ago.*

He thought she was married. *She wasn't.*

He was a gentleman. *Not really.*

Her mind reeled back and forth.

"If you wish me to begin with your study, I need to go downstairs for a broom," she said, pulling herself together.

Caelan shut the door after they both reentered the study. "My papers have to stay where they are. The piles may seem disordered, but they're not."

Clara firmed her lips into an obstinate line. "I can keep them in their piles, but they must be moved. This floor needs scrubbing."

He picked up her hand. "Soft and delicate. Designed for turning the pages of a book, not wielding a mop." He put it to his lips. "This isn't me kissing my housekeeper's hand, but a lady's hand. I seem to remember the gesture from my younger days."

"Nonsense!" Clara could feel herself turning pink, but she couldn't look away from his gaze. "My hands, like yours, are capable of doing anything from washing the floors to sorting these papers into separate boxes. Ripping gray sheets into rags. Tossing rotten rugs down the stairs."

The warmth in his eyes made her heart clench. All of a sudden, the room seemed very small and intimate. The longing she felt deep in her bones?

Madness.

CHAPTER 17

Caelan had never been a man who woke raging with lust. He considered the condition to be a scourge of boyhood that he had gratefully outgrown. Even in the first days of his marriage, he had leapt out of bed before Isla woke; she had remained there until a maid brought her breakfast on a silver tray.

Yet from the moment he'd woken this morning, he had wanted only one thing. He'd tented his kilt to the point of obscenity. When he walked into the courtyard and saw Clara at breakfast, he had to snatch a hunk of bread and retreat upstairs, because it was that or scandalize her maid.

Last night, when he'd helped her make up the bed, he'd watched her lean forward to tuck in the sheet—both of them doing that task for the first time in their lives—and tried unsuccessfully not to notice her gorgeous rear end.

Leaving her with a pail of hot water, he had walked down the steps to his study, imagining her unbuttoning her filthy pelisse and torn gown. Obviously, she planned to strip off every garment and wash thoroughly.

He had fallen onto his bed, carnal images racing through his mind. Clara's nipples would stiffen in the cool night air. Her wet hands would stroke every plush curve. He had a feeling she wouldn't be a lady in bed: not the woman who'd muttered "bollocks" when they couldn't get the sheet to tuck in properly.

Lewd fantasies crowded into his mind, plans to

excite her—and to satisfy her. He would begin by kissing her from head to foot, until she was wiggling against him and begging for more. Ravenous phrases streamed through his head, ready to breathe against her skin. Filthy words that would make a delicate lady faint, referring to filthy acts that a lady wouldn't contemplate.

But a *woman* with Clara's imagination? Who was fearless, bold enough to climb into an unknown carriage and let it take her to the Highlands? A woman who made jokes about naked chests being like chocolate and clearly liked his legs?

He had stroked himself senseless and was still panting when his tool rose back in the air, demanding attention. Again.

Like a damned boy of fifteen.

And now?

He could look into her green eyes every day for the rest of his life. By dawn's light. By candlelight. With all that sunlit hair billowing around her face.

"You are not truly married," he said, his voice deep and steady. Not accusatory but matter-of-fact. "Aye, you might have mouthed the words, but an unconsummated marriage is invalid. Did you know that?"

"That's not relevant to my circumstances," Clara said, obviously choosing her words carefully.

He felt a twinge of deep satisfaction. She might have fibbed about being married, and fibbed about being a housekeeper, but the real woman, the real Clara, was honest. What's more, she knew what she wanted: a castle and books. By God, he had a castle and books.

She wanted a man with a kilt?

He had that too.

"The point is relevant," he said, pulling himself together before he fell on her like a ravening beast. "I want to kiss you, but I would never kiss a married woman. A *truly* married woman. Are you truly married, Clara?"

She gulped.

"Clara?"

"No," she admitted.

He picked up her left hand, sliding his fingers down until he took hold of her ring and started easing it off.

She scowled at him. "What are you doing?"

"Throwing this in the rubbish."

"Absolutely not." She pulled her hand away from his.

"Why not? You're not married, or if you are, the union was never consummated. Which means you're not married."

"I need that ring. Everyone knows me as Mrs. Potts."

"I do not."

"Mrs. Gillan does," she retorted. "What's more, at the moment, I'm a housekeeper, not a lady. I don't have a chaperone. Without that ring, any random man who passes me in the street might pull me into an alley and kiss me. Or—or worse."

Caelan's jaw tightened. "Not if he hopes to see another dawn."

She gaped at him. "Don't be absurd! You're not my husband. You won't be walking next to me in the street, nor in church, for that matter. I'll be seated in the rear."

He felt an unfamiliar grin spread over his face. "You may not be my wife, but you're not my housekeeper, either. I think we can both agree on that. I am not paying you, which means you are not in my employ. So why are you cleaning my house?" He leaned in even farther, his eyes gleaming.

"I'm your friend."

That startled him. "*Friend*? I've never had a woman as a friend."

"This conversation is absurd," Clara said, her eyes unnervingly direct. "I fail to see why you are making such a fuss about my wedding ring." Apparently realizing that her headscarf was sagging to one side, she reached up and steadied the pile of hair.

"I wish to kiss you." With one long stride, he stood in front of her, tugging at the lacy cloth protecting her hair. To his satisfaction, it easily slipped off, freeing a torrent of curls that caught beams of sunlight. "Why would I say so if I didn't?"

"I've been thinking about that. Like Sleeping Beauty, you are waking up."

"I'm no beauty." Caelan ran a finger along her cheek. "You are, though."

"When Isla died, you went to sleep. Now you've woken up, and I'm the only unmarried—" She squeaked to a halt. "Oops."

"So you *are* unmarried." He felt satisfaction deep in his bones. "By the way, Isla has nothing to do with this. I don't want to hear her name from your lips."

She looked momentarily crushed before sympathy washed over her face.

"I didn't mean that as an insult," he added quickly.

"I completely understand. I really do, Caelan. I'm so sorry that you and—that your wife isn't alive to be here with you."

He cleared his throat. "I don't want sympathy. I have enough of that from every Highlander in these parts. I simply don't want to talk about Isla. Or your nonexistent spouse, for that matter. I'd prefer to kiss you."

"Why?"

Apparently he had to be less blunt. More complimentary. "I've never known anyone like you. Everything about you is kissable. Your crazy hair, your giggling mouth, your shining eyes, your soft curves."

She scowled at him—the list wasn't good enough.

He'd fallen out of the habit of wooing ladies, and besides, his mind was blurred by lust. What could he say?

You are Isla's opposite: Kiss me?

"There's no unmarried man in all Scotland who wouldn't want to kiss you," he said instead. "Your lower lip is the color of a wild strawberry."

She blinked at him uncertainly. Surely she knew . . . She had to know. Women always knew when they mesmerized a man.

He cleared his throat. "Would you prefer that I compliment your starlit hair?"

Her mouth curled into a reluctant smile. "Did you read that somewhere?"

"Maybe. Wild starlight?"

"And what, exactly, does that mean?"

He fiddled with one of her curls. "Your hair is luminous, as if it had captured light."

"Ah."

Clara stopped looking at Caelan, because holding his gaze led to madness. Something in his eyes made her want to throw herself into his arms.

Adventures were shocking. They came from

nowhere, like a helmet falling to earth. Frankly, everything Caelan said was as startling and unbelievable as that improbable meteor.

A new adventure was presenting itself.

He desired her.

Not another woman, in some other part of the room. *Her*, with her hair in a mess and her plainest dress on, without a corset, wearing boots, covered in dust, and despite a litany of silly remarks about fairy tales.

Even though he was in love with a dead woman.

"All right," she said, making up her mind. Now she thought of it, she ought to kiss another man, if only to banish the memory of Prince George.

When he stared silently, she clarified, "I wouldn't mind kissing you."

His eyes blazed, and a large hand reached out to tug her closer. His lips landed on hers softly, without the prince's sloppy urgency. Clara took in a deep breath, smelling the loch, not the dust. The man, not the laird.

Caelan. Not George.

His hands cupped her head as he murmured something, slanted his lips against hers. His tongue slid into her mouth, twining with hers.

Her mind began bouncing, trying to assess what was happening. She had never imagined that kissing was like breathing, except you were breathing someone else's air (another reason to be very glad that she'd escaped Prince George).

It was almost like talking. Except this kind of talking seemed to include a promise of some sort.

No, she had to stop being so fanciful. Caelan wasn't making a promise.

He was simply kissing her, the way her mother had warned that men might. That they *would*, if a lady ever gave them a chance.

"It's not merely that you haven't known a man," Caelan said. "You've never *kissed* a man, have you?"

"No," she admitted. "I haven't." Her stomach curled into a hard knot. Apparently she was rubbish at kissing, which didn't surprise her.

Prince George was the only man who'd ever indicated a wish to kiss her. His Majesty had lunged at her a year ago, but she had managed to whirl away, laughing as if he'd only been playing a game, waved goodbye, and run as fast as she could in the opposite direction.

"You're kissing me, but you're thinking of something else," Caelan continued.

She opened her mouth to defend herself—but he was right.

One side of his mouth crooked up, a surprising hint of vulnerability in his eyes. "Dreaming of a prince with sooty locks and a smooth forehead?"

That was unnervingly close to reality. "Actually, I was thinking about my mother's admonishments against kissing," she told him.

"No one is allowed to think about their parents while kissing. The fact you're able to think at all indicates my lack of practice."

His eyes fell to her lips, and his eyelids drooped. All of a sudden, Clara's mind craved his taste, reminding her that this was *her* adventure. He was right: her mother was irrelevant. She came up on her toes and wound her hands into his tousled hair.

His tongue slid inside her mouth as if it belonged there. She didn't think—she couldn't think. Not when they were both open-mouthed, tongues entwining, messy and sensual and full of want. Rather than assessing what they were doing, she felt it—felt him. Tasted him. Smelled him. Under the dust was a clean, male essence of Caelan that made her whimper against his lips.

"I'd like to take you against the wall," he groaned.

Her mind cleared. What had he said? *Take you . . .* that was clear. *Wall?* Not so much.

Caelan opened his eyes. "I shouldn't have said that."

He looked down at Clara, rueful that his stupidity had broken one of the most sensual kisses of his life. She looked astonished, as if the lovemaking potential of a wall had not occurred to her.

Yet she didn't look appalled. He recognized that puzzled frown from last night, when they were trying to figure out how to put on a sheet so that it stretched from top to bottom of the bed. After they'd made up Clara's bed, she had insisted that they change his sheets as well.

Caelan had agreed, mostly to see her bend over the mattress again. "I'm not always a gentleman," he admitted, his voice a husky murmur.

"I . . . I'm not sure . . ." Her brow knit in an enchanting fashion.

"Clara." He snatched her into another kiss, putting a hand on the middle of her back so he could bring her closer. She kissed him in return, melting against him, her tongue tangling with his. He heard her breath catch and quicken.

His tool was tenting his kilt. She tasted sweet and addictive, making him want to kiss her deeper and deeper. Wrap his hands around her arse and pull her higher. Place her on clean sheets and lick her from her collarbone to her toes. Bury his face in a cloud of spun sugar hair. Wrap it around his hands and—

"We can't go further than another kiss. Perhaps two," he said, his voice rumbling from deep in his chest. "Not until you're wearing *my* ring."

He was aching to rub against her. She was here, in his study, next to the bed . . .

Not yet.

Not here.

"It's morning, for God's sake," he said, trying to control himself before he lost his head and dove into another kiss. He did it anyway. He came out of the kiss slowly, and only because he had to allow her to breathe.

Clara's breasts rose as she gulped air, mesmerizing him as she stumbled back a step. "That's enough," she growled—if someone as sweet as sugar could be said to growl.

He reached down to adjust himself. Her eyes flicked down his front. Her brows drew together, so he took away his hands to allow her to see his whole length, straining against his kilt.

Her eyes widened.

"Do you want to get married first?" he asked, scarcely aware of the words as they fell out of his lips. The only thing he was—

"What are you talking about?"

"Marriage," he said, managing to get the word out.

"No, thank you."

Her firm answer fell on his head like a bucket of cold water. He'd learned as a young man that unmarried women dreamed of marrying him. Oh, if an English duke had strolled into a ballroom, he might have had competition.

But the only English lord he knew was old Bufford.

When the Laird of CaerLaven walked into a room, unmarried ladies simpered and beckoned. He had more land and money than most men in the Highlands, and he wasn't foul-looking.

The combination had apparently given him a swollen head, despite the fact that his previous marriage should have given him a more accurate assessment of his desirability.

All the hazy desire had disappeared from Clara's gaze, and she was eyeing him as if he were about to run amok. "Kisses are one thing; marriage is another. No, thank you."

"You may be wearing a ring, but you're not married."

"Well . . ."

One side of his mouth curled up despite himself. "Clara. You already admitted that you aren't married, and it wasn't a matter of consummation, either. You have never said vows to anyone, have you?"

"How did you know?"

He tipped up her chin. "Because you would never have kissed me if you'd vowed to love another man." Caelan would have bet his castle on that certainty.

A shadow crossed her eyes. "In my experience, people are perfectly willing to kiss others after they've said vows in a church."

"You are not one of them," Caelan stated. "I may not have known you long, but I know you all the same."

"You said those vows to Isla."

He flinched. "She died two years ago."

Clara took a deep breath. "I understand, Caelan. I think it's marvelous that you are waking up to life again."

"So you still insist that I'm the princess?"

She nodded. "I shall clear the brambles from this castle, but I won't marry a man in a glass coffin."

"That doesn't make sense."

"You don't even care to hear your late wife's name spoken aloud," she explained. "I don't want that in a husband. I am lucky enough to have control of my dowry. I have no need for a spouse."

Caelan managed to stop himself from growling before he reminded himself that Rome wasn't built, etcetera.

"I suspect my mother-in-law told you that she plans to marry me to a stonyhearted English-woman," he said wryly.

"She did. I'm not a candidate."

"Clara, I—"

"No."

Isla had looked at him with adoration, and Clara looked at him with hunger but *not* adoration. He could work with it.

He had to get her out of the castle, with all its memories of his late wife. There was nothing so adventuresome as waiting for a trout to nibble on one's fly and then fighting to bring the fish to shore. What was more, he could introduce her to the pool his grandfather had carved out of the rocks.

"I understand," Caelan said, making certain his tone was easy and cordial. "Let's go back to my of-fer to help you clean the study if you will go fishing with me."

Clara yanked her hand away. "Whether a woman is a housekeeper or a lady, she ought not to be dis-respected by an improper proposal!"

Caelan looked into her shocked eyes and burst out laughing again.

"I take it that you didn't mean unclothed," she said sheepishly.

"I did not, although like any man, I would celebrate if the lady in question wished to shed her garments."

"How can a lady possibly fish? Not having legs like tree trunks, she would be swept downstream!"

"You noticed my legs?"

"How could I not, given that you wear a kilt?"

Caelan grinned at her. "Prefer the kilt to breeches, do you?"

"I've always loved a man in a skirt," she blurted out. "I didn't mean that!" A rosy blush went up her cheeks.

"I thought you had never met a man in a skirt before me." He leaned in, bracing his arm on the door behind her. "I don't think you've ever *known* a man, married or not."

Clara winced. She wasn't a very good liar. "This is an inappropriate conversation," she announced. "We have to remove each book, dust it, wash the shelves, organize all the papers, wash down every surface, sweep, and then scrub the floor."

"I could send my coachman to the village to bring help," Caelan said, appalled by that list.

"Your mother-in-law is sending two maids, aprons, pails, and more, and I plan to put her staff to work helping Elsbeth with the other rooms. Still, I like your idea. I'll trade my labor *and* yours for a fishing lesson." She crossed her arms. "You and I will clean this room."

Caelan gave a painful thought to the contracts waiting on his desk before he nodded. His mother would faint at the idea of the Laird of CaerLaven engaging in manual labor; his father would have guffawed; Isla would have had hysterics.

"It's an adventure," Clara told him, obviously following his train of thought. "Neither of us has any experience cleaning other than last night. I suspect you grew up thinking the castle was cleaned by fairies—which is why you have done nothing about the state of your own home. You were waiting for house fairies to do it for you."

"Not fairies but broonies or brownies," Caelan told her. "Here in Scotland, a lucky family has a broonie who comes out at night to scrub down the place." He drew her into his arms, putting on a deliberately sultry tone. "I should like to offer a thank-you to my very own broonie."

She rolled her eyes and pushed him away before he could kiss her. "We'll start at the top and work down to the floor. First the highest shelves all the way around the room, and then around again to dust those within reach. We need rags, a pail of water, and a ladder." Which led to Caelan ripping one of his sheets into rags and spending the next few hours holding a ladder while Clara dusted.

She found the book collection fascinating and frequently paused to leaf through a volume; he was equally fascinated by her ankles. He had been dimly aware that women sought to cover their ankles—Isla had shrieked if a breeze stirred her hem—but he'd never understood why.

Now he did. Clara's gown was made of a heavy cloth that fell down past her ankles—except when she reached for a book. To his delight, she wore gossamer-weight silk stockings that no housekeeper possessed. The delicate knob on the side of her ankle was visible and lickable. Her silk slippers

were so supple that he could trace the arch of her
foot when she reached high for a volume. He would
have loved to kiss his way up that slender foot, lav-
ishing attention on her ankle. Kissing higher until
he reached the top of her stocking and undid the
bow with his teeth. Kissing higher . . .

After they were betrothed, of course.

True, he had thought to marry a mature and
rational woman, but as it turned out, he would
marry a woman who seemed to live in a fairy tale
because . . . because if he didn't marry Clara, some
other man would replace that fake ring on her finger and guard her from strangers in alleys. That
was unacceptable.

Some other man seeing her ankles?

Deeply unacceptable.

For the moment, he was content to steady the
ladder and gaze hungrily at every part of her that
he could see. She apparently wasn't wearing a corset, because whenever she moved, her voluptuous
breasts swayed. Every once in a while, she let out a
little crow and looked down in excitement, waving
a faded volume. That gave him the delicious curve
of her neck and a wobbling mound of fine-spun
hair, strands floating in the sunshine.

They had only one set of bookshelves left when
she climbed down the ladder and caught him smiling so widely that she raised an eyebrow.

"I love cleaning," he told her.

"I can't say I love it much, but I *do* love your library."

"I owe my broonie a kiss," he said, brushing
his lips against hers. This time she clung to him
rather than pushing him away, wrapping her arms
around his neck.

"You taste—" She broke away and pointed to the shelves. "Move the ladder there, if you please."

Caelan obediently moved it. "When we're married, will we dust the library once a month? Once a week?"

"I already refused your proposal." Then she narrowed her eyes. "This ladder is sound. Why don't you dust below while I dust above?"

"No." His voice was as uncompromising as hers had been when she rejected his proposal. "You're not going up a ladder without me at the bottom to catch you."

Caelan's voice had a possessive ring that Clara found stupidly erotic. What was erotic about wanting to make sure she was safe? "If you're worried about my falling down, *you* go up the ladder," she countered. "I'll hold it for you."

She watched him open his mouth to refuse— before a calculating light went through his eyes, and he grinned. "Good idea!" he said, bounding up the ladder. "Be sure to hold the ladder steady."

He was steady on his feet and the ladder perfectly sound. But she obediently moved into position below him. Caelan was a far more efficient duster than she; he snatched a stack of books, balanced them on the top rung, and washed the shelf, giving each volume a cursory swipe with a rag before replacing it.

"Aren't you glancing at the titles?" she asked.

"No. A few years ago I rearranged all the books. Everything is organized from 'Most Boring' at the top to 'Readable' at the bottom."

Clara was still giggling when he moved down a step, putting his thigh in front of her. His legs were thick and muscled, powerful limbs designed for bounding up mountains like a mountain goat.

She was still staring at his leg when he moved down another step. "See something you like?" Caelan asked, his voice as mischievous as a young boy's. She *did* like it. Being this close to him made her heart speed up and her limbs feel tender and unstable. Worse, she could feel her cheeks turn to rose.

He took down another stack of books without waiting for an answer, though she was perfectly aware that he kept glancing down at her.

"Tsk, tsk," he said, looking at a volume. "Burke's *Speech on Economical Reform* definitely belongs on the top shelf, don't you think?" He bounded back up the ladder, which let her look directly up his kilt.

She already knew he didn't wear smalls under his kilt. His bottom was surprisingly *round*. Plump and masculine and utterly unlike hers.

"Looking at my arse, are you?" His amused voice floated from above, and she jumped away from the ladder so quickly that she could have knocked him over.

"I'm sorry!" she gasped. "You moved and . . . I didn't mean to!"

He came down slowly, a smile in his eyes. "You're not wearing a corset, so we're even."

That smile gave her an odd sensation in her spine, of all places, and then between her legs.

When he said his broonie needed to kiss *him*, this time, she didn't hesitate. It was an adventure, after all. What an adventure. She cupped his face in her hands and brought her lips to his. When their tongues met, pleasure thrummed over her body in a way that erased her mother's warnings about kisses.

A few minutes later, they were still kissing, until Caelan stopped and said hoarsely, "Clara."

Only her name.

All of her delight in the *adventure* fled, as alarm slammed down her spine. The way he said her name? Groaned it?

"Cleaning!" she yelped, stumbling back.

He didn't say another word, just reaching for the rag and dipping in the pail. The water was brown with dust, so Clara ran down the stairs and fetched more. Mrs. Gillan's maids hadn't arrived yet, but Elsbeth had fashioned a mopstick out of the broom handle and rags. Clara brought it upstairs so they could wash the floor.

Two hours later, they were finished, the bookshelves shining and clean, the papers sorted into empty potato crates that Caelan had fetched from the pantry. Clara collapsed on the couch, and Caelan sank down beside her, his thigh touching hers.

She had to say something that would break this intolerable . . . *tension* between them. The feeling in the air made her want to squirm and press against his hip. She cleared her throat. "We should—"

Down below a little boy screamed, "Are you *serious*?"

"Fuck." The word flew out of Caelan's mouth without conscious volition. "Have you changed your mind about marrying me now that you know what an excellent cleaner I am?"

"No. I have a feeling that curse word is even worse than 'bugger.'"

"You'd be right. Don't repeat it, unless you want those around you to faint." Caelan leaned forward and dusted a kiss on her mouth. "Except in the bedchamber."

Her brows drew together in confusion.

Caelan rejected the impulse to pick her up in his arms and improve her vocabulary. "I'll explain it later. You just heard my nephew Alfie's favorite question. He exists in a state of constant skepticism."

She nodded, coiling up her hair before picking up the piece of lace and pinning it to the top of her head. It wasn't as neat as when her maid did it: loops of hair billowed to one side, like a mishappen cloud.

"Shall I accompany you downstairs and introduce you to my sister and nephew as Mrs. Potts, the housekeeper?" Caelan inquired. "Fiona, I should tell you, is the person who contacted an agency in London and chose the aforementioned woman."

"I gather from your expression that you think you're being amusing," Clara said. "There's no need to involve you in my untruths. I shall introduce myself." The bundle on her head swayed gently as she moved toward the door. "Then we shall begin cleaning the . . . the drawing room."

"Your profile is not unlike a helmet with a vast set of plumes." He caught Clara's hand as she turned away. "I'd prefer you didn't hoist any furniture out the window."

"I shall—" The defiance in her voice died at his expression. "Oh, very well. If you summon some grooms, I'd appreciate it if they could clear away the rotten furniture and carpets."

"I could help."

She gave him a wry smile. "I appreciate your help with this room, but you might be more useful organizing these papers."

Caelan watched her walk from the room. Walk *away* from him.

Later, his guests would leave.

Mrs. Gillan would not return with her maids until tomorrow. His sister and Alfie would climb back into their carriage. Elsbeth and the scullery maid would retire to sleep.

And he and Clara would go to bed.

Hopefully, together.

CHAPTER 18

*C*lara leaned against the curve of the stairs, desperately fanning her face. She felt as red as a beet, as if anyone who glimpsed her face would know that she had been hopelessly lusting after the master of the castle.

Surely no one could read her eyes. Or her expression. Yet she felt as if there was a sign on her forehead announcing . . . announcing what?

That the laird was recovering from his grief? That wasn't entirely accurate—Caelan still couldn't bear to hear Isla's name—but he was coming back to life.

She had to leave, and soon. She wasn't the cold-hearted Englishwoman Mrs. Gillan had in mind. It would destroy her to be forever compared to a beloved first wife, especially after she'd spent her life failing to become the perfect daughter whom her mother felt she deserved.

Yes, Caelan desired her. He had kissed her. And proposed . . . a marriage proposal of sorts, her very first one, even though Caelan hadn't technically asked her. He'd muttered "marriage," as if she were so desperate that she'd say yes to anything.

He had doubtlessly dropped to his knee in front of Isla, vowing love and adoration.

At that thought, she snapped herself upright and walked down into the kitchen. The floor was looking much better, and four maids in sturdy white aprons—including Elsbeth and Maisie—were busily scrubbing the walls.

"Mrs. Gillan's household staff arrived to help, bringing cleaning supplies," Elsbeth reported.

"Sally and Meg, this is Mrs. Potts, the laird's housekeeper."

Clara took a stab at her mother's housekeeper's austere expression, but when the girls curtsied, she gave it up and smiled instead. "It's so kind of you to help. I know the castle isn't in the best shape, but I have every faith that you will make it shine."

"We will," Elsbeth promised. "Perhaps you should join the laird's sister in the courtyard. Mind how you go: we had to prop a board at the threshold to keep those dogs from coming inside."

Clara stepped over the board and walked into the sunshine. Caelan's sister, Fiona, was a tall woman with flaming red hair, and the boy sitting on the flagstones with two puppies in his lap had to be Alfie. She suddenly remembered that she was a housekeeper and wiped away her welcoming smile. Instead she dropped a deep curtsy and murmured, "Good morning, m'lady. I am Mrs. Potts."

Fiona rose and walked toward her. "Good morning."

"You're quite dirty."

Clara blinked down at Alfie. He had his mother's hair with a curious little face, not handsome but expressive. "I have been cleaning."

"This house is filthy," Alfie informed her, nodding.

"Mrs. Potts, may I introduce my son, Master Alfie?" Fiona said.

Alfie jumped up and bowed, spilling puppies on the ground.

"One doesn't bow to a housekeeper," Clara said, smiling at him. "You might wish me good morning."

"You don't look like our housekeeper," Alfie observed. "Mrs. Wilson has an apron and a great many keys hanging around her waist. And her hair is different. And she's older."

"Alfie, do not make personal remarks of that nature," Fiona commanded.

He wrinkled his nose and scampered after a puppy.

"Breaking my own rule, I am rather surprised to discover how well you have aged, Mrs. Potts, based on the agency's précis of the many posts you have held." A smile flickered at the corners of Fiona's mouth.

Clara had the feeling that she would have liked her very much had they met under different circumstances. "English rain is good for the skin," she offered, wondering how old she was supposed to be.

"It rains all the time here, so it must be only London rain that offers a fountain of youth. My name, by the way, is Lady McIntyre. I'm the laird's sister."

Clara curtsied again. "M'lady. May I bring you a cup of tea?"

"No, no, I came to work," Fiona said, pulling a cap out of her pocket, slapping it on her head, and starting to jam locks of red hair under its gathered edge. "I have trouble getting all my hair confined by a cap, but from the looks of it, you have double the amount. Perhaps I should give up on caps and use scarves. To that point, I might warn you that some of your hair has escaped."

Clara raised her hands and discovered a wayward pouf of curls. "Mine is not always this frizzled," she said, pulling the fichu in place before adding quickly, "That is, your hair is lovely, m'lady."

"Oh, for goodness' sake. You're no more a

housekeeper than I am," Lady McIntyre said, grinning at her. "You can call me Fiona; what's your real name? I presume you're planning to marry my brother. Don't think I'll—"

"Are you *serious*?" Alfie exclaimed, popping up with a puppy in his arms. "My uncle is broken-hearted, you know. He wouldn't be a good person to marry. He told me himself. He's a broken man."

"Ah well, broken one moment, whole the next," his mother said. "In fact, Alfie, when it comes to love—"

Clara interrupted. "I have no desire to marry the laird."

As far as Alfie was concerned, that settled the question. He held up a plump, wiggling body. "Mama, did you see this puppy has two different colored eyes?"

"The laird described him as the smallest and naughtiest of the pack," Clara said, grateful for a new subject.

"I *love* him," Alfie declared.

His mother put her hands on her hips. "But you also love Wilhelmina . . . who is a chicken," she added for Clara's sake. "Dogs and chickens are not natural friends."

"That's true." Alfie put the puppy down. "He's very sweet, but he's not a chicken, is he? It's not the same."

"I've never met a chicken, only eaten them," Clara revealed.

He frowned at her. "That is not a kind remark, Mrs. Potts. My parents try to avoid the subject."

"We've been eating a great deal of duck," Fiona confirmed. "Now, it's time to begin cleaning. Shall we start at the very top, in her ladyship's inner sanctum?"

"What does that mean?" Alfie inquired.

"The room that your former aunt made in her own image," Fiona said.

"That's a funny thing to say. I'll stay here and play with the puppy, even though he's not a chicken."

Back in the kitchen, Maisie was scrubbing the chimney over the fireplace, while Elsbeth held the ladder steady.

"There's grease up there," Elsbeth said, waving at the chimneypiece. "We're going after it with cleaning vinegar, and if that doesn't work, a groom will have to go to the village and buy pumice paste."

Fiona walked ahead of Clara up the tower steps. "In time, Elsbeth will be an excellent housekeeper. My brother merely needs to hire a cook, a parlor maid, another scullery maid, a laundry maid, and a bootblack. Oh, and some footmen and a butler."

"A *butler*?" Clara tried to imagine all these people running around the castle. It would be very crowded. Very loud.

"Isla had four footmen and a butler, dressed in livery and silver-inlaid buttons," Fiona replied.

Clara couldn't make out her tone, but it didn't feel right to gossip about Caelan's wife. When they entered the upstairs bedchamber, Fiona looked around, eyes narrowed, as if she was about to burst into commentary. Clara headed her off. "Shall I summon grooms to break up the furniture and bring it downstairs?"

Fiona nodded. "This will be very satisfying." She walked over and shoved one of the remaining bedposts until it crashed to the mattress. "*Very* satisfying. Do you suppose this bed will fit through the window? We only have a few narrow windows like you see in most castles. One of our ancestors refused to believe that any clan would be stupid enough to shoot arrows at a CaerLaven castle, and so far, he's been right."

"The bedstead would have to be broken to pieces," Clara said doubtfully. She opened the wardrobe, which held garments laid out as if awaiting their mistress, except the mice had come along first. "Dear me."

"Those have to go," Fiona said decisively. "I'll put my coachman and groom to work, because Caelan's are doubtless lounging around the stables. I'm sure you've noticed that he prefers to have staff nowhere in sight." She pushed open the plated glass window and hollered down.

"Are you sure we should throw everything out?" Clara asked. "What if Caelan wants to keep some of his former wife's clothing as a memorial?"

Fiona's mouth curved. "*Caelan*, is it?"

Clara bit her lip uncomfortably. "When it was only the two of us, it was easier to address each other as friends. I don't intend to be a housekeeper for long," she added in a rush.

"No, because you intend to be a lady," Fiona said, chortling. "I shan't stop you. I think it will be marvelous for Caelan to put his woeful first marriage behind him."

"I wasn't referring to marriage. I already *am* a lady," Clara protested, deserting Mrs. Potts altogether.

Fiona patted her shoulder. "No one could mistake you for anything else. I'm on your side! Mind you, Mrs. Gillan may have some difficulty accepting that this is no longer 'Isla's castle,' as she's forever calling it."

Clara could feel herself turning red with embarrassment. Caelan's sister had obviously concluded that she had taken the position as housekeeper in order to finagle her way into marrying a lord. The very idea of people thinking she would "set her cap" at a handsome laird made her feel sick.

"Why on earth would Caelan want a garment like this?" Fiona held up a tattered bodice with silver lacing all down the front. "It's not good enough for rags. Isla was like a magpie, forever pecking at shiny things without knowing what had true value."

Thankfully, two men clattered into the room before Clara had to respond to that bald statement.

"Break up all the furniture," Fiona directed them. "Throw it down the stairs or out the window, whatever's easiest. Rug as well."

"No, carry the large pieces down the stairs," Clara interrupted. "Throwing pieces of wood out the window will crush Isla's flowers."

"Hmm," Fiona said. "Why don't I supervise emptying this room and the sitting room? You force Caelan to clean his study. Tell him that if he doesn't, I shall throw his papers out the window. *They* won't squash the flowers."

Clara opened her mouth to argue, but Fiona smirked. "You wouldn't dare to question me, would you, *Mrs. Potts*? Being as you are the housekeeper I hired all the way from London?"

At that, Clara turned around and ran down the stairs. The door to the study was open, and when she peeked inside, she found Alfie sitting on his uncle's lap, listening to a book. Her heart skipped a beat. The little boy had his cheek against Caelan's shoulder, his thin legs dangling as he listened intently.

"'The company were struck with terror and amazement,'" Caelan read.

He was reading aloud *The Castle of Otranto*! And—even better—the helmet would plummet down any moment. Caelan looked up and caught her eye, and suddenly all the knotted feeling in her stomach subsided.

All was well with the world when the laird's eyes were full of laughter.

Clara slipped through the door and closed it behind herself, because upstairs Fiona was directing the men to smash the bed.

"'Some of the company had run into the court, from whence was heard a confused noise of shrieks, horror, and surprise,'" Caelan read.

"Why?" Alfie interrupted.

"You have to wait and see."

He read until Manfred strode into the courtyard and discovered a mountain of sable plumes. "'What a sight for a father's eyes!—he beheld his child dashed to pieces, and almost buried under an enormous helmet.'"

"Are you *serious*?" Alfie cried, straightening up. "Mama won't be happy that you read me this story. I didn't sleep after she read me *Little Red Riding Hood*. I couldn't stop thinking about the wolf's 'ravenous teeth.'"

Clara couldn't stay silent because she knew that story by heart. "Don't you mean 'great teeth and ravenous appetite'?"

Alfie blinked at her. "I didn't see you come in. That's probably right." He leaned into the crook of

Caelan's arm. "I kept thinking about teeth all night, and I was a *nightmare* the next day."

Caelan tussled his hair. "Proud of being a pain in the arse, are you?"

"*Little Red Riding Hood* is a different type of story," Clara said, coming over and perching on the edge of the desk. "That story teaches you not to walk around by yourself because any forest might harbor wolves with ravenous appetites."

"Yes, that's what Mama said. Little Red Riding Hood got eaten up by a wolf that would like to eat me and Wilhelmina."

"But do you truly need to fear a helmet falling from the moon and crushing you?"

"I never considered the possibility before," Alfie pointed out logically.

"I'm much older than you," Caelan put in. "No helmets have tumbled out of the clouds, nor have any other pieces of armor."

"I suppose you can keep reading," Alfie conceded, "although my mother will not be pleased if I don't sleep."

"What about if Mrs. Potts reads to you?" Caelan said. "I have a lot of work to do, Alfie m'boy."

"Your sister is threatening to throw all your papers into the moat," Clara told him.

"She is not Mrs. Potts," Alfie stated, sliding off Caelan's knee. "A Mrs. can't become another Mrs. If she marries you, she'll be a lady, same as Mama."

Clara felt her face turning red with embarrassment. "Your sister jumped to an erroneous conclusion," she told Caelan.

"What was that?" he asked, his whole face alight with mischief.

"Lady McIntyre believes that I pretended to be a housekeeper in order to marry you," Clara said, gathering her dignity.

"Didn't you?" Alfie asked with interest. "Because there was another lady who did that last fall. When I decide to marry, I'll put out a sign, the way Papa did when he wanted to buy a new bed."

"Did he?" Clara said, desperate to change the subject.

On the other side of the door, a piece of furniture bounced down the steps with a tremendous splintering and cracking noise, followed by a pair of thundering feet.

"The wardrobe should go out the window," Caelan said. "Since we're on the subject, Mrs. Potts, do you recommend that I hang up a sign asking for a wife?"

"Only if you're desperate for a spouse," Clara said, choking back a nervous, breathy laugh. She felt hideously embarrassed.

If Mr. Cobbledick were here, she would climb into his carriage and leave this very hour.

Caelan stood up, setting Alfie on his feet. "I asked you to marry me before—"

"You announced your intention after kissing me. You did not ask me," she retorted.

"That worked for Sleeping Beauty," Alfie put in. "He kissed the princess, and then she woke up and got out of the glass coffin. That didn't happen to Uncle Caelan's wife, though," he said to Clara. "He loved her, but no one could kiss her awake."

Caelan's face closed like a trap at the mention of Isla. "Clara, would you please read aloud to Alfie? I have work that must be done."

Clara looked down at Alfie. "I would be happy to read to you."

"If Uncle Caelan is sitting at his desk, we'll have to sit on the floor, because two people can't sit on a bed together unless they're married," Alfie said.

"We'll make an exception," Caelan said, standing up with his nephew. He tossed him onto the bed. Alfie squawked with laughter—and the bed crashed to the floor.

Clara shrieked and ran toward the bed, but Alfie was laughing even harder. "Do you have no sturdy furniture in Scotland?" she asked, exasperated. Through the door, she could hear grooms thumping up the stairs again.

"I took this bed from one of the outbuildings," Caelan admitted, plucking his nephew out of the wreckage. "Actually, these parts are famous for furniture making. Plain pieces, but beautifully made."

Clara threw open the door and called, "Lady McIntyre! Your son has been in an accident!"

Fiona ran down the steps and stopped in the doorway, hands on her hips. "Alfie! I warned you before about jumping on beds."

"It's Uncle's fault," her son reported, pointing to the nest of dingy sheets and splintered wood. "He *threw* me, as if he was tossing me down from the moon."

"*Were* tossing me from the moon," Clara corrected him before she thought.

"Stop tossing my son about," Alfie's mother ordered her brother. She turned to Clara. "I thought you were going to call me Fiona, though you somehow neglected to tell me your name."

"Uncle calls her Clara," Alfie said cheerfully.

"He started reading me a book about a helmet that dashed a man to pieces. It even crushed his *eyeballs*."

Fiona raised a brow.

"It's a work of literature," Clara said hastily. "A novel by Horace Walpole."

"I could never see the point of literature," Fiona replied. "Where does it get you in the end?"

"To a place where giant helmets fall from the moon and squash people," Alfie said. "I'd like to be there. If I was a helmet, I would crash down on top of Mrs. Lowe."

"His schoolteacher," Fiona explained. "That's not kind, Alfie. I thought literature was supposed to have a civilizing influence."

"I want Clara to read to me, the way Uncle said she might," Alfie said.

"All right, *Clara*, would you please read to my son? You can sit in the desk chair, since it's apparently strong enough to hold two. I need you upstairs, Caelan." She would have been a good general. "I need to supervise the maids as they empty and scrub the dining room. You can oversee clearing the drawing room." She caught Caelan's arm and dragged him out of the room and up the steps.

Clara sat down and picked up the novel.

"Perhaps I'll stand next to you rather than sit on your lap. You are a strange lady, even if you may become my aunt," Alfie said, coming to her shoulder.

"I think that's an excellent plan," Clara said, tapping him on the nose. "Though I won't be your aunt. I plan to live in my own castle, which you would be welcome to visit anytime. Wilhelmina too," she added.

"That would be nice," he agreed. "We don't have a castle, but our house is much bigger than this, and Mama likes it better."

Clara couldn't imagine liking a plain house better than this fanciful castle. She opened the book. "'The horror of the spectacle, the ignorance of all around how this misfortune had happened—'"

"That's a good point," Alfie said, interrupting. "How did that helmet fall? It couldn't seriously happen, could it?"

"It could in the same world in which one can wake a sleeping princess with a kiss," Clara said. Outside the door, something that sounded like a heavy trunk was bumping down every step of the stairwell.

"If the princess was ready to wake, anything could have woken her," Alfie said in a knowing tone. "Like a bee sting, for example. That would be faster than a kiss. She might have slept right through a kiss. My mama kisses me at night when I'm asleep, and I never know."

Clara read aloud, with frequent breaks to discuss important points such as the fact that a big suit of armor implies a head. A *big* head. Alfie was very interested by her account of the giants in *Gulliver's Travels*, and Clara barely bit back an offer to read it next.

After that conversation, he climbed into her lap, admitting that his legs were getting tired. A few minutes later, his head grew heavy on her shoulder; she glanced down to find that he had fallen asleep.

In order to have a child, she'd have to marry, which meant she had to buy a husband, as her mother had suggested. She shouldn't have kissed

Caelan. It was giving him the wrong idea. It was giving *her* the wrong idea.

Fiona pushed open the door and beamed at Clara. "Napping, thank goodness. Alfie had a bad dream and a wakeful night."

Clara looked down at the small hand flattened on the page, as if to stop her reading without him. "He's a lovely boy, thoughtful and intelligent."

"I think so." Fiona sat on the desk. "So, Miss Clara not-Potts, what are your intentions toward my brother?"

"I don't intend to marry him," Clara said flatly. "In other circumstances, I might, but I don't want to marry a man who is still grieving his first wife."

"It's been two years," Fiona said, leaning forward as if she was about to offer an argument. "Clara—"

"No," she said, cutting her off. "I don't want to hear that it's time Caelan moved on, or that he needs an heir. Mrs. Gillan has already shared her views—and yours—on that subject. I'm not the right woman. I may be English, but I'm not stony-hearted."

Fiona opened her mouth to argue, but Clara narrowed her eyes.

"Rot," Fiona muttered. "I only know one other Englishwoman, and she has the same way of cutting off the simplest question. I was wondering if you—"

"No," Clara stated.

Fiona sighed. "Then I'll be taking that boy back home, because at this point the bedchamber, kitchen, dining room, and sitting room don't have more than a few sticks of furniture between them. Elsbeth is a treasure, but I suggest you confine the puppies to the courtyard. She was most unhappy when one snuck back inside and urinated on the hearth."

Clara felt a bolt of happiness, because though she'd had little to do with it, she was keeping her vow to Mrs. Gillan. By tomorrow, Isla's castle would be shining, albeit empty. "Thank you so much for helping. I feel guilty that I spent such an enjoyable hour reading to Alfie while the rest of the household was hard at work."

"It was only fair," Fiona said. "The castle was a CaerLaven disaster, so Caelan and I had to take responsibility. I should never have let the place lapse into a hovel. Listen, Clara, for all Mrs. Gillan proclaims this mess is the result of grief, she's wrong. Caelan has never had the slightest interest in showing off his wealth, and that includes maintaining a decent staff."

Clara looked down at the tousled red hair against her shoulder. She had the distinct impression that Alfie would take after his uncle in not caring for worldly displays.

"What about living in comfort?" she asked, unable to stop herself. "I do understand if the laird has no taste for luxury, but isn't it more pleasant to live in clean surroundings?"

"He was comfortable enough," Fiona said. "He's happiest when there aren't servants running about. He works all the time, you know: CaerLaven has long been the most prosperous estate in these parts, in terms of potato fields and livestock. Then he got interested in whisky, and now all the crofters are making money that way as well. He's the local magistrate, and he's writing two books."

Clara nodded.

"Caelan likes peace and quiet. I hope for his sake

that his next wife doesn't hire a flock of grooms the way Isla did." She looked as if she could have added more but thought better of it.

Clara had the idea that Fiona had been about to ask her if she wanted to leave the castle and sleep in their house. Which made sense, of course. Mrs. Potts might not need to be chaperoned, but Miss Vetry?

Yet she didn't want to leave.

She wanted to stay in the castle. She'd never had—never dreamed of—a friend like Caelan: someone to whom she could talk so easily, who made her laugh. Spending time with him was intoxicating.

"I am not going to marry your brother," Clara stated, so that Fiona understood. "He's great company. I just . . . like him."

"That will be a new experience for him," Fiona said wryly, standing up and shaking out her skirts before she bent over and touched her son on the cheek. "Wake up, sleepyhead. It's time to go home."

"Seriously?" Alfie mumbled. "No, thank you." His eyes didn't even open.

"What did you mean by that last comment, Fiona?" Clara asked.

"It was merely a comment on marriage, *Mrs. Potts*. Surely you agree with me?" Her mischievous expression was a perfect copy of her brother's. "Half the time I don't like my husband. You haven't met him yet, but Rory can be the most irritating man in the Highlands." With that, she woke up Alfie and took him downstairs.

Clara stayed where she was, trying to be rational. Mr. Cobbledick was due to return on Sunday, at which point she and Elsbeth would climb into his coach and leave to explore Scottish castles. If he was delayed along the route, she decided to move to Lavenween until he arrived.

That left one question: How much adventure did she want?

Caelan would kiss her again. She got up and straightened the line of potato boxes, still thinking about it. She was curious as well as desirous.

What if she never met another man like Caelan? She didn't want to break her own heart by marrying him, but surely . . .

Everything she had in mind was so shocking that her mother would faint. No, Lady Vetry would have hysterics, followed by a heart attack.

Of course Clara couldn't lose her virtue. For all his ruggedness, Caelan was still a gentleman, and he would insist on marrying her if that happened. She was lucky that no one except for Fiona knew she was staying at the castle. All the same, she had to leave in three days, when Mr. Cobbledick returned, because she had a suspicion that over time, Caelan could persuade her to do anything.

But a kiss or two? As long as she made sure things went no further?

Why not?

CHAPTER 19

On saying goodbye, Fiona suggested to Caelan that she take a carriage to Inverness the following Monday and return with a couple of maids, a cook, and a footman. "And perhaps a butler?"

"A butler?" He looked at her, aghast.

"The household quarters out by the stables are large enough, and in case you haven't noticed, you're to be a married man soon," his sister said, laughing like a hyena.

"Clara said no." Though he'd made up his mind to ask again, more romantically this time.

"So she told me. She didn't pretend to be a housekeeper in order to seduce you, did she?"

"She didn't even know who had hired 'Mrs. Potts.' She could have ended up anywhere in the Highlands." The idea made his stomach clench, because it would have been easy to find herself in danger.

"Clara can take care of herself," Fiona said, scoffing. "She may be small, but she's fierce. That's Shakespeare, isn't it? See, I know some literature!"

He shrugged. "Close enough."

"You'll have to convince her. Alfie, is that lump under your coat a puppy? Put it down, please."

"He loves me," Alfie said.

"He's too little to be away from his mother," Caelan told him.

"I could stay here with you tonight," Alfie said, turning to Caelan. "Not only because of Thursday."

"Thursday?"

"That's the puppy's name. What's more, Clara

has the book, the helmet book. What will we do without the story?" His face was woebegone.

"I would miss you if you moved in with my brother," his mother observed.

"If you ask Mrs. Potts, she may lend you the book so you can read it yourself," Caelan said.

"I can't read yet!" Alfie wailed.

"A good reason to pay more attention to Mrs. Lowe," Fiona said unsympathetically.

"Mama!"

"Return that puppy to its mother, please." After Alfie dashed off, Fiona turned back to Caelan. "I suppose once you marry Clara, I'll be hearing about any number of cracked plots."

"Yes," Caelan agreed. He didn't try to hide the jolt of happiness that thought gave him. Hell, who would have imagined that a woman with a carriage full of books might stop at his castle?

Fiona pointed out the obvious. "You could woo her by traveling to Inverness and bringing back half a bookstore."

"She brought the other half with her," Caelan said. "She arrived with stacks of books but left her clothing behind on the carriage." He hesitated and then said, "I don't know how to woo her, Fiona. You know what it was like with Isla."

"Not much wooing to be done when you're desperately in love," Fiona agreed.

"Something like that."

"Too late to change that story," his sister said, glancing at him. But she added, more softly, "Just because you didn't woo Isla doesn't mean you can't do it now. Considering the state of the castle, you should start by convincing Clara that you're not a beggar. Have you shown her the stables?"

"Not yet."

"I could bring over Isla's diamonds and Mother's rubies."

Caelan shook his head. "You can keep them."

"Nonsense. They belong to your next wife. I have my own set of rubies from Nan, remember?"

"I don't think Clara would like Isla's diamond circlet," Caelan said, trying to imagine it on top of a tall mop of sunlit hair.

Fiona nodded. "I suppose you're right. Jewels and French doodads won't do the trick."

Caelan didn't say a word, but somehow his sister caught his thought, because she poked him in the side and started laughing. "It's doing you good to have to chase a woman, rather than the other way around."

Alfie ran past them and disappeared into the carriage. "Goodbye, Uncle Caelan!"

"Seriously, I'm happy for you, darling boy," Fiona said, kissing his cheek.

"I'm no boy."

"You seem like it when you look at her," she chortled. "Puzzled, like a boy who's discovered girls. You'll figure it out. I like her."

"So do I." The words tumbled out of his lips. "She wants more."

"Then give her whatever she wants."

Easy for her to say.

He didn't want to play the part of Romeo again.

"Compliment her hair," Fiona advised. "Mountains of the stuff is a blessing and a curse. Hers is truly beautiful."

"I like her smile even better," he said, the words coming unbidden to his lips.

His sister beamed. "So do I."

The next few hours were spent tending the bonfire his grooms had made of the worm-ridden furniture, an irony that didn't escape him. If he'd been a fanciful man—which he was *not*—he'd have said that the flames were taunting him for his mistakes.

Such as marrying for love.

At last the fire dropped to smoldering, and he felt comfortable leaving it to his coachman. Long strides took him down the path to the loch, where he stripped and dove in, cold water breaking over his head.

Walking through the front door a half hour later, he saw that the flagstones in the corridor now shone a warm chestnut. All day the stone walls had reverberated with the clamor generated by people and furniture going up and down the steps. Now the only sound was a warbled ballad about a brokenhearted sailor.

In the kitchen, the old table was gone, as well as the broken-down chair. The bread oven was not only clean but held a sweet-smelling loaf wrapped in a clean napkin. He looked into the courtyard and found Elsbeth singing while hanging up a sheet as white as snow. Puppies tumbled around her feet.

"Where is Mrs. Potts?" he asked.

"She is taking a nap in the study, laird." Elsbeth showed no surprise at the idea of a housekeeper napping in the master's private room; Clara's disguise as Mrs. Potts had obviously been shattered.

"She will want a bath when she wakes. Can you please send a groom to the village to buy a tin tub for use until we receive the new bathtub?"

"I'll do so immediately."

"Was there something else?" he asked, because

she was giving him a minatory look that reminded him of his nanny.

"That shirt, my lord." She pointed to a large pot boiling over the fire.

He glanced down at linen spotted from loch water and not as white as it could have been. With a sigh, he yanked it over his head and tossed it to Elsbeth. He'd be lucky if any of his shirts survived the next few days.

Back in the kitchen, he realized that the ragged curtain had been torn down and the window glass scrubbed to a shine. The corner that used to hold battered pans was as empty as the dining room opposite, since the table and dusty wall hanging were gone and the stone walls free of cobwebs and grime.

When he was a boy, the dining room table had been a slab of oak passed down through the family. It had been nicked and dented but polished to a shine. Isla loathed it on sight, and so it had disappeared, replaced by a French table that belonged in a different sort of castle, with airy turrets and marble floors.

One level up, the drawing room seemed much larger without such formidable furniture. He paused, remembering Isla's joy when the round rug arrived. Her eyes had shone as she clapped her hands, her squeal echoing through the castle.

Further back, in his childhood, the family and dogs used to throng here, he and Fiona playing fiddlesticks, his mother reading, his father bellowing about a crofter who had angered him.

Finally he sighed and turned away, climbing up to the study.

The door was ajar, and he slipped through. The

shattered bed had been hauled away. One side of the room now held a long line of potato crates filled with paper.

Clara was lying on her side, curled on the red sofa that Isla had rejected as inelegant. A book had fallen from her fingers to the floor. Her kerchief had slipped off, and her hair lay against the red velvet like golden lace.

He walked over and came down on his haunches beside her. A smell of bleaching powder hung about her shoulders, overpowering the flowery aroma that had clung to her skin in the morning.

Taking ungentlemanly advantage of her slumber, he examined her face. She had absurd lashes, like butterfly wings.

From the moment Clara hollered "Bravo!" after he caught that trout, she'd surprised him again and again. His mother had read novels, but not with Clara's passion. Who else turned books into a filter through which she saw the world? To her, literature was a lens; seeing him in a kilt made her think of soldiers in *Macbeth*.

Through that lens, daily life became an adventure. And Caelan a hero, absurd though it seemed. He ran a finger down her cheek. "Clara."

When her eyes opened, she smiled hazily for a delicious moment. Blood rushed through his body, stiffening his cock and prickling his skin.

"Hello, laird," she murmured.

"*Caelan*," he corrected her.

"Lord MacCrae."

She was teasing him, laughter running under her voice like water in a shallow stream. Isla had never teased him. His first wife revered him, loved him, sometimes hated him. She had never laughed at him, teased him, or disagreed with him. Isla would have been greatly offended by Clara's manner. She would have stiffened and informed him later that Clara was impertinent and ill-bred.

He had a strong suspicion that Clara was a member of English nobility. Ill-bred she was not.

"My name is Caelan," he said stubbornly.

She stretched, arching her back so that her breasts—

He sprang up and walked away, rubbing the back of his neck.

"Have you been in the loch?" she asked, sounding more logical. Then, sitting up, "Why aren't you wearing a shirt?"

"I went for a swim to rid myself of ash and dirt after the bonfire. Elsbeth confiscated my shirt. I thought I'd grab one here, but I don't see any." Shirts and sheets had disappeared.

She yawned. "There are two in a box in the corner. I tried to make sure that Isla's flowers weren't damaged by furniture, Caelan, but I'm afraid that some were flattened on the west side. Hopefully the blooms will spring back up overnight."

He shrugged, walking over to the window and looking down. The moat looked the same to him. Off in the distance, he could see hazy smoke rising from the dying bonfire.

Behind him, Clara shook out her skirts and then walked over to stand beside him. Her hair had toppled over one shoulder, baring the curve of her neck, vulnerable yet strong. He wanted to lick it until she whimpered. Suck a purple patch that every man could see. Pull off that wedding ring and put his own in its place.

"Will you marry me?" he asked conversationally.

Next to him, she jumped and gave a little squeak of alarm. Not precisely what a man hoped to hear after he proposed.

"No."

"I'm asking the question, the way you suggested I should."

"Well, *don't*. I already refused. What will you do for furniture? The castle is rattling like an empty drum."

Caelan shrugged. "I've a crofter who can make me some."

"You'll have to sleep here." She nodded at the velvet sofa. "I tested it for you, and it's very comfortable."

"I've had many a nap there," he told her. "If you were ordering furniture—which you won't, because you refuse to marry me—what kind would you choose?"

She hesitated, and he nudged her shoulder with his own. "To put it another way, what kind of furniture will you order for your own castle?"

"I am tired," Clara said.

He wrapped an arm around her, pretending to steady her. "Well?"

"I need to take a bath."

"I asked Elsbeth to buy a tin tub to use until the other arrives. You're avoiding the question."

"I don't know, do I?" she burst out, frowning up at him. "I suppose . . . I suppose I want bookshelves like yours." She reached out and ran a hand over the shelves closest to them. "They're so beautifully curved. How on earth did you order something that fit the tower wall so precisely?"

"They were made by Auld Magnus, the same crofter who will be carving new beams over the winter. Now I'll be asking him for furniture as well."

"'Auld' as in old?" And at Caelan's nod, "You have bookshelves in the study, but I would put them in the bedrooms as well. What's a nursery without books?"

"I suppose you read in bed?"

"Of course I read in bed. Every night, even here." Clara sighed. "It's not safe to read by candlelight. You should order more oil lamps."

Caelan's fingers curved around her soft, rounded shoulder as he pictured Clara intent on a book, a flickering candle casting light on the page. Catching fire.

"Think of my hair," she continued blithely, having no idea of the knot in his stomach. "It would go up like a torch."

"You should never read while alone." He wrapped one hand around her bottom and lifted her up to the windowsill, leaning her against the glass. "I'm removing the candlestick from the nursery." He stepped forward, bumping into her knees.

"We shouldn't," she said, but her eyes didn't say no. They were wary but welcoming.

"Just a kiss." He bent to her lips with a mindless feeling of gratitude. "Tell me if I'm too rough," he murmured sometime later, but she couldn't answer if she'd wanted to, because he dove back into kissing her, and their breath was as tangled as their tongues.

A long time later, Clara drew away, gasping. Caelan tried to think what to say, because the only sentence in his head was *Will you marry me?*—and she'd already refused.

"I feel like the blaze that could have happened in my bed," she said abruptly. He started grinning as he watched her cheeks turn pink. "I didn't mean it that way!"

"I'd be happy to be the fire in your bed," Caelan said, chuckling deep in his chest, because she was so damn perfect. "I'll burn you up, lass."

"Good lord, that is terrible," she groaned.

"Might my kisses convince you to change your mind about marrying me?" When he nipped her earlobes, she shivered. "I'm not good with compliments, but if kisses would convince you, I'll happily stay here all night."

She shook her head before she gave the question any thought, but he knew more about her now. He had an idea about how to court her. As far as he could tell, no one had put her *first*. Not her mother, nor the man who sent her running to the Highlands.

That thought sent a chill through Caelan.

How was he any different? Isla had come first.

"If you married me, I'd be a jealous son of a bitch," he told her, choosing blunt truth. "I'd want to take you morning, noon, and night. I'd want to tup you in the courtyard under the apple tree."

"Play sacrificial maiden on that stone table?" She laughed.

She *laughed*. At that?

"Do you have any idea how extraordinary you are?" He kissed her again because kisses were so much clearer than words.

Courtship took time. Caelan knew that, but something about Clara drove him to a frenzy, and it wasn't due to the absurd notion that he was waking up after two years. It was all *her*: the woman who mocked him, refused him, kissed him, told him stories. "I thought I'd show you around the stables," he said when they finally drew apart again. "The estate isn't only a decrepit castle."

"The castle is *not* decrepit, merely dusty," Clara stated. "Are the stables far away?"

He lifted her down from the windowsill, took her hand, and drew her out of the room. "Around the castle in the other direction from the loch. I know you're tired, but a walk in the twilight will do you good."

As they walked around the moat, she pointed out the crushed flowers. "Hopefully they'll recover by tomorrow. Bluebells seem to be rugged, for all they look so delicate."

Like you, he thought, but he didn't say it. They were Isla's flowers, after all. "They have grown like weeds," he said instead. "It's—well, the soil is rich, isn't?"

"Because this used to be a moat? Did water from the loch run around the castle?"

He shook his head. "Not for one hundred years. But what did, and does, run off here are the privies."

Clara giggled. "Isla's moat is so beautiful because the toilets empty out here?"

"Hundreds of years of CaerLaven shite, if you'll forgive the vulgarity of it."

She was laughing so hard that she couldn't get her breath.

Caelan caught her around the waist and started kissing her neck. "Fiona told me I should give you compliments. I don't think she'd approve of this conversation about shite."

He began nipping her neck with his teeth and then licking the sting away. It fogged his mind. "I never told Isla why they grew so well. She couldn't get them to thrive in the courtyard. She would have said I was being vulgar if I told her the truth."

"Well, you were. Are."

He tightened his arms around her and kissed her temples.

"You don't want me to say her name aloud," Clara said, after a while.

"I'm trying to work it out in my head."

"I didn't know your wife, but she loved beauty, didn't she? She loved your beauty, and she made you an elegant home, a fairy-tale castle."

"All those things are true."

"I would prefer to be comfortable rather than elegant, though I am very appreciative of people like Isla who create beauty wherever they are."

"I wish she could hear you talk about her."

Frankly, Clara was very glad that Isla *wasn't* there since she wouldn't appreciate her husband hugging another woman.

"Life is messy," Caelan added. "Privies make flowers grow. Yet Isla couldn't tolerate even a mention of shite in her presence. As if we didn't all do it."

Clara didn't know what to say. "I suspect many ladies would dislike the reference," she offered.

"Did you know that Versailles, the French palace that Isla most fancied, stunk like a privy? People squatted wherever to do their business. Isla imagined perfection, but things never are, are they?"

"Rarely," Clara agreed. "My mother had a perfect daughter in mind, but that's not the daughter she got."

Caelan took her hand but without saying anything, which she appreciated.

The path continued into the woods. "A track goes through the forest to the village, but it takes two hours," he said a while later, "whereas it's fifteen minutes by carriage through the pass. The pass isn't safe on horseback, though. If a horse shied, horse and rider might pitch straight down the side. Rory and I should dig into the mountain and create a wider road, but neither of us minds being cut off now and then."

They broke out of the shadow of trees into the pasture that housed the castle's outbuildings.

"We still call this the stables, but other buildings have joined the stables proper," Caelan announced, feeling a beat of pride. He'd inherited the castle, but he'd designed the rest himself.

Clara's eyes rounded. "It's like a small village!"

"We're standing at the middle of two horseshoes, facing opposite directions," he explained. "That curve to your right holds the actual stables, with room for horses, some cattle, a pig or two, and a yard in front. The smithy's there and a few out-buildings. The curve facing the other direction is a servants' hall, with a kitchen, buttery, and laundry, bedrooms on the second floor, and a kitchen garden in front."

"I love the balcony that runs in front of the bedrooms. Why on earth were your sheets being sent to the village if you have a laundry?"

"I don't have a laundry maid. The rooms are all empty except for the one shared by Elsbeth and Maisie. The coachman beds down over the stables with a couple of grooms."

"The household deserted you after Isla died, when you were distraught with grief? Do those people still live around here?"

She sounded as fierce as a Scotswoman. He couldn't help laughing. "It wasn't like that. 'Twas a terrible shock for everyone, as Isla fell ill one morning and was gone two days later."

Clara squeezed his hand. "I'm sorry."

"I didn't know what to do with myself. The butler disappeared a week later, and the housekeeper with him. Isla's personal maid left and took a good deal of Isla's things. I didn't discover it for a week, and then I couldn't see chasing after the woman all the way to Glasgow. Besides, what was I to do with a silver brush and mirror?"

"Without a mistress of the house or a housekeeper, the rest of the staff drifted away," Clara guessed.

He nodded. "I wasn't throwing myself around sobbing, but no one wanted to be around me, and that's the truth. Everywhere I went, people were grieving for Isla and bemoaning my broken heart. I couldn't go to the pub without someone weeping on my shoulder. It became easier to stay in the study and be by myself, so I wrote my first book."

"It sounds dreadfully lonely."

"That first year, Fiona came every day with Alfie. She sent Rory around too, until I begged him to stop wasting my time. He was mad for fly-fishing, and after a while, he got me interested."

"And now you're writing a book about it."

"Only because so much of what has been written is total rubbish. Here's the laundry," he said, showing her a spacious room with two stone sinks and a huge table for ironing.

"The table is lovely," Clara said. "Auld Magnus?"

"Aye. He lives in one of the crofter's cottages for free, and when I need furniture, he makes me something. CaerLaven hosts around fifteen crofter families, give or take."

"Did the household servants live in the south tower before you built this?"

"When my mother was alive, yes, but Fiona wanted a bigger household. We sunk lead pipes from the castle to here and threaded bell pulls so that we could ring for help. Most of the staff preferred to live here. Scots don't like being locked up like birds in cages. This way, the household is living close by, but each person has their own door."

Clara nodded. "Sparrows rather than canaries?"

"Exactly. Want a look at their kitchen?"

She glanced around at the stove, the fireplace, the cupboard, the sturdy dishes. "I'm going to say the obvious, Caelan. This is much cleaner and nicer than the castle's kitchen."

"It wasn't a matter of grief," he said, unable to keep his voice from sharpening. "I never liked having people racketing about until I couldn't even think. And I dinnae give a damn about dirt. As long as I have a cup of tea in the morning, I'm set."

She nodded and walked back out into the courtyard. "Where are the crofters' cottages?"

"They're spread around the estate, each man having his own plot of land." He gestured to the west. "We brew whisky back in the woods, since it makes a stench. The crofters took up brewing with a will. Most of them have a still of their own."

"Fiona told me that your people are all wealthy thanks to that brewing. I do believe you're the best laird I know," Clara said, smiling up at him.

"I'd take that as a great compliment if I didn't suspect that I'm the *only* laird you know."

"I read," Clara protested, unsurprisingly. "More

than a few novelists write about the sad state of servants abused by their masters. Or merely bellowed at, as in my mother's household."

Her mother sounded like a harridan. Deciding not to share that observation, he said, "I'd like to take you fishing one of these mornings."

"You've no need to fish for your breakfast any longer. Elsbeth could bring back seeds from the market tomorrow so your kitchen garden has something growing in it."

"Fishing is a joy, and I want to teach you," Caelan said. "What if there's a storm and we can't get over the pass? We might starve."

She rolled her eyes. "We'd take the path through the woods. You'd never let me—I mean, anyone—starve."

He let the truth slip from his lips. "I'd never let *you* starve. I don't care so much about the rest of the Highlanders."

Clara squinted at him. "I'm not marrying you, remember? Think of it like the first half of *Love in Excess*, when D'Elmont quickly falls for a couple of women, only to discover that his true love is Melliora."

Showing remarkable self-restraint, Caelan managed not to laugh. Instead he drew her so close that their bodies touched. "Do you think I could fall for a woman with such a fanciful name?"

"My mother regretted naming me Clara. She thought having a servant's name had made me—"

She broke off, a good thing because Caelan was on the verge of deciding that he needed to travel down to London and have words with her mother. You couldn't challenge a lady to a duel, but you could chastise her. Fiercely.

"Luckily, I adore the name Clara," Caelan murmured, tightening his arms. To his infinite pleasure, she relaxed against him.

One side of her mouth curled up. "Oh, you do, do you?"

He nodded. "I fantasize about making love to a woman with that name. In fact, it could be that I only want women named Clara." His voice had dropped into a deep tone that said a great deal without words.

She stilled. Then: "You might wish to warn Fiona. She's hiring maids for you, and she might come home with a Clara. *Two* Claras."

"Clara is a lovely name," he said, tipping up her chin. "The best name."

She cleared her throat. "We should return to the castle. Elsbeth was heating a bath for me—a proper one, rather than a pailful of water."

"Sure you don't want to try the loch?" he offered.

"No!"

"We could wear clothing?"

"Absolutely not!"

CHAPTER 20

April 21, 1803

$\mathcal{F}$riday was spent working shoulder to shoulder with Caelan in his study, sorting papers while maids scrubbed the castle top to bottom.

"What is in this pile?" Clara asked, picking up a potato crate and bringing it over to the sofa.

Caelan glanced over. "Legal documents dating to my father and grandfather."

She picked up an old piece of parchment and read aloud, "'James MacCrae, Laird and Liege-lord of CaerLaven, and Helen McFee, both in this parish, gave up their names to the proclaimed in order to be married.' Ancestors?"

He nodded.

"What does it mean to be a liege-lord?"

"It means that our crofters have sworn allegiance, or at least they did once. A great many of those papers will probably refer to judicial decisions."

Clara chose another sheet. "The wife of John Austyn defamed one of her neighbors, calling Margaret Waryn a strumpet because she supposedly bedded John 'in the fields.' Your grandfather's note says she should display penitence in the kirk."

"I hate adjudicating that sort of thing," Caelan said with feeling.

"I think it's fascinating," Clara said. She was still puzzling through the text. "What do you think a 'hoorcope' is? Also, she called Margaret a 'strong lady.' How is that an insult?"

"If you married me, you could attend the franchise

court at my side," Caelan said, tossing two papers into the box they'd designated for paid invoices. "Help me adjudicate cases."

She wrinkled her nose. "Enticing as that sounds, the answer is still no."

"Isla refused to attend," Caelan admitted.

Clara got up and fetched another pile of papers. She didn't care to hear anything else about his dead wife.

"Sorry," he muttered.

"For what?" she asked, forcing herself to meet his eyes. "It's natural that you often think of her—and that's why you shouldn't marry right now, Caelan, no matter whether two years have passed or no. Some love is so deep that grief follows its own timeline."

He frowned. "What are you talking about?"

"I can't imagine the heroes of my best-loved novels taking a new wife. One of my favorite heroes, Simon Bawburgh, had to go through *so much* to win his bride, Anne. If she died—and I hate to even think of it—he would be crushed. Two years later, he might feel more alive, but he couldn't stop thinking of her."

He peered at her. "You aren't getting tearful about a fictional man with an unfortunate name, are you?"

Clara cleared her throat. "Of course not!"

She was a bit tearful, but only about Caelan and *his* love story.

By the time they put the last paper in the last box, oil lamps were burning all around the room, since Caelan had removed the candlesticks and replaced them with lamps.

"Thank goodness," Clara said, collapsing onto the red sofa.

Caelan sat beside her. "Some of those papers hadn't been touched since my grandfather was last in this room."

"Your *great*-grandfather," Clara said. "Don't forget that pile we found under the table."

He took her hand. "We're grimy." He turned over her hand to show her that their fingertips were inky black.

"When your new bath arrives, you'll be able to pump hot water from the roof," she told him. "You could sink into the tub and let all this wash away."

"Fiona reckons it's better than a tin bath."

"She says it's wonderful. I might do the same when I find my own castle."

She heard his breath hitch. Then he said, very quietly, "So you do mean to live in a castle?"

Clara nodded.

"And fill it with books?"

Her nod was a bit more tentative, as his eyes were fierce.

"I'm offering you all that and myself in the bargain, and it's not good enough, even when I throw in the excitement of the franchise court, watching crofters berate each other for stealing each other's cows and sometimes, their wives?"

Clara's breath caught in her lungs. Could there be a hint of vulnerability in his eyes? Impossible. He was the Romeo of the Highlands.

"There's Alfie too," Caelan added. "There isn't a boy like him in all Scotland. The minute he learns to read, Fiona will have to confiscate all the candles in the house, or he'll be reading under the covers and setting the house on fire."

She managed a smile. "I wouldn't be surprised."

"*Seriously*, can't you see how much he needs an

aunt to talk to him about books?" he demanded. "Fiona was never one for book-learning."

The image was so lovely she could scarcely bear it. Caelan put an arm around her shoulders and settled her head into the curve of his shoulder. He put his chin on the top of her head.

"You could read to Alfie, and then we'd send him and Wilhelmina home across the fields, and we could cook a trout that we caught earlier in the day."

"I don't know how to fish!" Clara said, a hint of laughter in her voice.

"I'm teaching you tomorrow morning. But to go back to our marriage, after we sent Alfie home, we'd make love all night long." His thumb brushed her lips and then pressed her chin up. "I could make you happy, Clara. I would do anything in my power to give you whatever you wanted."

Her smile wobbled, because the one thing she wanted, he *couldn't* give her. "I'd like someone to fall madly in love with me," she said, trying to sound light.

A terrible silence followed.

Clara managed a nod. "After such a joyful union, you will never experience the same again."

He opened his mouth, but she continued. "Still, you won't be alone forever, Caelan. You have to promise me that you won't allow your castle to fall into disorder again. What if it frightens off your next wife, a delicate lady?"

He was pressing kisses on her forehead. "You weren't frightened." A big hand wound into the tangle of her hair. "*I* wasn't frightened by your hair, even though you assured me that every gentleman in London would be appalled. I love your pouf."

Clara's heart thumped, but she couldn't say that

loving her hair was like loving *her*, especially after Prince George's nauseating compliments about angelic curls.

"I'm sorry, but that's not enough," she said, stirring. He let her go. She stood up and looked down at him. How could she have thought Mylchreest was handsome? No one's face compared with Caelan's.

She ran her fingers lightly down his cheekbones. "Now that you've woken up, every unmarried woman in the Highlands will be looking at you. Desiring you." Her voice was embarrassingly thick.

"Not you?" She couldn't make out his expression.

She didn't want to lie to him again. She couldn't stop a wry smile. "Oh, I desire you, Caelan. I thought I knew what a beautiful man looked like, and then I met you."

"Well, then—"

"I want my husband to be in love with me."

His jaw was tight, but he nodded.

"I could live not far away," she offered. "We could be friends, you and I."

"*And* your husband?"

"Perhaps I won't marry," Clara said airily. "What I'm saying is that . . . is that I would be honored to be your friend. I've never met anyone like you. Someone I can talk to so easily."

His tight mouth eased slightly. "I'd rather you were my wife."

"I want what Isla had," she said, the truth coming straight from her heart. "I would want you to fall to your knees and tell me that you're desperately in love with me. And you couldn't do that, could you?"

"Couldn't you give us a chance?"

"It would be so lonely," she said.

He frowned.

"I can't imagine anything lonelier than being married to someone who was settling for second-best. No matter how close a friend he was. I couldn't bear it, Caelan." Her smile was wobbly, but she forced herself to look up. His expression made her stomach clench into a knot. He understood.

In a perfect world, in a novel, he would have fallen to his knees and said that she would never be second-best. But he couldn't say that, could he? Caelan was honest to the bone.

"I'll teach you to fish in the morning," he said instead.

"Marvelous," Clara replied, her voice faint. "I can't wait."

CHAPTER 21

April 22, 1803

𝒯he next morning, as Elsbeth helped Clara dress, Caelan kept shouting up the stairs every ten minutes, informing them both that the fish were biting, and it was *time to go.*

"Are you sure you want to indulge him?" Elsbeth asked in a hushed voice.

"Indulge him?"

"My older sister says that it's better to curb male expectations. Women have to train men to behave, especially when the man in question is the master of the house. I tried to follow her advice in my last position, but it didn't work."

"Is your sister also a housekeeper?"

"Aye, she is. After me mum died, she took care of our da and me. Then she took a husband, but because she didn't train him in time, she chucked him out and took up a position with two old ladies. This way she doesn't have to fuss about men at all."

"What if she moved here to become the laird's housekeeper?" Clara asked, inspired. "I'm worried that the castle will fall into disrepair once we leave."

Elsbeth hesitated.

"*You* want to be his housekeeper," Clara guessed. "Of course you do!"

"I do enjoy being your maid," Elsbeth said. Their eyes met in the mirror as she added a few more pins to keep Clara's curls in place. "Your hair poses an unusual challenge. But I like cleaning more. Cooking, too. The laird says he doesn't want a large household. I thought I could be his cook as well, since he likes plain cooking."

"He has simple tastes," Clara said rather hollowly. She had pictured herself and Elsbeth tooling about in Mr. Cobbledick's carriage, but Elsbeth's eyes were shining at the idea of running Caelan's castle.

"He said that as long as I bring him a cup of tea when he shouts for it, we'll get along fine."

Down below, Caelan shouted, "I will leave without you, Clara. I'm serious!"

Elsbeth shook her head, one side of her mouth crooking up. "He's awfully opinionated about the things he wants."

Clara blinked at her. Surely she couldn't mean . . . Yes, Elsbeth *did* mean that, because her maid's eyes were mischievous.

"Some men are like that," Elsbeth said demurely. "They know exactly what they want." She tucked in a last pin. "Generally speaking, they get it."

"There you are," Caelan said impatiently when Clara reached the bottom of the stairs. He eyed her. "What on earth took so long? You aren't wearing any of those face paints, or a frilly gown, or any such foolishness."

"No, I'm not," Clara said, walking past him into the kitchen. "I haven't eaten."

"I made you a piece of bread and cheese," Caelan said. He waved a cloth wrapped around a lump.

Clara opened her mouth to protest, but he caught her hand and drew her out of the castle's perpetually open front door, over the moat.

The last thing she saw was Elsbeth laughing.

"When you're fishing for trout," Caelan said informatively, striding along the path, "morning is best. In the afternoon, the trout come up to sip insects from the surface, so that can work too. Do you know what a fly is?"

"Two wings and a buzzing noise," Clara said, dropping his hand so that she could eat her bread and cheese.

That led to an avalanche of information about horsehair and silk threads. She let him lecture her, enjoying the way the smoky brown tree trunks stood out against pale green leaves and lush moss starred with tiny white flowers. "Did Isla try to plant bluebells here?" she asked.

"I don't think so. She rarely came this way. She thought the loch was loud and cold, and raw trout were slimy. She didn't like me to go fishing."

A few minutes later, Clara stood on the riverbank, watching as Caelan cast a rod over the stream. "See how my fly floats? A trout beneath the surface will think it's a mayfly or a large midge."

"What about a trout above the surface?" She burst out laughing at his expression. "There *are* flying fish, you know. I've read about them."

He snorted. "In the same book in which you read about giants? Your turn." He handed her the rod. "Nudge it up so it looks as if the mayfly is bobbing up and down." He cast his second rod into the loch.

Twenty minutes later, Clara moved to sit on a large slab of rock, jamming her rod between two smaller stones at her feet. "The fish aren't interested," she said, propping her chin on her hands. "I wonder what would happen if the mayfly floated below the surface of the water, or if it were brightly colored? If I were a fish, I'd be intrigued by a golden mayfly since I wouldn't have seen it before. You could use a shiny bead."

"Would you try to swallow a golden fly?" Caelan objected, not without justification.

Clara tried not to obsess over his body as he flipped his line across the water again, because that was uncouth and unladylike and plain bad manners. "Why not? If I were a trout, I'd be horribly bored. If I dismantled that mouse reticule you saw, I could use beads from its eyes and wire from its whiskers to make a better fly."

"Better?" he growled, but then laughed. "All right, you make a better fly, Mrs. Potts."

"We can have a contest," Clara cried, inspired. "You can wade out into the water and try to catch a fish with your fly and then with mine. Frankly, I don't think trout are lurking by the shore."

"You may be right," Caelan said, bobbing his rod again.

"Thankfully, I have a book with me," Clara said, pulling it from her pocket. "Would you like to hear *Elizabeth; or, the Exiles of Siberia*? The bookseller in Glasgow described it as 'wildly romantic and irreproachably moral.' The cover claims that the story is 'founded on facts,' but we should take that with a grain of salt."

"Flying squirrels!" Caelan exclaimed after a few minutes. "There's no such thing. Squirrels don't have wings any more than fish do."

Clara shrugged. "Helmets are rarely found on the moon."

"So this family is in exile, pretending to be named Springer?" he said sometime later. "Elizabeth Springer . . . meet Clara Potts!"

"Not fair," Clara said. "Surely you don't think I am disguised due to 'some great criminality' or 'unjust tyranny'?"

"I'm reserving judgment until you finally decide to tell me why you fled to the Highlands," Caelan said. "Though I admit that the heroine's description as 'docile and submissive' doesn't suit you. I prefer the mother. What do you think past 'the first season of youth' signifies? Is she forty or eighty?"

"She's old, like me," Clara said.

"*Old?* You're not old!"

"Twenty-five is a spinster."

"Nonsense. What was that last sentence again?"

"'Studious to gratify every wish of her husband, be it ever so trifling, she watched his every look, to learn what could promote his comfort or pleasure.'" Clara rolled her eyes. "That's absurd. I've never seen anyone behave like that."

"Isla—" Caelan said, and then stopped.

"She was in love with you," Clara said hastily, trying to cover up her embarrassment. She never should have assumed that his experience of marriage bore any relation to depressing London marriages. "I imagine people in love often study each other's wishes. I wouldn't know. I shouldn't have ventured an opinion."

"So no one's fallen in love with you?"

Could there be a more humiliating topic of conversation? "No," she said flatly.

"And you haven't felt the emotion yourself?"

She shook her head. After all, what she felt for Caelan was raw desire with a dollop of affection, which was not the same as being *in love*.

Caelan nodded, looking unsurprised.

At least he accepted the truth, unlike Prince George with his loathsome attempt to convince random bachelors that they should fall in love with her. Or buy her outright. "You and Isla were very lucky."

He glanced at her. "Any number of men will fall desperately in love with you, Clara, if you give them a chance."

All evidence to the contrary. But she didn't say it.

"Would you mind if I waded into the stream?" he asked, tactfully changing the subject.

"Are you planning to strip off your clothing? I could return to the castle."

"No, don't leave," he said, his eyes flashing to hers. His expression was warm. More than warm. "Hell, I'll go into the stream in my kilt if you want me to, although Elsbeth will lecture me about pleats. I like to talk to you and fish at the same time."

Clara bit back a smile. She felt warm, but it wasn't infatuation. It was . . . friendship. Lovely, giddy-making friendship.

"I want to hear more about the heroine in that novel," Caelan added. "She's planning to make her way to Petersburg alone, which reminds me alarmingly of a young lady I heard about who hopped into a strange carriage and made her way to the Highlands."

"Pooh!" Clara said, giggling.

"If you don't mind, I'll take off my shirt and kilt. I'll keep my smalls on."

Clara nodded, her cheeks heating—because how could she say no? She wanted him to take his clothes off. Of course she did. Any woman under the age of eighty would nod. The fact his thick thighs made her feel achy was natural, albeit embarrassing.

He yanked off his boots, threw his garments onto a bush, and waded into the loch.

Rather than returning to the novel, Clara found herself considering Caelan's propensity to strip off his clothing. He wasn't thinking about her as a vulnerable woman when he disrobed. When he inquired whether she'd be affronted, it didn't occur to him that his almost-naked body might seem dangerous.

Because he wouldn't have dreamed of snatching at her, the way Prince George had done.

If she warned him not to strip in front of other women, he'd probably be irritated, the way he had been when people thought he'd let the castle go to ruin because he was brokenhearted. She believed him, as far as that went. He preferred to be alone, and he didn't mind dust. He preferred to be naked.

Truly, his second wife would be a very lucky woman, as long as she didn't mind the fact that the lovely Isla had apparently *studied to gratify* his every wish. He had done the same for her. That much was obvious, given the dreadful stuffed owl in their bedchamber.

How could he sleep with those yellow eyes gleaming at him in the night?

"Go on," Caelan said, bracing himself against the current and glancing at her over his shoulder. "Do you want to bet that Elizabeth is about to meet a young man?"

His smalls were made of light cotton; now they were wet, and the garment clung to his arse in a truly scandalous manner.

Clara looked hastily down at the book. "She'll either meet the hero—or the villain." Sure enough, Elizabeth ventured out at night and encountered a man.

"An extremely foolish decision," Caelan said, interrupting, the way his nephew did. "Don't ever wander into these woods by yourself at night."

"I'm not sure about that," Clara said, laughing at

him. "What if I met a man like this? 'His countenance was youthful and his air majestic.'"

"The only man you'd meet in my woods is me," Caelan said. He struck a pose. "I've entered the story! Barring the youthful countenance, of course."

"You're youthful enough," Clara said. "But majestic?" She eyed him. His smalls were clinging to his thighs. Truthfully, he *was* majestic, like an elk on a mountaintop—which was such a foolish comparison that she would rather have died than repeat it.

His mouth twisted. "Let's keep reading and see if the fellow knows how to fish."

She was startled by a flash of darkness in his eyes, but she must have been wrong, because he started laughing when the hero's first reaction was to scold Elizabeth: "'You should not have ventured here alone . . . You run great hazard.'"

"Didn't I say as much when you first turned up at the loch by yourself, and me as naked as a jaybird?"

Clara was glad that his wry expression had disappeared; there was something about it she didn't like. "I don't remember that," she said with dignity.

"There I was, naked. And there you were, utterly delicious. That fellow thinks her a 'vision,' and that's exactly what I thought of you."

"Angelic?" she asked, and now *her* voice was dry.

"Actually, I thought you were a lady of the evening," Caelan said, throwing her a laughing glance. "Hired by Fiona to prove a point."

Clara wasn't sure what to make of that. Torie's husband had had a gorgeous mistress, but comparing her to Clara would have been likening an eagle to a sparrow.

"I do have something in common with the heroine of this novel," she said, changing the subject. "Elizabeth's hair reaches in large ringlets 'almost to the ground.' Mine goes out rather than down, but we both have too much hair."

"As to that, I—" At that moment, Caelan braced his feet and snapped his line. Once the trout was out of the water, she could see it was much larger than the one he'd caught when they first met.

"Bravo!" Clara shouted.

"Lunch," Caelan said a moment later, wading in to shore, looking very satisfied.

She took one look at his drenched smalls and turned away. His stomach was sculpted in the front in a way that caused water to run in rivulets as if down shallow canals.

"Right," she said briskly. "Will you chop off its head?"

"I thought you might want to do that." Caelan threw the fish down on the butchery rock and conked it on the head with a rock until its tail stopped flapping. "Since you have ambitions to be a housekeeper and all."

Clara looked down at the fish, which seemed to stare back at her with a cold eye.

"Adventure!" Caelan prompted, amusement bubbling in his voice.

He didn't think she'd do it. "Right." Clara took the knife. "What do I do?"

He bent his head and kissed her fleetingly on the mouth.

"One does not kiss one's housekeeper."

"Nor one's fishmonger, but I am mad with desire."

His husky voice made Clara feel so shy that she turned back to the fish, adjusting her grip on the knife. "I'm going to chop off the head, because his expression reminds me of a man I don't like, with large, staring eyes." She thumped down with the knife.

Caelan picked up the fish head, laughing hard. "So the fish had an expression, did he?"

"He eyed me in an impertinent fashion. I'm sorry his head ended up in your lap." She cut off the fish's tail and then followed Caelan's instructions. Her hands grew slimy, abruptly reminding her that she'd stopped agonizing over the seagull's shite, to use the Scottish term.

Later they cooked the trout in the outdoor fireplace. Clara didn't let herself think about the way Caelan kept touching her and kissing her, little kisses on the top of her head, on her nose, lightly on her mouth.

They liked each other. At one point, after she told him the fish was the best she'd ever tasted, he had a look in his eye as if—

But he turned away, remarking it was marvelous she wasn't revolted by raw fish. Her mind kept going back to the idea of marrying him. He *had asked her*, after all. An impossibly handsome, brilliant laird had asked her to marry him. Her first proposal.

Yet she had to be pragmatic about the depth of the relationship Caelan was offering, and her ability to be happy in such a union. She would always be second to his real wife, the one he had fallen in love with, wooed, and cherished.

She couldn't take that—and she had to keep reminding herself of that fact.

A lesser man might have pretended to feel more than desire, but Caelan hadn't. She deserved more than a man who winced at the mention of his lost beloved's name. Actually, if she happened to marry another widower, it wouldn't matter . . . because she wouldn't fall in love with him.

But Caelan? It *would* matter with him, although she refused to allow herself to voice why.

The light dwindled down to flickering candles while they sat in the courtyard, talking of everything from their parents to their schooling.

"I can't believe you read so much, since Lady Vetry kept firing your governesses," Caelan said, turning a glass in the candlelight so the red wine gleamed like banked embers.

"I can't believe that you were able to live in such disarray, if not plain squalor," she retorted. Then she jolted, remembering Isla's death. "I didn't mean—"

"It wasn't grief," he said impatiently. "I told you that, didn't I? What's more, I told you before that I'm hardly a gentleman, Clara, and I meant it. Isla found life with me a terrible shock." He eyed her over his glass. "You seem fairly unmoved."

"You're a gentleman in the ways that matter," Clara told him. "You love and protect your family, and you would never threaten a woman."

"I did kiss you," he prompted, a wicked light brewing in his eyes. "I would do more if you allowed me."

"But only if I allowed you. I can trust you. That's the definition of a gentleman. Of a hero, in any of my books. The happy books, at least."

He rose and then sat down on the stone bench beside her. "The evening air is growing colder, and I'm sure that a gentleman would offer his bodily warmth under these circumstances."

She relaxed against his side, relishing his arm

around her, not because he was warm, but because he smelled *so good*. "You may hold me," she observed a few minutes later, because somehow she had ended up on his lap. "But that's all, Caelan. Sunday morning I'll accompany you to the kirk, and after the service I'll leave with Mr. Cobbledick."

His back stiffened; she found herself stroking his arm the way one might an agitated cat.

"I'm sorry," she said. "I like you a great deal . . . so much. But I can't marry you. I want more than you can offer."

His arms tightened around her. "I can't fight with that." He sounded tired all of a sudden. "What if I read more novels?" he suggested.

Clara's heart squeezed into a little ball. She turned to look up at his face. "You will find a woman who is perfect for you."

"Never."

She bit her lip because he sounded so *certain*. "Why not?" She couldn't stop herself from running her hand through his rumpled hair.

He shrugged, which Clara took to mean that all his love died with Isla. She couldn't argue with that, so she said it was time for bed. They went up the stairs, and he handed her a lantern rather than a candle so that she didn't set her pouf of hair alight.

When he left her at the nursery floor and continued up to the next level, Clara swallowed hard. She'd never been able to stop loving her mother, no matter the clear evidence that her feelings weren't shared.

She couldn't do that to herself again—yet if she

was honest with herself, she had already fallen desperately in love with Caelan.

As wildly in love as he had been with Isla, back when she was the "bonniest lass in the whole of Scotland," according to her mother. Even thinking of Caelan's expression when he told her about Isla's death made her feel sick.

No one could choose their parents. But one could choose how much anguish to feel as an adult, as a wife, and Clara was determined to make wise choices. Her throat tightened up at the idea of leaving the castle, but she'd made up her mind.

She would find—not anyone better, because there was no one better than Caelan—a man who wouldn't rip her heart to pieces because he couldn't bear to hear his dead wife's name spoken aloud.

CHAPTER 22

April 23, 1803

Caelan was in a temper that he couldn't shake. Clara refused to marry him. She had refused him last night, and she had refused him again this morning. She had even refused him in front of Elsbeth, though the lass might well believe they'd spent the night together.

Which they hadn't.

And for what reason? The stupidity of that idea about falling in love. He'd lain awake half the night weighing the advisability of telling her that he *might* fall in love. Yet he didn't believe it, and there was nothing worse than starting a marriage with a lie.

Clara knew what she wanted, and it was more than a castle and some books. She wanted a man at her feet, stars in his eyes.

He sat in the coach, drumming his fingers on one leg as the carriage rattled through the pass. "You do mean to stay in Lavenween? You won't leave immediately?"

Clara had been looking out the window, down into the depths of the ravine, but she glanced over at him. "Only until Mr. Cobbledick arrives back from Glasgow. He may be there already."

That wasn't enough time to woo her into changing her mind. Damn it, he was going to have to follow her.

"You can have this carriage," he said, exasperated. "I can't let you run off with a stranger. Who knows what will—"

"There's no question of you *allowing me*," Clara said, cutting into his sentence. "You have no claim over me, laird, and you would do well to remember it." She cast him a defiant—albeit sweet—look.

Caelan went back to drumming his fingers. Damn it, he wanted her more than . . . more than any woman he'd ever . . . But he couldn't—

Clara would never believe him anyway. She didn't care about his type of *wanting*. She wanted romance. The great love of the ages. He'd never been good at that, not with Isla and not now. It wasn't in him.

How could he say that to her? Clara was certain that he had loved Isla with all his heart. Even if he said that he hadn't, he wasn't about to start languishing for her. Ready to kill himself for love or some such shite.

A greedy voice in his heart—or maybe his loins—persistently suggested romantic gestures. *Buy some flowers. Root up Isla's flowers and plant new ones instead.*

That would be idiotic. Clara loved the way the castle swam in a blue ocean. He hadn't noticed the watery effect until she pointed it out, but now he did. She made him see things differently.

Clara stared out the window all the way to Lavenween. Her heart was aching, but she had set her course. After church, she would stay with Fiona until Mr. Cobbledick returned to take her over the mountains, away from the castle. She had put on a traveling gown in case he was already in the village, along with a gathered cap fit for a housekeeper for wearing in church.

Caelan walked into the kirk looking extremely handsome, his kilt in perfect pleats, his shirt and

cravat snowy white and starched. He had slung
an adorable bag called a sporran around his hips.
Clara tried to distract herself with the idea of stealing it and embroidering a face—with whiskers—on
the front.

The village priest, Father Boggs, was an elderly
man who greeted "Mrs. Potts" with kindness but
turned to the laird. She faded back as parishioners
clustered around him, chattering about a man
whose heart was broken, about a roof that had
fallen in, about the churchyard gate that had been
repaired. Caelan was obviously the heart of the
village.

He turned, looking for her, but Clara shook her
head. No housekeeper sat with her master. Caelan's
face darkened to a scowl, but Mr. and Mrs. Gillan
were waiting in the first pew with Fiona, Alfie, and
a man she assumed to be Rory. As Clara watched,
Caelan bent his head and whispered something to
his nephew.

Sure enough, Alfie dashed back down the aisle
and said, very loudly, "Future Aunt Clara, why
won't you sit with me?"

Elsbeth giggled, and Maisie gasped audibly. Everyone in the pew before them turned around, their
bonnets quivering with interest. In fact, everyone
in the small church craned their necks.

"Please don't address me in that absurd fashion.
I sit here because I choose to," Clara said with as
much dignity as she could, speaking not merely to
Alfie but to his uncle.

Alfie tugged at her hand. "*Seriously*? Rather than
sitting with me?"

Behind him, the church door opened again, and

a rustle went through the congregation. Clara glanced up—and her mouth fell open.

Her best friend Torie's sister, Leonora, was proceeding into the church on the arm of an elderly man whom Clara knew well, because she'd danced with Lord Bufford numerous times.

Her heart sank; the game was up.

One moment Leonora presented the picture of saintly devotion, a pearl-studded prayer book clasped in her gloved hand—and the next she dropped that prayer book to the stone floor. "Clara Vetry!" she cried. "What on earth are you doing here?" Her eyes narrowed. "And what in the world are you *wearing*?"

Clara rose to her feet and moved into the aisle, hardly noticing that Alfie was still clinging to her hand. "Good morning, Lord and Lady Bufford." She dropped a curtsy.

"Oh my goodness," Leonora cried. "You've become a governess! Torie has been so worried about you. The only thing your mama would disclose was that you'd decided to move to Scotland, but we never imagined she had thrown you into such common circumstances!" She turned to her husband. "Bufford, you must *do* something!"

"Good morning, Miss Vetry," her spouse said, giving Clara one of his measured smiles. "I am happy to see you in my favorite part of this country."

Politic, but not to the point.

A comfortingly large person loomed up at her shoulder. "Good morning, Lord and Lady Bufford." Caelan's voice was practically purring with satisfaction.

"Need we have this conversation in front of the entire village?" Clara hissed.

"Everyone will know by day's end, anyway," Leonora said, waving her hand. "Lavenween is not like London. Truly, Clara, what *are* you doing? The *Honorable Miss Vetry* engaging in menial labor?"

"The Honorable Miss Vetry?" Caelan repeated. "My, my."

Clara threw him a scathing look.

"We were informed of Prince George's reproachable behavior," Lord Bufford said in the same magisterial tone with which he presumably addressed the House of Lords. "I consider the future of the English monarchy to be in grave danger."

"Never mind that," his wife cried. "Clara, you take off that dreadful cap this moment!"

Clara opened her mouth, but Torie's older sister had never been one to mince words; Leonora reached out and tugged the cap off. Elsbeth had done her best, but Clara's curls sprang out of their confines.

"What has happened to your hair!" Leonora cried, sounding even more horrified.

"I love her curls," Fiona said, joining the group, deep amusement in her voice.

"So do I," Alfie piped up. "She looks like Wilhelmina."

"You should never compare a lady to a chicken," Leonora told him, not unkindly.

"I believe the service shall be delayed," Fiona said. "Perhaps you might go outside and see how Wilhelmina is doing, Alfie."

Clara was burning with embarrassment. Seemingly unperturbed, the minister had wandered down from the altar and was chatting with the few

parishioners who weren't riveted by the drama, because they were too old to overhear the commotion.

"I chose not to visit my great-aunt as my mother wished," Clara explained, seeing no way around it. "Instead, I arrived at Lord MacCrae's castle."

"Arrived at *MacCrae's* castle?" Leonora's eyes widened. "The laird has no children." She looked from Clara to Elsbeth and Maisie, horror growing on her face.

"As my housekeeper," Caelan confirmed helpfully. "That's why she's wearing that ugly cap."

Back at the castle, he'd looked a perfect Highland gentleman, but now his hair was disheveled, and his jaw was beginning to darken. He looked considerably happier, though.

"I'm sure the service should begin," Clara announced.

"We have time," Caelan said, his eyes sparking with enjoyment.

"Yes, we *do* have time," Leonora said bossily.

Torie used to complain about her older sister's imperious ways, and Clara started feeling very sympathetic.

"Laird, are you saying that a young English lady arrived alone at the MacCrae castle, a dwelling so disgraceful that the whole of Scotland knew of its condition?" Leonora asked.

"That's an exaggeration, and anyway, it's clean now!" Clara said, unable to stop herself.

"You have been *cleaning*," Leonora cried, hand on her heart. "Lady Vetry would be horrified!"

Who knew that Torie's sister could be so dramatic? Clara's impression had been that Leonora was cool and buttoned-down, but perhaps marriage had changed her.

"She has been cleaning," Caelan confirmed.

Clara glanced at him, and her heart skipped a beat. He was grinning, a wide smile that she'd only seen once or twice.

"Am I to understand that your housekeeper is actually a lady?" Mrs. Gillan said, squeezing in beside Fiona. She looked not only interested but thrilled.

"I didn't pretend to be his housekeeper in order to marry the laird," Clara told her. "I was pretending to be Mrs. Potts, but I had no idea who owned the castle."

"Of course you didn't," Fiona put in, her eyes twinkling.

"Mrs. Potts?" Leonora cried. "The lady with whom Prince George fell desperately in love is being addressed as Mrs. Potts?"

Caelan's body stiffened. "Prince George? Isn't the man married?"

"More to the point," Leonora said, "*you* are not married, laird, and the Honorable Miss Vetry has been living under your roof without a chaperone!"

"My maid—" Clara started.

Caelan's deep voice cut in. "Aye, and it's a burden to my conscience now I know the truth. She did indeed spend a night under my roof without another soul in the castle other than myself. After she came across me fishing."

Leonora shuddered. "Everyone in this parish knows to avoid the loch for that very reason."

Fiona chuckled and elbowed her brother. "I warned you, didn't I?"

Revelations were rolling downhill like an avalanche. Torie would say that Leonora had the bit in her mouth and was running amok.

"We can settle this problem immediately," Caelan said, his voice smooth as silk.

"The answer is *no*," Clara said roundly.

Lord Bufford had been watching placidly, leaning on his cane, but he straightened. "I fear that you have no choice, Miss Vetry. I would be doing grave injustice to the memory of your father if I allowed your reputation to be ruined."

"My father is long dead," Clara cried. "I don't want to marry the laird!"

"You could have left my brother's castle the moment you understood that he didn't have another woman under his roof," Fiona pointed out. Like her dratted brother, her tone was richly amused. "You didn't. You could have stayed with me."

Caelan's grin flaunted his satisfaction at this turn of events. "Without even knowing her title, I asked her to marry me," he said virtuously.

Defense came from an unlikely corner. "The lass shouldn't be forced to marry," Mrs. Gillan said. "Didn't I tell you, laird, that a warmhearted woman would be crushed by marriage to you, when you're still grieving my daughter? Who's to say when your heart will mend?" She moved to stand beside Clara. "It wouldn't be fair."

"What if Miss Vetry *wanted* to marry my brother?" Fiona asked Mrs. Gillan.

"That would be different. She's a good lass and worked hard the last few days, for all she's a lady."

A horrified noise came from Leonora's lips.

"Aye, for all she's a lady," Mrs. Gillan repeated. "She'd be a good wife to the laird. I wouldn't want her to be forced into it, under the circumstances." She crossed her arms over her chest and gave Leonora a fierce look. "It wouldn't be fair."

"Fairness is not relevant when a lady's reputation has been marred," Lord Bufford stated. "Lord MacCrae, perhaps you might speak to your fiancée privately, after which Mr. Boggs will conduct the marriage ceremony."

Clara gaped. "What?"

"We hold to the old ways in Scotland. Two people merely need declare themselves before at least two witnesses. I think we all agree that the situation is such that time is of the essence."

"Except I'm not declaring myself," Clara snapped. Her glorious adventure lay in shards at her feet. She scowled at Leonora. "Torie would not agree with you, and you're being frightfully bossy."

"My sister is not here, and no matter her opinion, the rest of polite society would agree with me. Look around you, Clara. If you don't marry the laird, the news will travel to Inverness and then to Glasgow, and from there to London."

Clara opened her mouth to say that she didn't care, but Leonora wasn't finished. "From there, it will come to your mother's ears and to those of her friends. You may have reason to dislike your mother, as she appears to have thrown you out of the house, but I have known you for years, Clara. You would never allow her to be rejected by society due to her daughter's reputation as a fallen woman. My guess is that your assault on Prince George has been difficult for her to negotiate."

"Assault on Prince George?" Fiona muttered. "Damn it, I knew I liked you, Clara."

Caelan leaned forward and said quietly, "Bravo."

"Lady Vetry would never again be invited to one of the queen's drawing rooms, which I believe she much enjoys," Leonora continued. "No doubt the prince behaved reprehensibly, but the scandal arose from the fact you struck His Majesty."

"Excellent," Fiona said.

But Clara's heart plummeted. Leonora was right. It was as if *she'd* fallen from the moon and instead of crushing a prince, crushed herself. Crushed her dreams of adventure, her dreams of a castle of her own.

"I believe I shall take up Lord Bufford's excellent suggestion," Caelan said. He glanced over at the minister. "Mr. Boggs, please begin the service. The Honorable Miss Vetry and I shall return."

He reached out, caught Clara's hand, and drew her toward the door.

CHAPTER 23

*C*aelan walked down the steps from the kirk, knowing in his bones that the conversation ahead of him was the most significant of his life.

Betrothing himself to Isla had been an easy decision. She had been delightfully pretty, and his mother liked her. After his father died, suddenly every single woman in Scotland seemed to be chasing him. Isla felt like a safe choice.

But Clara?

Her face was stoic, but he could see pain in her eyes. She'd gone pale when Leonora's arguments hit home. She wanted her own castle and books, not his. Not theirs.

No, that wasn't it. She wanted to marry a man who would fall on his knees at her feet.

He pushed open the cemetery gate and ushered her inside. Alfie was off in one corner, dangling a worm before Wilhelmina's beak and trying to lure her to eat it.

As he looked down at Clara, a silent curse resounded in his heart. Isla's grave was directly in front of the gate, and she was staring at it.

"It's hers, isn't it?" Clara asked. Her voice had a small tremor. "Did you plant all those flowers?"

"Isla's mother and I transplanted them from the moat. Mrs. Gillan makes certain that they flourish."

"Isla was a lucky woman to be so loved," Clara said hollowly.

Caelan nodded.

"I'm not saying that I'm unlucky," she added.

"You are not the sort of person who complains." He took her hand again and drew her into the opposite corner from Alfie, far away from Isla's grave.

"Would gossip about my stay in your castle really travel to Glasgow and beyond?" Her eyes looked glossy, as if she were about to cry.

"Did you see the women sitting directly behind the front pew?"

"I noticed the plumes on their bonnets."

"A group of hopeful ladies have undertaken to make the journey from Inverness weekly, in hopes that I will fall madly in love with one of them or decide I need a second wife and pick one at random."

"Brave of them," Clara said.

He raised an eyebrow.

"Considering the infamous state of your castle."

His heart thumped at the wry note in her voice. "Astonishing, isn't it? Of course, after today, I am unlikely to attract a respectable lady."

"Don't you dare try to make me feel guilty about *you* as well as my mother." She glared at him.

"My point is that this gossip will be considered fascinating in Inverness and beyond. Lady Bufford is right that it will eventually make its way to London. How on earth do you know her ladyship well enough to call her Leonora?"

"She is my best friend's sister."

"The odds of that were very small," Caelan said.

Her shoulders were drooping. He couldn't bear it. "It wouldn't be so terrible to be my lady. You wanted a castle. And books. And a man in a skirt." Damn it, he sounded as if he was pleading. Begging. "You like me." Her lips were trembling, so he added, "I landed a fish, looked up and there you were. Like an angel on the riverbank."

"Don't," she said. "That's—that's what Prince George used to say about me."

"Right. I want to hear about that scandal. I suppose I can't go to London and shoot a member of royalty. Besides"—he couldn't help grinning—"it sounds as if you took care of him yourself. You rebuffed him."

"With my reticule," she said, a trace of pride in her eyes.

"There's my girl," he said, the words rolling out of his mouth without forethought. "What did he do to you? I'm still available to shoot him. Most of Scotland would approve."

One side of her mouth curled into a shaky smile. "Nothing warranting homicide. He . . . he sang about me, not a nice song. Then a pigeon shat on me, to use your word. On my breast. He took out a handkerchief." She pressed her lips together.

"He used it as an excuse to take liberties," Caelan said, his fists curling.

"Yes," she confirmed.

He stepped closer. "If you want him dead, I'm your man."

"I don't."

"Because that would be even worse for your mother?"

"No, because I don't want you to be hanged. I like you. I truly do." She seemed to be turning pink. "I think that we . . . We both like books."

"And kissing," he prompted, as she appeared to have lost her train of thought.

"I don't know why I'm being so silly. I never

truly believed I could marry for love. I *hoped* that I would, but mostly I wanted to find a spouse well-bred enough to make my mother proud. Hopefully a man who could fend off Prince George."

He bared his teeth. "As I said—"

"I hit him," she said fiercely. "I took care of myself." Her eyes had darkened to the color of the loch at twilight. "That's the scandal that sent me to Scotland. It was not merely that the prince groped me—society had watched him hound me for three years. The scandal was because I struck him."

"In those earlier years, no one courted you because the prince had staked a claim," he said, grasping the extent of the prince's obsession.

"Something like that."

"I should go down there. Shooting him would be doing the women of England a favor."

Her eyes shone with tears, and they tore at his soul. "I wanted what you and Isla had, but I'm so lucky to have a dowry and books, and—"

"Me?" Caelan handed her a handkerchief. "Don't forget Wilhelmina, your favorite chicken. There's Alfie, and Fiona, Elsbeth and Maisie. I promise to hire Mr. Cobbledick. Even Mrs. Gillan, who stood up for you today in fine style."

"I *am* lucky," she said, obviously trying to convince herself.

Caelan sighed. It was time to come clean. "I had known Isla since she was five years old. Marrying her—"

"I'd rather not discuss Isla!"

"My point is that—"

"I mean it," Clara interrupted, her mouth compressing into a tight line.

Caelan decided to abandon the point and move

on. "I like you. *You*, Clara. I like you very much."
He studied her face, memorizing every feature in
case she fled for the nearest carriage. "I love your
imagination and your sense of humor. I love the
fact that dreadful as your mother seems to be, you
grew tearful over the idea of her ostracization. I
think that you are incredibly beautiful."

She wrinkled her nose.

"Not only your hair and the glorious breasts that
drove a future king to madness. Your lips, nose,
chin, curves, shoulders . . . all of you." He hesitated
and then told her the truth, because that mattered
in marriage. "Would you settle for an absurdly
affectionate husband who feels riveted by desire
whenever he looks at you?"

Thankfully, her lips eased. "I'm in this situation
because of decisions that *I* made. What would you
have done when we first met if I'd introduced myself as the Honorable Miss Clara Vetry?"

"Summoned the carriage and sent you wherever
you wished to go," Caelan said. "Instead, the improbable Mrs. Potts followed me back to the castle."

"I did, didn't I?"

"When I didn't have a bathtub, you could have
confessed all and left."

"I could have moved to Fiona's house."

"You remained in an echoing and empty castle
and kissed me. Many times." He took her hands
in his. "Please marry me, Clara. *Not* because of
your mother, and not because we are madly attracted to each other, and not even because I like
you so much."

Her eyes were shining now. "Why, then?"

"I have things you want," he offered, feeling
awkward.

"The castle? The books?"

"My legs. You like me in a kilt."

"Your chest is also worth consideration," she said, a smile deep in her eyes.

"But mostly, you can be yourself with me, Clara," he said, putting his cards on the table. "Read books all day long, if you wish. Hire a housekeeper who is literate, though I think that Elsbeth has laid claim to the position, and I'm not sure of her schooling. Bring me tea and seduce me on the only sofa we have in the castle. Tell me stories about helmets and witches and sighing portraits. *Please*."

"Oh." Now her eyes looked starry.

"Please, Clara." He didn't go down on one knee, like a prince before a princess, but he hesitated long enough to see acceptance in her eyes before he gave her a kiss that commanded and begged, both at once.

"I did promise to make you a better fly for fishing," she whispered.

"Promise to teach our daughters to slap any man who takes advantage, future king or no?"

Her smile made his chest hurt, which was absurd. Still, it was that beautiful. He turned around, not letting go of her in case she changed her mind.

"Alfie," he shouted. "Come on, lad! I'm about to marry your future aunt."

The boy looked over. "Now?"

He nodded. "Now."

Alfie jumped up. "She can't marry you looking like that!"

Clara felt a pulse of dismay. True, she was wearing her drab traveling gown. Alfie's eyes were on her head, and her hair must look dreadful, given

Leonora's appalled expression. She put her hands up and tried to bundle it together. "Elsbeth carries pins."

"No," Caelan said. "I love your hair. It's as wild as a Scottish moor."

"She needs flowers in her hair," Alfie said with authority. "That's what brides do. Wear, I mean. Wait a second." He dashed over to the lilac bush and broke off a branch. "Here, Uncle Caelan, put these in her hair. I'd do it, but she'd have to sit in the grass so I could reach her."

"Would you mind?" Caelan asked her.

Her mother would *die*.

"I would love that," Clara said.

"I wish Wilhelmina could come into the church to see you get married," Alfie said.

"She can be my maid of honor. You are a lovely boy," Clara said, smiling at him. "I'm so happy to become part of your family." He darted forward and wrapped his arms around her waist, and they stayed like that while Caelan wove sweet-smelling white lilac blossoms into the floaty mass of her hair.

The kirk had emptied by the time the three of them (and Wilhelmina) walked back through the door. The fashionably dressed women from Inverness had departed, leaving only family and the Buffords.

"The villagers and crofters are preparing a celebration," Fiona whispered to Caelan, before she turned to Clara. "You look so beautiful!"

The windows of the kirk were old and warped, but enough sun came through the panes that Clara's hair turned to spun gold as they knelt before the rail. Caelan couldn't stop smiling as Mr. Boggs declared them husband and wife.

Afterward, he didn't let go of her hand. She couldn't leave for England now. She had vowed to stay with him. Anyone could tell that when Clara promised something, she kept her word.

"Everyone is waiting in the pub," Fiona told him after they signed the parish book.

"Not the castle?"

She shook her head. "You don't have chairs, let alone a bed big enough for the two of you, remember?"

He had forgotten.

His sister grinned. "Not to worry."

CHAPTER 24

Clara had been to many English weddings as her friends found husbands. These ceremonious, dignified weddings were held in the morning and followed by ceremonious and grave wedding breakfasts during which champagne was the drink of choice.

After her wedding, she and Caelan walked down the village street between a corridor of people cheering and pelting them with blossoms. Once they arrived in the pub, it became clear that whisky was the champagne of Scotland.

"You're a Highlander now," a Mr. McCurdy told her as he handed her a glass, smiling so widely that she could see his back teeth. "I pride myself that mine is a trifle sweet, perfect for a lady. I introduced a touch of honey."

Clara took a hearty sip and had a hard time not spitting it out. Only her mother's drilling in ladylike behavior came to her rescue. "It's . . . lovely," she managed. "Very pungent."

Mr. McCurdy's forehead wrinkled. "'Pungent,' eh? One of those English words I don't know. I'll use it in me text. We have to write up a description when we sell it down to the Brits."

He was shouldered aside by a man who introduced himself as Mr. Monro.

"I'd be right grateful for an English word that might describe mine," he said, holding out a glass. "I heard you are a great reader, and the laird himself told me that you have the best vocabulary in these parts. I smoked clover leaves over my brew to add a smoky flavor."

That whisky was, hands down, the worst thing that Clara had ever tasted. The only thing she could say was that the sip landed warmly in her stomach, but Mr. Monro's hopeful eyes were fixed on her face. Thankfully, Walter Scott's poetry came to mind.

"Rugged," she said, managing not to shudder. "Deep and broad."

That was met with delight.

Mr. Halidon was next. Clara sampled his dreadful brew. "Gallant and wild."

"Wild?" Mr. Halidon looked somewhat surprised.

"Like a wild harp wakened by the winds."

An arm closed around her waist. "Are you trying to intoxicate my bride, Mr. Halidon?" Caelan asked.

"Nay, we're giving her the tiniest sips," he protested. "She has a way with words that's like a verist Scottish minstrel, laird. To quote the bard himself, 'Liquor guid to fire his bluid!'"

"Shakespeare?" Clara asked.

"Nay, Robert Burns," Mr. Halidon said, shaking his head. "Only poet worth reading, especially when he's talking of poor man's wine. 'Whether thro' wimplin' worms thou jink, or, richly brown, ream owre the brink.'"

"I have no idea what you just said," Clara confessed.

"Scots dialect," Caelan said, pulling her even closer, until their hips touched. "Shall we try the next?"

Six or seven more men were ranged behind Mr. Halidon, chattering as they waited. "Oh, my," Clara breathed, wondering how much poetry she could remember.

"I can tell them that you've had all the drink you

can stomach," Caelan said, bending down to nuzzle her hair.

She shook her head. "I'm a Scotswoman now."

"You could merely wet your lips. Though a befuddled Clara might be very enjoyable."

She poked him. "Stop making fun of me, you fiend!"

Caelan's rumbling laughter broke out, and Mr. Halidon's face brightened. "Ach, but it's a year and a day since we heard the laird laughing, is it not? I'm thinking that good Scottish whisky would better any wedding night."

The whole of them spontaneously burst into song. "'We'll drink a cup of kindness yet, for the sake of auld lang syne.'"

Clara didn't know what to make of it—or even what the words meant—but when they all raised their glasses, she drank with them, finishing Mr. Halidon's sample. The whisky burned to the pit of her stomach. It seemed to taste slightly better now; perhaps she was getting used to it.

"Off with you," Caelan said, shaking hands with him. "Let's have the next one."

From then on, Clara sipped each whisky, and Caelan tossed off the glass. He and the crofter in question would have a learned conversation about peat and malt, while Clara desperately summoned up lines from poetry.

Walter Scott's "Glenfinlas" proved very useful, as she proclaimed Mr. Hay's whisky had "potent tone." Mr. Annard was somewhat taken aback by "rapture's glow," especially when Caelan couldn't stop laughing. But Mr. Shaw rejoiced at "dark and deep."

After the last crofter had come and gone, Caelan

handed her a glass of his own MacCrae whisky just as the wives claimed her. They drew her over to a table and told her stories about Caelan as a boy. Very kindly, no one mentioned Isla's name. Fiona introduced an elderly woman, Mrs. Baldy, who looked at her defensively and said that the castle steps were more than she could manage most days.

Clara took her hand and confessed that she had made the laird change his own sheets, which caused all the women to scream so boisterously with laughter that a few of their husbands came around and demanded to know the jest.

Mrs. Gillan took the opportunity to whisper that she was glad Caelan had married her, because he did need an heir.

Clara nodded, feeling unsettled all of a sudden. It was one thing to kiss Caelan, but children?

Mrs. Gillan frowned. "Oh my goodness." She turned her head. "Fiona, do come here, if you would!"

After this many rounds of ale and samples of local whisky, titles had gone by the wayside. Fiona wobbled on her way across the pub, gathered Clara into her arms, and whispered sweetly, "Now my wee brother will be happy again."

Wee brother?

Clara stole a look at Caelan. His shoulders were larger than anyone's in the room, a realization that made her smile like a goose, especially when their eyes met and his conveyed that he was equally pleased with her shape.

That wasn't a small thing, she thought blurrily.

Mrs. Gillan wrapped a hand around her wrist. "Come along, Fiona!" she said, pulling Clara into the snug, off the main room.

Fiona wandered after them. "Has anyone seen my son? Or a rabbity chicken?"

"He's fine," Mrs. Gillan said, closing the door. "Now, Fiona, we have a task before us."

"We do? I thought we took care of it. The bed should be up by now."

"That's the problem," Mrs. Gillan said impatiently. She, if no one else, had stayed sober.

"I apologize for marrying Isla's husband," Clara said impulsively, sinking onto a bench. "I *am* sorry for your loss, Mrs. Gillan."

The older woman smiled, her eyes clear. "Isla adored Caelan from the time they were wee ones. She never would have begrudged him a wife and children."

"We won't have the same kind of marriage," Clara said. "He feels affection for me. Maybe he called it 'great affection.'"

Fiona sighed loudly. "My brother. Blind as a mole and always has been."

"Dear Clara's mother is not here," Mrs. Gillan said to Fiona.

"Leonora says that the woman's a right—" Fiona caught herself. "That is, Lady Bufford has a low opinion of your mother, Clara." She took a swallow of whisky. "'Lady Vetry' sounds like a frosty evening."

"Fiona!" Mrs. Gillan frowned at her.

"Hmmm?"

"Perhaps I should return to the other room," Clara said. She was starting to feel a little queasy.

"No one has told this poor lass about the wedding night," Mrs. Gillan burst out. "Fiona, you're as drunk as a boiled owl!"

"Am not," Fiona said, blinking owlishly at Clara.

"Wedding night, eh? My brother didn't manage to talk you into making love on that red sofa of his?"

"No," Clara said.

Fiona hooted with laughter. "His seduction skills need work. Maybe Rory can give him some pointers."

"The laird would never take advantage of a young woman under his own roof, no matter what the gossips say," Mrs. Gillan snapped.

"He didn't," Clara assured her. "He's very honest. Honorable. He was very truthful. Perhaps too truthful."

"You're drunk as well," Mrs. Gillan observed.

"I believe it is the fault of Caelan's whisky," Clara told her, putting the glass down. "I don't want to hurt his feelings, but I don't think anyone will buy it, as it tastes disgusting. Luckily I have a dowry. We can afford to buy some furniture." She blinked, focusing on Mrs. Gillan's face. "Perhaps not as lovely as that which Isla chose."

"Never mind that," Fiona said. "Let's get going with the explanations, because I should find out what happened to Alfie."

"He's under a bench against the wall," Clara told her. "He has Wilhelmina with him, and last I looked, they were both sleeping."

"Ach, it's a marvelous mother that you'll be," Fiona said, sighing. "Now, listen to me. You know that a man has a thing down there, don't you?" She waved in the general area of Clara's waist.

Clara picked up her glass of whisky and took another gulp, shuddering as it went down her throat. "I know all about it because Prince George showed me a vase."

"What?" Mrs. Gillan frowned.

"A man's tool can be a wee bit dismaying," Fiona

said, ignoring Clara's mention of a vase. "That tool does fit inside a woman, even when it seems as if it wouldn't and couldn't."

Clara smiled. "I've already seen my husband without clothing."

Mrs. Gillan gasped. "No!"

"He was in the loch," Clara explained. "I slapped my hands over my eyes, but it was too late. I shouldn't have looked, but it all happened so fast."

Mrs. Gillan was aghast.

"That's why I'm not worried. He's much more reasonably sized than I would have feared considering how tall he is. The vase was very misleading."

"Vase?" Fiona asked.

"A Roman vase." Clara lowered her voice and whispered, "The men had preposterous *things* in the front of them. Big as . . . as carrots. No, bigger. Obviously, the depiction was false."

She reminded herself not to say anything more about Caelan's size, not to his sister and mother-in-law. It would be a secret between them.

"I warned my brother that he would be scandalizing innocents," Fiona said, giggling madly, "but I didn't take the effect of cold water into account."

"The advice I gave my darling Isla—"

"Mrs. Gillan!" Fiona's voice was very sharp. "I don't mean to be unkind, but that is inappropriate."

Mrs. Gillan started. "Of course, you're right! 'Twas a totally different circumstance, was it not? I'm a beast to have raised the subject."

Clara nodded. "They were in love. Different circumstances. Kissing Caelan is scorching, so she . . . it . . ."

"The bride is *drunk*," Fiona said, giggling some more.

Clara decided it would be comfortable to lie down on the bench. "It's been a very stressful day. I'll rest my head for a moment."

"Scorching?" Mrs. Gillan repeated.

"Well, thank goodness they have that going for them," Fiona snapped. She sounded a great deal more sober. "Mrs. Gillan, I shall say this to you once and trust that you don't disappoint me."

"Yes?"

"Isla, your darling Isla, is dead. If my equally darling brother is to have a happy marriage and a happy life, we must stop talking about how perfect Isla was and referring to the great love affair of their marriage."

"I know," Mrs. Gillan said.

She sounded so chastised that Clara groggily opened her eyes and thought about saying she didn't mind talking about Isla. But it wasn't true. She didn't want to ever talk about her. "I know she was everything to Caelan," she said instead. "He told me that I can't say her name. Aloud. To him." She heaved a sigh.

"That fool," Fiona hissed.

"Oh dear," Mrs. Gillan muttered.

"Most people don't marry for love," Clara told them. "He told me that too, and he's right. My parents certainly didn't."

"Neither did ours," Fiona replied. "But Clara, darling, feelings can change. No one knows how they'll feel on their first anniversary."

"How did you feel?" Clara said. She propped herself up enough to pick up her glass and take a sip of Caelan's whisky. It was so awful that it jolted her awake.

"Well, I was in love when I married," Fiona said awkwardly. "I'd known Rory since we were children, you see."

"Just like Isla and Caelan," Clara said before she could stop herself.

Mrs. Gillan looked uncomfortable. "As Fiona said, we should let the past stay in the past."

Clara managed to give her a weak smile, mostly because she'd suddenly remembered her mother's command to marry someone ferocious. She had the feeling that Caelan qualified. But then, Lady Vetry would consider this marriage further evidence that her daughter was "impetuous and thoughtless." Clara shivered to imagine Lady Vetry's comments. Not that it mattered, because she was a Scotswoman now.

Mrs. Gillan, despite her tragedy, had been far kinder than her mother would have been.

"Perhaps I'll take a nap. A *wee* nap," Clara said, determined to start using more words like "wee" and prove herself Scots that way, because she would never love whisky.

SOMETIME LATER SHE woke up in the carriage, snugly held in Caelan's arms. "My head is terribly foggy."

He laughed and kissed her forehead. "Thanks to all that whisky."

"I feel very warm," Clara told him. "Very . . . *affectionate.*" She closed her eyes and turned her head toward his chest. "You smell delicious, do you know that?"

"*Clara.*" His voice rasped.

She didn't pay much attention, because she was sniffing him. "I like the way you smell. That's a good thing about our marriage." She raised a finger in the air and managed to focus on it. "One good thing."

"Surely not the only good thing?"

"No, there's the way you look. I love your shoulders. And the size of you, ah, privately. Just right for me, because I'm rather small." Remembering that might be an insult, she looked up at him hazily. "I apologize if that sounded belittling."

He looked confused, so she drew a finger down his brow and his powerful nose. "You're beautiful," she said dreamily, half aware that she would be terribly embarrassed in the morning. "Your legs, your arse—I apologize for being so vulgar—your shoulders from the back *and* the front. I feel achy looking at you."

"Do you?" His voice was almost a croon. "I wish you hadn't drunk so much whisky, Clara."

"I couldn't say no," she told him. "You have so many crofters, and they each have their own whisky. I am so sorry to tell you this, Caelan, but it all tasted dreadful."

His eyes were dancing. "Every single one?"

"Including yours," Clara said. "I'm only telling you the truth because I'm a trifle foxed, but whisky is *awful*." She thought about it. "Perhaps better after the tenth glass, but I had to tell some terrible fibs this afternoon. I told every single man that their whisky was outstanding. Remarkable. Incredible."

"I was standing next to you, remember? You were eloquent and kind."

"You're laughing at me," Clara muttered, turning to nestle her face against his chest again.

His arm tightened, and he bent down, his lips brushing against her ear. "If you weren't drunk, I'd make love to you in this carriage."

"What? You can't do that," Clara said, blinking at him.

"Why not?" His teeth nipped her ear lobe.

Clara felt it like a jolt through her body. *"That* made me feel—" She broke off, not sure how to describe it.

"Like?" His voice was gravelly and low.

"I couldn't say it aloud," she told him, her mother's most forbidding expression floating through her mind.

"Maybe later," Caelan said. He rearranged her in his lap so she was more upright. "I'll kiss you when you're sober."

"All right," Clara said, putting her head against his shoulder. She wasn't entirely comfortable, so she wiggled side to side.

Caelan uttered a guttural sound that made her eyes blink open.

"Are you quite all right?" She drew up her knees and put her feet on the seat.

"Yes."

It was one word, but something in his tone shimmered through her body in a peculiar way. Or perhaps that was the fact the carriage was swaying so much.

"Are we going through the pass now?" she asked.

He didn't even glance out the window. "Aye."

"I like it when you talk like that. 'Aye,'" she said, trying it out, but it didn't sound right.

"Like a Scotsman?" he asked. "You wouldn't prefer that I spoke like a Lowlander or an Englishman?"

"Why would I?" Clara asked. "That would be like asking you to wear breeches instead of your kilt." Sleep was coming over her like a thick woolen blanket.

"Isla did."

"Say something else to me."

"'So fair art thou, my bonnie lass,'" Caelan said, kissing her forehead.

"That's nice," Clara said.

His deep voice rumbled into her dreams.

CHAPTER 25

April 24, 1803

Clara's headache woke her. She forced her eyelids open and stared at the beams above. If she remembered correctly, they weren't infested by worms, but something else . . . Termites? Termites that shat on the bed.

Which is when she realized that a heavy arm was pinning her down. She turned her head carefully—because her skull might crack open—and found her husband lying on his stomach, his head turned away from her. Nut-brown, tousled hair spread over white sheets—

White?

Very white pillows and sheets.

She sat up, and Caelan's arm slid away. They were in the top room, the one that used to have the owl and Isla's fancy furniture, now empty except for a bed that hadn't been there yesterday.

Through open windows, she could see smoky green woods and the loch beyond. Birds were singing, and pink-tinged clouds floated over the water.

A hand drew her down against a warm chest. A naked chest. Clara squeaked and jerked back. "Caelan!"

"Wife."

She hurdled straight out of the bed, the heavy mass of her hair whipping around her shoulders. She was wearing a chemise, but Caelan . . . Caelan had turned on his back and pushed down the sheet to his waist. He was naked.

"Oh my goodness," she breathed, staring at him. She had no words to articulate what she felt about his muscled chest. The *hair* on his chest. The golden color of his skin against all those white pillows. His wicked smile.

"Where did this bed come from?" she managed. It was made from ruddy chestnut wood with a gracefully curved top and bottom. And it was low, perfect for a shorter person like herself, unlike the fancy bed—

She pushed the thought away. No Isla.

"Auld Magnus gave it to us," Caelan said, folding his arms behind his head.

"It's beautiful." She ran a hand along the curved baseboard. "We should thank him today, don't you think? What a marvelous wedding present."

"The sheets are from the villagers. You'll love this, Clara. Your Mr. Cobbledick arrived at the castle when we were at church. Today a tub to collect rainwater and a stove to heat the water will be set up on the roof. Elsbeth informed me last night that once the ceramic—not glass—bathtub is installed, our privy should be referred to as a water closet."

Clara's mind reeled. "I don't remember hearing that. Actually, I don't remember much after falling asleep in the pub."

"Aye, you were drunk as a lord," her husband said comfortably.

"Everyone saw? Mr. Cobbledick?"

"No one was surprised you were jug-bitten. They reckoned that you drank two or three glasses more than any woman in recent memory. Many a Scotswoman can hold her drink, but you've struck a blow for the reputation of all Englishwomen."

Clara shuddered at the memory. "As long as everyone understands that I'm not doing it again. I shan't be tasting *anyone's* whisky, even if it's your own blend. Is Elsbeth downstairs? I'd love some tea."

"You ordered me to send the household home last night," Caelan said, grinning. "I'm not sure I've got the wording right, but the gist was that you refused to consummate your marriage with anyone else on the premises. Then you washed your face, climbed into bed, and fell asleep like a baby."

Her eyes widened. "I have *no memory* of saying anything of that nature."

"Your first command as the lady of the castle," he told her, flat-out laughing now.

Clara moaned. "This is so embarrassing." She hesitated. "We didn't . . . Did we?"

"Not yet. We both need to be awake."

"Right," she said, turning away hurriedly. "I'll go down to the nursery to brush my teeth."

"Elsbeth brought your things upstairs. Not your trunk, but the rest. We'll have to order a wardrobe for your clothing."

"Oh, not like—" She stopped.

A heavy silence filled the room.

"Perhaps a smaller wardrobe," Clara said, adding awkwardly, "Less imposing."

"Auld Magnus makes some beautiful dressers. Your gowns would have to be folded rather than laid flat."

"That would be fine," Clara said. She hurriedly changed the subject. "Did you see the color of the clouds over the loch?"

He didn't look, just kept his eyes on her. "Pink, are they?"

Clara's stomach was twisting, and her knees felt

wobbly. "Yes," she said rather faintly. "At any rate, did you say that no one is in the castle?"

"I did." He threw back the white coverlet and swung his legs out of the bed, reaching for his kilt.

Clara hastily turned away. "I'll make a cup of tea," she said hurriedly, starting to move toward the door. "No, I have to brush my teeth first." She fled into the privy. A pitcher of water had been left on the windowsill, along with two toothbrushes and two bowls of tooth powder.

Caelan reached over her shoulder and picked up his toothbrush. He briskly poured a little water over it and dipped it into her pot of toothpaste powder. Clara stared at him mutely.

"Oil of peppermint?" he asked, brushing vigorously.

She nodded. Somehow this felt more intimate than lying next to him in bed, which had been unnerving enough.

He pushed over an enameled bowl. "Clove oil."

They used each other's tooth powder and then walked back into the chamber. Clara headed straight for the door.

"You're going downstairs in your chemise?" Caelan observed, following her. "And me in naught but my kilt? I like it."

"I need tea," Clara said, trotting down the steps in her bare feet. Her headache was beginning to ease, but she wanted to be out of the bedroom. The whole situation was too overwhelming.

The door to the drawing room stood open. Clara glanced in and froze. The red sofa that used to be in the study now sat under a window with two comfortable chairs to its sides. A simple but beautifully made table held her stacked books along with a couple of whisky decanters, while another group of chairs was clustered before the fireplace.

"Round about here, we set up a newlywed couple," Caelan said at her shoulder. "Everyone knew the castle was empty. Those who don't have much will have brought us some potatoes or a jar of honey." He grinned. "A jug of their whisky."

"If Mrs. Baldy offered her services as a cook, I refuse."

"Elsbeth says she can make a good porridge, and Mr. Cobbledick says her cracklings are addictive. But if you wish, we can hire a proper cook from Inverness, one who knows how to pot mackerel."

She rolled her eyes at him.

"I'm hungering for orange fritters." His expression was hungry, all right. That was a ray of happiness in the midst of Clara's anxiety: her husband might have lost the great love of his life, but he was still hungry for *her*.

Her bare toes curled thinking of it..

The ragged silk carpet had been replaced by a wool rug in a teal-green plaid. Rather than majestic and royal, it looked homey and toasty warm.

"The plaid of the McIntyre clan, as it was donated by Fiona," Caelan said. "If you care for the idea, I'd prefer a rug woven in the MacCrae tartan. Or we can order another round one from France."

"I'd love a rug in the color of your kilt. We need a bookcase or two in here, and a few small tables for lamps, but otherwise it's perfect. Do you think we need curtains?"

She glanced over her shoulder when he didn't answer.

"I do not, as my wife's chemise is translucent in the morning sunshine."

"Oh!" No wonder he'd had that smile.

Clara rushed past him and down the steps to the kitchen. A sturdy table and chairs stood in the middle of the room. The pantry door was ajar, and even from the door she could see baskets piled high with potatoes alongside tin boxes of tea, sugar, and oats.

"This was so kind of them," she breathed. "We must visit each person and say thank you, don't you think?"

"Aye, they would love that," Caelan said.

"If Elsbeth and Maisie did stay away from the castle, we have a helpful broonie. The tea kettle is hot."

"They may have crept in this morning," Caelan agreed.

"Easy to do as the front door doesn't close." Clara turned to find teacups and stopped short. New dishes were stacked in the cupboard: sturdy pieces that would stand the test of time, not gold-rimmed plates chosen for prestige.

"My goodness," she said, taking down a plate to look at it. "They gave us crockery."

What happened to Isla's French plates? She couldn't ask without saying her name aloud. Happiness seemed to be floating in the air, and she didn't want to ruin it.

"A local pottery, Jamieson's, works in salt-glazed stoneware. You'll like this: Jamieson's daughter Grisel oversees the whiteware pottery. I'd guess every family gave us a plate or two. They all use it themselves."

"They shouldn't have," Clara said, carefully replacing the plate.

"Why not? They're happy that we are marrying. They'd rather their laird wasn't living in a pigsty. Do you know what Auld Magnus said about you?"

She shook her head.

"'But to see her was to love her.'"

Clara felt herself turning pink. "That's terribly kind of him. And quite poetic."

"We love a good poem in the Highlands. By the way, Alfie has shared the story of the homicidal suit of armor with everyone his age, and they with their parents. Most of the village is waiting for the next installment. Fiona told him that he's not allowed to plague you until you've been married for two days."

Clara measured out tea leaves and poured steaming water over them. "I like Alfie."

"Aye. He could use a cousin or two. Or six. We could fill up the south tower."

"How do you like your tea?" Clara felt too shy to look at him.

Caelan sat down. "Strong and black."

After she joined him at the table, a warm foot nudged one of hers. She startled.

"Head still hurting?"

She darted a look at Caelan from under her lashes. He had stubble on his chin and hair that was going every which way, yet he was more handsome than he'd been in church. She nodded, afraid that her voice would give away her feelings.

Her lust, to label it correctly. Something along those lines. Deep affection. Embarrassingly deep affection.

"I don't want to drink whisky again. I mean it."

"You kept it down," her husband said cheerfully. He got up, went to the larder, and came back with a hunk of bread.

Clara closed her eyes. "No, thank you." She tried

digging her fingers into her temples, but it didn't seem to help with the drumbeat.

Caelan was chuckling in a very unkind manner.

"I'm rethinking the idea of marriage," Clara said weakly. "Your laughter isn't charming or gentlemanly, in case you're wondering."

"I have a solution for wha' ails ye."

"I do like it when you speak like that," Clara said. But she didn't open her eyes.

One arm went under her knees and another around her back. "We'll go out into the fresh air." He paused. "Unless you'll vomit on me."

"Probably not," Clara said tentatively.

Something touched her forehead, and Clara had the idea that he'd kissed her. She leaned her head against his shoulder. The subject of kisses was so complicated—and enticing—that she scarcely noticed as Caelan bore her out of the house.

"I luve the fact—"

"*Luve*?" she interrupted.

"Aye."

"That is so . . ." But she kept her eyes closed because it was embarrassing to feel this affectionate.

No, lustful. Aching. More so every time he spoke with that deep Scottish accent, so she concentrated on praying that she'd get her composure back. Somehow.

Meanwhile he kept walking, and unless she was mistaken, dropping kisses on her forehead and nose every few steps. Her eyes popped open when she heard the rushing of the loch. "No!" she gasped, stiffening.

"Not unless you want to," Caelan said. "But, lass, I wud like a bath." He carefully set Clara down.

"*Wud,*" she said, distracted. "Would?"

"Aye. Head still hurting?"

She nodded. It wasn't entirely true. Perhaps a little true.

"You're looking fishy around the gills," Caelan said, smiling down at her. "Swimming is an excellent cure."

"No, thank you. I'd be swept into the mouth of a great whale."

"There's a bathing hole around the bend, and I promise to fight off any hungry whales."

"I'll think about it when I see it," Clara decided.

This time, when he picked her up, she wasn't even startled; presumably, at some point she'd get used to a man who liked to open his arms and catch her against his chest. Caelan began walking on the side of the turquoise-colored loch, following a path that curved along the shore.

Clara focused on his smell because it made her feel safe. "You know what you said about feeling affection for me?"

"Hmm," Caelan said.

"Affection is everything," Clara told him, realizing the truth as she said it aloud. "Love is nothing. My mother would say she *loves* me." When he didn't respond, she opened her eyes. He had stopped walking and was gazing down at her, very sober.

"Lass." His husky voice had deepened.

"You might not believe it—sometimes I don't—but the truth is that she probably does love me. She doesn't *like* me very much, and my point is that you don't feel affection unless you like someone. I would prefer that my husband felt affection and liked me, even if he didn't love me."

That wasn't entirely true—she could hear the falsity in her own voice—but it was braver to say and less humiliating.

"Shall we have a bath now?" Caelan asked, avoiding the whole tricky subject.

He placed her gently on her feet. Sure enough, someone had quarried a small pool out of rock, around the size of four bathtubs.

"It truly is a bathing pool," Clara said, walking to the edge. The water here was paler than turquoise, with glints of gold, as if shards of light shimmered beneath the surface. "Is it deep?"

"Not even over my head. My grandfather had men chisel it from the rock whenever they had a spare moment, but there weren't many such minutes," Caelan said.

"The water looks like a shawl sewn over with gold sequins. Blue is the most expensive dye, you know." She put her bare, dusty foot into the chilly water. "I'm not sure—" But she said it while turning to face him, and the words died in her mouth.

Caelan had unbuckled his kilt and thrown it over a bush. His chest muscles ranged down in organized squares. Below that . . .

"What?" Clara yelped.

He raised an eyebrow.

"What is *that*?"

CHAPTER 26

Clara gaped at her husband, who put his hands on his hips, eyes amused. "It's called a 'cock' or a 'tool.'"

"No," she breathed.

"'Bagpipe'?" he offered. "'Trumpet'?"

"That's *not* what I saw before," Clara said, putting her own hands on her hips as well.

"Really?"

"It was small and chubby and . . . and *not* . . . *that*."

Caelan started howling with laughter, but his cock stayed big and upright.

"We were *here*," she said. "Right here. You were in the water, and that part of you was not frightening."

He was laughing in an unhinged way, joyful glee that practically echoed off the mountains behind them.

"Oh, for goodness' sake," Clara said crossly. "There's no need to make fun. How should I know that you were capable of such transformation?" She felt so filled up with irritation that she could have burst. "I wouldn't have married you!"

His laughter stopped. "Do you find me repulsive?" Something went through his eyes that she didn't care for.

She made herself look at his body. That part was standing up, away from his stomach. It was strangely appealing, the size between what she'd seen that day in the loch and the curved monstrosities on Roman vases. It looked warm and eager.

Her heart was thumping and her fingers trembling, because she would have liked to touch him, shameful as that was.

"No," she said finally. "I had thought you and I would easily fit. I was mistaken. But no, you're not revolting. Not at all." Between her legs she felt soft and uncertain. Vulnerable. She forced herself to look away, because she could stand there for an hour, gaping at him like a boy at a puppet show. "I was surprised."

Whatever that expression had been in Caelan's eyes, it disappeared. He took a step toward her. "This is what a man looks like when he desires a woman. There'll never be a time in my life when I don't get a cock-rise from holding you in my arms, Clara. I promise we'll fit."

She swallowed, aware she'd begun trembling again, and not from fear.

"Time to bathe," he said, taking another step. "May I remove your chemise? I promise not to jump on you like a ravening wolf." He laughed. "Nor a yearning wolf."

"How can we bathe without soap?" Her brain was taken up with the difference between yearning and *need*, which was so much more graceless and embarrassing than *yearning*.

Yearning sounded almost romantic. *Need* sounded like *desperation*, a humiliating word.

Caelan took a few more steps, and then his cock brushed against her chemise, against her stomach, against her body.

She looked down. "Impossible," she told him, trying to be polite as well as resolute. "I married you thinking that you were—you had—one thing, and you have another. It's not your fault. Or mine," she added. "No one tells girls anything."

"Nor men," Caelan said. "No one told me the world held an Englishwoman with wild hair, with curves like the sides of a violin, and a giggle that would melt me. I would have moved to London years ago." He smiled at her, the devil in his eyes. "Your chemise?"

She fidgeted. "I thought we'd do this in the dark under the sheets."

"We will," he said, perfectly agreeable. "I'm not consummating our marriage in the loch."

"Our bodies don't look the same," she said, blurting it out. "I'm not—" She veered away from thinking of willowy Isla. She probably pranced naked around the room, whereas Clara had curves and rolls and shaky bits.

"*Moladh an Tighearn*," Caelan said in a rumble. "'Thank the gud lord,' in Gaelic," he added. "Lass, I wouldn't want you to look like anything but yourself."

Clara gave him an uncertain smile. Was she—a woman who came to the Highlands by herself— such a frightened ninny?

The answer was yes, but she took off her chemise and tossed it toward a bush as Caelan had done with his kilt. Naturally it fell to the ground. She ignored the shrinking knot in her stomach that told her to run back down the path and all the way to London, steeling herself because if she saw a hint of disappointment in Caelan's face, it would be awful.

His eyes were wild and dark, and they weren't merely focused on her breasts. He rubbed a thumb over his mouth as his gaze jumped here and there, as if all parts of her were pleasing. Not merely her body, either. Her hair and her face.

"*Losa Crìosd,*" he breathed.

"You have to speak English," she said, her voice ragged and breathy.

"May I touch you?"

"We are married," Clara said, dimpling at him. Who would have thought that taking her clothing *off* would make her feel comfortable?

She'd always known that Prince George would grab her breasts if he had the chance, but Caelan put his hands on her cheeks and tilted her head up. "I'll never get used to your mouth," he muttered.

Their lips clung until Clara swiped his lips with her tongue, as he had taught her. After that, the kiss was deep and wet and hungry. At first his hands stayed on her face, slanting her to the angle he wanted so he could take her mouth and her breath. But slowly his hands slid into her hair.

"I don't want you to wear that cap ever again," he said, guttural and low. "You'll wear your hair loose. You're not my housekeeper. You're my wild huntress."

Even in the midst of a rush of desire, Clara found herself giggling. "Will I sail away on the midnight wind, then?"

His hands left her hair and swept down her back, pressing above her arse until she curved into his body. "Fuck, no. You'll never leave me, Clara. Do you hear?"

The rough note in his voice made her blink at him.

"Never leave me," he repeated.

"All right," Clara agreed. "I won't. I love—the castle, Caelan." Just in time, she stopped herself from blurting out that she loved *him*. "Where would I go?" She started rubbing his arms in an entirely ineffectual wish to take away that ferocity in his eyes. He must be thinking of Isla.

"You'll go nowhere without me." One of his hands pressed her close, while the other wound into the mass of her hair and gently tugged her head back so he could lick his way into her mouth again.

"I'll be damned if I consummate my marriage on a bare rock," Caelan muttered, long minutes later.

"I need a bath before . . . before," Clara said. How was she supposed to refer to the act? *Making love* wouldn't be the right phrase, but inquiring about a different label might make it sound as if she were begging for love.

She cleared her throat, her toes curling on the smooth rock. "Does one walk right into the pool?"

Caelan was frowning at her, trying to figure something out. "Yes."

She nodded and turned to the water.

She heard a choked noise and looked back over her shoulder. Caelan's eyes were on her arse. A flush had come up in his cheeks. Clara gave him a saucy smile and flipped her hair over her shoulder. It drifted down, tickling the small of her back.

"An' aren't you as lovely as the morning star," he muttered, covetous and happy at once. He shook himself and strode to the water's edge, taking her hand.

"I've never bathed like this," Clara confided, words rushing out of her mouth because she was in the grip of overwhelming new emotions. That wasn't what she truly meant. She meant: *I've never been looked at by a man. I've never been touched by a man. I've never had my clothes off before a man.*

And:

I've never felt such a potent sensation between my legs, and I'm not sure I like it.

A big hand wrapped around hers, and Caelan tugged her gently into water that splashed over her ankles.

"Trust me?"

"That's a monumental question," she said, smiling a bit.

"No," he said. Then: "Yes?"

"I trust you," she said, fast and true.

Of course one of his arms curled under her knees, and she found herself against his naked chest. While her husband walked steadily into the water, Clara inspected the plated muscles that made up the upper half of his body. "May I?" Her fingers hovered over his shoulder.

"Clara."

"Yes?"

"I'm yours. My body is yours. Whatever you want or desire or dream about, I'll do my damnedest to give it to you."

She barely caught back a nervous *Even though I'm not* . . . "Thank you!" she said instead, summoning up a smile.

"What did I say wrong?" He stopped walking, frowning. "I don't mean that I'll treat your body like a plaything, Clara. I won't disrespect you." Then he grinned. "But you can treat mine that way. I don't mind."

She liked that—but he kept going. "It's not my first time, after all."

True.

"Have you made love to many women other than . . ." She faltered, because she did want to keep to his edict and not speak Isla's name aloud.

Caelan was up to his waist in the water; he waded to one side and sat on a flat rock. Water splashed over Clara's belly, and her legs dipped into the water. It wasn't horribly cold. She'd become used to chilly baths on her trip to Scotland.

"Before my betrothal to Isla. But afterwards, no."

"You were grieving."

"I did have an offer or two."

"Let me guess," Clara said with a giggle. "Young Ross's wife before she ran off with the knife sharpener? I heard all about her last night."

Caelan scooped up some water and poured it onto her thigh. "Aye, she tripped and fell into my arms."

"But you didn't?"

"Nay."

Of course he hadn't. He was grieving.

His palm was rubbing circles on her thigh, warming her skin. "You might be thinking it was because of a broken heart, but that's not the truth of it."

Clara's heart thumped. "Oh?" she said, trying not to pry.

"I didn't want her," he said, his fingers sliding up her thigh. "She only wanted me because I was the laird."

Clara didn't believe that for a moment. Women would desire Caelan if he was a chimney sweep. "Stop touching me like that. I can't think straight."

"Aye."

Clara reached up and tugged on a lock of his hair. "Look at me."

"Always."

She could feel the lingering caress of each of his fingers, cool against her flesh. "I love that I married a writer."

"Not that *I married a laird*?"

"My mother thought the word was 'lard,'" Clara said. She put an arm around his neck and smiled. "The title wasn't something I dreamed about."

He cleared his throat. "I should get into the pool and cool down, Clara."

"Are there fish?" She peered down, but up close the water looked like melted pearls.

"Only small ones," Caelan said.

"Right," Clara said. *Adventure*, she reminded herself, sliding off his knees and yelping because the water splashed as high as her breasts. Caelan went straight under and came up shaking his hair, scattering drops through the air.

"Now what's funny?" he asked.

"You could be a shaggy dog who strayed into the Round Pond in Hyde Park."

"You could be a mermaid who strayed into my loch."

Clara took a breath and dropped under the surface. From below, the water was foggy green. Her hair floated out and then slapped back against her shoulders when she came up for a breath. Water sluiced off her breasts. They didn't feel heavy and unfashionable now; all the depictions of mermaids she'd seen gave them curves and breasts.

Her husband was standing, his chest glistening wet. The whole of him, the flow of muscle from his big arms to his chest, to the way it narrowed to his hips . . . It was all glorious.

"A ravishing mermaid," Caelan said, the English words rolling with a Gaelic intonation.

Clara smiled. "Have you soap to spare for a wayward sea creature who happened into your pool?"

"Aye." He splashed back to the flat rock and flipped open a tin box, tossing her a pale pink ball.

Clara raised it to her nose. It smelled like honey. Surely it wasn't Isla's.

"My mother used to make these from iris root and the nectar of Highland bees," Caelan said. "There's a fellow in the market who sells them. May I?"

Not Isla's. Clara felt a pulse of relief as she placed the ball in his outstretched hand. He rolled it in his palms and set it back on the rock. It didn't foam like English soap; instead, his fingers spread a light paste down the back of her neck to her shoulders and down her back. He picked up the ball again and washed the front of her neck, then paused.

"Would you prefer to wash your breasts yourself?"

Clara took a deep breath, but his eyes didn't stray from her face. "It's fine," she said awkwardly.

His hands slid down her breasts and over her nipples. She could see his breath coming quickly, but he looked at her face. She shivered . . . but the memory of the prince's fingers was gone. Not merely retreated in the face of Caelan's caress, but truly gone.

"You're grinning again," he observed.

"I don't feel the pigeon droppings any longer. I finally washed it off."

He nodded. "Excellent. Sometime you'll have to tell me what happened."

Clara shrugged. "You know it all. Does Scotland have pigeons? I haven't seen any."

"Yup." Caelan's hands were on her waist now, sliding around to her back. More soap, and his hands slid underwater, shaping the globes of her bottom. Clara squeaked and nearly jumped away.

"There's my good girl," he murmured, leaning down to kiss her. Clara almost bristled at being praised like a child for something unchildish—but his hands had slid down and around, and she gasped instead.

When he knelt in the shallow water, it put his chin just above the surface. Even while his hands were rubbing her legs, his lips slipped over her belly, stubble sparking her skin to life. Clara twisted in his caress, gasping something incoherent.

Something that sounded unnervingly like "Please."

Caelan stood up a moment later, grabbing the soap and rubbing his body.

"Don't I get to wash you?" Clara asked.

"Next time. Let's go back to the castle."

"I have to wash my hair."

"Later."

Clara bit her lip.

"Do you wash your hair every day?"

"Yes."

"You *are* a lady," he groaned.

Keen desire receded from his eyes, thankfully, because it was making Clara anxious. She didn't want to fail at making love. But she had no idea what to do.

In bed, that is. With him.

His soapy hands began working over her scalp; it felt so wonderful that she gasped and leaned against him. "I can't work through your hair," he said a while later. "Was it tangled by the water?"

"It got tangled on the journey," Clara confessed. "Elsbeth has been combing through a portion every day, but I'm thinking of cutting it off."

"No," Caelan said firmly.

He splashed back to the bank and the tin box, pulling out a small bottle.

"What's that?" Clara asked.

"An oil made from cloudberries. Close your eyes in case it drips."

His hands stroked over her scalp—and then hit the tangles. On the trip to Scotland, Clara had soaped, rinsed, and hoped for the best, but now Caelan began effortlessly teasing the strands free.

Five minutes later he was halfway down her back, but Clara was shivering. "Perhaps we could finish later?"

"Sorry," he said, startled. In one smooth gesture, he lifted her up onto the bank and jumped after. "What if we dry in the sun?" He moved behind her.

"Do you think anyone from the household will come looking for us? Perhaps I should put on my chemise."

"No one will come here unless I give permission."

She nodded, hoping that was the case. "What do you do when you're not writing?"

"Manage the crofters, the whisky, fishing," he said absent-mindedly. "Franchise court once a month."

She had the feeling he did far more, but he interrupted the thought by stroking his finger down a long, untangled strand of her hair. "You did it!" she cried, looking over her shoulder.

"Not all of it yet." He dropped a kiss on her lips.

It took another half hour or even more, but finally Clara's hair was sleek and tangle-free. "Thank you!" She ran her fingers through her hair. It didn't feel too oily. "I love this scent. I'll let it dry like this. Could we take the bottle back to the castle with us?"

She lifted her arms and ran her hands back from her forehead. Her hair was already drying, turning to sleek waves.

"Of course," Caelan said, sounding strangled.

Clara stood up, grabbed her chemise, and put it on. "Why on earth did you have oil in that box, anyway?" She glanced at his waist. "Do you *truly* call that your bagpipes?"

"Don't dimple at me, lass," Caelan said. "It might be the straw that breaks my self-control. I don't call it 'bagpipes,' no. I can't say I talk about it much. 'Cock,' I suppose."

"Very Shakespearean," Clara said, giggling. "I don't suppose you swear 'by cock'?"

"We've no need for Englishmen to tell us our body parts," Caelan said. "Our own Robert Burns wrote a whole song encouraging Johnnie to 'cock up your beaver.'"

Clara frowned.

"There's some that think Robbie was talking about furry hats," Caelan said. "But we in the Highlands know where a cock likes to go."

Despite herself, Clara glanced down at her legs. "You're talking about my cunny, I take it."

"I am. I had the oil here because I use it to satisfy myself," he said bluntly.

She opened her mouth and closed it again.

"Want to see?"

CHAPTER 27

*C*aelan's blood was pounding through his body with an urgency he'd never experienced before.

Clara's eyes were huge, but she nodded. Her hair was dampening her chemise, making it cling to her body. She looked like the embodiment of his dreams.

"I'd be in this state anyway, but you smell like *me*. Like me when I'm coming in the open air."

She turned pink. "I don't understand. Why don't you touch yourself in privacy, in your own bed?"

"As you do?" He held his breath.

She made a strangled sound in her throat. "You shouldn't ask me that!"

"I shared a bed with my wife."

If he hadn't had his eyes on her face, he wouldn't have seen the wince that went through her whole body. They were man and wife, and at some point they had to talk about his first marriage, about Isla, for all he hated the idea.

"When I was widowed, I brought in that old bed and moved to the study. Mrs. Baldy would bring me meals there. Weeks passed when I left the room only to go fishing or to the kirk. I felt most alive here, in the water."

Her eyes filled with tears. "That's heartbreaking, Caelan. I'm so, so sorry. I wish that Isla hadn't—"

Without thinking, he lifted his hand. "Don't be."

"I'm sorry," she said with a gasp. "I didn't mean to say her name."

"What?" He shook his head. "I don't want to discuss her now, not with you and me here, and you so damn beautiful, and me—well, I'm so damned naked."

"You are very naked," Clara agreed.

Thankfully, she didn't sound destroyed. His wife was a resilient woman, with all the best qualities of a Scotswoman. She must have been tough to have survived her mother and that bloody prince.

"That's why I don't allow the household to wander over here without notice. After fishing, I always come here for a bath."

"And to practice your bagpipes!"

He jerked his head up, startled. Clara was giggling madly.

"I love that sound, lass. Did anyone ever tell you that your moods change so quickly that they could give a man whiplash?"

"No one pays attention to my moods," she said blithely and without a hint of self-pity. "Last night when I was drunk, I must have sounded like a proper ninny."

"You didn't," he told her. "A whole pub full of men fell in love with you and your giggles."

"Pooh," she said, shrugging it off as a fib and smiling at him, dimples in play.

His cock responded the way a lad's might at a sketch of a breast. Happiness, *her* happiness, affected him like an aphrodisiac.

"Weren't you planning to show me something?" she asked, her eyes mischievous.

Caelan upended the bottle into his palm and stroked down his cock. Even that one stroke brought him to the edge of coming. He clenched his teeth, watching as her curious eyes ranged over his body and froze on the broad head of his cock above the clutch of his hand. She didn't look distressed or disgusted, although the mushroom top was red with blood, and likely his face was too.

"I'm about to make a mess," he said, the words strangled in the back of his throat.

To his infinite shock, she came toward him. "May I?"

His hand fell away before she finished the sentence. Her hand wrapped around him and then his heart caught as disappointment filled her face.

"I don't think this will work between us," she said.

Nausea gripped him, his heart pounded in his ears with a sickening beat. "It's not as bad as it looks."

"Bad?" She looked startled. "What's bad about it?" She added another hand below the first. "You're too big, and that's a fact. When I saw you fishing, I thought that you and I were perfectly suited." Her cheeks were rosy. "I shouldn't have been thinking that. It wasn't ladylike or polite, because you didn't know I was there."

Relief felt like a benediction. He dragged heated air into his lungs before he fell into a faint. "You're not disgusted?"

"Did I look disgusted?" She tightened her hand. Caelan bit back a groan. He would come. Soon.

"No," he rasped. "Maybe?"

"If I wasn't a small person, I'd be—"

"Do that again," he groaned, unable to stop himself.

She did. He caught an arm around her and took her lips in one of the deepest kisses of his life. His other hand closed around hers, and he began coming in waves such as he'd never experienced before, his cock trapped between their bodies, against her softness, pulsing through her palm.

He couldn't speak afterward for gasping; the orgasm turned him inside out. He thought he was finished, but her hand shifted, and one last spurt burned its way up his cock.

"Bluidy hell," he whispered a moment later.

Rather than springing away from the mess he'd made, she leaned against him. They stayed like that, no sound but a lark singing far up in the blue sky. "Clara," he said finally.

Her face tilted up to his, and what he saw there shocked him to the core. Her cheeks were flushed, her lips parted, eyes glossy. When he looked down between their bodies, her hands had slipped away from him, and one was curled tightly between her legs, over her chemise.

He lost himself for a moment, blinded with relief, his whole body simmering with joy. "Darling," he said low and soft, like a man trying to lure a wild creature. "Will you let me help you, please? You're so fucking beautiful. You ruined me, and I can't leave you wanting. I can't."

"You said not on a rock," she whispered.

"There's moss," he managed. He pulled off her chemise, wet with his come, and threw it to the side, snatching his kilt. Then he drew her into the woods until he could toss the kilt down on the moss and set her down as carefully as an egg.

"What are you doing?" she asked.

"This."

He fell on his knees before her and pushed open her legs. Clara squeaked and reached down to cover herself.

"No." He took her hand and nipped her palm. "You're so beautiful, glistening in the sunlight, wanting me."

She made a stifled noise. When he glanced up, she had her hands over her face, as if she were pretending to be somewhere else.

Caelan settled down on his stomach, crushing his cock, which had risen straight up as if that orgasm never happened. First he looked at Clara's pink fluted beauty, and then he leaned in, delicately running his tongue up the heart of her.

She gasped, and her hands fell off her face. She came up on her elbows. "Caelan," she said hoarsely. "Are you sure we should be doing this? Is it allowed?"

"Every good Scotsman knows the art," Caelan told her. "Can't say about the British. If they have rules, we don't bother with them."

"I'm not sure," Clara whispered.

"I'll stop if you don't like it," Caelan said, as soothing as he could be. He bent his neck, and what he did next must have pleased her, because she sank back and covered her eyes again.

In a matter of minutes, Clara's hips were twisting, and she had her hands over her mouth instead of her eyes. When he added a finger and then two, cursing silently at how small she was, she flung her arms over her head. "This is bliss," she said hoarsely. "Come here!"

"Nay, we canna do that, lass. Not in the out-of-doors, your first time."

"*Aye*, and I say we will," his little wife ordered, her eyes wild. "I don't know how to put this politely, Caelan. I might shock you to the bone, but come *here*."

No man had ever been as lucky as he. She was so beautiful, her hair curling around her like a mermaid, covering her breasts.

"Don't you want to?" she cried.

"Jesus, take you, my new wife, on my kilt? On my land?"

She stared at him. "Well, then?"

"It's your first time, you, a delicate lady."

"I'm not feeling delicate, more like empty, wanting, lustful. Not ladylike things."

He came up on his knees and paused to lavish attention on her breasts until he had her crying out again. It wrecked him to feel her open for his cock, to nudge inside, sink farther.

"Bluidy hell," he groaned, about halfway. "I don't know if I can do it."

"You're too big," Clara whispered. "I knew it."

"Does it hurt?"

"No! It's merely impossible." She arched, wiggling her hips. "Frankly, it will never work—"

It did work.

His cock slid home. She abruptly stopped talking.

"Lass," he said hoarsely. "Clara. Tell me it's possible."

"Well."

He braced himself over her with his elbows in the moss. "We could go back to the castle and go to bed. Or try again tomorrow."

Who would have thought her green eyes could darken to the color of fir trees? Become ferocious? "Caelan."

"Aye?"

"If this is all there is to it, you'll need to leave me to a bout of grieving. If there's more, get going and do more, because I thought there was more." She frowned, taking one arm off his neck and threading it between their bodies. "I can help."

Her head fell back, her face slackening with bliss as her fingers drifted over the place where they joined. "Who would have thought it'd feel so good to have you inside?"

Joy was not an elusive emotion in Caelan's life. He'd been lucky in small things: the joy of catching a fish, throwing his nephew into the air, writing a sentence he liked.

But this?

Delight burned down his spine. He came up on his knees, sank even deeper, put his hands on her hips and tilted Clara's hips up.

"Oh, my," she breathed.

He grinned and pumped into her.

"Oh, my."

It took some adjusting to find the perfect angle, the one that made her start whimpering, broken words bursting from her lips, her hips arching frantically to meet his.

He asked her twice if it hurt before she threatened to swat him. It felt awkward when he balanced on one elbow and bent his head, but when his mouth closed over her nipple, and she screamed?

Glory.

Sometime later, he was braced on his elbows so that he could kiss her, and she had wound her legs around his hips. Short legs, the right length. Everything about her was right.

Clara's hands were on his bottom, her eyes squeezed shut, sweaty cheeks, luscious hair everywhere, the two of them so wet that obscene noises echoed into the quiet woods . . . Somehow he hung on until she sucked in a breath and shrieked like a teakettle. He might have to tell the household to stay in the stables, not just away from the loch.

Her cunny tightened around him and he knew he was stretching her, but she had promised it didn't hurt, and elation poured from his loins in a burning flood.

When he could see again, and think again, he found his wife giggling. He was so deep inside her that he could *feel* her laughter. He'd only just come, but his cock stiffened.

"Stop," he whispered, kissing her.

"Stop what?" she asked a while later.

He was hard again, still inside her to the hilt. He didn't have the words. Any words.

Clara looked at his face and broke into a proper belly laugh that sent sensation down his cock.

"Oh, heaven above," he rasped, and started pumping because he literally couldn't do anything else. He felt between them, his fingers sliding in the warm mess they'd made together until he brushed her the right way.

Her laughter died, and her legs came up. He caught her right knee and pushed it back a bit. Clara's eyes opened wider. She started talking—of course she was talking. He wanted to listen. He *would* listen next time.

But this time, it was all he could do to move, keep moving, keep going, until thankfully she started pulsing around his cock, and he let go of his control. Again and again and again until his body emptied out and he was lying on her, barely propping himself up so she could breathe.

Trying to catch his own breath, shaking.

"Clara." He meant to say things with her name that he couldn't put into words.

"It's all very untidy." She put a hand between their legs and brought it up, glossy and wet, and then—dancing eyes on his face—rubbed her fingers against her breast.

He groaned. "You were the Honorable Miss Clara Vetry, pursued by royalty. You are a lady. You rubbed my . . . *me* into your breast. That was not ladylike."

"I feel shameless," she told him. "Also, as if I'd like another bath."

He was filled with wild gratitude, but words failed him still. He carried her back into the pool, half expecting the water to hiss and boil. Instead their sweat washed away, and he felt like a man newborn.

The luckiest man in the whole damn world.

The only man with a mermaid who rubbed soap all over him, even the inelegant parts, her curious fingers leaving little trails of fire.

When they emerged from the loch again, he wound his kilt around her waist rather than his.

"I can't walk into the castle like this!" Clara cried, her eyes large as she looked down at her breasts.

"You are ravishingly bare-breasted like an Amazon warrior. And you're wearing my kilt." He brushed back a thick curl of hair so he could see her nipples. "When I'm on my deathbed, I'll be thinking of you at this very moment."

To his shock, her eyes blurred with tears, and she stepped closer, throwing her arms around his neck. "I know you're living with fear of mortality," she said earnestly. "I promise I'm not planning to die for years and years, and you won't either."

Once again, he—a man writing two books—couldn't find words to express what he felt, not with his wee wife in his arms, her breasts against his chest, his kilt around her hips. Clara came up on her toes and dotted his jawline with kisses until he tucked his chin down so he could take her mouth.

They stopped kissing when she said "Tea" against his lips.

"You have a proper addiction to the stuff," he whispered, grinning. "I'll have to send someone to the tea auction in Glasgow."

"I can do without. I'm afraid it's very expensive."

"I told you before that I've a great deal of money. All that whisky you were tasting last night sells like hotcakes, but we charge a great deal more than we could make for bread. Londoners are perishingly fond of the brew, and they'll pay a king's ransom for it."

"You shall have whisky, and I shall have tea," she said, twinkling at him.

He tapped her nose and then kissed it. "We smuggle the whisky out of the Highlands, because the Scots parliament in its infinite wisdom decided to tax the brew, and I've no wish to give them my proceeds. I send one wagon with a few barrels down to Edinburgh to sell on to the magistrates, which means CaerLaven brewers haven't had any problems with enforcement."

"I have a large dowry," Clara said shyly.

Caelan had the vague feeling that fine London gentlemen might think a lady should say nothing of money, but he was of the opinion that more was always welcome. "Excellent. We'll need it to buy kilts for our fourteen children, so they don't wander around naked like their parents."

"We should go back home," Clara said, stepping away and winding her arms around her bosom, as if it were a crime for birds to glimpse her nipples.

"I'll bring toweling next time," he promised.

"I don't think we have any," Clara said. "Mrs. Gillan said that Isl—her daughter's linens were her pride and joy, but I couldn't help noticing that the only sheets in the house are fit for rags."

"I suspect they went out the back door with the bacon," he said. "The Baldy family is a terrible one for taking a *pochle* here or there, a *pochle* being a small thing taken without permission. I dinnae care. I'm a heedless man, and if I had enough books, paper, and ink, I reckon I'd be happy in prison, except that I couldn't fish."

Clara's eyes were fixed on his face, as if she could see to the heart of him. If she *had* that ability, she'd see that he would break out of any prison in the land to get home to his wife. The wife wearing his kilt.

"You truly didn't notice that you were eating off battered tin rather than fine china?" she asked, knitting her brow.

"I'm a rough sort of man," he said apologetically. "A brute, at the heart. Isla did her best to shape me into something better, but it didn't take. 'Twas a terrible frustration to her."

She opened her mouth as if to say something, but thought better of it, slipping her hand in his, which meant he got to see her breasts again.

"If I'm too much of a beast, tell me," he said. "On

my own, I'm happy standing about with my parts hanging down."

Clara being Clara, she laughed. "Your parts aren't hanging down."

"They never will, not when you're standing there in the altogether, but for my kilt," he said. "Smelling like the loch, sunshine, cloudberries. *You*."

To his utter delight, she reached out and wrapped her fingers around one of his balls. He squeezed her other hand because it was that or fall to his knees as her delicate hand cupped him below.

"They're in a different position than . . . than when I first saw you in the loch."

"You don't mind?"

She made a funny little snorting noise. When he bent to look into her eyes, they were foggy and hungry, and her fingers were caressing his balls, which were aching as they never had before. As if they might implode from lust.

"How can you ask that?" she said, a bit scolding, as if he were the craziest man on the island.

Clara was sore. She had to be sore because she was so small, and it had been her first time, first two times. "Tea?"

She blinked and nodded. "Tea." Her hand went away, and he barely stopped himself from begging for more.

"Later," Clara said, as if she knew exactly what he was thinking. She was flushed, like a woman who was having a filthy daydream about her husband. And she threw him a mischievous look that promised all the things she knew nothing about yet. All the things he'd ever dreamed of. The things willing women did with men.

Caelan couldn't help thinking that his wife was a miracle from God himself, with his kilt slipping down her hips, her creamy skin glowing, her eyes soft with desire.

It was one of the best moments of his life and no mistake.

CHAPTER 28

As they walked back to the castle, Clara's legs felt wobbly as a newborn calf's. Her hand was tucked into Caelan's. Obviously if she stumbled and fell, he would catch her in his arms before she hit the ground.

He'd probably always pick her up if she fell.

It was such a new thought that she put it away to think about later.

The castle was as empty as when they'd left it. "The staff didn't return," she said, marveling at the empty kitchen, filled only with specks of dust floating through rays of sunlight. Her mother's house had bustled from dawn to dusk, brimming with people scouring, polishing, and cooking.

"You told them to stay away," Caelan reminded her. "Would you like me to ring for the household? Cobbledick's our butler, and his postillion is now our footman. We have Maisie and Elsbeth and a maid from Fiona's household. What other staff would you like?" He paused. "We used to have four footmen and a boy whose only task was to run back and forth from here to the stables."

"I'm not sure what Mr. Cobbledick will do all day, let alone four footmen. Anyone can come in the front door, since I still haven't seen it closed. You don't have any silver for him to polish, which is what my mother's butler did most of the day."

"Actually, there's a load of silver locked in a trunk. Mrs. Baldy would never touch something so expensive."

"It's such a small castle," she said apologetically.

"Perhaps we could go upstairs to the sitting room and read for a while before the household returns? I'm uncomfortable being in a kitchen without a gown."

"Only that I'm properly ravenous."

"The basket has made a reappearance." Clara walked over to the sideboard and opened it. "Bread, cheese, a jar of water. Some tarts."

"Excellent." Caelan grabbed it. "Let's go."

Clara followed her naked husband up the stairs, her eyes fixed on his arse. It was a very, very fine bottom, not that she had never given thought before to rear ends. Now she had definite opinions, and they all involved muscled globes that flexed with every step.

"Will you teach me to make flies today?" she asked his back.

"Yes. We'll go out to the loch tomorrow at sunrise—" He stopped and turned around. "Ladies aren't up at that hour. Elsbeth will serve you breakfast on a tray."

He kept climbing while Clara enjoyed the way his arse moved and thought about sunrise. Maybe she should pretend to be ladylike, so that he wouldn't guess she was greedy to spend time with him.

She couldn't bear to be pitied for the sad condition of being madly in love with him. The very idea sent a bolt of humiliation through her, reminding her of the way polite society had pitied her in London. The men who asked her for dances out of pity. The ladies who introduced their widowed and elderly second cousins once removed.

"Actually, I wake up early," she said casually. "My mother didn't believe in unmarried ladies being served meals in their beds."

He glanced at her. "So I understand, but now you're married."

"I get out of bed when I wake up." Compelled by honesty, she added, "Some days I go to bed for a nap after lunch and then read all afternoon."

He made a deep, happy sound in his throat as he rounded the curve leading to the nursery landing.

"I also occasionally claim to have a headache and eat my supper off a tray in bed," she confessed. "Lady Vetry did not approve, as she thought I was avoiding society, but in reality, I merely wanted to read."

"You refer to your mother as Lady Vetry?" He walked into the nursery, empty but for her trunk. He threw it open. "Where are your chemises?"

"My mother models herself on Queen Elizabeth," Clara said.

He cleared his throat. "My late wife modeled herself on Marie Antoinette."

Clara did not want to talk about Isla. "The top shelf comes out," she explained, showing him. He put it to the side, revealing a pile of gowns and below them, floaty pieces of light cotton trimmed with lace and embroidery.

He picked up the top one and shook it out before he yanked it over her head.

"Do you want to see my reticules?" She removed the chemises and put them to the side, uncovering her cat reticule. "This is my favorite."

It was shaped like a circle on which she had embroidered cat features, with shiny beads for the eyes. "The whiskers were bent by travel," she explained, straightening them.

Caelan took it from her and turned it in his

hands. "It's as clever and darling as you are," he said, obviously meaning it.

Clara beamed at him. "I slapped Prince George with a mouse, and Lord Boden with a rabbit."

"Excellent," Caelan said, his voice edging into darkness.

"I protected myself," she reminded him.

His mouth eased in a rueful quirk. "I shall enjoy being married to a warrior." He picked up his kilt and slung it over his shoulder. "Do you mind if I don't dress?"

"I don't mind," Clara said, trying to stop herself from ogling him.

"I could put on a pair of smalls."

"If there's someone else in the castle, you must wear your kilt," Clara said. She looked down at herself. "If anyone but you saw me in this chemise, I'd die of humiliation." This chemise was tight across her breasts.

His face grew instantly dark. "*No one* will see you like that. I'd have to kill him."

"What about all those servants you were talking about?" Clara inquired, heading down to the study as he picked up the basket.

"They'll have to stay out of this tower unless we invite them in," Caelan stated. "What would you think of that? The north tower for us, for the family. Perhaps the south tower, as well."

"Someone has to wash the floors and change the sheets," Clara said practically. "You and I aren't the best at it, and I've no wish to improve my skills in that area."

"All right, they can come in for an hour or so in the morning, but no more."

"What about my bath?"

"I'll be doing that for you," Caelan said instantly.

"My hair?" Clara asked skeptically, walking into the sitting room.

"Every day." He dropped the basket next to the sofa and drew her down to sit beside him. "No one will see your hair like this, either. All tangled up from my hands and looking as if you'd been tupped on your back in the woods."

Clara's stomach clenched into a happy knot, because he had liked it. That. With her. She wasn't always confident, but she wasn't one to overlook an obvious truth, either. They'd have a good marriage, because surely that was good enough.

They ate bread and cheese, and drank water from a well that Caelan said had been sunk into the rock by his great-great-grandfather. "It's one of the secrets of my whisky," he told her. "Don't go telling that to anyone." She laughed at his mock ferocious command and settled down to read with her head against his shoulder.

Caelan picked up a book about fly-fishing, and they read in silence until Clara exclaimed at the villain's perfidy.

"He should be shot," Caelan agreed once she explained it.

"Probably the squire will kill him," she said. "It would be more interesting if the heroine snatched his revolver and took the man's life herself."

"Bloodthirsty, aren't you?" Caelan asked.

Clara beamed, because he looked so affectionate that her heart was bounding all over the place.

A while later, he let out a low curse, which led to him explaining that Ferguson—an idiot who knew nothing about the ways of fish—had been mad enough to put clear-cut foolery down in black and white, which led to Caelan fetching his horse-hair and silken ties and showing Clara how to make a fly.

"You want it to float on the surface?" she asked, tucking and tying the horsehair the way he showed her.

"Your fingers are incredibly nimble," he said. "I'll be damned if that isn't the neatest fly I've ever seen."

"I could do better," Clara said, fluffing up the horsehair "wings." She ran back up to her trunk and fetched down her least favorite reticule: the mouse that slapped Prince George, missing a few whiskers after the last carriage ride with her mother.

"I like this mouse," Caelan said, turning the bag over.

Clara briskly extracted a whisker. "I can use one of these."

"What for?"

She plucked off a bead and wired it to the fly, holding it up. "This will glint in the sun."

"It's beautiful, but it won't float," Caelan said. "I love that you made it for me, though."

He started kissing her, and it wasn't until some-time later that she managed to point out that be-ing light, it might float just *under* the surface of the water. "You're going to fish with mine, and then yours, remember? I can't help you write about whisky, but I can make you a better fly."

He burst out laughing. "I love your confidence, lass. You don't want to try out your own fly?"

"I don't wish to be washed down to Inverness."

"I'd never let you go," Caelan said casually.

The words felt so good—especially because of the memory of that carriage ride with Lady Vetry, which had clarified how easily her mother had dismissed her from her life.

"What are you thinking about?" Caelan asked.

She curled up her legs and settled her back against his stomach. "Nothing."

Ferguson's discourse on brown trout hit the floor as his arms went around her. "Lass. Tell me."

"Lady Vetry—my mother—said that she would decide whether or not to acknowledge me in the future based on who I marry," she said finally.

His chin came down on the top of her head. "Will I pass, do you think?"

"Well, you are a *lard*," she said teasingly. But then she added, "This sounds awful, but I think I don't wish to approach her. What if she decided our children were ungainly and eccentric? What if my daughters grow up to have my figure rather than hers?"

"We shall rejoice, as will young Scottish males," Caelan said, holding her very tightly. "Did I tell you that I want to fill the whole south tower with children? Three per floor."

"Please tell me that the servants are allowed to freely range in that tower," Clara said. "From what the villagers told me about you as a boy, the children will create mayhem. What if one takes after Alfie and invites a chicken to live with them?"

"I was a mad scamp. Perhaps a nanny and a governess could share one floor," Caelan allowed.

"What were your parents like?" Clara asked.

"To my mind, my father was overly fond of hitting me and sometimes even Fiona."

"Oh, Caelan." She picked his hand up off her stomach and kissed his palm.

"The man couldn't stop himself. He had a terrible temper."

"It's lucky for him that he's not alive, or I'd be tempted to topple him into the loch," Clara said.

He burst out laughing, and they went back to their books.

At some point, his arm slackened, and Clara looked up to find that Caelan's brow had unknit in sleep.

She couldn't help wishing with all her heart that he'd never had a dark moment at the hands of his father—or fate. It was an absurd thought that confirmed how desperately she had fallen in love with her husband.

Who wouldn't? Mrs. Gillan had described Isla as adoring Caelan from the time she was a young girl. Clara sent a quick prayer up to her, an apology with a dusting of sorrow, because the poor woman must have hated leaving her husband.

If only Clara could figure out how to suppress these unruly feelings, she'd be fine. Affection and desire were the emotions offered, and they were *amazing*.

Dismissing the thought, she turned to her side, because she had an uneasy feeling that the wetness between her thighs might mark the sofa. She woke up an hour later to find the crisis imminent. She leapt from the sofa, waking Caelan. He stretched and came to his feet slowly, smiling.

"If you'll excuse me, I'll go upstairs to the privy." She felt ferociously embarrassed, but marriage must often be embarrassing. After all, in a week or so she'd have her courses, and he'd have to be told, wouldn't he?

Unless she was already pregnant. Surely not.

"I could take a piss myself," he said, and flinched. "That was vulgar, and I apologize for it."

"It's not that," Clara blurted out—and bit her lip, wanting to throw herself out the window. "I need to wash," she said, because he looked puzzled.

"We just had a bath, lass." His jaw tightened. "Is it something to do with that feckless royal—"

"No!" she said quickly. "I'm a bit . . ." She waved her hand around her middle. "I'll go downstairs for a pitcher of water."

To her surprise, he backed her up against the stone wall, his eyes glinting. Before she knew what he was thinking, a big hand yanked up her chemise and cupped her below. "I made a mess of you, didn't I, lass? It's my fault that there's seed in your pretty little cunny."

His fingers slid through her folds, and it was a good thing the wall was behind her, because Clara gasped and melted against the stone. Caelan started kissing her, fierce and hungry, as if he couldn't stop himself. All the time his fingers were stroking her, until her knees became so weak that he was supporting her with a hand under her bum.

"You like this, don't you?" he growled. "You're wet and hot, and I can feel your hips jerking when I touch you."

"Yes," she breathed, twisting. "Oh, Caelan, you're making me—"

"You're getting wetter, lass, so I'm making things worse. But maybe you like it so much that you don't mind, eh?"

Clara was breathless, her whole body concentrating on his fingers. "No, I don't mind," she whispered, the words quavering into the open air. And then, with a groan, "This is so embarrassing."

Caelan didn't give a damn, that was clear. "You'd let me pull you up and take you against the wall," he crooned. "You'd beg me for it, wouldn't you?"

"That's what you meant!" she burst out. "You said that before, and I didn't—"

So he showed her, catching her up in one arm and rubbing against her until there was nothing for it but his sliding inside. She winced, and he stopped, apologizing, beginning to pull back, except she gave him a fierce "Don't move."

They stayed still for a while, his body pinning hers against the wall, Caelan whispering things against her lips about how she was destroying him. Offering to stop, and Clara repeating, "No, don't move."

Staying together until the pain drifted away, leaving her legs restless. She curled them around his hips, arching her back and nudging him.

Caelan didn't say anything, just looked into her eyes and began gently easing back and forth, until Clara lost all her embarrassment and cried, "We can't keep doing this."

He froze, looking stricken.

"I need something more," she told him. "Harder, maybe."

"Oh, God, you're telling me what you want," he groaned. "So slick and wanting, and now you're cross at me because I'm not satisfying you."

"I certainly am not!" Clara said, humiliated again.

"Yes, you are. Because I'm your husband, and it's

my job to give you everything you want." Clara didn't pay much attention, because he tilted her body and thrust home.

"*That*," she gasped.

"I'll give it to you. Remember that word you wanted me to define?"

Clara had no idea how he could be thinking of vocabulary at a time like this, but she managed to shake her head.

"You want me to *fuck* you," he crooned, low and sweet. "That's what I'm doing, Clara. Taking you against the wall, fucking you the way you want, because you *do* want it, don't you? You want me to give it to you."

In the back of her mind, Clara thought his voice was even more intense than it had been when they made love earlier, by the loch. But the thought slipped away because he nipped her lip and thrust again.

"Ah," she gasped. "Yes. Please."

He gave it to her, over and over and over, making her cry every time he bottomed out, as flame slowly built in her spine. In this position, Clara wasn't able to move. He had tucked his arms under her knees and was holding her legs so wide, in such a lewd position, that she found herself pretending she wasn't in the room, doing this incredibly embarrassing thing in the broad daylight.

Except she *was* in the room.

What's more, Caelan's face was lit with hunger and joy and affection, and that was the best expression she'd ever seen on his face. On anyone's face.

"You're going to come, aren't you?" he demanded hoarsely. "Not by touching yourself, and because

I'm holding up your legs, I can't touch you, either. You're greedy to come around my cock."

Clara couldn't answer. In fact, she was vaguely surprised that he had so much to say, because it felt as if air was sobbing through her lungs, and she couldn't put words together. She was aching now, everything tense and waiting for pleasure to start rolling from her toes.

Finally it began. "Oh!" she cried, her fingers digging into his shoulders. And then, very quietly, "That's lovely. *Please.*"

"Begging me," he groaned. Then they were both coming, because she could feel him pulsing inside her, his lips pressed against her forehead, his hips moving convulsively.

A while later, he put her on the couch, a whole stream of Gaelic coming from his lips. He was shaking a bit and kept kissing her face in an erratic way, as if he couldn't stop himself. Clara figured whatever he was saying must have been positive.

He'd liked it, that was clear. He might not feel the same way about her that he had about Isla, but he liked that with her, Clara. Doing that.

Then he fetched a pitcher of water and washed her gently, finally pulling a clean chemise over her head.

"Sofa or bedroom?" he asked.

"I'd like to go to bed," she confessed. "If you don't need help with your papers."

Caelan picked her up as if he existed for that reason alone and strode up the steps. "Tomorrow, perhaps. I'll put you in bed, and then I'll ring for the staff." He headed upstairs.

"Elsbeth is very young," Clara said, not wanting

her maid to guess that consummating her marriage had worn her out. She could feel her whisky headache creeping back.

"I'll bring you tea later," he said. "First order of the day is setting up the stove on the roof for your bath. I could bring you toast."

"I may never eat again," Clara said, her nausea returning at the thought of bread.

All afternoon she drowsed amidst a cloud of white sheets and pillows, dreamily listening to voices echoing around the castle. Gaelic curses heralded a stove going up to the battlements, followed by a tin basin that clanked against the stone walls, then pipes that did the same.

She felt weightless, as if she were floating on a warm ocean. Was it so exhausting to make love? Or was it the whisky? Or the newness, the strangeness of it all? Caelan's voice wove among the others, laughing as he ordered the men about. She had the feeling they were teasing him and was doubly glad to be hidden in her room.

Her headache tightened around her forehead, and with it came a terrible lethargy and a strain of melancholy. She was married to a man she liked and admired—and with whom she was madly in love. Many people in London society would say that it was more than she, Clara Vetry, could have hoped for.

"I brought up a gown. We've installed the heating apparatus on the roof. Next we need to pipe the privy—excuse me, the water closet—so you'll have to move to the study," Caelan announced, coming through the door with some clothing over his arm.

Clara blinked awake. "Of course," she said,

swinging her legs off the side of the bed. "I've been a dreadful slug-a-bed, lying about while everyone is working."

He laughed. "They're still talking about your prowess with whisky. I have a pot of steaming tea waiting for you in the study because the maids are scrubbing the drawing room."

"Perhaps," Clara said tentatively, "we might call it the sitting room, as your mother did?" An expression shot across his face too quickly to interpret, and besides, her eyes were tired. "No drawing room has a kilted rug," she added, trying to clarify that her suggestion had nothing to do with Isla's ambitions for the castle.

"Shall I carry you downstairs?"

"No," she said hastily.

He held out her corset upside down, but Clara took one look and knew with a deep certainty that lacing it up would make her vomit. Instead she pulled the gown over her head and poked at her chemise until it wasn't visible under the neckline. She pushed her hair behind her shoulders, resisted the inclination to slap her own forehead in hopes the ache would go away, and followed Caelan down the steps to the study.

He poured her a cup of tea and walked out again. She stared balefully at the wooden door. What right had he to be so cheerful? He'd easily drunk three times as much whisky as she had. The very thought made her gorge rise.

People trotted up and down the steps outside the door while Clara forced herself to keep reading about Felicity's woeful adventures. The girl was a terrible crier. This or that person would be mean to her, and she would dissolve into tears, coming home "like a nesting bird" to the squire's "broad trunk."

Clara fell asleep again thinking about whether Caelan's legs qualified him for treehood, just as his land made him a laird.

CHAPTER 29

*I*n the following few days, Clara learned several important things, to wit:

First and foremost, her husband wanted to make love all the time. He called it that other, rougher word that sent sparks down her legs every time he muttered it in her ear and led her into the bedroom.

Second, their household staff was perfectly happy to be banished to the stable area. Elsbeth showed every sign of becoming a formidable housekeeper. Mr. Cobbledick had taken on the role of butler with gusto. One of his first actions was to hire a second scullery maid and a boot boy to support his daughter as the south tower was emptied and scrubbed.

And third . . .

And third, she was deliriously in love. She choked back "I love you" once on the first day of their marriage, twice on the second, thrice on the third. It was absurd.

This morning she'd removed herself from her husband's company in order to stifle the truth from leaping out of her mouth unbidden. Having carried several reticules down to the courtyard, she was seated under the tree, apple blossoms drifting around her slippers as she turned horsehair, silk thread, thin wire, and beads into flies—some bigger, some smaller.

She looked up when Cobbledick—no longer *Mr.* Cobbledick, except to the household—entered the courtyard. "Lady McIntyre and Master Alfie." As butler, his mustache not only curled, but ended in sharp points, and he wore a coat with shiny buttons.

Alfie ran out of the kitchen, Wilhelmina bouncing at his hip, feathers bursting out of her bag. "Where's Thursday? And the other puppies?" he shrieked.

"They've moved out to the stables," Clara said, standing up and kissing him on the forehead. "Perhaps you might set Wilhelmina down, since they aren't here?"

"That's a good idea," Alfie said, unceremoniously yanking his chicken out and putting her on the ground.

"Look whose carriage followed ours," Fiona said, strolling into the courtyard followed by Mrs. Gillan.

"Good morning, Mrs. Gillan, Fiona," Clara said, curtsying. "Cobbledick, will you please fetch us tea and scones?"

Fiona ignored the curtsy and gave her a hug. "These are adorable," she said, sitting down at the table and picking up a reticule. "What is this one?"

"That's obviously a rabbit, Mama," Alfie said. "This is a cat, and that's a dog. This one is sad because he lost both eyes."

"That used to be a mouse," Clara explained.

"Isla used to have a subscription to *The Lady's Magazine*, which had lovely patterns for embroidered seat covers," Mrs. Gillan said.

"Alas, these reticules represent the whole of my ladylike skills."

"Did you take the kitty to the most fashionable resorts in London?" Fiona asked, slinging it over her wrist.

"The queen herself was complimentary when I brought it to one of her drawing rooms," Clara said, dismissing Prince George's sour comment from her head. "One of her ladies-in-waiting requested a mouse reticule."

"That bag has been in the presence of a queen," Mrs. Gillan mused. "My daughter would have loved to know that."

Fiona cleared her throat. "Mrs. Gillan."

"Will you make me a chicken *re-ti-cule*?" Alfie asked, pronouncing it carefully. "Please, Aunt Clara?"

"Reticules are worn by ladies," Fiona said.

"I need one that Wilhelmina can travel in," Alfie said, ignoring the question of gendered garments. "She's grown so much that her tail feathers get squished."

They all looked at the chicken, pecking contentedly in a corner of the courtyard.

"She's the biggest chicken I've ever seen," Mrs. Gillan confirmed.

"I feed her a lot. All the time."

"We've been discussing the fact that Wilhelmina is of an age where she'd like to live with other chickens," his mother said. "She's a good-natured bird, but she dislikes being carried about, doesn't she?"

"She clucks in a very disagreeable manner," Alfie told Mrs. Gillan and Clara, his mouth drooping.

"I could make you a sporran, like your uncle wears to the kirk," Clara said, inspired.

Fiona burst out laughing.

"You mean the pocket that Papa wears with his kilt?" Alfie asked. "Could you give it a beak like a chicken? I have a Sunday kilt too. That would mean Wilhelmina would be at church with me!"

"I could make you one that looked like Wilhelmina, but it wouldn't be large enough to hold her," Clara said.

"She's a very unusual-looking chicken, because she's half rabbit. Look at her head."

They all looked; Wilhelmina's plumes were swaying in the breeze, not unlike those of the infamous helmet. "I could sew feathers to the top of your sporran," Clara suggested, "Unfortunately I didn't bring any plumed bonnets."

"Don't look at me," Fiona said. "Plumes would make me look even taller than I already am."

"I have Isla's French bonnets," Mrs. Gillan said. "I can donate plumes for the sporran."

"Are you sure you couldn't make a sporran big enough for Wilhelmina to ride in?" Alfie asked.

"Yes, because she needs to be free," Clara said. "I'll make it big enough to carry a book, how's that?"

"I don't *have* any books."

"Well, I have a lovely new copy of *The Castle of Otranto* that you may have."

He jumped up and grabbed her around the waist. "Thank you, Aunt Clara!"

"Alfie talks about that blasted armor day and night," Fiona said. "It's been hard to keep him away from you long enough that you and Caelan could have a honeymoon."

Mrs. Gillan made a clucking sound, not unlike Wilhelmina when faced with Alfie's traveling bag. "Yesterday, everyone in the bakery was talking about that armor."

"If you run to the study and ask your uncle for the book, I can read a chapter aloud," Clara told Alfie.

The little boy dashed off, skidding through the

kitchen and apologizing to Elsbeth for nearly knocking her over. "It's a very small kitchen, isn't it?" he said, his clear, piping voice carrying out into the courtyard.

"Thankfully, there's a second kitchen in the other tower," Mrs. Gillan commented. "I know that Isla—" She stopped because Fiona bent over the table, looking like one of the furies in Clara's illustrated book of Greek myths.

"Enough is enough," Fiona said, slapping her palm on the table. "You have a choice, Mrs. Gillan. You can continue to nurture the illusion that your daughter's marriage was utterly perfect—even though *no one's is perfect!*—or you can accept that she is gone, and your son-in-law has married again."

Mrs. Gillan winced.

"It's up to you," Fiona said, not unsympathetically. "But I will say that you're needed here. Clara doesn't know a thing about the Highlands. She doesn't have a mother in this country, and I doubt she ever will. *You* took on that role after the wedding."

"I did, didn't I?" Mrs. Gillan said, looking startled.

"Caelan is very fond of you and your husband. But if you continually bring Isla into the conversation, he and Clara will draw away. Their children won't want to hear about their father's first love, no matter how romantic."

Silence fell. Then, when Clara was about to change the subject, Mrs. Gillan said heavily, "You're right."

Clara let out a silent breath.

"You can be a grandmother to Caelan's children and Alfie, a beloved part of our family," Fiona said, "or you can be one of the people in the village whom we greet on a Sunday. That may be what you wish to be, Mrs. Gillan, and there's nothing wrong with that. You can nurture Isla's memory. But you can't ruin Caelan's life with your memories. I won't let you."

"I understand."

"We who knew Isla will never forget her. Clara won't forget her, either, because Clara is the sweetest woman in the world, Mrs. Gillan. You can see that. She would hurt herself over and over, talking to you about Isla's virtues, but Caelan wouldn't put up with it. You know he wouldn't."

"Caelan cannot tell me what to do," Clara interjected.

"Nay, she is right," Mrs. Gillan said. She reached across the table and took Clara's hand. "I've been foolish."

"You've been *grieving*," Clara insisted.

"Part of my heart will always grieve for my daughter, but I don't want to live in the past. We love Caelan, and you too, Fiona, and Alfie. It's been a joy to be part of your lives."

Clara swallowed hard. "Of course."

Mrs. Gillan nodded. "That's settled, then. I'll call you Clara." She smiled. "Mrs. Potts never did set right with me."

Fiona was not one to linger over delicate issues. "What are you doing with these little bobbly things, Clara?" she asked, sorting through the four flies Clara had made so far.

"Making flies for fishing." She held up her favorite. "I think that trout will like this better than the ones Caelan tied."

Fiona laughed. "I've seen Rory messing about

with horsehair. Maybe I'll make one and best my husband as well."

"I have the book!" Alfie cried, throwing himself out of the kitchen.

"We could have a fishing contest," Clara suggested. "I've seen them on the banks of the Thames, men all lined up with their fishing poles."

"Make my bag first, please," Alfie implored. "My sporran that looks like Wilhelmina."

"My son will be quite a sight with a tuft of feathers adorning the sporran covering his privates," Fiona said, her grin showing that she didn't care a whit. "It'd be very kind of you to make him one, Clara."

"I think the greatest kindness would be allowing me to be a grandmother to this lovely boy," Mrs. Gillan said. "And a mother to you, Clara, as much as you'd like."

"That's enough crying," Alfie said, frowning. "It's time to read!"

CHAPTER 30

$\mathcal{A}$fternoon sun was pouring into the bedchamber when Clara woke from a nap a week later. The castle was quiet. Hopefully no one would see her tangled hair, wrinkled gown, and missing stays.

Blissfully, the kitchen was empty. She pottered about, pushing baskets of vegetables in the pantry into a straight line. Three large tins of tea stood on one of the shelves, and freshly baked bread was wrapped in a snowy-white cloth. A rich lamb stew was bubbling on the stove.

She cut herself a slice of bread and cheese and went out the courtyard door. Caelan was sitting at the table, so concentrated on his writing that he didn't hear her footsteps.

"Hello," she said, walking over to him.

He looked up and smiled. His expression was heart-soothing as he pulled her down to sit next to him on the stone bench, leaning over to take a big bite of her bread. "Turns out Maisie the scullery maid knows how to bake."

"Have they left for the day?"

He nodded. "I promised Elsbeth that I'd braid your hair at bedtime."

"Do you know how?" she asked, startled.

"I learned when my sister was six. After Mother died, Fiona used to crawl into my bed and sleep with me. If her hair wasn't braided, I'd roll on it and wake her up."

"Didn't you have a nanny?"

"On and off. My father was difficult to live with

and had trouble keeping servants. Luckily, Fiona began escaping over to the McIntyre estate."

"Before she married Rory?"

"Long before, by the age of ten. Sometimes Fiona wouldn't come home for weeks at a time, but my father scarcely noticed. Or he noticed," Caelan corrected himself, "but he didn't care much. She was a girl who would never bring in a big dowry because she wasn't beautiful, to his mind."

"That's awful," Clara said, putting down her bread. "She *is* beautiful. Her mouth looks as if it was made for laughing. Plus her hair is gorgeous, and she's so tall and strong."

He wound an arm around her waist, picked up her bread, and had another large bite. "My father was a fool."

"I'd be sorry to agree, but the evidence seems to suggest you're right," Clara said.

"When our children come along, they will *all* be beautiful, no matter if they have turnip noses."

"Or hair that resembles a cat hit by a lightning bolt," Clara agreed.

"Did someone say that about your hair?"

She shook her head. "My hair was always pinned to my scalp, with just enough curls showing to allow me to collect compliments about angels. That is what I privately think about my hair. I'm not very elegant when I'm by myself." She pushed it back over one shoulder.

He tipped up her face. "I adore your catlike hair." His lips ghosted down her cheeks, slipped sideways to her lips. The kiss was not gentle and not slow, and yet Clara didn't care; the moment his tongue caressed hers, heat burst over her body, and her breath became a gasp, then a whimper.

Caelan turned sideways and brought her onto his lap, pulling her back against his chest before he spread his legs, pulling hers apart at the same time.

"What are you doing?" Clara whispered, shifting her hips because she could feel him throbbing against her arse.

He laughed, the sound rough and joyous, floating freely. "No one is here but us, so we can do whatever we want."

Clara registered that her husband would never want servants within shouting distance.

"Someday we'll have children, and we won't be able to do this in the courtyard. We should enjoy it while we can." Caelan tugged up her gown until they could see her pale legs on top of his bronzed ones. His hands closed around her inner thighs and slid upward, slow and caressing.

"Oh my goodness," Clara whispered. She couldn't look away from his brawny callused fingers lingering on her legs.

"How can you say you're not elegant?" he asked in her ear, his voice a rasp. "Your thighs have the most sensual curve I've seen in my life. And here—" He ran a hand under her bunched-up skirt and tapped her intimately. A surprised cry escaped her lips as his simple touch sent warmth down her legs. He did it again, and again, until she was breathing hard. Her bones felt as if they'd curved into his body.

She could dimly hear a bird in the apple tree singing itself to sleep, but mostly she was focused on the delicious heat that was flickering to her toes with every tap.

"I can't believe you're doing that," she said, dizzy with desire, arching back against his chest, her legs easing wider, head against his shoulder. "More," she whispered.

His whole hand licked between her legs, and then he stuck a finger in his mouth and sucked. "I love the way you taste. The way you sound. The curve of your thigh. The way you throw yourself into pleasure."

He put his other hand on one of her breasts, and the first returned to languid strokes. Clara stopped thinking altogether, her body chasing a glow that began in her legs and spread from the pressure of his fingers. One minute she was incoherently feeling as if she were drowning in sensation, and the next fire rushed up from her toes until she cried out and jerked against his hand.

Afterward, it took long moments for her heart to return to a steady rhythm. She put her legs together and turned to the side, registering that he was *so hard*. "Shall we make love?" she whispered, amending the question quickly: "I mean, shall we have sex?"

"If you move your delicious arse off my lap, I'll probably die."

She giggled. "That's oddly specific." She leaned her cheek against his chest and then wiggled her bottom, for the fun of it. Also because he felt good.

"You want me," Caelan said roughly. "You want me, don't you? You want my cock. You want me to lick you and fuck you."

His voice was so intense, and his words so vulgar, that Clara instantly thought a proper lady would demur.

"I—"

He didn't wait for a reply. "You want me to spread your legs and take you to bed," he rumbled. "Or take you here in the courtyard, because I think you're throbbing, aching, waiting for me to touch you."

It was true, but also wildly irritating. She couldn't figure out *why*. Was it because ladies weren't supposed to feel this way? Or if they did feel this way, it should never, ever have been spoken aloud, let alone celebrated?

"You're making me feel unladylike." She tugged her skirts lower on her legs.

"You aren't a lady," he said. "Not you, Clara. You're an adventurer, remember?"

Well, that was true, but something about all of this was making her uneasy, and the sensual excitement in her body drained away. She stirred and then made herself stand up, grabbing the edge of the table because her knees felt weak.

She shook down her skirts and sat back down on the bench beside him. Caelan didn't seem cross because she had removed her bottom from his lap.

Instead, he looked sympathetic. "Is it hard to hear the truth aloud?"

"It's embarrassing." She fiddled with her skirts and pushed her hair behind her shoulders again. "It's the way you said it," she burst out. "As if . . . You weren't *comparing* me, were you?"

It was a stupid thought that had leapt into her head, but his eyes changed. His whole face changed, and her heart sank. "Oh, no," she whispered. "You were. To Isla." It wasn't a question.

Because of course *she* was a strumpet, and *Isla* had been a lady. Her face burned with humiliation.

Caelan swallowed so hard that she saw his Adam's apple bobble. "I was thinking of Isla . . . Well, not as such, but—"

"You were thinking of her," Clara said curtly.

His face stilled, and his brows drew together. "I didn't mean to."

"But you did. You were comparing us. I understand that Isla was far more ladylike than I am." Clara smoothed her skirts over her thighs. She was desperately trying to be reasonable. Caelan hadn't been criticizing her, after all. It wasn't his fault that his comments aligned with her mother's dismay at her eccentricity, her large breasts, her unruly hair, all the *wrongness* of her.

None of that was his fault.

Caelan's eyes were so dark that she couldn't read them. "It wasn't meant as a criticism."

"I understand," Clara said. "I gather you meant it as a compliment. Well, not exactly a compliment."

"It's about me, not you," he cut in.

"What?"

"Isla fell in love with me when she was eleven, and I was thirteen."

"I know that," Clara said, desperate not to hear any more about the greatest love story of the Highlands. Maybe some other moment, when she didn't feel so raw. "Mrs. Gillan told me."

"She was very young and *very* ladylike. I had no interest—until I came back from university, and there she was, the prettiest girl I'd ever seen."

Clara ground her teeth. Why hadn't she held her tongue?

"My sister was in love with Rory, and Isla was her closest friend. Our parents had passed away, and before I turned around, everything had been settled. We were all in love."

A breeze rattled over the courtyard, and a few blossoms landed in his hair and stuck there, like fallen stars. He was so handsome that Clara couldn't breathe—or was she choked by the specter of Isla's perfection, still haunting her husband's heart? If she cried out "Please don't go on, kiss me instead," he would know the truth: she was mortifyingly in love, easily as in love as Isla ever was—that is, if Isla felt as if every bone in her body would break if—

Well, if he died.

Her mind was rabbiting in circles, trying to imagine what he was thinking. Caelan was looking down at his hands. His bare hands. Had he worn a wedding ring after marrying Isla? After she'd died, what had he done with it? Was it hidden in a box somewhere in their home, or was it too painful a reminder for him to keep? Had he buried it with her ring or cast it into the loch? Clara felt so sick, she might throw up that bread and cheese that seemed so delicious a few minutes ago.

"Mrs. Gillan was rightly punctilious, and the two of us were prudish," Caelan said, looking up. "Fiona was forever running off giggling to meet Rory in a barn, but Isla and I—weren't. Which was fine, absolutely fine, because Isla was only sixteen and so delicate. I was fascinated by how different she was from me. How ladylike."

"Ah." The comparison was there to hand; who could expect him not to make it? Would he ever wear a ring again, or had the chances of that died with Isla too? She looked down at her own bare hands. Caelan seemed to have forgotten about giving her one to replace the old one.

"Our wedding night was difficult for both of us," Caelan said, his voice tired.

Clara had to bite her lip hard because of surprise and sadness. "I imagine it's a shock for many ladies," she prompted after he sat silently for a few minutes, shoulders slumped.

"I have chest hair, thick thighs, and large private parts as you noticed."

Clara nodded. "Isla was shocked?"

"Revolted, more like," Caelan said flatly. "She kept saying that if only I looked like her, it would be fine. But of course, I didn't. I wasn't soft and pink and all the rest of it. There's nothing soft about me."

"Oh," Clara breathed. "I'm so sorry, for both of you."

"We'd been married three years, and people were beginning to wonder why she never quickened," he said, looking away. "That would never happen if two people sleep next to each other like a marble couple on a tomb."

Clara frowned, trying to imagine such a tomb.

"The husband is in armor, and the wife holds a prayer book," Caelan said, his voice a dark rumble. "I might as well have worn armor to bed for all the interaction we had after the first few months."

Clara reached out and gripped his hand.

"Isla adored the story of our love. She clung to me and kissed me in public. But in private? She was never unkind, but you can sense revulsion, can't you? She hated the way I smelled, and she thought my muscles brutish and my tongue fleshy."

Clara loved the way he smelled, even when he was sweaty and fishy and had the loch in his hair. "I'm sorry."

"When you desire me, it goes to my head," Caelan said flatly.

"I can imagine," Clara said. "It must have been awful for you." She hesitated, and then said it.

"Heartbreaking, and then your heart broke again when she died."

"Aye. I did love her, and she loved me."

When Clara managed a smile, it felt like one of the more triumphant achievements of her life, right along with slapping Prince George with her reticule.

"I think I should dress," she said, standing up. "I promised Mrs. Gillan that I would visit her in the village today, and it's already afternoon." She hesitated and then leaned over and kissed her husband on the cheek.

Inside, she felt sick. What had happened to Caelan and Isla wasn't anyone's fault; it was fate. Fate had given Clara to a mother who couldn't help comparing her to the better, more ladylike daughter she wished she had. And then fate went ahead and gave her to Caelan, to a man who compared her to the ladylike wife who died.

No, that wasn't fair. He liked bedding her, even if she wasn't the prettiest lass in all the Highlands. She would not allow herself to lapse into a morass of self-pity.

"I'm so sorry that you and Isla weren't suited in that way," she said, to make certain that he knew she wasn't bitter.

He nodded. "Must you go to the village? Elsbeth left stew for us on the stove."

"Just for an hour," she said firmly.

"It's not because you're hurt?"

"I'm a grown woman, and I was well aware of your feelings for Isla before we married. Making—*having sex* is a delightful part of our married life, which is good. Of course."

Caelan's eyes had tightened, but she couldn't tell

whether that was because he was remembering Isla or thinking about his married life with Clara. Either way, she didn't want to know.

"I'll fetch Elsbeth, and we'll leave from the stables," she said. Then she left, because that was something a grown woman could do. When Lady Vetry used to be disappointed, Clara had never been able to leave.

But as a wife, not a daughter?

She could turn her back and walk straight out of the house, grabbing her pink pelisse from a hook. Naturally it began raining when she was on the path, but by the time she was climbing into the coach, the coin-sized drops of water on her coat were already drying, and she had stopped shivering.

"You don't have a bonnet," Elsbeth said. "You'll catch your death of cold."

"I would be grateful if you would pin up my hair," Clara said.

Elsbeth had begun carrying hairpins wherever she went. She instantly moved to sit on the seat beside her and started twisting and pinning. At some point, Clara might have to hire a personal maid, but the castle was small enough that Elsbeth was comfortable being housekeeper and maid.

When they were rattling over the high pass, Elsbeth said, "So, are you beginning to train the laird, my lady?"

"Aye," Clara said, using that word for the first time in her life. She was a Scotswoman now. She almost sounded like one.

CHAPTER 31

$\mathcal{B}$y the time they arrived in the village, rain was coming down in sheets, and they were both soaked the moment they stepped out of the carriage.

Mrs. Gillan ran into the foyer as a footman took Clara's drenched pelisse. "You're wet as a hen. I have your dear sister-in-law here as well. She ducked in when the rain began."

Sure enough, Fiona stuck her head out of the drawing room. "Hello, dear! It's coming down buckets, isn't it?"

Elsbeth went downstairs to dry off and Mrs. Gillan took Clara upstairs, Fiona trailing behind. They walked into a bedchamber that felt as if it were designed for a princess. The curtains and bed hangings were embroidered with roses, and an artist had painted thickets of the flowers around the walls.

Mrs. Gillan picked up a fluffy pink shawl and wrapped it around Clara's shoulders. "We'll be lucky if you don't catch a cold. I'll fetch you some dry clothing and some tea."

When their hostess was safely downstairs, Clara cleared her throat. "Fiona, do you happen to know whether this was Isla's chamber?"

"It wasn't," Fiona said, glancing around. "It's a bit much, isn't it? I hardly need to say that Isla had a hand in the decorating. I was very fond of her, but I'd be the first to say that she had mad ideas. She was like a magpie, wanting everything shiny and pretty."

Clara sat down on the bed and burst into tears.

"Bugger it," Fiona exclaimed. She sat down, gave Clara a one-armed hug, and patted her shoulder.

"What on earth happened?" she asked, pressing a handkerchief into her hands when Clara finally stopped heaving with sobs.

"I can't be Isla," Clara hiccupped. "I wouldn't say this to anyone else, but you know it's true. I will have to live my whole life not being Isla." She stopped and mopped away some more tears. "I won't spend my life moping, but it's *so hard!*"

"Bugger it," Fiona muttered again. "My brother is an idiot, but things will be better. I promise they will."

Clara was so tired that she fell backward and stared up at the ceiling. "I suppose you're right," she said drearily. "If you'll forgive me saying it, I wish that I hadn't married Caelan."

"I'm so grateful you did. I think the two of you will have a wonderful life together," Fiona said stoutly.

"Perhaps." The crying made her sound croaky.

"Caelan will be a marvelous husband and father, by which I mean he's nothing like our father. Did you have a wrangle?"

"Not really. He was comparing the two of us, and I realized that even when . . . even when we're together *intimately*, he's still thinking about her."

Fiona drew in a sharp breath. "He didn't! Not at that moment!"

"He was thinking about it, and I guessed," Clara said miserably.

"My brother is naught but a daft eejit."

"His comparison wasn't negative. I know it's selfish, but I always thought my husband would be mine alone." She caught her breath on another sob.

Fiona cleared her throat. "My understanding was that Isla wasn't welcoming in the bedchamber. She was fastidious, even as a young girl, and bed play isn't."

Clara gulped. She couldn't repeat what Caelan had confided. "Caelan told me Isla was very elegant," she said instead. "A true lady."

"She was a dreamer. She grew up here, in the village, and yet she thought she could live like Marie Antoinette," Fiona said. "Never mind the fact that Marie lost her head. Isla wanted the grandeur, not the reality."

Mrs. Gillan bustled back in just as Clara sat up and said, "The most important thing is that Caelan still loves Isla so deeply. He told me so this afternoon, and I simply couldn't bear it."

Mrs. Gillan's eyes widened in horror, and she dropped into a chair, pressing a handkerchief into Clara's hands. "I miss Isla too. But that man has got to pull himself together. Allowing the castle to go to rack and ruin!" She took in a deep breath. *"Insulting his wife!"*

Clara sniffed. "He didn't mean it as an insult. He's helpless, because Isla meant so much to him."

"He's a fool is what he is," Fiona said ferociously. "Anyone in that church could tell that my brother is mad for you."

"I won't say it wasn't difficult for me to accept," Mrs. Gillan agreed, "but life has to go on. I don't want the laird throwing himself on my daughter's grave like some witless version of Romeo. He should be a *man*."

"He's manly," Clara said wearily. Then she blurted out the truth. "I'm in love with him, as much as Isla ever was, I'd guess. I'm such a fool, because he told me that he'd never fall in love again. I knew that he'd never return my feelings, and I married him anyway."

"He'll love you in time, Clara. Give him a chance. Men are slow."

"You didn't have much choice about the marriage," Mrs. Gillan added. "If I understood Lady Bufford, your mother would have suffered had you not married the laird."

"Lady Vetry doesn't care much about me," Clara confessed, more tears welling up. "She would have disowned me, and society would have exonerated her. She's always been ashamed of me, and I'm sure that she was relieved to be rid of me. Another scandal would have put an end to society's questions about where I am and what I am doing."

"Are you talking about your *mother*?" Mrs. Gillan sounded horrified.

Fiona wrapped her arms around Clara. "Thank goodness you found your way to the Highlands."

Clara wiped away a few more tears. "I've been a disappointment because she always . . . Well, the truth is that she would have loved a daughter like Isla. Beautiful, fashionable, ladylike."

"You *are* beautiful," Fiona said. "Haven't you noticed the way Caelan watches you? How all the men do, for that matter? Except my husband."

Mrs. Gillan sat on the edge of Clara's bed and took her hand. Clara gave her a wavering smile. "Lord, but you do have a lovely smile," Mrs. Gillan said. "Isla had loved the laird since she was a little girl, and he came to love her back, but he wasn't *mad* for her, if you know what I mean. It would have been very distressing for her if he was."

"I see," Clara murmured. A germ of hope lit her

breast, but she ruthlessly crushed it. Caelan might be mad for his current wife—but to be brutally honest, he was mad for the way Clara desired him.

That wasn't like being desired for oneself. For who she was. Tears welled in her eyes again.

"Enough of that," Mrs. Gillan said bracingly. "This house has seen all the tears it can bear."

Clara nodded.

"When you have a baby, I claim the right to be its grandmother," Mrs. Gillan continued. "I've no doubt that Isla is up in heaven, praying for that. I think she sent you to the Highlands so that you could alight at Caelan's gate, clean up her castle, and have babies."

It sounded nice, if improbable.

Rain began lashing the windows. Clara hunched her shoulders. "Mrs. Gillan, would it be a terrible imposition if I had a bath? I am wet through to my chemise. I love my pelisse, but it is truly an inadequate garment in a storm."

"Of course!" She jumped to her feet and yanked on a bell pull. "I'll tell your maid and have the footmen bring in a bathtub immediately."

Fiona kissed her cheek. "I'll be running out to my carriage the moment the storm lets up, as Rory frets about the pass in the rain. But I'll visit you tomorrow."

"You can visit her here," Mrs. Gillan said. "Clara will have a bath and go to bed. You'll be running a fever next."

"I'm never ill. My voice is hoarse from all the crying."

"I'm a mother, and I know best."

Clara almost protested, but then she saw that Mrs. Gillan's eyes were sharp with nerves that had more to do with Isla's fever than Clara. She soon found herself bundled into bed in a clean, pressed nightgown, being spoon-fed chicken soup by Elsbeth.

"I'm not ill," Clara told her maid. "We should return home."

"Mrs. Gillan already sent a groom through the woods to tell the laird that you're spending the night here."

She didn't want to go home. By tomorrow her feelings wouldn't be so raw, and she could go back to pretending that she didn't love her husband. "May I have some more tea, please?"

It was comforting to be wrapped up in warm blankets while Elsbeth braided her damp hair and told her stories she had gleaned about the Gillan household. "'Twas terrible when their daughter died. Isla was the apple of their eye. Their two other children both died at birth."

"How dreadful," Clara said.

"From the sound of it, that girl had a charmed life. She went from her mother's house to her husband's and always had everything she wanted. This is a pretty room, isn't it?"

"Fiona said this wasn't Isla's room."

"Aye, hers is down the corridor painted in bluebells. They brought an artist all the way from Inverness to paint flowers on the walls because she loved them so much. It goes to show," Elsbeth said thoughtfully, tying off Clara's braids with a bit of worsted. "I would have been wildly jealous of her when I was a girl, thinking that she had everything—the handsome laird in love with her and the parents who gave her whatever she wanted—but she didn't have them for long, did she?"

"No."

"The master was lucky that he met you," Elsbeth said.

Clara couldn't bring herself to answer.

Mrs. Gillan trotted in a few minutes later, holding a tray with two bowls. "I brought more chicken soup. I haven't been eating as much as I ought." She looked ruefully at her wrists. "My arms are thin as twigs."

So they both ate soup while Mrs. Gillan told stories about how naughty Caelan and Rory had been as young lads. Clara fell asleep in the midst of a story about how they had cut all the flowers in the churchyard and presented them to Rory's mother for her birthday.

CHAPTER 32

In the middle of the night, Clara opened her eyes and saw Caelan standing by her bedside. She blinked—and he was gone when her eyes opened again. The dream was so eerie.

Only then did she realize that despite the moonlight pouring through the bedroom windows, she could hear urgent voices and booted feet downstairs. She stared at the rose-painted walls in confusion before her mind steadied, and she remembered where she was. She swung back her covers and got out of bed; the voices sounded serious, and she could hear Mrs. Gillan above the rest.

A robe had been left for her on a chair. She tied it around her waist and padded down the stairs in her bare feet, walking into the sitting room. Two men stood with their backs to Clara, bringing with them the smell of fresh rain.

Her hosts were next to the window, Mrs. Gillan clutching her husband's arm with one hand.

Clara hesitated, but after all, she was the laird's wife. "Is something wrong?"

All four looked to her, their faces pinched and fearful. A beat of dread shot through Clara's body. "What is it?" she demanded.

"It's the laird," one of the men said. "His carriage."

"What happened to his carriage?"

Mrs. Gillan moaned, the sound so loud that her husband started.

"It's down the ravine," the other man said, his

Scottish burr making it sound as if he was making a fateful statement. Which would imply . . .

"No!" The sound broke directly from Clara's chest.

"This is the lady of CaerLaven," Mr. Gillan said, his voice sharp. "Lady MacCrae, the laird's wife."

"Apologies, my lady," the first man said. "I'd no idea. We came to tell Gillan here, as he heads up the local burgh council. The road's out. We've closed it just past the village."

"Could be that the laird survived the fall," the second added hesitantly. "He's a strong man."

"My husband cannot have been in the carriage," Clara stated. "He told me that the pass was too dangerous in a storm. He wouldn't have risked it."

"I told him to come!" Mrs. Gillan cried, her voice breaking. "I told him you had a fever! He came because of my message."

Clara stared at her white face without seeing it, thoughts whirling like a blinding snowstorm.

"A fever like Isla's," Mrs. Gillan added. "I thought he'd come in the morning. But I never imagined—"

"I wish to be taken there now," Clara ordered, cutting her off and turning to the men.

One mouth fell open. "In the morning, perhaps—"

"Now." She spoke with every bit of arrogance she'd inherited from generations of English ancestors ordering people around. "I will dress with expedience, and you will take me to the pass."

The men turned to Mr. Gillan.

"Take her!" Mrs. Gillan said shrilly. "*You* take her," she said to her husband. "On horseback; it'll be faster since they've closed the road. The Clydesdale can bear the weight of you both."

Clara whirled and ran back up the stairs. She threw her damp pelisse over her nightgown and buttoned it with shaking fingers. She couldn't get one garter to tie, so she left a stocking on the floor and pushed a bare foot into her boot. She was back down the steps in three minutes, finding Mr. Gillan shrugging on a topcoat.

In years after, Clara never forgot the horror of that ride. The rain had stopped, but the road was sodden and thick with mud that slid sluggishly under the horse's hooves. The drumbeat of hooves splashing into muck drowned out every sound but the frantic thumping of her heart.

As they left the village, branches arched over the road, shaking rainwater down their necks. Clara was soon shivering, her pelisse soaked once again. She kept leaning forward, as if she could push the sturdy beast to go faster. Her breath was ragged, and her chest hurt.

It was impossible. Impossible.

Caelan had told her . . .

He had told her that the pass was dangerous. So it must have been someone else in his carriage. Someone had stolen the carriage and driven it from the castle. Her mind rejected that as foolish; who would do such a thing?

Perhaps one of the crofters' wives was having difficulty giving birth. She and Caelan had met all of them in the days after the wedding, and two were quite advanced in their pregnancies. Caelan wouldn't have accompanied the man and his wife. He would be safe at home.

At length they emerged onto the main road, skirted the barrier, and followed the road along the mountain. It trailed alongside the rocky cliff, moonlight making the chasm to their right look like the depths of hell.

Clara turned her head away, her body trembling. Single pine trees clung to the side of the ravine until they clustered into a forest at its bottom. Moonlight reflected off a thick cloud of fog far below that swirled amidst the tops of trees. Clara found herself thinking the fog could be the murky water around a drowned man's fingers. She forced herself to stare at the horse's mane.

As they rounded another corner, she abruptly saw torches and heard men's voices shouting. Her mind was still spinning tales, insisting that Caelan would never set out in the rain to cross the pass. He wouldn't, not even if he were afraid she was dying, like his wife.

The other wife. The real wife.

She was the second wife. He didn't care enough. Therefore, *he was safe.*

He had to be safe, because otherwise the world would break in two. Not her heart, because that wasn't big enough. The whole of everything had to go if the most intelligent, thoughtful, affectionate—

Why on earth had she cared if Caelan mourned his first wife as long as he lived? Was she mad? He had been in her bed, and she loved him. That was enough. As long as he was safe—

He had to be safe.

Pushing her fear away again, she concentrated on the plodding steps of the horse carrying them along the road. They drew slowly closer to the torch burning golden against the drenched and dripping pines that spilled down into the ravine.

They turned one final bend and caught sight of a mound of mud lying across the road. Clara flung

herself off the horse, barely hearing Mr. Gillan's
startled exclamation. She landed with a jolt that
rattled her teeth and ran forward, ignoring the way
mud sucked at her boots. Her heart hammered in
her chest. She broke into the circle of light and—

Saw.

The carriage was far below, barely visible. It was
lying on its side, ghostly in the pale light of the
moon. It must have gone with the mudslide, skat-
ing on top but falling at a steep pitch, crashing between trees and somehow arriving at the bottom
in one piece.

It *wasn't* Caelan's burial place; it wasn't, because
she refused to believe it.

Trees stood upright all the way down, some of
them bent but still holding against the brown
slurry of mud that had flowed around them.

The men were clustered together, their backs to
her, thick ropes looped over their shoulders. She
felt a bolt of anger at them for chattering when they
could be climbing down the slope. What if Caelan
was breathing his last right now?

What if he was desperately injured and lying
there cold and alone, with only a few minutes left?

Clara flung herself at the edge. It was the work
of a moment to grab a tree that had been pushed
sideways and begin to climb down the hill, moving
from that tree to grasp a root sticking out from the
mud. She dropped from the root to another tree,
feeling strong and invincible. Let the men chatter,
trying to figure out an easier way to descend into
the ravine.

She was going to find Caelan. She would *always*
go to him.

Above her, Mr. Gillan had sounded the alarm,

since rough male voices began bawling down at her, sounding so Scottish that she couldn't understand anything they said. Her hands were freezing, brown mud slicking along her palms. She was feeling along a tree root, moving to her right where she could see another tree that would take her down several feet.

Men were shouting, but she ignored them. They were cowards.

"Clara!"

And then, stronger, a roar, "Clara! Clara, you little fool, don't move!"

Her heart gave one enormous thump and then steadied. She tilted her head back, but all she could see were black forms against flickering torches. That voice sounded like . . . It couldn't be.

Yet she stilled, clinging to a wet piece of root. Suddenly she felt how stiff, almost frozen her hands had become, barring the warm blood that dripped down her sleeve. One of her palms had been torn by a rough twig. Her wet skirts were wrapped around her ankles.

"*Clara*, do you hear me?" Caelan bellowed.

She tried to piece it together in her mind. Her lips moved. "You're alive?" It came out a breath, surely inaudible above.

She could see men running around with ropes.

A slick of heat swept over her body, a glow of humiliation that chased away the chill. She *had* been a fool. He was there, safe, and she'd idiotically thrown herself over the edge like . . . like Juliet, and she'd always thought that girl was the stupidest of Shakespeare's heroines.

She didn't have the excuse of being thirteen. Now everyone up above would know that she loved a man famous for his devotion to his first wife. Her breath sounded harsh in her ears.

With another sickening jolt, she realized that Caelan would know too. There was no way he wouldn't guess how she felt about him.

All the same, she'd happily accept humiliation over his death.

"Don't move," he called down, gentler now. "For the love of God, Clara, don't move a finger, or you'll bring the rest of the hillside down on your head."

She stopped looking up, because it occurred to her that perhaps the weight of her head tipped backward would encourage the root she was clutching to give way.

Up above, they argued for a moment until Caelan cut through the noise by barking an order. "Draw the two of us up!" Peeping from below while trying to keep her neck straight, Clara made out that he had tied a rope around his waist and slung the end over a stout tree branch.

One of the men protested.

"Don't you understand, you bawbag, she's mine," Caelan snarled. "I'm going after her *now*."

Clara stared at the muddy slope before her face. Possession was nine-tenths of the law, and he was hers too. He could mourn Isla as much as he wished. She would never whine about it, even to herself. She would help him tend the flowers on Isla's grave.

She dared to peep up again and saw Caelan swing out from the road. The rope snapped taut and then swung him back to the cliff, his boots slapping into the earth as he swung away again. Mud splattered her face, and the root flexed under her fingers.

"Lower!" he shouted.

An arm whipped around her waist, and a voice

growled, "I have you." He kicked off again just as the mud before her eyes began to flow slowly down, like dirty water but thicker.

Clara let out a stifled cry, turned her head away, and clung to him with all her might.

"Up," Caelan bawled. And to her, "I have you, Clara. I have you." His arms were like steel bars encircling her, and her head nestled into a dip in his shoulder that felt like hers. At the edge of the pass, men were grunting in unison as they pulled them up, like deckhands hauling on a sail.

"I thought you were dying," she whispered, her voice cracking.

"I would have been *dead*," Caelan replied, sounding exasperated. "It's a long way down."

"What if you hadn't? What if you had a few minutes left? I couldn't let you die alone." She was shaking again. "I want . . ."

"I know what you want," Caelan said, a ghost of a chuckle in his voice. "Lord knows we have enough rainwater for a week of baths."

"No." She cleared her throat. "I thought you were *dead*, Caelan. I want a kiss."

"Oh, you'll have those."

He sounded faintly amused, damn him. They were above the lip of the crevasse now. She could make out the sweaty faces of men straining at the rope, and then Caelan's coachman lunged forward, grabbed his master's legs, and hauled him onto the road.

When they landed on the ground, Clara's knees crumpled, but Caelan held her up. The men burst out in Gaelic. He thanked them, and then laughed, and for a moment she hated him, truly hated him. He could have died. Her stupidity could have killed the two of them, even if he hadn't been in the carriage.

"Aye, you're all right," he said. "We're an excellent pair. I threw myself on a grave, and she threw herself down a ravine."

The comparison was painful—and so sudden—that she flinched. His arms tightened. Behind them, the second landslide must have gained speed; a tree gave way with a splintering crash.

"That's your carriage gone, laird," a man standing at the edge shouted.

"Thank God we had time to free the horses," Caelan said.

Clara turned about, still in his embrace, and forced herself to smile at their rescuers. "I can't thank you enough for saving my life. I was . . . I was extremely foolish and lucky that you were there."

They didn't seem scornful; they were beaming, which eased her humiliation.

"I'll be taking my wife home now," Caelan said, his arms still clamping her to his chest.

Mr. Gillan offered up his horse, and someone else spoke in a burr that Clara's exhausted brain couldn't unravel. Her husband laughed again and swept her up in his arms.

"Good enough?" he demanded.

The men were applauding and shouting as he turned and began tramping back across the mud to where Mr. Gillan's patient horse waited, reins looped on his neck. Caelan hoisted her up and then swung behind, pulling her body back against his.

Tears began to slide down Clara's face because he was *alive*. Warm and alive.

"I would stop and kiss the living daylights out of you, but they're all watching," Caelan said, his voice rough, not laughing. "I thought my bloody heart would stop when I saw you down there, Clara." His arms tightened, and he buried his face in her hair, which had unraveled from her braids and was floating free around her head and shoulders.

"Where shall we go now?" she asked, keeping her voice steady because she didn't want him to know she was crying.

"Home," he said, picking up the reins with one hand. "Through the forest. It'll take us two or three hours, but I'll be damned if we have the conversation we need to have in one of Gillan's beds."

"Mrs. Gillan shouldn't have sent you that message," Clara said. "I don't have a fever. I'm not dying like Isla."

"When her man showed up, it crossed my mind to go through the woods, but instead I flung myself into the carriage so I could bring you home or to a doctor—and honestly, get to you quicker," he said wryly. His left arm tightened around her waist, and he murmured something about irrationality into her hair.

"How did you escape before the mudslide?"

"I was riding on the box. The coachman and I didn't like the look of the slope up above. We tried backing up, but the horses were terrified, pitching and rearing. We barely got them out of the traces when the mud gave way. After the carriage went over, we took the horses back to the castle to get men and ropes for towing, which is why the villagers thought we'd gone over. We had just returned when you threw yourself over the edge."

Clara had been trembling, but now she was visibly shaking.

"What happened to your stocking?" Caelan asked.

She glanced down at her ankle, ghostlike in the moonlight. "I was in a hurry, and I couldn't tie one of my garters." She felt another stab of embarrassment. The men must think her utterly mad. Idiotic.

"Is your ankle cold?"

She considered that. Parts of her body—her heart—still felt as if they weren't hers. Her palm stung. Her ankle was the least of it. "I'm fine."

"We're quite a couple," Caelan said, pushing back some of her hair to kiss her on the temple. "The difference being that I tripped on a chicken, whereas you threw yourself down a ravine. I am honored, Clara."

Humiliation felt like a black chasm as big as the ravine, one that she might fall into and never get out of. This was even worse than when Lady Jersey informed Prince George that his vulgar singing had upset Clara.

Caelan knew. He was *honored* by the fact she . . .

"It's all right," she said, steadying her voice. "I do love you. I'm somewhat—no, desperately in love with you. I couldn't help it. I know you don't feel the same. You told me as much, and I wish you didn't know how I feel, in case it makes you feel guilty. But now you do." Her voice wound down like a children's toy.

He had his face buried in her hair again, the horse ambling along on his own. "I can't talk about it without seeing your eyes."

"Could we please not make a fuss?" Her voice wavered, and she steadied it. "I'll be a nine days' wonder in the village."

"Far beyond," Caelan said. "This'll reach Glasgow. Scotsmen love a story more than anything, and this one has love and death."

"Wonderful," she muttered. Exhaustion had set in now, along with the wet and cold. Her body was starting to ache: her arms, her palm, even her stomach as she'd apparently scraped over a tree. She turned her head against her husband's chest and took in Caelan's blissfully sweaty, spicy smell. "Do you mind if I have a nap?"

He kissed her forehead again. "Would you prefer to return to the village? This horse has to be the slowest I've ever ridden, but I wouldn't like to kick it to a trot with two of us on his back. We have several hours to go."

"No, I want to be at home," Clara said. "Please."

"If it's a home, Isla made it—"

"I don't want to talk about Isla," Clara interrupted. "You told me not to speak her name to you. Now I'm saying the same to you." She'd straightened so she could see his face, but he tugged her back against him.

"We have to talk about Isla," he stated. "We should have done so earlier."

"We already did." Clara closed her eyes. How could she be so irrational and contrary? Only an hour ago, she'd sworn that if Caelan lived, she would help tend the flowers on Isla's grave. Now anger was burning in her belly again.

It wasn't all at her husband. She was so *tired*, not merely bone-weary but soul-weary as well, because although Caelan would be horrified at the comparison, their relationship wasn't terribly different from hers with her mother.

She could never catch up, never be the best. Isla made a home.

"I tried to make the castle a home," she whispered, but so quietly that he couldn't hear her over the clopping of the horse's hooves. "I tried."

CHAPTER 33

*C*lara woke occasionally during that long ride, but the world was gray and wet whenever she opened her eyes, and her body ached more rather than less. Finally the horse plodded over gravel, and she opened her eyes. The sun was rising in the east, over the loch. The sky was pink, and the castle seemed to have sprung out of a fairy tale.

"There's no spire," she told Caelan.

"What did you say?" He sounded weary.

"There should be a spire with a flag. A thin flag."

He got down, keeping a hand on her waist. "You are worn out."

"My eyelids hurt."

He plucked her off the horse and started for the front door.

"Cobbledick, I'm afraid that my lady has had an exhausting night."

The butler's broad, whiskered face swam in front of Clara's eyes. "If you'll allow me, my lady?"

"I'm too tired to welcome you, but I will."

A large hand wrapped around her forehead, deliciously chilled—and disappeared. "Fever. You'd best bring her upstairs, laird."

Caelan started up the stairs. "You have a fever, Clara." His voice was strained and low.

"Don't worry about it," she said. "It's not like Isla's fever. I'm sturdy. Horribly sturdy. You should have heard my mother on the subject of my hips."

His grip tightened, and if she hadn't been so fuzzy with exhaustion, she might have thought he growled deep in his throat.

"My daughter won't be back until midmorning, since she'll be coming through the woods. She's not the best rider," Mr. Cobbledick said.

"I'm so glad you're here, my friend," Clara said, reaching out blindly. Her head hurt more every time she opened her eyes.

A big, cool hand encircled hers. "You've got the laird in a fine state, lass."

"I like your brass buttons," she told him dreamily.

"I can see from your husband's face that it's lucky I'm an old man," the butler said, chuckling. "I'll set the grooms to heating water on the roof if you'd like a bath, laird. We finally have the piping sorted out."

"Not fair," Clara managed. "I wanted the first bath in the new bathtub."

The bedchamber door closed with a snap that made her startle.

Then Caelan was gathering her up again, his lips cool against her forehead. "Would you like a bath now, darling?" he asked, and asked again, because she couldn't seem to understand.

"Too tired," Clara said, and then in a fit of generosity, "*You* go first. It's your bathtub, after all." Something important was swimming through her head and finally surfaced. "Don't tell Mrs. Gillan that I'm ill," she whispered, somewhat surprised to find that her voice was hoarse. "The fever will terrify her. I know you think she is possessed by grief for Isla, but she's like you, coming alive again, and she's been very kind."

"Both of us . . ." he began, saying something, but Clara's mind drifted. He was talking about the bathtub, *their* bathtub apparently.

Sometime later Elsbeth appeared, washing her

face and binding up her palm. Then her maid was gone, but Caelan was lying beside her in the bed, her head nestled into the dip of his shoulder. She felt a twinge of happiness, but he was too hot, so she pushed him away.

Then she was standing upright, her legs trembling, while Caelan changed the sheets. She began to giggle, thinking of her first night in the castle. He turned around and lifted her back onto the bed, shaking his head when she kept hoarsely giggling.

"What?" he asked.

"You're making the bed."

"You sweated through the sheets." His hand curled around her forehead again.

"Were you sleeping with your hand on my face last night?" she asked, thinking about it.

"Only part of the night."

Later that day she thought Mrs. Gillan was offering her calf's-foot jelly. "You don't know how to make it. And I don't like it anyway."

Mrs. Gillan was sniffling into Caelan's shoulder. He hadn't obeyed her when she said not to tell his former mother-in-law. Perhaps she forgot to say it.

She fell asleep thinking about it. Caelan wouldn't want to be planting flowers on her grave as well.

The thought stuck with her, and the next time she woke, when he offered her water, she said, "Don't plant flowers on my grave."

"You are not going to die," he said, his voice deep.

"If I do, I don't want flowers."

"Why not?" He wrung out a cloth and draped it over her forehead. Water trickled into her hair.

"No one would sit there," she explained. "My

mother wouldn't care, would she? I don't mind that now, but after I'm dead? Maybe no stone, either."

He was frowning at her so hard that his brows almost met. "What are you talking about, Clara?"

She fell asleep. He asked her again when she woke up, but the thought was gone. "I'm not very flowery," she rasped, trying to remember. "Perhaps some moss? I like the moss in the woods."

"You are not dying," he stated.

"Of course I'm not! That was your idea, not mine." She wasn't quite as sleepy now, but she closed her eyes anyway, because he seemed so fierce.

Clara woke with a start in the middle of the night. An oil lamp had been turned low on a side table that must have been made by Auld Magnus, because the legs had a gentle curve. Caelan was lying on his stomach beside her, his hand wrapped around her right wrist. She needed to use the privy desperately.

When she tried to ease away, his grip tightened, but he didn't wake.

She reached down to uncurl his fingers, which woke him up. "I'm sorry," she whispered. "I have to use the privy."

Caelan sat up, blinking. "Clara?"

"Yes, it's Clara," she said, thinking that she was lucky he didn't mutter Isla's name in his sleep. Or worse, during an intimate moment.

"You seem—" He dropped her wrist and put his hand on her forehead. "Your fever has broken."

"If you'll excuse me," Clara said, sliding to the edge of the bed, "I'll go over into that room. By myself." A faint memory lurked of him carrying her into the privy, and she didn't want to ever repeat that experience.

"Oh my God." It was a groan, and he fell back onto the pillows.

She got up and tested her balance. Weak and a little tired, but fine. She used the privy and eyed the new tub, deciding it could wait until after she'd had some tea. Her throat wasn't sore, but hot tea felt like a necessity. Then she went over to wash her hands, raised her eyes to the glass, and squealed in shock.

Caelan ripped open the door. "What?"

"My hair," Clara gasped. "What happened to it?"

His whole body relaxed. "I put it in braids, but they hurt your head. I washed it yesterday, and that happened afterwards."

Her hair reached out from her head like the nimbus around the moon on a foggy night.

"You bathed me?"

"Aye. You told me that I couldn't use the tub without you, so we both got in there. You slept through most of it." He had dark circles under his eyes, and his chin was shadowed with beard. "Your hair billowed out when I tried to dry it."

"Thank you for taking such good care of me. Oh dear." She patted her hair.

"Have you ever seen a tumbleweed?" Caelan asked.

She frowned at him. "Please don't describe one. Would you mind propping me up for a minute? My legs are absurdly weak."

He was there in a heartbeat, winding his arms around her.

"I have to brush my teeth," Clara muttered, trying not to breathe in his direction.

"I'll do the same with my free hand," he said, picking up his toothbrush.

"You are rather unkempt," she said, around her

toothbrush. "Are you growing a beard? I'd rather you didn't."

"I'll shave it off later," he promised.

She spat out her favorite peppermint tooth powder and washed her face, trying to ignore her hair. Then Caelan picked her up and carried her into the bedroom. "Tea!" she commanded.

"In two minutes. I need to know you're . . . you're all right. Please."

"Has Elsbeth returned from Mrs. Gillan's? I thought she was here, but maybe not."

"It's been five days," Caelan said, sitting on the bed and arranging her in his lap so she was tucked against him, head on his shoulder.

"Five days?" Her voice squeaked. "Impossible." Memory returned with a rush, and she said, "Your carriage crashed to the bottom of the ravine!" Her cheeks heated at the memory of how stupid she'd been. "On the good side, I slept through five days of gossip about my foolish behavior," she said, trying to sound amused.

"You could have died of the fever." His voice sounded hollow.

"Nonsense! I merely had a cold, and my mother would say I deserved it after throwing myself into freezing mud. Not my finest hour," she admitted. "You called me a fool, and you were right."

He didn't answer, so after a bit she twisted in his arms. His jaw was clenched, and his eyes . . .

"You're crying," she whispered, brushing a tear away. "Were you—you must have been afraid of losing a second wife. I'm so sorry, Caelan. I would never want to cause you any anxiety."

"If I had lost you." He stopped, his Adam's apple bobbing as he swallowed.

"I know," Clara said, kissing his throat. "You've already been through such a heartbreak."

"No," he burst out.

She froze. What on earth was going on? "It must have reminded you of the past," she revised, remembering her stout vow to herself that she wouldn't be jealous of Isla any longer. "We should talk about Isla more often," she said, taking a deep breath. "I've been cowardly, and I regret that. I apologize. She was such an important part of your life, and if you want to speak of her, you should feel free to do so."

He had buried his face in her hair, holding her tightly. Of course men did not like to be seen crying. Luckily she had enough hair to mop up any amount of tears.

"No more self-pity," she told him, because she might as well tell him all the truth. He already knew her deficits.

"I've never seen you whine about anything," Caelan said.

"I was envious of Isla. Jealous of what you both had." He didn't comment, and she wanted all the truth in the open. He might as well pity her for the whole of it. "You went to your knees, asking for her hand, because you were in love." It felt unbearable, but since she'd vowed to be truthful, she added, "I wanted that, but I know that's not . . . Anyway, we have something good too."

"Aren't you going to ask me why I was crying?"

"I don't need to," she told him. "I mean . . . unless you want to talk to me about Isla, and I'm absolutely fine with that! I don't need a ring, either."

Caelan picked up her left hand and stared at it.

Then he moved Clara so that she was seated opposite him. She tried to brush the cloud of hair behind her shoulder but gave up.

"It's true that when I asked Isla to marry me, I went on one knee and promised eternal love."

Clara told herself that she had a lifetime in front of her in which to get used to hearing about Isla. She reached out and took his hand. "We don't need to have this conversation now. A cup of tea would do both of us good." She began to scramble off the bed, but his large hand curled around her knee.

"Clara."

She stilled. "Yes?"

"I was not *in* love with her. With Isla."

Her mouth fell open. "What?"

"I was infatuated when I returned from college. My father was dying, and she was a gorgeous princess who would scarcely allow me to touch her fingers. The afternoon when she said that she loved me was one of the most delightful days of my life."

"I can imagine." Her voice rasped a bit. Maybe she should stop reading books with romantic endings.

"But by the time we married? I felt differently. She said she loved me, but the actual *me*, a man who sweats and shits and swears every day? A man who would like to make love to his wife every day as well? Even before our wretched wedding night, I knew we were in trouble."

Clara bit her lip.

"I might have fallen in love with Isla after the ceremony, but we never connected in ways that would make it possible. She used to promise that we'd have sex on Sunday after church or after she had her monthly . . . except we never did, because she couldn't bring herself to do it. After she explained that it was too distasteful, I stopped asking."

Clara was so stupefied that she sat there blinking at him for a moment. Then she cleared her throat. "I understand why you were so pleased by my response," she said, trying to find the right words. "It wasn't mature of me to be hurt by the comparison."

Especially since he wasn't—*he wasn't in love with Isla*?

She could hardly make sense of the words. Everyone was wrong? For a moment she thought perhaps he was trying to make her feel better, but no. Caelan wouldn't lie to her. He truly hadn't been in love with his wife.

Astonishing.

CHAPTER 34

*C*aelan stared at his wife in perplexity. He was bolloxing it up; he wasn't making himself clear. Clara was smiling, but he saw pain deep in her eyes. Why was her heart aching now, when he was telling her that she'd been wrong about Isla?

That the *world* had been wrong about his relationship with his first wife, and that Clara wouldn't live in her shadow?

"How have I hurt you?" he asked. "I did something wrong . . . What?"

Her smile wobbled. "It isn't your fault."

"You must tell me so I don't do it again."

"It was merely you thinking about Isla while having sex with me," she whispered.

"Making love," Caelan corrected her.

"It was entirely natural of you to compare us. It's a shock to hear that you weren't in love with Isla. Everyone thinks . . ."

As her voice dwindled away, Caelan couldn't help scowling. "Sometimes I loathe living in this neck of the woods, and that's a fact. The villagers think they know everything about me. They watch like hawks, waiting to winkle out an emotion they can chew over for a few months."

"I've given them plenty to think about," Clara said. "Throwing myself over a cliff and all."

"I threw myself after you," he pointed out.

"Thank you for saving my life," she said, as if prompted.

"I will always save your life, if I can," Caelan told her. *"Always."*

"I heard you, up on the cliff, shouting to all those men that I was yours." She dimpled at him. "I was never happier to be a possession."

"You were climbing down to me, not to save me, but because you thought I was dying." He swallowed hard. "You were coming to be with me so I wouldn't be alone while I breathed my last."

"Foolishly," she muttered. "Since you were safe and sound on the road."

He couldn't bear not touching her. He gathered her up and tipped them both backward on the bed so that he could prop himself on one elbow next to her. "Do you know what that means to me, Clara?"

"You're honored," she said obediently. "You are flattered, and now you know how I feel about you, which is embarrassing, but I suppose—"

Caelan groaned low in his throat and cut her off with a kiss. He slung one of his legs over her hips, propped his elbows on either side of her head, and cupped his hands around her head . . . Telling himself all the while that she was safe and well and exactly where he wanted her to be. Their tongues lapped and lingered, a smoldering kiss that made desire spark in his blood.

"Open your eyes, darling," he whispered, his voice ragged. Butterfly eyelashes opened. "Terror roared through me when I saw you down on that slope. I've never felt that. Ever." He captured her mouth again, trying to tell her everything without putting it into words.

But Clara being Clara, she kissed him for a minute, drew away, and said, "What do you mean?"

"My marriage was lived out within the myth of a perfect love story," he said bluntly. "It was important to Isla that everyone around us continued to believe. But here? In the castle? We had nothing in common. She spent her days dreaming of being Marie Antoinette, and I'm a simple Scottish laird, when you get down to it. I had the money to make the castle over the way she wanted, but I couldn't change myself."

"Let me guess: she wanted you to wear clothing while fishing," Clara said, obviously trying to make him feel better.

He refused to smile. He wanted to get the truth out and never discuss it again. "After a month or two of marriage, Isla confessed that she had decided to marry me at the age of nine not because she adored me—which would have been absurd at that age anyway—but because I was the highest she could achieve, since her parents didn't have the money or bloodlines to give her a Glasgow debut.

"We may have slept in the same room, but we rarely talked," he continued, voice even. "Sometimes she would tell me details about the French queen, usually after she managed to find a new book. I would ask her for advice with the crofters, but she didn't care for them."

"'Let them eat cake'?" Clara asked, eyes large.

"She didn't care what they ate, as long as they didn't come too close, or smell too strongly, or appear too needy. My father was a tight man who had left the crofters with crumbling houses and little to wear. I was trying to make things right. It didn't interest her."

Clara buried her hand in his hair, but what helped most was the sympathy in her eyes. Not sympathy for an emotion he didn't feel, but sympathy for his wretched marriage, to call a spade a spade.

"When Isla fell ill, I put my head in to say goodbye, but frankly, she often enjoyed a day or two lounging in bed, complaining of feeling weak, bathed in perfume and sipping French cognac but never Scottish whisky. I left for Inverness, and by the time I returned two days later, she had slipped into unconsciousness."

He paused for a moment. "I was deeply sorry that Isla died, and I was very moved by her parents' grief. I never claimed to be heartbroken, but people awarded me the label and pointed to my every action as evidence. If I rubbed my eye, I was fighting tears. If I drank a glass of whisky, I was drinking away my sorrows. We're a nation of overly dramatic people."

Clara stretched up to kiss his chin. "That sounds incredibly difficult."

"I stopped having a pint at the pub to deny the crofters food for more rumors, but that gave rise to the claim that I was so hobbled by grief that I refused to leave CaerLaven. Whatever I did, they assumed I was a broken man, that I let the castle go to rack and ruin because I was broken."

Her eyes met his, clear and direct, blue-green, like the loch in summer. "If you weren't grieving, Caelan, then why *did* the castle become so dilapidated?"

He moved his shoulders uncomfortably. "I didn't pay attention."

"I have an idea."

"Not the princess and the brambles again?"

"I think you were punishing yourself for not loving your wife enough. Which isn't fair, Caelan, because I don't think she loved you, either. Not the way you deserve to be loved—and desired."

His breath caught. "The way you love me?"

Her smile nestled into his heart. "Yes, and desire you too. I came along, unable to hide my lust for your manly thighs—"

"It wasn't just that, Clara, no matter what you think. You *know* what you feel, and you don't disguise it, the way I've done for years."

"There's no disguising my emotions when you're as impetuous as I am," she admitted. "If I had the presence of mind to think ahead, I wouldn't have thrown myself off a cliff."

"You weren't the only one who pitched themselves off that cliff. We could have thrown ropes down to you, and you could have eased a loop over your shoulders, and we could have drawn you up. The slope wouldn't have collapsed, except I crashed into it like a man possessed on the way down to you."

"But perhaps it would have," Clara said, gulping. "How could I get a rope over my shoulders and hold onto that root?"

"You were holding onto a *root*?" He felt the blood drain from his face.

She nodded. "Thank you for coming for me."

"I came because I'm head over heels in love with you." He said it flatly, his eyes on hers. He had to make sure that she understood that Isla was far in the background.

"What?"

"Madly in love." He could hear the deep truth in his own voice. "When I saw you clinging to the cliff, I knew that I'd rather die with you than stay behind. If we had gone down in that mudslide, as long as I had you in my arms, I would have been— not content, but accepting. You by yourself? No. That was unacceptable."

"Oh," she whispered, her beautiful lower lip trembling. "I felt like that too, but then I felt so reckless and stupid. If I had waited or asked, they would have told me you weren't in the carriage."

"If you weren't so impetuous, you would never have claimed to be Mrs. Potts and jumped in a carriage to Scotland."

"Or slapped the heir to the throne, which sent me on the way to that carriage," she said, one side of her mouth quirking up.

"I knew within a minute of your arrival at the loch that you were never leaving the Highlands. My decision was as impetuous as yours; I simply kept it to myself. You stated exactly what you wanted—a castle and books—and I decided on the spot that I would do anything to convince you to stay with me."

"I do love the castle," she said, dimpling.

"And *me*. You wanted *me*, the man I am, not the perfect hero of some storybook, though you have arguably read more of those than anyone in this country. Even with all the sweet-talking men with smooth foreheads you've read about, you didn't want *that*. You wanted me: naked, hairy, standing in a loch."

She was turning pink. "Well, that's true."

Caelan dropped his head so he could kiss her neck. "Do you know what a gift that is? To be wanted for oneself? I was in a frenzy when you kept planning to jaunt around the Highlands with Mr. Cobbledick. I couldn't sleep at night, thinking of some other Scottish bastard with a castle—there are hundreds of us—getting a glimpse of you."

She began giggling, and it felt as if starlight was floating through the room. "You thought they'd see a cloud of tumbleweed hair and throw themselves at my feet?"

"I would have," Caelan said. "You know when I landed that fish and walked out of the loch, the first time we met?"

Clara nodded.

"I wanted to kiss you," he said, his voice aching. "I've never experienced such an impetuous desire in my life."

"Oh," she said.

"I knelt before Isla in her parents' sitting room because that's what she wanted: the laird at her feet. But you, Clara . . . I had the chance to marry you, and I leaped at it. I forgot about giving you a ring." He picked up her hand and kissed it. "It's because I'm a fool who doesn't think about jewelry, love, not anything to do with my vows. I meant every word of them."

He thought he saw trust in her smile.

"We'll go to Inverness and pick out a ring. I'd happily go on my knees. It'd be Caelan, not the laird, at your feet, begging for your hand."

She stopped smiling, and tears welled up in her eyes. "Truly?"

"If you said no," he told her, "I wouldn't accept it. Now that you've been down a cliff for me, and I for you?" He bent his head and nipped her bottom lip. "If you leave the castle, so do I. If you move to Inverness, my carriage will follow yours. If you find another laird, you can expect to see him dead in the square."

Clara giggled. "You'd never kill a man, Caelan."

It was just as well that she didn't know what he was capable of. He would kill another man, and quickly, if that man injured Clara. Without remorse.

"If you hadn't gotten the better of that feckless English prince, I'd have gone down to London and taken him out with one shot from a moving carriage."

"*Boastful*," she said, her eyes loving him. The warmth of it spread over his skin like sunlight.

"You were so sick," he said, putting kisses on her cheeks, her eyelids, her forehead. "I cannae take it when you're sick, Clara, I truly can't." His lips slid to hers, and she put her arms around his neck.

"You didn't leave me when I was ill, did you?" she whispered. "You do love me."

"I couldn't leave you in case someone made a mistake caring for you," he admitted. "The village doubtless thinks I'm mad. 'Twas a shock for Mrs. Gillan. She was stunned to hear I'd washed your hair."

"I nearly died of whooping cough when I was a child," Clara blurted out.

He breathed a curse.

"My parents moved the whole household to the country after I was diagnosed so that no one else would catch it. My nanny and a maid stayed behind with me, but the maid ran away the next day."

"But *children* die of whooping cough, not adults," Caelan said, astounded.

"I still remember how empty the house sounded, and the fact that everyone thought I was about to die. That's one reason why I launched off that cliff. I would never leave you to die alone."

Then she kissed him, and that kiss—that kiss was everything his first marriage wasn't.

If Isla could see him now, not having bathed since the day before, lying naked on top of a woman, she would shudder. She *had* loved him, though. Perhaps she would smile and be grateful it wasn't her lying beneath him.

But Clara? Clara pulled at him until their bodies aligned, and then her eyelids drooped, and their kiss turned frantic and hungry. Sometime later, he pushed up her right leg, and they both looked down to where they were almost joined.

"Please," Clara begged. "Please, Caelan."

"You're asking me to make love," he told her. "Not that we haven't been doing it all along, but I wasn't man enough to call it that before."

"I didn't mind when you called it *fucking*," his wife said, demure and wicked all at once.

His control snapped, and he thrust into her over and over until their bodies were sweaty and they were panting in unison. Finally he pulsed inside her, and she screamed. Loudly.

Thank God he'd banished the servants the night before. The thought was dim, because Caelan was still shuddering, both hands wrapped around his wife's round arse so that he could hold her body up and make love to her in the way she loved best . . .

Take her.

Make her his.

"I love you," he said after he dropped back down to the bed, one arm around her sweaty body to stop her from going anywhere. "Don't ever get a fever again. No more cliffs, either."

"I promise," she said obediently.

His little wife was never obedient—more the opposite: forcing him to make beds and fall in love and swing down a rope like a maniac.

"I loved you at first sight," he told her, to make sure she knew the truth. "I didn't want to accept it, because I'd gone off the idea of love. I told you on the way home from the pass, but you were already sick. Since you love literature, I told you by way of a poem. 'So fair art thou, my bonnie lass.'"

"You said that after our wedding," Clara said, dimpling at him.

"I told you the rest on the way home five days ago. 'So deep in luve am I, And I will luve thee still, my dear, Till a' the seas gang dry.'"

After Caelan mopped her tears, he said, "I think we'll stay in the tower for a few days. By ourselves."

"I can finish reading you Jacqueline's adventures," Clara offered.

"I never knew sweat could taste so sweet," Caelan said, licking across her breast to her nipple. "Yours is sweet and salty and tastes like Clara."

Her knees came up on either side of his hips as if she was made for him. She was so wet that he slid home, his heart raw with emotion and splintered by feeling.

"You've broken me," Caelan said into her ear.

Clara's hands slid down his back and landed on his arse. "You don't *feel* broken," she said, laughter in her eyes, arching up to meet him. "I suspect you could pull yourself together long enough to . . ." Then she put her lips to his ear and told him about things that she wanted that had nothing to do with a castle or books.

Everything to do with him.

EPILOGUE

A few years later

$\mathcal{I}$t was the day of the annual CaerLaven Fly-Fishing Contest, attended by the village and crofters, as well as passionate fishermen who began turning up after Caelan's book went into its third printing, begging to be taught how to create a "sinking fly," the kind that brown trout devoured.

If—and only if—they contributed to the local school fund, Clara would sit down and show them how to make one of her signature flies that gleamed under the surface, luring trout into recklessly biting. If they were particularly generous in their donation, she might gift them with one of her reticules, which were proudly carried by every woman in the vicinity of CaerLaven.

This year, as had become custom, Cobbledick had taken Clara's newest fly into the stream while Caelan and Rory wielded their own creations. For the first time, Alfie had been judged strong enough to brave the current without his father or uncle at arm's length. He was still slender, but thanks to his passion for fly-fishing, his legs had far more strength than those of other boys his age.

Fishermen were standing up and down the whole loch, but only MacCraes and McIntyres were allowed to fish the patch closest to the castle path.

Family members who weren't in the water watched from chairs set on the shore, except for Clara, who sat on a flat stone to make sure that her son, Angus, wasn't swallowing river rocks; he put everything in his mouth these days. Thankfully, he was preoccupied with Thursday, the blue-and-green-eyed puppy who was as beloved as Wilhelmina. Belying Alfie's fears that his rabbity chicken would be teased by the other hens, she had readily established herself as the queen of the coop.

Mrs. Gillan was rocking a baby and crooning a lullaby in one chair, while Fiona sat in another, a child at her breast.

"Such a greedy little pig," Fiona said happily, propping her son against her shoulder so she could burp him.

At the sound of her voice, small hands burst from the bundle Mrs. Gillan held, a wail emerging shortly thereafter.

Clara laughed. "Maggie is just as greedy."

Fiona rolled her eyes and traded bundles with Mrs. Gillan. "How's yours doing?"

Clara eased back the blanket covering the baby she held. "Catherine is sleeping, like the sweet honeybee she is."

"I don't know how I'd survive without both of you," Fiona said. "I'm so grateful." Her eyes welled up. "No one thought they would live, not all three of them."

Clara grinned at her. In the last four months, Fiona, Clara, and Mrs. Gillan had lived together, rotating the triplets on and off their mother's breasts. Luckily, Clara and Caelan had been blessed with a sweet-natured, placid child. As long as Thursday was allowed inside the house, Angus was as happy to play in the McIntyre kitchen as his own.

When she glanced down at him again, he'd toppled over and fallen peacefully asleep, his head on

Thursday's stomach. The dog looked up at her, his blue-and-green eyes seeming to twinkle.

Out in the loch, a sudden roar echoed over the water. "Is that Caelan?" Clara asked.

"Rory?" Fiona was wiping up some spilt milk.

"No, it's Alfie—and it's a big one," Mrs. Gillan exclaimed.

Clara jumped to her feet. Out in the stream, Rory had splashed over to help his son land a huge brown trout. "Bravo!" she shouted.

Catherine stretched a tiny fist and blinked open her eyes. Her hair stood out around her head in red corkscrew curls. "Hello, beautiful girl," Clara said.

The baby blinked and then smiled, a wide, gummy smile.

"Guess what? Your older brother won the annual fishing contest! Your uncle will be very, very cross."

"No, I will not," said a deep voice in her ear. "Alfie won with one of my floating flies, after all." Since it was a public occasion, Caelan was dressed, though his breeches and white shirt clung to his body. "I'm all wet," he said unnecessarily.

"I see that."

His eyes were ravenous—not surprising, considering that Cobbledick had routed the household out of bed at dawn to set up the fishing contest. "Perhaps you could escort me back home to change my clothing."

Mrs. Gillan smiled. "I'll take Catherine and keep an eye on Angus."

"You'll find rusks and milk in the basket," Clara said. "If you need more help, Elsbeth is down the stream to the right, cheering on James."

"My best footman," Fiona said mournfully. "I

suspect he'll be leaving and coming over to live with you soon."

"He'll never talk Elsbeth into leaving the castle," Caelan said, taking Catherine in his arms and kissing her forehead before he settled the baby into Mrs. Gillan's free elbow. Then he picked up his wife and carried her off down the path, ignoring the excitement behind him as Alfie waded to shore, his huge catch held high.

Clara was entirely unsurprised when Caelan only waited until they were around the bend, hidden by the trees, before he put her down and kissed her so fiercely that she found herself backed against a trunk.

"Really?" she murmured, her heart thudding.

"I love you," he groaned, yanking up her skirts. "I know I'm a beast, Clara. I can't help it. I see you all round and rosy with one child at your feet and another in your womb, and I feel like stripping myself naked and painting myself blue and laying siege to your castle."

"I wouldn't mind that," Clara said, giggling, and then gasping, as he pinned her to the tree.

"You're hardly a gentleman," she whispered, cupping his face in her hands and kissing him, "but I'm hardly a lady, either."

A NOTE ABOUT HEROES, HEROINES, AND SEXUAL MORES

*L*ately I've taken a deep dive into eighteenth-century novels featuring heroes with "manly curling locks like jet" and beautiful, beleaguered heroines. I found myself particularly curious about the effect reading these novels may have had on young women at the time: on one side, fictional ladies were rigidly chaste and prudish (à la Isla); on the other, they readily climbed into breeches and set out on adventures (à la Clara). These heroines were always in danger of being accosted and were not infrequently raped; yet the novels did nothing to teach young women about sex, beyond commands to avoid "allurements" and to never indulge a man's passion.

When I dreamed up the plot of this novel, I had two characters in mind: a young woman who throws herself into a carriage bound for Scotland, and a laird who doesn't want the pleats on his kilt getting wet while fly-fishing. Caelan and Clara are antiheroes, compared to the novels of their time. They embrace the *messiness* of life, the impulsive, improper delight that people in love can take in each other. They also, crucially, learn to talk to each other about sex.

On a historical note, Prince George was an oaf and a sexual harasser, who occasionally found himself at an event with both his longtime mistress, Lady Jersey, and his unfortunate wife, Princess Caroline. Some of the novels and poems mentioned here were published a year or two after 1803, but within the decade. Scottish whisky was indeed brewed in secondhand madeira casks, assisting the country's dominance in whisky production to this day. Caelan's crofters would have survived the potato famine looming in 1846 thanks to their laird's fascination with the brew and his support of their experimentation, not to mention his lady's adroit use of poetry to describe their creations.

Discover more from *New York Times* bestselling author
ELOISA JAMES

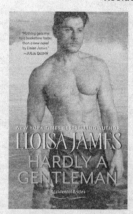
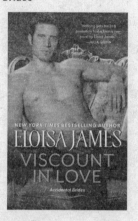